Surviving the Dead Volume I:
No Easy Hope

By:

James N. Cook

Also by James N. Cook:

Surviving the Dead Volume II:

This Shattered Land

COPYRIGHT

FIRST EDITION

Library of Congress Cataloguing-in-Publication Data has been applied for.

Epub Edition © NOVEMBER 2011

Prologue

Gabriel raised the stock of the Belgian P90 assault rifle to his shoulder, took aim, and squeezed the trigger. The weapon's silencer muffled most of the noise from the shot. It made a dull crack, like an empty box dropped on a concrete floor, followed by the metallic clang of the next round going into the chamber. He moved the barrel a few inches to the left and fired again.

Crack-clang.

"You are way too good with that thing," I said. "Scary good."

Gabriel lowered his rifle and grinned as he looked at his handiwork. Two dead bodies lay face down on the ground about forty yards ahead of us on the other side of the perimeter fence. Both had gaping exit wounds visible on the backs of their heads, and a rust colored sludge began to ooze from their broken skulls, staining the snow beneath. Cold mountain air stung my nostrils with the acrid scent of cordite as Gabriel turned to face me, still smiling. His white teeth stood out in contrast to his dark black beard, and his bright gray eyes twinkled with humor.

"You didn't think it was too scary last week when I saved your ass from getting eaten," he said, his breath rising around his face in a thick fog.

It was a cold late December morning, and the sun was just beginning to crest the peaks in the distance. Reddish-gold shafts of light pierced the gloom, sparkling against the snow and frozen tree limbs. The air was biting cold, but not bad enough to get its teeth past my heavy winter coat.

"First of all, you didn't save me from anything," I said. "I knew those two walkers were behind me, and I would have killed them right after I finished dealing with the one crawling under the fence. Second, those shots went by close enough to tickle me. You know how to say 'duck', right? Maybe you should try that next time."

Gabriel laughed. "Hey, I was just trying to help you out."

"You're an ass, Gabe. I hope you know that."

We made our way down to the fence, snow crunching under our boots as we walked. The incident Gabe referred to happened a little over a week ago as he and I were coming back from an unsuccessful scouting trip. We were making a circuit of the ten-foot steel fence that encircles the mountaintop, and as we approached the main gate, we spotted a crawler trying to pull itself under the bottom rail. It heard us coming, and started hauling itself across the ground.

At the same time, I heard rustling in the evergreens to my right, and turned around to see two walking maggot farms stumbling in my direction. They must have heard the other one moan, and set off in the direction of the sound. I decided to deal with the crawler first, before it made too much more noise. The other undead probably wouldn't start moaning until they actually saw me.

I drew my small-sword from its sheath on my back as I approached the crawler. The small-sword is a descendant of the rapier style swords that were popular in Europe a few centuries ago, but unlike the rapier, a small-sword does not have sharp edges. It does, however, have a very sharp tip, and due to the triangular shape of the blade, it is slender and narrow, but as strong and durable as a suspension spring. Despite its name, a small-sword is actually twenty-seven inches from cross guard to tip, making it the perfect weapon for skewering undead eyeballs and rotten brain matter.

I kicked the crawler over onto its back, planted a boot on its withered neck, lined the sword up with its left eye, and plunged the blade downward. A quick twist of the ornate handle scrambled its brain, and the crawler went limp. Just as I was about to turn around and deal with the two walkers behind me, I heard the familiar *thump-clang* of Gabriel's P90, and the distinctive *thup-thup* of bullets passing by close to my head. Two bodies crumpled to the dirt a few feet behind me. I shot Gabriel an irritated glance.

"Cut that one close enough, asshole?"

"They were getting too close," he said. "You can't let them do that."

"I knew they were there, Gabe, I had plenty of time. Next time just say something first."

I have the utmost confidence in Gabe's marksmanship, but I do not like being downrange of anyone firing a weapon if I can help it. Gabe brought my thoughts back to the present by tapping me on the shoulder and pointing a gloved finger down the mountainside.

"More of 'em coming. Guess they didn't want their friends here to have all the fun."

I looked where Gabe was pointing and saw a loose knot of five ghouls staggering their way toward us. They looked to be about a hundred yards away.

"I wish like hell I could figure out how they keep finding us," I said. "You think they know we're here somehow?"

"I doubt it," Gabe replied. "Probably just wandering around looking for food, chasing deer or something."

I had seen the remains of a few animals unlucky enough to be blindsided by the walking meat sacks, and although it was not a pretty sight, it was encouraging to see direct evidence that the Reanimation Phage does not affect animals. Gabe has known for years that the infection only affects humans, and has told me as much many times, but it was still nice to confirm it for myself. Undead people are bad enough. The last thing I want to encounter is a revenant mountain lion or brown bear.

Gabe shifted his P90 around to his back and held out a hand for my hunting rifle.

"No way, dude," I said. "You already got to have some fun this morning. Besides, I need the target practice." Gabe frowned, but dropped his hand.

"Fine, but try not to waste too much ammo. We've only got a few hundred rounds left for that thing," he said.

I put one hand on a fence rail and rested the forearm of the rifle between my thumb and forefinger, tucked the stock firmly into my right shoulder, and peered through the scope. I lined up the crosshairs slightly above the forehead of the lead walker to compensate for the drop of the projectile, and concentrated on timing its jerky, uncoordinated movements. Through the magnified view of the scope, I could see that the undead shuffling in front had been a tall, lean young man before it died. The tattered remains of a business suit flapped around its grayish skin, and its shoes had long since fallen apart, leaving its ruined feet exposed to the elements. A lime green tie dangled listlessly from its neck in the frigid wind.

I let out half a breath, held it, and squeezed the trigger. The stock bucked backward into my shoulder, and even with a silencer on the barrel, the rifle's report was loud enough to make me flinch. Through the scope, I saw the dead man in the suit collapse, his brain matter splattering the face of the corpse behind him in specks of gray and brown.

"Nice shot," Gabe said, peering through his binoculars. "See if you can do it four more times."

I worked the bolt of the rifle, chambering another round. The next three undead dropped with one shot each, but on the last target, my aim was slightly low and the bullet punched a hole through the ghoul's cheekbone. It staggered backward, then righted itself and doggedly trudged forward. Most of the left half of its face was gone, but its brain remained intact. The hunting rifle was out of ammunition, so I handed it to Gabriel and reached back for my sword.

"No sense wasting any more ammo on just one," I said. "Reload that for me?"

Gabe slung the hunting rifle over his shoulder and opened the cover to my backpack, taking out a handful of thirty-ought six rounds. I stuck the point of my sword into the frozen ground, propped the handle up against a steel fencepost, and crossed my forearms over the rail as I watched the corpse stagger up the mountain.

"You making any progress on that journal of yours?" Gabe asked as he reloaded the Winchester.

"Yeah, I guess. Mostly simple stuff. Supply and ammo inventories, places we've scouted already, fresh water and building materials, things like that."

"I thought you were going to write about what happened to you after the Outbreak."

I turned my head to look at him. "It's not my favorite subject."

"Mine either. But it might be a good way to pass the time."

I watched the big man thumb a few rounds into the Winchester's magazine, and then looked thoughtfully back out at the frost white shimmer of the surrounding woodlands. A gentle easterly breeze blew in, sending small swirls of powdery snow dancing through the air.

Good that the wind is blowing east, I thought. *That'll keep the worst of the radiation away from us.*

Gabe finished loading the rifle, worked the bolt to chamber a round, and handed it back to me. I slung the strap across my chest to leave my hands free as the walker shuffled to within ten yards of the fence. I was expecting it to start moaning and gurgling, and frowned when it didn't. Holding up a hand to shield my eyes from the sun, I saw the reason why the ghoul was so quiet—its throat had been torn out.

It wore the tattered remains of a police officer's uniform, and gaped at us with wide, bloodshot eyes turned milky white, mouth hanging open, a look of perpetual hunger contorting its wasted features into something sub-human. It ran into the fence rails and began to heave against them, reaching bone-white arms through the gaps.

I brought my sword up and drove the point through the walker's eye, giving the blade a practiced twist as it went in. When I felt it hit the backside of the creature's skull, I quickly drew back, covering an arm over my face to avoid splatter. The corpse shuddered, tottered for a moment, and then crumpled to the ground. I reached a hand under the lowest rail in the fence and started pulling it toward me.

"What're you doin'?" Gabe asked.

"He's still got his duty belt on. I want to see if it has anything useful on it," I replied.

Gabe bent down and helped me pull the body to the fence, dragging it close enough for me to reach through and unbuckle the duty belt. After some tugging and cursing on my part, I finally managed to rip it free and pull it off the corpse.

I stood up and looked it over. Leather attachments for handcuffs, a radio, and a taser were all empty, but the expandable baton was still in its sheath, along with a rusted can of pepper spray. Most importantly, the pistol was still in its holster, which I recognized it as a Sig Sauer 9mm with a magazine in it, and two more magazines on the backside of the belt.

"Well I'll be damned," I said, holding up the belt for Gabe to see. "Look what we got here."

"Nice. Let's hope it still works."

I nodded in agreement. A serviceable pistol and forty-five rounds of ammo was more than we had scored on our last two scouting trips. I stepped behind Gabe and put the duty belt in his pack.

The rest of the patrol passed without incident, and the good fortune of finding the dead cop's weapon buoyed our spirits. Life had been tough over the past few months, and any stroke of good luck was a welcome change.

After we finished patrolling, we loaded the body closest to the fence onto a makeshift sled and dumped it over the sheer cliff that made up the entire western face of the mountain. It tumbled down gracelessly, taking its place among a steadily growing heap of corpses lying broken on the rocks below.

Rest easy, friend, and thanks for the gear.

"What do you want to do about the bodies down the hill?" I asked, as we walked back toward the gate.

"I'm too tired and hungry to drag those sons of bitches all the way up here," Gabe replied. "Let's just fire up the truck and use the winch."

Normally I would have protested the use of precious fuel, but the morning was cold, and the rumbling of my empty stomach was becoming a distraction. I grunted in agreement and went into the cabin to get the keys. We pulled the Tacoma up to the eastern side of the fence and used the winch mounted on the front to haul the bodies up to the gate. I would have checked them to see if they still had anything useful, but like most infected, their clothing had been reduced to shreds. It wasn't worth the effort.

After the last of the morning's casualties had been disposed of, Gabe and I parked the truck under the carport and went inside to make breakfast.

To avoid tracking in mud, we left our boots just inside the door, hung our guns up on hooks set into the wall, and propped our swords up in a corner. Gabe squatted down by the stove to get a fire going, while I grabbed a few strips of dried meat and some canned potatoes from the pantry. Taking the lid off a rain barrel, I ladled clean water into a pot with the dried meat, then poured some more water into a larger pot and set both of them on the stove.

"What's the hot water for?" Gabe asked.

"Tea."

He rocked back on his heels and looked over his shoulder. "What's the occasion?"

"When was the last time you looked at a calendar?"

He shrugged. "Not sure. Couple weeks, maybe."

I chuckled, shaking my head. "Well, Merry Christmas."

He looked bewildered for a moment, then laughed.

"No shit. Man, I totally forgot. Christmas..." He shook his head and went back to feeding little sticks into the kindling. As the fire grew, he motioned toward a stack of firewood a few feet away.

"You feel like going out and cutting down some more wood today? Between what's here in the cabin and under the tarp out back, we've got about three days' worth. Maybe more if we start sleeping down in the bunker."

"Yeah, might as well," I replied. "We're gonna need it sooner or later. Better get it done while the weather is tolerable."

Our underground shelter stayed a constant 60 degrees, but since we had finished work on the perimeter fence, we preferred to sleep aboveground in the cabin. It saved electricity, which was a lot tougher to come by than firewood.

Once Gabe had the fire burning brightly, he tossed a few larger pieces of wood into the stove and shut the door, twisting the air valve open to keep it fed. By the time breakfast was ready, the cabin had warmed considerably, and Gabe and I were able to hang up our heavy coats before sitting down to eat. I poured the tea into a pair of metal cups and handed one to Gabe.

"To Christmas," I said, holding mine up, "and being alive to see it."

"To Christmas." Gabe clinked his cup against mine, and we took a sip.

"Mmm, good lord, I forgot how good this stuff is," I said.

"Tell you what," Gabe said, "come the spring thaw, we should shoot down the river over to Marion. Remember that store there, Heavenly Leaves, or something like that?"

"Marion is that little town just west of here right? About fifteen miles or so down the river?"

Gabe nodded.

"Might not be a bad idea," I said.

It would be a risk canoeing all the way to Marion, but then again, anything was a risk these days. And besides, a little caffeine pick-me-up is always welcome on the trail.

We finished the meal in companionable silence, eating the canned goods and splitting up the boiled meat. Gabe lifted the pot to pour some of the broth into my empty cup, but I stopped him.

"Nope, that's all yours buddy. My Christmas present to you."

Gabe chuckled. "Damn, now I gotta get you something."

I pointed toward his pack. "You get that Sig we found this morning in working condition, and get those bullets cleaned up, and we'll call it even."

"You got a deal."

Gabe poured the rest of the broth into his cup and sat back in his chair, drinking it in little sips. When boiled in clean water, smoked venison makes a nice savory broth. Water gets boring after a while, and most of the food we ate didn't have much flavor to it. Dried meat and canned vegetables will keep you alive, but without spices and salt to add flavor, their taste leaves a lot to be desired. Gabe had a few barrels of salt in the underground shelter, but we didn't waste it on edible food. We only used it to preserve meat from wild game we hunted in the forest, or caught from nearby lakes and streams.

After breakfast, we spent the rest of the morning cleaning the guns we brought with us on patrol, and then set to cleaning our hand weapons. My small-sword is easy to maintain, as it doesn't have any edges that require sharpening. All I have to do is wipe smears of brain matter off the last seven or eight inches, and run a steel file over the tip to keep it nice and pointy. Gabe's Falcata, however, with its high-carbon steel and sweeping leaf-shaped blade, takes quite a bit more work to keep sharp.

The sword was a custom job I had commissioned for him as a birthday present three years ago, which was about a year and a half before the end of civilization.

A few months before Gabriel's birthday that year, I had driven up to Morganton from my house in Charlotte to give him a hand clearing some brush from a piece of his land. The part of his property that we worked on had once been farmland, but over forty years had passed since the last time anything had been planted there, and where crops had once grown, there were now tall grass, saplings, and scrub brush.

I brought along a military issue machete that my father gave me when I was a boy, and a short axe to cut down the more sturdy growth. Gabe came to his front door carrying only a kukri machete, which at first, I thought would be too short to do any good on the thick shrubbery. But after seeing it in action, I was surprised at the amount of cutting force it could generate, even joking to Gabe that his machete looked like what would happen if a battle-axe and a broadsword had a kid.

Gabe held up the blade and said, "You know, this thing is just a baby compared to what the Spanish used to make. They had a sword with a design a lot like this one called a Falcata. I wish I could get my hands on a good replica. I've wanted one of those things since I learned about them in..." he paused for a moment. The smile faded from his face before he continued, "Anyway, it'd be nice to have one."

That was all I needed to hear.

I placed a call to a guy I knew who worked at Legion Forge, a small company that specialized in making functional custom replicas of historical weapons, and directed him to a website with the sword's original design. The smith cut the weapon from 5160 high carbon spring steel, heat tempered the blade to strengthen it, and polished the razor-sharp blade to a high, glossy sheen. He also made a horse-head shaped pommel and cross guard out of ornately cast bronze, and fashioned a handle for it from leather and wire wrapped sharkskin over sandalwood grips. The finished product was a gorgeous piece of craftsmanship, and I would be lying if I said that I didn't briefly consider keeping it for myself. But only briefly.

Later, on his birthday, Gabe heard me pulling into his driveway and stepped out onto the front porch to greet me.

"Happy birthday motherfucker!" I shouted as I got out of my truck. Gabe stopped and blinked a couple of times.

"Shit, it is my birthday, isn't it?" he said. "I literally turned thirty-six before I knew it."

I shoved the box into his hands as I went through the front door. Gabe followed me in and set the box down on the table, while I poured a couple of fingers of whiskey into two glasses and handed him one.

"Go on, open it," I said.

I watched him, waiting for his reaction when he peeled away the wrapping paper and opened the box. He didn't move or say anything for a moment, he just sat there, staring silently. Finally, he reached in, took the sword out, and drew it from its sheath.

The mirror-polished blade reflected the lamplight, sending a bright yellow ray dancing around on the wall behind me. Gabe ran a thumb over the sword's centimeter-thick spine, and raised it to eye level to examine the shining, razor-keen edge.

"Where the hell did you get this thing?" he asked.

"The guys at Legion Forge made it for me. You like it?"

"Shit yeah. Is this for me?"

"No Gabe, I boxed it up, gift-wrapped it, and drove my ass up here on your birthday just show it to you. Yes, genius, it's for you."

We spent the rest of the night putting away whiskey and rummaging through Gabe's garage looking for things to cut apart. The next morning, bleary-eyed and nursing hangovers, we spent several painful hours cleaning up the colossal mess we had made, and trying to remember what the hell we had done with the sword. After almost giving it up for gone, Gabe spotted it buried halfway through a tree branch nearly fifty feet off the ground. Neither one of us could remember how it had gotten there.

Gabe brought me out of my reverie by throwing a piece of oil soaked cloth at my head.

"Hey, space cadet, what are you grinning about over there?"

"Just remembering the day I gave you that sword."

Gabe paused for a moment, then laughed and shook his head. "I hope you can remember more of it than I can. We were so drunk I'm surprised we didn't cut our own fool heads off. It took me two days to get over that hangover."

He made another pass over the blade with a sharpening stone.

"I have to say though, this thing has served me pretty well since the world went to shit."

His smile faded as he tested the edge of the blade with his thumb, and then returned it to its sheath. He propped the sword up against the wall, then stood up to move back to his chair.

"You know, you really should put something together to post to the Net," Gabe said, jerking a thumb toward the laptop. "Once we get past the Appalachian range we'll be able to get a signal. We should tell people about everything we've seen."

"If you're so concerned about it," I said, "why don't you write something down?"

"Because you're better at it, college boy. Besides, I got bullets to polish."

Gabe walked over to his pack and took out the duty belt we had found that morning. He removed the pistol and the ammo magazines, picked up a cleaning kit, and sat down in front of the stove to begin working on them.

I watched him for a few moments, wondering where to start. Finally, with nothing better to do, I sat down with the laptop, took a breath, flexed my fingers, and began to write.

Book I

Our world has passed away,
in wantonness o'erthrown,
there is nothing left today,
but steel and fire and stone...

Comfort, content, delight,
The ages slow bought gain,
They shriveled in a night,
Only ourselves remain…

-Rudyard Kipling
For All We Have and Are

Chapter 1

Divestiture

I was a wealthy man before the Outbreak. Well, wealthy in monetary terms. I had almost no family by the time the world ended, and being an only child when my parents died, my only family was my Grandmother and my uncle Roger. No wife, no children, not even a dog. Just a big empty house and a pickup truck. My life could have been a joke about a bad country-western song.

My grandfather was a successful attorney, and when his heart gave out on him, he left everything he had to the woman who had stood by him for more than forty years. Grandma didn't do much with her wealth—she was active within her church, and donated to a few charities—but nothing too extravagant. When she passed, she split the money between my uncle Robert and me.

It was a strange adjustment; one day I was a corporate salary man, and the next I had inherited more than twelve million dollars in bond investments and several pieces of real estate. I didn't want to maintain more than one or two homes, and the idea of dealing with renters appealed not at all, so I decided it would be best if I kept the two best properties for myself and sold off the rest.

That was how I met Gabriel.

He bought a large swath of land and a cabin just outside of Morganton from me. The first time I met him, I had driven to the cabin to clean it up in anticipation of a potential buyer coming to see it with his realtor. My agent had told me that they would not be arriving until late in the afternoon, so imagine my surprise when I got there and saw a silver Taurus sitting in the driveway, and two people standing on the porch staring at me. One of them was a petite Asian woman in a smart looking pantsuit, and the other was a tall, powerfully built, scruffy looking man in jeans and a t-shirt.

As I stepped up onto the low porch, swallowing my irritation and managing a smile, the Asian realtor pounced forward and held out a perfectly manicured hand.

"Hi, I'm Kristina. You must be Mr. Riordan, right?" she said, even pronouncing my last name correctly (REAR-dun).

I shook her hand and breathed in the flowery scent of her perfume. She had gorgeous almond shaped eyes, flawless cinnamon skin, and adorable little dimples in her cheeks.

"Yes, that's right. I was just about to get the place cleaned up for you folks. I wasn't expecting you so early," I replied.

"Oh, that's alright, Mr. Garrett is more interested in the layout of the property than in the cabin itself."

She gestured toward the big, grumpy-looking guy. I remember thinking that I was more interested in her layout than I was in selling a house right about then. As I was surreptitiously checking her left hand for any rings, old tall, dark and ugly made his way over, offering a massive, scarred hand.

"Hi there, Gabriel Garrett, nice to meet you," he rumbled.

His voice seemed to start somewhere about six feet underneath his scuffed boots, and issued forth in a resonant, albeit gravelly, baritone. I shook his hand and tried not to wince at the strength of his grip. I am neither a small nor a weak man, but I knew without question that Gabriel could have crushed every bone in my hand if he had wanted to.

"Eric Riordan, nice to meet you Mr. Garrett," I said, resisting the urge rub my hand when he released the handshake.

"Please, call me Gabe," he said. "This is a nice place you have here."

"I wish I could take credit for it, but it belonged to my grandfather," I replied. "The place is old, but it's well built. Back in Grandpa's day, people took pride in their work and appreciated good craftsmanship. At least that's what he used to tell me. He also used to tell me that Jimmy Carter was a communist, and that people should have to pass a written exam before being allowed to vote, so I took everything he said with a grain of salt."

Gabriel laughed, and it was like listening to rocks rattling around in the bottom of a barrel. He sounded much older than he looked, and I noticed that he had two thin, ragged scars that started just under his right eye and cut through his short beard all the way down to his jaw. It occurred to me that Mr. Garrett might have been in a scrape or two over the years.

"Well, your grandfather had good taste in land, at least," Gabriel said. "This cabin is in a good location. It's not near any major highways, there's only one road on the mountain that leads up here, and I don't think there are any neighbors for a few miles in any direction. Looks like the kind of place a man could go and get away for a while."

Gabriel had just described all of the reasons why I had decided to sell the property to begin with. It was remote, isolated, and much too far away from civilization to suit my taste. I couldn't help but wonder why the big man wanted to live so far out of the way.

Kristina chimed in, "Why don't we go ahead and take a look inside the cabin?"

I nodded, and gestured toward the door. "Sure, let's go on in."

Holding the door open as she walked inside, I couldn't help but notice the way Kristina's hips and butt filled out her tight-fitting pants. Gabe followed her in, and I spent a few seconds looking around for a light switch before remembering that the cabin had no electricity. As I had feared, a thick layer of pale gray dust blanketed everything around us.

Gabriel stood for a moment in the middle of the common room, silently looking around and nodding to himself. His broad frame seemed ridiculously huge in contrast to the small space. He went to either end of the cabin to take a brief look into the bedrooms, then stopped at the wood stove near the back wall and squatted down in front of it. The cast iron hinges on the door made a loud metallic squeal as he opened it and looked inside.

I looked over at Kristina, who was standing in a corner of the kitchen with her hands primly clasped behind her back watching Gabriel, no doubt gauging his reaction. Her smile looked a bit strained, and she seemed unimpressed with the décor. Gabriel stood up from in front of the stove and planted his feet in the center of the room, hands on his hips.

"It's perfect," he said. "I'll take it."

No one was more surprised than me. Kristina rescued the moment from becoming awkward.

"That fantastic, Mr. Garrett, but we haven't had time to put together an offer," she said. "Are you sure you don't want more time to think about it?"

"Oh, that won't be necessary," Gabriel replied. "I'll just pay the list price."

"Well that's great," I said, jumping in. "Do you need time to put together financing?"

"Nope, that won't be necessary either. I'll be paying by certified check. That work for you, Mr. Riordan?"

I smiled. "That would be just fine, Gabe, and please call me Eric."

I turned to Kristina, and I would not have been surprised if she had started jumping up and down and clapping her hands in excitement. She was looking at receiving a substantial commission; the cabin sat on over two hundred acres of land, and the price tag was in the high six-figures.

"Well, pretty lady, I think we just made your job a lot easier."

She beamed a smile that made me feel warm all the way down to my toes.

"Yeah, I guess you did. Tell you what, when we get back to town I'll make a few calls and see if we can set up a closing date," she said.

We filed out of the cabin and I followed them over to their car. I thanked Gabriel for being such an easy guy to work with, and endured the pain of another one of his handshakes, then turned my attention to the lovely Kristina.

"It was really nice meeting you," I said. "I hope I get to see you again soon."

She took my hand and covered it with both of hers. "It was very nice meeting you too, Eric, and don't worry. You'll see me at the closing."

I stepped back as Gabriel folded his massive bulk into the passenger's side of the car, and Kristina favored me with another glacier-melting smile before sliding into the driver's seat. I waved as they pulled away, thinking it was good that I ran into them when I did. It would have been a shame to waste my day cleaning only to realize that I could have sold the place without getting my hands dirty.

I got into my truck, turned my satellite radio to a folk music station, and backed out onto the narrow mountain road. As I drove toward the highway, I began to wonder about Gabriel's sudden offer to buy the property at its list price. He must have been a wealthy man to be shelling out damn near a million dollars in one sitting. A man with that much money could buy a nice two-story colonial or something down in Morganton. Why would he want to spend his money on a ratty old cabin out in the middle of nowhere? The place didn't even have a working toilet.

After a few moments of pondering, I dismissed the thought with a shrug. My goal was to sell the property, and that's what I had done. Gabriel could be a damn drug dealer for all I cared, as long as his check cleared. I tapped my feet to the radio, and thought about what I was going to do with an extra million bucks in my pocket.

A few days later, Kristina called to let me know that she had set up a closing date.

"That's great," I said, "although I have to admit that I'm looking forward to seeing you again more than I am to selling the cabin. Do I really have to wait until the closing, or could I take you out to dinner tomorrow night?"

"Dinner would be really nice, but if we're going on a date, we should wait until after the closing. Conflict of interest, and all that" she replied.

Score!

"I understand," I said. "Until then, I'll just have to look forward to the closing."

"So will I. Goodbye, handsome." She hung up.

A couple of weeks later, I made the drive back up to Kristina's realty office for the closing. Gabriel was already there lounging in the lobby, his massive bulk straining the legs of a plush red chair. He stood up to greet me as I came through the door, holding out a massive paw. As I shook his hand, I was again reminded of his immense strength.

"Nice to see you again Eric," he said. "We waiting for your agent to get here before we start?"

"Bruce will be joining us by conference call," I replied. "Honestly, I don't think the little jerk deserves his commission considering that he hasn't done any work for this sale. I'd rather spend that money taking your agent out to dinner."

Gabe laughed, and gave me a wink. "She is a beauty, ain't she? You gonna try to get a piece of that?"

I laughed, surprised by his candor. "God I hope so. If I strike out, maybe you should ask her out."

"Oh hell no, not me. I'd break that poor little thing in half. I like my women with a little more meat on them."

I heard the sound of high heels clicking on tile, and a moment later Kristina came around the corner.

"Mr. Riordan, it's good to see you again," she said. "Thank you for coming today, I know it's a bit of a drive for you."

"No problem at all," I said.

"Should we go ahead and get started?"

"After you, sir." I motioned for Gabriel to proceed ahead.

Kristina turned to go back down the hall and Gabriel followed. The closing went as painlessly as could be expected, which wasn't saying much. One of the assistants for the attorney handling the transaction came into the office and went over the paperwork with us, pointing out places to initial and sign.

As I worked, I kept missing things because I was too busy staring at Kristina. She was wearing a light blue blouse that cinched nicely around her trim waist and a short gray skirt that showed off her sculpted legs. At one point, she caught me looking and stared me straight in the eye as she slowly stretched her feet out, crossed her thighs the other way, and let her hands linger close to her hips after smoothing down the fabric of her skirt.

I looked away and tried to concentrate on filling out paperwork to stifle the stiffening feeling in my groin. Gabe caught my attention as he reached for a bottle of water sitting next to him on the table, and when I glanced up, I saw that he was smirking at me.

I got through the rest of the closing by focusing on what the office assistant was saying, and making a conscious effort not to look at Kristina and her killer legs. As we finished the last of the paperwork, I stood up and offered a hand to Gabe, bracing myself for the bone crushing pressure I was about to feel.

"Gabe, it's been a pleasure doing business with you. What do you say I buy you lunch as a thank you?"

"Sounds like a winner," he said. "I skipped breakfast this morning. I could go for a bite to eat."

I looked over at Kristina. "Care to join us?"

"Not this time, I'm afraid. I have a lot of work to do in the office today. Could I take a rain check?" She replied.

"Okay, but I'm gonna hold you to it. You owe me one meal, my treat of course."

"You have my number. Give me a call." She gave me another gorgeous smile, picked up a stack of papers, and brushed past me out of the conference room. I was admiring her petite backside when Gabe leaned over and whispered, "Down boy."

I turned to him as the office assistant opened the door for us to leave.

"Did you catch that thing with the legs?"

"Yeah, I caught that. To tell the truth, I was having a hard time not staring myself."

"I'm asking out tomorrow," I said. "I'd be an idiot not to."

We piled into truck, and at Gabe's recommendation, I drove us to a nearby sandwich shop. I ordered us a couple of beers, even though it was only one-thirty in the afternoon, and Gabriel and I sat in our booth munching on meatball subs and fries. We finished our food, ordered more beer, and talked about movies, girls, food, sports, and everything in between. I was happy to find that Gabe was an avid mixed martial arts fan, and we both had the same favorite fighters. It was a rare thing to find another fan who liked the sport as much as I did, so I decided to invite him over to watch the next ultimate fighting event at my house in Morganton.

"I might just do that," he said, after thinking about it for a moment. "I haven't seen any fights in a long time. You got my phone number or email address?"

We exchanged information, and then left the sandwich shop so that I could drive him back to his truck at the realty office. I told him to give me a ring if he needed any help moving in to his new home and waved as he drove away.

On the night of the fights a couple of weeks later, I drove back up to my little vacation house and gave Gabe a call. He arrived an hour before the event started, so I gave him a tour of the property. He was impressed with the outdoor fireplace that doubled as a grill, and with the kegerator in the living room. I poured us a couple of beers and settled down in front of the television.

During the fights, Gabe impressed me with his knowledge of striking and Jiu Jitsu. I told him that I was a purple belt, but had stopped training a few months back when my sensei was killed in a car accident. Gabe nodded solemnly as I told him about how good of a teacher Luis had been. He was only forty-two when he passed—far too young for a good man like him to be taken from the world. That got me on the subject of my grandmother, and finally my parents.

"Seems like you've seen more than your share of grief," Gabe said, his Kentucky accent becoming thicker the more he drank.

"You're telling me," I said. "You should probably avoid getting too friendly with me, you might be the next one to drop."

Gabe chuckled. "I'm too ugly to die. At least you know how to find some humor in it. Losing people, that is."

"Yeah, well, you either learn to laugh or you lose your mind."

"Amen to that."

A moment passed in silence. "You ever lose anybody?" I asked.

Gabe's eyes grew distant. "Yeah, too damn many. My old man died in a coal mining accident when I was eight, and my mom and I moved in with my uncle Aaron in Louisville. Mom died from cancer when I was eighteen, and Uncle Aaron had a heart attack when I was twenty-three. Got no other family."

"Damn, dude, that's tough. I'm sorry to hear that. I know how you feel though, my only living relative is my uncle Roger, and we hardly ever talk."

Gabe shifted in his seat for a moment and decided to change the subject. "Whatever happened between you and Kristina?" he asked. "Did you ever take her out?"

"Yeah, we did the whole dinner and a movie thing a couple of times. I got a little tongue and over-the-sweater action on the second date. I called her up a week after that, thinking that I'm finally going to get her in bed, and she tells me she can't go because she has a date with someone else that night."

"No shit?" Gabe let out a snort. "Fuckin' women."

"Yeah, no kidding. I told her to have a nice life and deleted her number from my phone."

"That's too bad for you man, I bet she would have been a tiger in the bed. She has that look."

"Don't I know it. She was a great kisser. Made me wonder what else she was good at."

Gabe gave me a sidelong glance and pushed his tongue against his cheek, making it bulge out to the side. I snorted and handed him another beer.

For the rest of the evening, anyone listening to us would have thought that Gabriel and I had known each other for years. We quickly settled into an easy camaraderie, and Gabriel drank at least a gallon of beer. After the fights, he stood up from his chair and swayed unsteadily on his feet.

"Shit, man, I'm not sure I can drive home," he said, stumbling toward the bathroom.

I thought about the man that killed my parents, and did not want Gabriel driving drunk.

"Don't sweat it dude, you can crash in the spare bedroom," I said.

"Cool. 'Preciate it," Gabe called over his shoulder, shutting the bathroom door.

We both woke up the next morning nursing hangovers, so I drove us into Morganton to get some grease and cholesterol to soak up the booze in our blood. After breakfast, Gabriel climbed slowly into his truck and invited me to go shooting at a firearms range with him the next day. I had not been shooting in years, and looked forward to knocking the rust off my marksmanship skills. Later, as I drove back to the cabin, I mused that it was nice to have someone to hang out with for a change. I had been spending too much time alone, and needed to do something social once in a while.

Some friendships happen slowly, over time, and some develop quickly. Even though I had barely spent any time with the Gabe, I felt like I had known him for years. Maybe it was because we had so many of the same hobbies and interests, or maybe we had both lost so many loved ones and were tired of feeling alone in the world. Probably, it was both. Either way, over the next three years, he and I started hanging out more and more often. We hiked hundreds of miles of trails that crisscrossed the southern Appalachians, frequented the local shooting ranges, and wreaked havoc at bars and taverns all over the mountains and piedmont.

Not long after we started hanging out, Gabriel and I began exchanging fighting techniques. I was a decent grappler, and a competent striker, but Gabriel made me look like a complete amateur. He is a hell of a lot faster than his size would suggest, and his technique is nearly flawless. In addition to black belt level Jiu Jitsu skills, he is an expert striker and is downright terrifying with a blade. He had also started competing in freestyle wrestling when he was nine, and kept at it until he graduated from high school and joined the Marines.

When it came to his service in the military, he was reluctant to talk about it for a long time. I had often heard that combat veterans did not like to discuss their experiences, and Gabe's behavior seemed to bear that out. As time went on, Gabe gradually began to open up about some of the things he saw and did during the war. It seemed to help him, somewhat, to share his experiences. In light of all he had been through, Gabriel began to make more sense as a person, but I always got the feeling there was something he wasn't telling me, some secret he was hiding.

That all changed one night almost three years to the day from the first time I met him.

We were sitting on the back patio of my house in Morganton, drinking liberally from a bottle of Kentucky bourbon, and watching a low fire burn in the outdoor fireplace to ward off the last of the stubborn winter chill. Gabe was telling me about the first and second battles of Fallujah, where he had served in the First Marine Expeditionary Unit at as a scout sniper. The operations were long and brutal, and Gabe had racked up more kills than he cared to remember.

"I still see them sometimes, the men I killed," he said. "I lie down and try to sleep, and I see their faces. No matter how many times I did it, pulling the trigger never got any easier. Even though the man on the business end of my rifle would have done the same to me given the chance, I was still taking a human life out of the world. I was killing someone's brother, or son, or father. Even the worst of men have somebody that cares about them."

"Yeah, but the guys you took down are the kind of people that the world is better off without," I replied.

"How do you know that?" Gabe shot me a piercing stare. "Put yourself in their place for a minute. A bunch of foreigners come into town and take over everything. They set up shop in your church, start laying down curfews, and confiscate people's property. They go after the people that try to fight them, and wind up killing a bunch of non-combatants. Not just men, but women and children too. How long do you think you'd be willing to put up with that shit? How long would it be until you picked up a rifle and started trying to chase the invaders out of your home?"

I thought about that for a moment, trying to imagine what it would be like to live through a foreign occupation. I remembered all the times my mother had told me never to judge a man until I had walked a mile in his shoes. Maybe Gabriel had a point.

"I don't know," I replied. "I guess I never thought about it that way."

Gabriel looked away, anger fading from his expression. "Yeah, well, it's all in the past now. My soldiering days are over, thank God. As bad as it was, Fallujah wasn't the worst of it for me. When I went to work for Aegis…" He stopped mid-sentence. He glanced at me, and shook his head.

"Never mind, I don't want to talk about that."

"That's bullshit," I said. "You wouldn't have brought it up if you didn't want to talk about it." I turned and leaned toward Gabriel.

"Gabe, we've been friends for a while now, and I've gotten to know you pretty well. I can tell that whatever happened when you worked for Aegis is eating away at you. You can't just carry that shit around forever, man. Get it out of your head. Drag it out, and stop letting it ruin your life."

Gabriel passed a hand over his face, his palm making a loud rasping sound on his beard stubble.

"You don't understand Eric, I can't talk about it. If the wrong people found out, things could get real bad for me and whoever I tell. You're better off not knowing, it's safer that way."

"Safer? What are they gonna do, take me away and lock me up?"

He shot me a level stare. "Yes, or worse."

That stopped me. I looked at Gabe for a moment, and then sat back in my chair.

What the hell had he been involved in? What could be so bad that the government would kill or imprison people to cover it up? I had seen enough evidence to know that those things happened from time to time—usually as the result of a colossal fuck-up—but sometimes agencies of the federal government did terrible things. In recent years, exposés about declassified government documents revealing secret military operations had filled the news. It was not far-fetched to believe that Gabriel might have been caught up in something like that.

Gabe watched me as I pondered, and after a few moments, turned away and stared at the fire. The light from the flames cast twisting patters of shadow over his weathered face, casting his grey eyes in an ethereal glow.

"Trust me, Eric," he said, "there are some things you are better off not knowing about."

I felt a swell of pity for my friend, but I was also curious to know what could possibly be worse for a man to go through than the horrors of war.

"Listen Gabe, I'm a grown man. I can make my own decisions, and I can take care of myself. I know how to keep my mouth shut, and I'm not stupid enough to think that the government can't touch me. You need to talk about this stuff, and I'm willing to listen."

Gabe looked at me for a moment, his expression unreadable, and then said, "Okay. I'll tell you some of it, but there are some things that I will have to leave out. Some things are just too dangerous to talk about."

"I'm listening."

He nodded and continued, "Aegis isn't just a private security firm. They do wet work for the CIA and the NSA. Strictly off the record shit. Not even Congress knows about it. I have no idea how they cover up all of the funding that they get, but I know it's a shitload of money."

"What's wet work?" I asked.

"Killing people. Wet work refers to any kind of mission where the operatives are sent in with the specific directive of killing people, and keeping it quiet."

My eyebrows went up. "Oh...wow. That's crazy."

"You're telling me. Anyway, on some missions we worked closely with a liaison from the Center for Disease Control. At least that's where he said he was from, I have my doubts about that. Those missions were usually pretty simple. When a lethal infectious disease broke out somewhere, and it needed to be kept quiet, strike teams went in to contain or eradicate it. I was a sniper on one of the strike teams."

"How do you eradicate a disease?"

"You kill the carriers and burn their bodies."

Suddenly, I began to understand why Gabe was so reluctant to talk about this.

"How many of these missions did you go on?" I asked.

Gabe shook his head, "I don't know. Too damn many."

"What kinds of diseases did these people get? They must have been pretty bad for the government to send death squads after them."

"You have no idea. It was awful. Bubonic plague, weaponized smallpox, mutated strains of Ebola…all kinds of nasty shit."

"Wait, you said weaponized smallpox? How does that work?"

"Airborne strains dispersed with bombs. Terrible shit. Light one off over a major city, and you have an instant epidemic. Panic, death, looting, rioting, it's like Armageddon in a bottle."

I thought back to when Gabe bought the cabin from me, thought about what he was telling me, and could almost hear the click in my head as all the mental cogs finally tumbled into place.

"Is that why you bought your cabin from me? So you could get away if something like that happened?" I asked.

He nodded. "Yep. I don't want to be anywhere near a city if an outbreak happens."

"Do you think that's really likely? I mean, it seems like something out of a horror movie."

Gabe looked at me, his expression grave. "Not only could it happen, I firmly believe it is only a matter of time until it happens. It's not a question of if, but when. The weaponized versions of these diseases are just too damn easy to make. Any country with half-assed medical laboratories can manufacture the shit." He jabbed a finger into the table beside him. "Mark my words, there will be a pandemic. Probably within our lifetime."

I absorbed that for a moment. "So what should people do? I mean, how do you prepare for something like that?"

Gabe shook his head. "People can't do anything about it. People are lazy and stupid, and don't even want to acknowledge that this kind of shit exists. Now an individual person, with the right knowledge, could do a lot to prepare..."

Gabe looked thoughtful for a moment, then abruptly stood up and pulled his cell phone out of his pocket.

"A few years back I wrote down some things I figured I should do to get ready, just in case. I even made lists of supplies I wanted to have. I'm going to email it to you, just in case you want to go ahead and take some precautions of your own."

I got out my phone and opened the email Gabe sent me. We sat outside on my patio long into the night discussing Gabriel's work with Aegis, and what I should do to prepare for the worst. At one point, I noticed that Gabe's survival items included a list of weapons that are illegal in most states that function well with silencers on them.

"Why would I need silencers on all these guns?" I asked.

"Trust me, you don't want to know. I'll buy it all for you, and keep it at my place until you can come pick them up. But you'll have to pay me back."

Gabe noticed my surprise and held up a hand. "It's cool. I know a guy."

I thought about pressing him further on that point, but decided against it. I already had a lot of information to digest, and I wasn't eager to add anything else to the pile. I went over a couple more items on the list, and then decided to ask Gabe a question that I had been holding in for a long time.

"Where do you get your money from Gabe?"

He looked up from his phone, momentarily taken aback by the change of subject.

"I mean, you've told me this much right?" I said. "You already know where my money came from."

Gabe was silent a moment before responding. "I'll answer that, but first you have to answer a question for me."

"Shoot."

"You've known me for over three years, why haven't you ever asked before?"

I shrugged, "I don't know, I guess I figured you'd get around to it sooner or later. It didn't really seem that important until now."

Gabe nodded. "I stole it."

I blinked.

"You stole it? From who?"

Gabe smiled, showing sharp white teeth against the firelight.

"From Aegis. Not long before I quit the company, I was working physical security on a shipment of gold bullion in Afghanistan. I never knew for certain, but I suspected they were using the gold to bribe tribal leaders in the region into giving up intel on insurgent troop deployment, and then selling the info back to Coalition forces. Taliban raiders attacked our convoy one night, and I managed to escape in one of the trucks. When I got far enough away to feel safe, I checked the cargo and saw that I had run off with a shitload of gold. I got on the truck's satellite phone and called a former associate of mine who works in the money laundering business. He got in touch with some of his contacts in the region and helped me smuggle the gold out of Afghanistan, then laundered it through several accounts in Switzerland and the Cayman Islands. By the time I gave my partner his cut, and transferred the rest into my own accounts, it was squeaky clean."

"What did Aegis do when they found out?" I asked.

"They didn't. I told them I left the truck out in the desert after it ran out of gas, and made my way back to civilization on foot. I was only about fifty miles from Kandahar, so it wasn't that difficult of a story to believe. They asked me what happened to the cargo, and I told them that I didn't know. I guess they figured the Taliban found it. Either way, they never traced it back to me."

"How much was it worth?"

"I walked away with about seven million and some change."

I whistled. "Not bad for a day's work."

"The way I see it, the fuckers owed me at least that much after everything I did for them. I considered it a severance package."

"And how long was it from then until you left Aegis and bought my cabin from me?"

"About six months, give or take."

"And all this time you never thought to tell me about any of this?"

Gabe smiled and shrugged. "You never asked."

Chapter 2

Outbreak

A year later, when the proverbial shit hit the fan, I was at my home near Charlotte sitting on the couch and flipping through the HD sports channels. My cell phone started buzzing on the coffee table, and when I picked it up, I saw Gabe's number on the display.

"Hey Gabe, what's going on?"

"Are you near a television?" he replied.

"Uh, yeah, I'm watching TV right now. Why?"

"Something bad is happening down in Atlanta. Have you caught any of the news today?"

"No, I haven't. What's going on?"

"Turn on CNN, Eric. It's happening."

Those words brought an abrupt, screeching halt to the last good day I would have for a very long time. I went silent for a long moment, breathing shallow and feeling like someone had just kicked me hard in the gut.

"Eric, you still there?"

"I'm still here, just give me a minute." My voice squeezed through a clenched throat.

I put down my cell phone and leaned forward on the couch. *Calm down, man.* I thought. *Maybe he's wrong; maybe it's not that bad. Just turn on the news and see what's going on.*

I took a few deep breaths, sat up straight, and reached for the remote. I told myself that Gabe was just being paranoid, that he was overreacting. It couldn't possibly be that nameless, dreadful thing that I had spent the last year of my life living in fear of. Over the next hour, as I watched the tragedy in Atlanta unfold, I was slowly forced to begin accepting the awful, gut-wrenching truth.

I was wrong. It was that bad.

But that's getting ahead of what happened.

Before I started losing my shit, I turned the channel to CNN. Anderson Cooper was mid-sentence talking about a large riot that had broken out in downtown Atlanta.

"...any information about the cause of these riots?" A graphic appeared on the screen announcing the name of a reporter from CNN's Atlanta office. She was at the scene of the incident and speaking live via cell phone to the news studio.

"We don't have any information at this time about what caused this outbreak of violence, but we do know that it started in downtown Atlanta and has spread outward from there. Police have established barricades outside the riot zone on all of the streets that access the downtown area. Authorities are trying to keep the activity from spreading to other areas of the city, but it seems to be doing so in spite of their efforts." She paused for a long moment, and then said, "Okay, I just got word that we should have a video feed available in just a few moments."

Anderson toned in gravely, "Alright folks, we're going to take a quick break. Hopefully when we return, we'll have a video feed from Atlanta so that we can get a more accurate assessment of events unfolding there. Please stay with us." As the network went to commercial, I picked the phone back up.

"Gabe, they're talking about a riot. How bad can that be?" I asked.

"You know what's in Atlanta, right?" he replied.

"Coca Cola and fat people?"

"Do I sound like I'm in the mood for fucking jokes, Eric?" he nearly shouted. "I'm talking about Aegis and the goddamn Center for Disease Control."

"Okay, okay, sorry. Don't flip out on me. What do you think happened?"

Gabe didn't reply for a moment. I could hear him breathing on the other line as he considered what to say next.

"Fuck it," he snapped, as though coming to a decision. "I think something that the CDC lab rats used to call the Reanimation Phage has broken out in Atlanta. If it has, and I think I'm right on this one, then all of North and South America is in deep trouble. Maybe even the rest of the world."

"Okay," I said. "First of all, what the hell is a Reanimation Page, and why is it a threat to two continents?"

"Phage, not Page, dumbass," Gabe replied crossly. "I've had to fight it more times than I can count, and it's worse than anything you can imagine. This thing getting loose in a heavily populated area is a disaster. It's my worst nightmare come to life."

My level of anxiety went from an eight on a scale of ten to about a sixteen.

"Okay, what is this thing? And why do you think it's what's causing the trouble in Atlanta?"

"I got a call from a former co-worker of mine just before the news outlets caught wind of what's going on down there. He had just put a bullet in his best friend's head, and was about to bug out of the city. He said it was definitely Red Plague, and if this thing is loose in Atlanta, then shit is about to get real dangerous, real fast."

My mind was reeling. Red Plague? Reanimation Phage? What the heck is a phage? I was about to ask Gabe to explain what the hell he was talking about when Anderson Cooper came back on the air.

"Okay folks, we've managed to establish a live video feed on the ground in Atlanta at the scene of the riot." Anderson's eyes were wide, and his skin had gone as pale as his prematurely gray hair. To his credit, he managed to keep his voice level.

"I need to warn the viewers at home that some of the images you are about to see are extremely graphic. If you have any young children watching this with you, please use discretion before allowing them to see footage we're about to air. Again, what you're about to see is extremely graphic, and may not be suitable for some viewers."

The broadcast cut to a pretty blond reporter standing in front of a police barricade. There were emergency vehicles, police cars, and dozens of cops running around behind her with a few high-ranking police officers barking out orders. I could see that most of the officers had taken up defensive positions behind the cars with their weapons aimed at a large crowd of people approaching in the distance. Tall buildings and storefronts lined the cordoned off street, and it looked as though they were somewhere on the outskirts of downtown Atlanta. The reporter was looking into the camera adjusting her hair.

"Are we on?" she asked. At some unseen signal off camera, she went into reporter mode and began describing the scene unfolding behind her. I muted the television as she started talking.

"Gabe, what are you talking about? What the hell is the Red Plague? Why did your friend shoot somebody?" I asked.

"Eric, I don't have time to explain everything right now. How are you as far as supplies for your shelter?"

"Why do you ask? Damn it Gabe, tell me what's going on."

Cold fingers of dread started to work their way into my stomach. Ever since Gabriel told me about his work with Aegis, I had worried that one of the deadly diseases he had fought to contain might get loose. What little he'd told me about it had been enough to keep me awake at night for weeks after our discussion.

"Look Eric, I'm going to tell you some things that are going to sound pretty crazy. Hold off on your usual smart ass remarks, and just listen," he said.

"Okay, I'm listening. Just so you know, you are seriously freaking me out right now."

"Good. If I'm right, then you need to be scared. We all do. Okay, first of all….hey, are you still watching the news?"

Without realizing it, I had started pacing the room and was standing near the kitchen entrance. It's something I do when I'm nervous. When I turned around to go back to the living room, what I saw on the television nearly made me drop my phone.

The sound was still muted, but I could see that the blond reporter was obviously distressed and shouting at the camera. I snatched the remote from the coffee table and turned the volume back on. The sound of gunfire, and lots of it, made it impossible to hear what she was trying to say as she mouthed something unintelligible and pointed in the opposite direction of where the camera was aiming. The camera quickly panned around to the police barricade where a crowd of people had reached the emergency vehicles lined up across the street. The officers behind the barricade had opened up on the crowd with shotguns, and my heart leapt in my chest in horror until I noticed that they were firing non-lethal bean-bag rounds. I would have breathed a sigh of relief, if not for the fact that the crowd-control bags were bouncing off the people nearest the barricade without noticeable effect.

As strange as that was, the people in the crowd were even stranger. Despite the fusillade that the police were sending at them, they just kept moving forward, shuffling along as a single mass, their movements oddly jerky and spasmodic. As they grew closer to the barricade, the cameras panned away from the cops and zoomed in on the rioters.

That was when I noticed the blood.

Near the front, a morbidly obese woman had a massive section of her throat and face missing. I could see her teeth through a gaping hole in her cheek, and the muscles of her neck were visible through the ragged tears where her skin used to be. Her eyes were blood red and wide open, her expression slack, yet somehow menacing. Most of the other people in the camera shot were in similar condition or worse, having suffered deep, vicious wounds.

The crowd started pushing its way through the barricade. I don't mean over, or around, but actually through the barricade. The mass of humanity pressing on the vehicles in front of them was so powerful that they were shifting the rear ends of the cars forward against the police officers. As crazy as it was, I remember thinking to myself: That kind of makes sense. The engine is in the front, so the rear end should move first.

In the front ranks, the force of the mob had crushed dozens of people against tons of heavy steel, their bones snapping visibly and popping out of torn skin, but they didn't scream, or even seem to be aware of what was happening to them. They kept surging forward trying to get to the cops who were desperately emptying their shotguns at point blank range. A voice near the camera shouted, "Fuck this shit!"

The camera panned over to one of the cops as he dropped his shotgun, pulled his sidearm, and started firing at a man close in front of him. Blood sprayed from the man's chest, and his body jerked with the impacts, but he just kept surging forward as though nothing had happened. In the background, the sound of the blond reporter's screaming became audible over the cacophony of gunfire, and an older cop with a bald scalp turned around and began shouting at her and her crew.

"Run! Just run! Get the hell out of here!"

As he turned back around, a little old lady—who couldn't have weighed a quarter of what the large cop weighed— grabbed him by the shirt and started pulling herself closer, lips peeled back over yellow teeth. The cop dropped his shotgun and tried to push her away, but she kept pulling, bending his straining arms. His eyes widened in disbelief at being overpowered until the little woman's mouth locked onto his chest, bit down, and ripped out a gobbet of bleeding flesh right through his uniform. Gore dribbled down her chin, and strips of skin and muscle tissue disappeared as she threw back her head like a crocodile and swallowed it down.

Blood poured in great spurting gouts from the cop's chest as he howled in agony and pushed against the old woman's throat with one big hand. The adrenalin of pain lent strength to his arms, and he managed to force her head away, create distance, and reach down to pull his sidearm. He placed the barrel against her wrinkled forehead, let out a guttural cry of pure rage, and pulled the trigger. The bullet, as well as about a pound of crimson brain matter and bone, burst from the back of her head and left a crater in its wake. The old woman collapsed in a limp heap of bloody flesh, but the man behind her, who was missing most of the skin and muscle on his arms, stepped over the woman's corpse and reached for the wounded officer.

The cop staggered backward in horror, dropped his gun, and ran away from the mob as fast as his legs would carry him, all the while keeping one hand pressed over the bleeding wound on his chest whimpering "Ohgodohgodohgodwhat the FUCK!" as he fled.

The cameraman, having seen enough to know not to stick around any longer, dropped his camera, turned, and followed the bleeding cop as he ran away. The broadcast abruptly cut back to the studio and Anderson Cooper, who sat stock still behind his desk looking both stunned and horrified at the same time.

I know he eventually got himself together and started talking again, but I didn't catch any of it because I was too busy spraying cool ranch Doritos all over the back of my Belmont leather sofa. Cramp-inducing retches kept me bent double until I had purged every scrap of material out of my stomach, and when the vomiting subsided, I hit the ground and crawled backward until my back touched the living room wall.

Somehow, in the midst of all this, I managed to hang on to my cell phone. I could hear a tiny Gabriel voice in my palm, but could not make out what he was saying. I brought the phone back up to my ear.

"Eric? Eric? Are you still there? Can you hear me?"

"I'm here," I croaked.

"Did you see that? What just happened on TV, did you see that?" he asked.

"Yes, I saw it, Gabe." I wiped a handful of puke from my chin and flung it to the floor. "Dude, if you have any idea what the lovely fuck is going on down in Atlanta, I would really appreciate an explanation."

I heard Gabe take a deep breath.

"It's a disease."

"What is?"

"All those people you saw? The ones that were torn up and bleeding? They're infected."

I blew out an exasperated hiss. "Infected with WHAT Gabe? You're not making any sense."

"It's highly contagious, and spreads through direct fluid transfer," he went on, as if he hadn't heard me. "If an infected person bites you, you're infected too. Sometimes just a scratch is enough, if they have infected tissue in their nails. There is no cure for this disease, and anyone who gets it is as good as dead. And as bad as that is, it's not the worst of it. Sometimes it takes a few hours, sometimes it only takes a few seconds, but after the infected person dies, they reanimate."

"What do you mean, reanimate?" I asked.

"I mean they come back to life, sort of."

It was a long instant before I responded. "That's insane, Gabe. That's not possible."

"I know it sounds crazy, but I've seen this thing with my own eyes, Eric. And now, so have you. You don't have to take my word for it, just watch the news. Sooner or later, you'll figure out that I'm telling the truth. Just don't take too long about it, whether or not you survive the next few months will depend on what you do in the next few days."

Looking back, I was definitely in shock at the time, but something in the primordial lizard part of my brain that controls my survival function was alert, listening, and taking notes. I had known Gabe for four years by then, we had become good friends, and he wouldn't be trying so hard to get me to believe him if he didn't think it was really true. That worried me a great deal.

"Okay, assuming I believe any of this crazy shit, what do I need to do?"

"Your bunker. How are you as far as supplies?" he asked.

"I have about three months' worth."

"Good," he said. "Did you get one of those radios I told you about? The kind you can wind up to power?"

"Yeah, I did." I had actually gotten two of them, among other things.

"Okay, great. If the Phage makes it to Charlotte, get to your shelter and monitor the emergency broadcast bands. That will let you to keep track of what's going on in the rest of the country. Once you seal the entrance, do not leave your shelter for any reason until you're down to a week's worth of supplies. Make sure you ration your food, and be especially careful with your water. Where you live, clean water may be a hard thing to come by in the near future, so don't forget to connect your gutters to your rain cistern."

"I'll do that," I replied. A network of pipes connected to the gutters on my house and garage into a filtration system in a survival bunker beneath my back yard. The tank could hold five hundred gallons.

Gabe said, "Make sure you fill that thing up as soon as we're off the phone. While you're at it, fill up all of your bathtubs, sinks, buckets, and anything else you can find that will hold water. And I do mean absolutely anything that will hold water. Pretty soon, clean water is going to be more valuable than gold. After you do that, get as much of your food and water that's in the house into the shelter as quickly as you can, and DO NOT tell anyone about what you're doing, unless you plan on taking them into the shelter with you. If you're going to let Vanessa in on any of this, now would be a good time to do it."

Vanessa was my sort-of love interest at the time. A practical-minded girl, it was going to be difficult to explain any of this to her. I wasn't even sure if I understood it myself.

"Yeah, about that, what if she doesn't believe me?" I said. "I mean, it's not as if I can force her into the shelter. This is hard for me to believe, and I've been preparing for the possibility that something like this could happen for over a year now. How am I supposed to convince her?"

There was a silence before Gabe replied. He had long ago made his opinion known about Vanessa, and I got the feeling he was choosing his words carefully.

"I don't know what to tell you, bud," he said. "If you don't think she believes you, then don't tell her where to find the shelter. The more people who know about it, the more problems you're going to have once the dying starts. Everyone will be desperate, scared shitless, and there will be thousands of refugees trying to find a safe place to hide. If any of them catch up to you, they might not take no for an answer. Know what I mean?"

I nodded, even though I knew Gabe couldn't see it. "Alright, I'll deal with that when I get to it. For now, let's go back to that disease you were talking about. What in God's name are we dealing with here? You think this thing kills people and brings them back to life? Is that why those people on the news weren't hurt when the cops shot them, because they're already dead?"

"That's right. Remember that old woman, the one the cop shot in the head? That's the only way to put someone down once they reanimate—massive brain trauma. Just busting open the skull won't get the job done. You have to penetrate deep and destroy the brain tissue. A bullet to the head works best, but beheading them or severing the brain stem works too. A sharp object through the eye is another way to go, but be careful to get it in good and deep. You want to touch the back of the skull."

Listening to Gabe describe various methods of destroying the human brain did very little to ease my mounting fear. I had only fought in anger twice in my entire life, and although I could handle myself pretty well, I had most certainly never done any of the things that Gabe was describing. I was guessing that he probably hadn't been as lucky as I had in that regard.

"You said earlier that you had seen this disease before. What is it? How could something like this get loose? Doesn't the government know about it?" I asked.

I got up off the floor and made my way into the bathroom, putting the cell phone on speaker along the way. Cupping a hand under the faucet, I rinsed the puke out of my mouth and washed stinking, stringy residue off my face. As I grabbed a towel to dry off, Gabriel began speaking again.

"I don't know what it is. It's not a virus or a bacteria, at least not like any that have ever been studied before. It is some kind of microscopic organism, similar to a bacteriophage, but it doesn't really fit into any of the scientific categories that I know of. Whatever it is, the shit is lethal, and you do not want to be exposed to it. And if you do, you'll know it. First you get lethargic and feverish, then you go into convulsions, and after the convulsions subside, you die. After a while, your body will get back up, and will have only the most basic functions available to it."

"Like what?" I asked.

"Those who reanimate can walk, see, smell, hear, and control their limbs. They don't seem to feel pain, and they will eat any living thing they can get their hands on, but they're drawn most strongly to human beings. I've seen these things munching on dead bodies, and as soon as they spot a living human, they forget the corpse and go after the person. They're determined sons of bitches too. You can fire a cannonball right through the middle of one of 'em, and the only thing it'll do is piss it off. That being said, they get distracted easy, and don't seem to be able to communicate amongst one another. They don't behave in any sort of coordinated manner with the other dead, but they don't go after each other either. I don't know why."

"How is it possible that these things exist and no one knows about them?" I asked. "For Christ's sake, we're talking about a germ that brings dead people back to life."

"They're not really alive," Gabe replied. "They move, eat, and can even make some kind of weird moaning sound, but their hearts don't beat. Their blood doesn't flow. It doesn't make any sense that they should be able to function, but they can, and they can somehow sustain themselves by eating living things."

"But why have I never heard about any of this before? Why hasn't the government warned people about it? I gather from what you've been telling me that they definitely know it exists."

"The government has been very hush about this thing for as long as I have known about it," Gabe answered. "When I left Aegis, it was made very clear to me that if I ever tried to go public with what I know, that I would be dealt with harshly. I even had to sign a non-disclosure contract, as if the threat of being killed wasn't enough to keep me quiet. I think I understand, though, why they were so concerned." Gabe took a deep breath.

"After being sent on a few missions to eradicate outbreaks, I started to get suspicious about the circumstances surrounding them. These outbreaks were always in some backwater, isolated community in a third world country with no strategic or diplomatic value to the U.S. The first few were small scale, but they got bigger and worse as time went on. Larger communities, more people, varying levels of infrastructure, it was just too damned convenient. I got the feeling that these outbreaks were not an accident, and that the guys on the strike teams were being used as guinea pigs in some kind of experiment. I think some agency of the government, acting without sanction, wanted to know what it would take to contain this disease if it ever got loose on U.S. soil. The outbreaks were all just a ruse to run field tests. That was the reason I finally left Aegis. I just couldn't deal with it any longer."

I sat down heavily on the toilet and stared into space while the implications sank in. If what Gabe said was true, then government agencies had been callously killing innocent people just to test out ways to contain a disease. I looked up from where I had been staring and saw my face in the mirror. I was wide-eyed and pale; much like Anderson Cooper after seeing the footage of the riot in Atlanta. My irises looked like dark blue pebbles against a blood-shot background. I replaced the towel on its rack and went back into the living room.

"I can't say this with any degree of certainty," Gabe continued, "but I think that the government might have a hand in this. I think either they created it, or they know how it was created. Maybe they were doing medical research on tissue regeneration and it went wrong, maybe it's some kind of biological weapon they were developing, maybe it came from fucking outer space and the Department of Defense just wanted to see what it could do. I don't know. Wherever it came from, it looks like the lab rats at the CDC didn't keep a tight enough leash on it, and it managed to get out. If this thing spreads as fast as I think it can, the government may not be able to stop it."

As I entered the living room, I sidestepped the puddle of vomit behind my couch and saw that the news was still airing footage of the carnage unfolding in different parts of Atlanta. Shots from a helicopter showed smoke rising from several buildings in downtown, people running panicked through the streets, massive vehicle pileups halting traffic on most of the major streets and highways, and in the midst of all this, everyone was trying to get out of the city on the same few roads, and no one was able to get anywhere. Cars sat immobile in long lines at every intersection and on every highway while frustrated, frightened, and angry drivers honked horns, yelled at each other, got into fights, and did every stupid thing that a person can possibly do to make a bad situation worse. The graphic on the bottom of the screen read that looting and vandalism had broken out all over the city, and that hospitals were quickly filling up with casualties of the spreading chaos.

"What's going to happen if the government can't stop this thing from spreading?" I asked. "Is there a vaccine or something to keep people from getting infected? If the government created this shit, then they should know how to stop it, right?"

"I don't think so," Gabriel replied. "I think they might have bitten off more than they can chew with this one. If they can't stop this outbreak, then within a few months there won't be much left of civilization in this part of the world. That's assuming it doesn't somehow manage to spread outside of North and South America."

"So what are you telling me Gabe? Is this the fucking end of the world or something?"

"It might be Eric, it might be. God, I hope I'm wrong, but I have a really bad feeling about this."

I stood in my living room staring at the television, rooted to the spot with my phone pressed against my ear, and felt a coldness creep slowly into my hands and face. I couldn't think of anything to say, and the line carried only the sound of breathing for long seconds before Gabe finally spoke up.

"Listen, my brain is pretty fried right now," he said. "I need to go soon, and start getting ready, but first I need to send you some information. Years ago, back when I first left Aegis, I wrote down everything I knew about Red Plague and how to fight it. Do you have enough ink and paper in your printer for a large document?"

"Yeah, I do. Are you going to email it to me?"

"Yes. It's a fairly long document so make sure you load up the paper tray. Reading it is secondary to getting your bunker ready; I don't know how much time you have until the outbreak makes its way to Charlotte. It may be a few weeks, it may only be a few days, but it will reach you, and if you are not prepared, then you might not survive. If there is anyone other than Vanessa that you want to get into the bunker with you, then you need to call them as soon as you get off the phone with me. Your house is a pretty good distance away from the most populated part of the city, so if there is any reason you can think of for which you need to go into town, do it now. In a few days the roads probably won't be safe to travel on."

"Okay, I'll do that," I said. "Jesus, man, this is some heavy shit."

"I know, man, believe me, I know." Gabe said. He sounded tired. "Just do everything I told you to do, okay? Call me when you get the document printed so I that will know for sure that you have it. Handle whatever business you have to as quickly as you can, then get the fuck into your shelter."

"Yeah, I got it," I replied. "Hey Gabe?"

"Yeah?"

"Thanks for calling me, bro. I appreciate you trying to help me."

"Forget about it," he said impatiently. "Just do what I asked you to do, okay?"

"Alright, I will. I'll call you to let you know when I get your email."

"Okay. Good luck out there buddy. Before this is over, I think you're going to need it."

"I hope you're wrong, man, but thanks anyway. Later."

Chapter 3

Preparations

After I hung up the phone, I turned my attention back to the television. Another hour of watching the destruction running rampant in Atlanta gave me a headache, so I turned the TV off and decided to get moving. While logging on to my computer to check my email, I called Vanessa's cell phone and got her voice mail.

Goddamn it Vanessa, answer your phone for a change. I hung up on the recording and sent her a text asking her to call me as soon as she could. I didn't bother with leaving her a voice message—she never checked it.

With that done, I downloaded the document Gabe sent me to my desktop and started printing it. My overgrown friend had not been lying when he said it was a long one, the damn thing took ninety-three pages to print. As I was punching holes in the pages to clip them into a binder, my cell phone came to life with Vanessa's ring tone.

"Vanessa, thank God you called back."

"Oh my God, Eric, have you been watching the news?" she asked, her voice shaky. "Something really bad is going on in Atlanta. I swear I just saw people like, eating each other or something."

"I know," I said. "I've been watching. Are you doing okay?"

"I'm fine. I'm just a little…freaked out. This is surreal; it feels like September eleventh all over again."

"Babe, I think I might have an idea of what's happening, and I think it's actually worse than that," I said.

She didn't say anything for a moment, and I could almost see her brows coming together in confusion. "I'm sorry, what? What the hell are you talking about?"

I sighed. "Listen, do you remember my friend Gabriel? The kind of tall, dark-haired, rough-looking guy?"

"You mean that creepy survivalist with all the scars? The guy that lives all alone in the woods, and is probably a serial killer or something? Yeah, I remember him. Why?"

I didn't realize Vanessa had such a low opinion of him.

"He called me today and told me some things I think you need to know. He used to work with the CDC in Atlanta, and he knows what's causing all the trouble down there. It's pretty serious, babe. I think you should come over so we can talk about it. It's the kind of thing that needs to be discussed face to face."

"That guy used to work for the CDC? What is he, a doctor or something?" she asked.

"No, he's not," I said. "He didn't work for the CDC, he worked with them. He was a private security contractor, and his employer did a lot of stuff for the government."

"So he's a mercenary? Christ Eric, why are you friends with him?" Vanessa was very left wing when it came to politics.

"No, Vanessa, he's not a mercenary, not anymore at least. He doesn't work for that company anymore. Look, I don't have time to explain all of this right now. Can you please just come over so that we can talk?"

"Okay, fine," she said. "I'll let my boss know, and I'll be over in about an hour."

"Alright. See you soon. Bye." I hung up and put my cell phone in my pocket.

I lived on the north side of Charlotte, and it would take a while for Vanessa to drive up there from the office building where she worked in Ballantyne. Meanwhile, I had things to do.

My garage stood about a football field away from my back patio, separated by a broad expanse of bright green, well-tended lawn that I took pride in nurturing myself. I went out my back door and crossed it at a jog, my mind on the small structure buried beneath me. Inside the garage, I grabbed a crowbar from a hanger on the wall and carried it behind the building to one of the two hidden entrances to my emergency shelter.

Shortly after Gabe told me about his work with Aegis, he gave me a brochure for the company that installed a similar shelter on his property and suggested that I purchase one of my own. I took his advice—in fact, I bought two of them. One here in Charlotte, and the other at my house in Morganton. There were times when, after realizing how much money I spent on them, I felt like a paranoid idiot. After all, who devotes so much time and expense to something they would probably never need? In light of recent events, however, I was beginning to feel vindicated.

If you were to remove all of the dirt from my back yard, you would see two things that look like oversized shipping containers standing side by side with a short tunnel connecting them, kind of like a giant H. The containers are made of galvanized steel covered with a thick coat of fiberglass to prevent corrosion. They are set into a concrete foundation, and surrounded by gravel up to the roof, which reaches its highest point three feet under the surface of my lawn. One of the compartments is finished to look like the interior of a small two-bedroom house, albeit with exposed wiring and plumbing, while the other is a bare-bones storage unit.

The company that installed them had dug one hell of a big hole in my back yard to pour in the foundation, before spending the next week anchoring in the compartments, wiring everything up, connecting the plumbing, and testing the security system. They also set up the solar panels on my roof, and a few small wind turbines atop the garage. Fast and efficient, it had been an impressive operation to watch.

One of the entrances to the shelter was hidden under a shallow concrete slab beneath the back door to the garage. Designed to be heavy, but manageable, it had enough bulk to keep anyone from trying to move it, but was light enough that I could lift it if need be.

I set the binder containing Gabe's document on the ground before putting the lever end of the crowbar under the slab and pushing down. Instead of the slab lifting up, the crowbar sank into the dirt. Cursing, I threw the crowbar down and looked around for something to use as a fulcrum. Near the tree line a few feet behind the garage, I found a short length of two by four left over from when I had the house built, placed it under the bar, and this time when I pressed down, the bottom edge of the slab lifted a few inches off the ground. I put my foot on the bar to hold it in place, and strained with both arms to lift it up. It was heavy, but I managed to get it upright. The slab was attached to a sturdy hinge that could hold it up once lifted, and underneath was the entrance to the shelter.

It was a simple steel hatch that looked like the kind of thing one would see on the deck of a warship. Both the handle for lifting it, and the bar used to prop the slab in place, lay recessed into the surface so that the false threshold would lie flush on top of it. I lifted the bar and wedged it into a notch in the concrete to make sure the slab wouldn't fall on me while I worked, and then pulled up on the handle to open the hatch. Upon reaching the bottom, I reached out to my right and flipped a light switch.

Compact fluorescents in the ceiling of the narrow tunnel illuminated the off-white paint on the galvanized steel walls. I walked down the tunnel to the heavy steel security door at the end and pulled a thin chain from around my neck. Using the key hanging from it, I unlocked the cover to a keypad, dialed in the combination, and listened as the magnetic lock disengaged. I closed the cover to the keypad, locked it, and slipped the chain back around my neck.

As I entered the storage unit, I flipped another light switch and illuminated the interior. To my right was the five hundred gallon water drum, which connected to a series of pipes that in turn connected to the gutters on my house and garage. Although filling it with rainwater was a nice option to have, it also had a connection that ran from the well pump. Being that my house was too far away from town to connect to city water, I'd hired a company to dig a well and install an electric pump for it. At my request, they had also installed a hand pump that I could use just in case the power went out. I turned a valve to the tap water setting, and then turned another to start the water flowing.

The rest of the storage unit was mostly filled with shelves that held containers of canned food, military surplus MRE's (meals ready to eat), tea, flour, sugar, toilet paper, paper towels, and various other things that I thought might be useful in an emergency. A series of three metal closets with padlocked doors lined the wall at the other end of the unit, each bearing a small placard that read WEAPONS on the first one, AMMUNITION on the second, and EQUIPMENT on the third.

While the tank filled up, I went to the bedroom in the living quarters and put the binder containing Gabe's document on the table beside the bed, then went back into the storage area and grabbed a heavy electric powered winch from a shelf by the door. I lugged it up the ladder and mounted it onto a bracket on the back wall of the garage, unclipped the hook from the winch cable, and plugged the power cord into an electrical outlet close by.

Picking my crowbar up from beside the hatch, I put it back on its hook in the garage and then rolled a wheelbarrow into my kitchen through the back door. I took the stairs two at a time to the upstairs bathroom, closed the drain, and filled both the tub and the sink up with cold water. I did the same to the downstairs bathroom, but left the sink in the half-bath empty. I wanted to keep at least one bathroom usable. After that, I started loading things into my wheelbarrow, starting with the heavy stuff first.

Over the next hour and a half, I used an old canvas bucket to lower all the food, beverages, and other necessities from the house with the exception of some stuff to make sandwiches, a few bottles of water, and some tea. Everything else went onto the already crowded shelves. That done, I put away the winch and resealed the entrances.

As I was fitting the concrete slab back into place over the hatch, I remembered that I was supposed to call Gabe to let him know that I had printed his email. After fussing with the dirt and grass around the entry to make it look like it hadn't been disturbed, I went back into the house and grabbed my phone.

Gabe answered on the first ring. "Took you long enough. I was getting ready to call you."

"Yeah, sorry about that. I actually printed your email out about an hour and a half ago. I got to moving things into the shelter and forgot about calling. "

"How much longer before you go underground?" he asked.

"I'm waiting on Vanessa to get here. She said she would be here in an hour, but that was about an hour and a half ago."

Gabe snorted. "Reminds me of my ex-wife. Women have a distorted sense of time."

I hadn't known that Gabe had ever been married.

"I'm not too worried about it. Vanessa will probably be late to her own funeral." Just as I said that, I heard the sound of a car coming up the driveway.

"Speak of the devil, looks like she just rolled up. I'm going to go talk to her. You doing okay, man?"

"No, Eric, I'm pretty fucking far from okay. I've got to finish some things up, let me know how things go with Vanessa."

"Will do. Let me know if there is anything I can do to help you, okay?" I replied.

"I'll be fine, worry about yourself. Talk to you in a little bit." He hung up.

I went to the front door and opened it just as Vanessa was getting out of her car. She had changed out of her work clothes and was wearing a pink tank top with a pair of jeans and flip-flops. On most girls, an outfit like that would look casual, but on her, it looked stunning. The tank top showed off her bronze skin, as well as the heavy swell of her breasts, and contrasted wonderfully with raven black hair that hung well past her shoulders. As fantastic as her body was, her eyes were her best feature. They were an iridescent shade of green, like the color of a forest on a cloudy day.

Gabriel had once pointed out that he suspected Vanessa was only with me because I had money, and bought her lots of nice things. I told him that I didn't really care, and that I would put up with her for as long as she was willing to put up with me. Maybe that made me a chump, but I doubt that any man who laid eyes on Vanessa would have blamed me. Other than Gabriel.

I waited for her on my front porch as she got her purse out of the back seat. She came to the door and I put my arms around her, breathing in the scent of her perfume.

"You doing okay, babe?" I asked.

"Yeah, I'm just kind of freaked out about what I saw on the news earlier," she said as she hugged me back. "I watched TV while I was getting ready to come over. It looks like Atlanta is getting worse."

"Come on inside, I'll put on some tea."

I held the door open and went inside after her. Vanessa went into the living room and stopped in front of the large puddle of coagulated vomit behind the sofa.

"Oh my god, that is so gross. Did you do that?" she said, pointing one manicured fingertip at the puddle.

"Uh, yeah...I kind of have a bad reaction to the sight of blood. I saw something on the news earlier that...you know what, just go sit down. I'll clean it up."

"Why didn't you clean it up before now? God, it stinks." She put a dainty hand over her nose as she sidestepped the vomit and sat down on the couch.

"Sorry, I got distracted."

Preparing for what could possibly be the end of the world made a little puke on the hardwood floor seem like a trivial matter. I went into the kitchen and got a dustpan, some spray cleaner, a cleaning bucket, and a roll of paper towels. While I was cleaning half-digested tortilla chips from my living room floor, Vanessa turned on the television and began flipping through channels. It seemed that every network had stopped their regular programming to show footage of the chaos in Atlanta.

Multiple news helicopters showed bird's-eye view footage of the rioting that had spread far beyond downtown. Nearly half of the city was on fire, huge clouds of black smoke obscured the streets, and panic-stricken people ran away from flame-engulfed buildings and suffocating clouds of smoke. Reports from the ground showed police and emergency workers being overwhelmed, while everywhere in the city, reports were coming in of people attacking one another. One of the news networks had to cut away when two men covered in blood and gore dragged a field reporter to the ground, tore out his throat, and ripped off half of his face. He tried to scream, but only an agonized gurgle and a dark spray of blood came out of his mouth.

The broadcast switched to the Atlanta Chief of Police telling people to get off the streets, stay in their homes, and lock their doors. The governor of Georgia had declared a state of emergency and requested federal aid. National Guard units were mobilizing, while police and emergency responders from other jurisdictions headed for the city to help contain the growing disaster. A spokesperson for FEMA came on the air and stated that they were sending aid to Atlanta as soon as possible.

By that point, I had finished cleaning up the vomit from behind the couch, washed my hands, and put some water on the stove to boil. Back in the living room, Vanessa's face had gone white, and her eyes were wide with shock. I took her hand in mine, removed the remote control from her grip, and gently pulled her up from the sofa.

"Come on babe, let's go in the kitchen and talk about this." I wanted to get her away from the television and try to calm her down.

As I led her out of the living room and into the kitchen, she kept her hand pressed over her mouth and stared into space like she was catatonic. I was beginning to worry that she was in shock. I sat her down at the small table beside a window that overlooks the back yard.

"Vanessa?"

Nothing.

I nudged her shoulder. "Babe, you okay?"

The light came back into her eyes, and she took her hand away from her mouth. Placing her palms flat on the table, she took a few deep breaths, and then looked up at me.

She said, "You told me earlier that you know what's happening."

I turned away from her, walked back over to the stove, took two cups down from a cabinet, and placed a bag of Earl Gray into each one. The kettle began to whistle, so I took it off the stove and poured hot water over the tea, then spooned in some sugar. Brown, ribbon-like swirls diffused from the leaves, darkening the water in elegant little circles. Vanessa stared at me expectantly, but when I tried to call up a good way to start, I got a dial tone. I let a few seconds tick by, and finally decided that, in this case, honesty was the best policy.

"What I'm about to tell you is going to sound pretty unbelievable," I said.

"Is it more unbelievable than people eating each other? 'Cause I've seen some of that today," she replied.

Good point. "Everything I know about this, I learned from Gabriel, and I don't think he would lie to me."

"Really?" Her single raised eyebrow wasn't so sure. I shot her a look, and she held up a hand.

"Fine. What did he tell you?"

I laid it out for her. Everything Gabriel had told me a year ago, and everything he told me that day. I left out the part about the two hidden shelters—not to mention all the illegal weapons—and when I finished, she nodded slowly, and turned her head to stare out the kitchen window.

"You know, if I hadn't spent most of today watching what's going on in Atlanta, I would have told you that Gabriel is a fucking lunatic," she said. "I would have said that you should stop talking to that guy, and tell him to stay away from you. But after what I've seen today...I don't know. Maybe he's on to something. It would certainly explain why he went up into the mountains to live by himself."

She drummed her fingernails on the tabletop, the smooth curve of her chin resting in the palm of one hand, and stayed that way for a while. I watched the light play over her eyes as a cloud moved in and obscured the sunlight shining through the window. Finally, she stood up, walked over to me, and gave me a peck on the cheek.

"I'm going to go home and call my parents. I'll tell them what you told me, and see if I can get them to believe it. Give me a call tomorrow, okay?" she said.

"Vanessa, I think it would be better if you stayed with me. If Gabe is right, then this thing is going to spread fast, and it could reach Charlotte in a couple of days. You'll be safe here; this place is rigged up like a fortress."

Vanessa bowed her head for a moment, and when she looked back up to me, her beautiful green eyes were sad. She laid one cool hand against the side of my face.

"Eric, you are a really, really nice guy, and I like you a lot. But if what's happening is everything that you and Gabriel seem to think it is, then I should probably go and be with my family right now."

She took her hand from my face and walked back to the living room. I trailed after her until she picked up her purse from the foyer table and stopped in front of the doorway.

"Don't forget to call me tomorrow, okay?" she said.

"I won't."

She walked out the door and got into her car. I stepped outside and watched her back out of the drive, waving as she pulled away. When she was gone, I went back inside and shut the door behind me.

It was the last time I would see her alive.

Chapter 4

Watching, Waiting, and Worrying

After Vanessa left, I went back in the house and sat down on the living room couch. Her dismissive departure had left a sour taste in my mouth, and the pervading smell of all-purpose cleaner and vomit only made it worse. I needed a distraction, so I picked up the phone and called Gabriel.

"How'd it go?" he asked.

"Shitty," I replied. "She left a few seconds ago. Said she needed to be with her family."

"How much did you tell her?"

"All of it, pretty much, except the part about the shelter."

"Good. I don't think you should tell her about that."

"You know, I'm starting to think you might have been right about her. The way she reacted to what I told her, and the way she said goodbye...it was weird. It was like she became a different person, like flipping a switch or something."

"She doesn't care about you, Eric, not like you deserve. I know she's a looker, but looks ain't everything, friend. Besides, we got more important things to worry about right now. What do you plan on doing next?"

"I'm going to take a few laps around the house and see if there is anything that I missed. I haven't decided if I'm staying in the house or the shelter tonight."

"My vote is for the shelter," Gabe said. "Better safe than sorry. That's what I'll be doing."

"Yeah, not a bad idea," I replied. "I'm going to watch the news and try to keep track of what's going on down in Georgia. Hopefully the authorities can get a handle on this thing before it gets out of control."

I heard Gabe let out a hissing sigh. His voice held a note of resignation. "I got news for you, Eric. It's already out of control. There are too many infected to contain as it is, and I have a feeling that what we're seeing now is only the beginning. If you get the chance tonight, read that email I sent you. It should answer a lot of questions."

"About what?" I asked.

"About me, about my life, about the things I've seen, and about what lies ahead for all of us. About why I helped you buy all those nice toys of yours, and why I told you about the bunker here on my property. You are, by the way, the only person who knows it exists, so let's keep it that way. Okay?"

"Speaking of, do you think I should go ahead and drive up to Morganton? My shelter there is just as good as the one here," I said.

"I would stay in Charlotte for now. When things get bad, people will quite literally head for the hills. Your place up here is too close to town, people might get funny ideas. You're better off where you are for the time being, assuming you stay in your damn shelter like I told you to."

"Will do. I'm gonna let you go so I can finish up around the house. I'll give you a call in the morning. You should try to get some rest."

"I'll do my best. Talk to you tomorrow." He hung up.

I put my cell phone back down on the coffee table and considered what to do next. It was only a little after three forty-five in the afternoon, and there was plenty of daylight left. I needed to make the most of it. I made a few passes through my house trying to find anything else I should take down into the shelter with me, but decided I had moved everything that was worth moving.

With nothing else to do, I went into the kitchen, sat down at the table, and stared out the window at my lawn. Looking down, I traced my finger along the windowsill, lingering for a moment over a little metal square that lay flush against the cool white surface. To the unknowing eye, it looked like a piece of decorative material, but in reality, it was a sensor for a contact alarm. A few years ago, I had gotten tired of living in my old condo in Dilworth, of being packed in top and bottom with other people and their daily dramas, and had decided to use some of my wealth to build the house that now stood around me.

A massive two-story, it boasted four bedrooms, two bathrooms, a home gym, an office, a game room, and a display area for the different things that I collected. I owned quite a few valuable possessions, and at Gabriel's suggestion, I had the construction company build the house to specifications that made it just next door to a fortress.

It was built of the most durable, strong, and flame resistant materials the builders could find. All of the windows were made of thick ballistic glass tough enough to stop a bullet, and the doors were strong enough to stand up to just about anything but a tank. Even the walls were armored with steel and fiberglass, and designed to be bullet resistant. It had cost me a pretty penny, but I slept well at night.

The icing on the cake was a sophisticated security system that had cost almost as much as the house itself. After the installers finished with it, Gabe had driven down to inspect their work and had pronounced it 'serviceable'. High praise, coming from Gabe.

I armed the security system from my cellphone, and then went to the fridge to get something to eat. I had taken most of the food in the house down to the shelter, but there were still cold cuts and some bread in the cupboard. I made myself a sandwich and ate it standing by the kitchen counter, too hungry to bother taking it into the living room. After I finished, I turned the TV back on and watched with growing concern as the situation in Atlanta continued to deteriorate.

Just as Gabe said it would, it soon became clear that everything he had told me about the Reanimation Phage was true. News networks aired near-constant footage of the infected attacking anyone they could get their hands on, and the anemic efforts of law enforcement and armed civilians to stop them. For the most part, all they succeeded in doing was adding their own reanimated flesh to the ranks of the undead. Even the National Guard was having problems, as evidenced by the number of walking dead wearing ACU's and Kevlar helmets.

The networks brought on so-called 'experts' to explain why the violence had spread so far, so quickly. Their reasons varied, covering everything from mass hysteria to airborne diseases that affected the brain. A representative for Homeland Security suggested it could possibly be some kind of neurotoxin released by terrorists, sparking an entirely new round of speculation and debate.

I would have laughed at all of them, if the implications weren't so dire. It was obvious that no one had the faintest clue what was really happening, and if the scientists, doctors, and various government officials that the public depended on to handle situations like this did not understand what they were facing, then it was unlikely that they would be able to do anything to halt the spread of the disease. I began to understand why Gabe was so afraid of this thing.

I turned off the TV and went through a door in the kitchen. I had one last thing to do before I settled down for the evening.

My laundry room was in the basement, and like everything else in the house, nothing inside of it looked out of the ordinary. Looks, however, can be deceiving. I pulled the dryer out from the wall a few feet and pressed a hidden switch behind it that was designed to look like an electrical outlet. A small biometric scanner read my fingerprints, and I heard a click as the locks disengaged. Pulling aside the piece of fake drywall that covered the entrance to the underground shelter, I opened the steel hatch and crawled backward through the opening before pulling the dryer back into position and replacing the fake sheetrock. On the wall to my left was a locked keypad. I opened it, keyed in the code, and then kicked backward to open the second hatch behind me.

I crawled backward into the short tunnel, then stood up and flipped on the lights. After closing all of the hatches and securing them, I unlocked the door that opened into the living compartment side of the shelter and stepped through the narrow doorway. Inside was a nicely furnished room complete with a couch, recliner, end tables, lamps, and a large entertainment center. Next to that was a desk with two computers: one a large iMac desktop, and the other a PC laptop. I fired up the laptop and opened a software application that accessed the security system.

All of the magnetic locks were engaged, and the water tank had shut off automatically once it was full. I brought up a screen that showed the view through all of the security cameras hidden on the property, both on the inside and outside of the house. Each camera's field of view occupied a little box on the screen, and I could enlarge any one of them with a mouse click. A quick scan showed me that I was alone, so I switched to a menu that controlled the DVRs.

I planned to check the recorded video every day, so to avoid taxing the DVRs' memory capacity, I set them to store twenty-four hours' worth of footage before purging, and then set the computer to give off an audible alarm if anything triggered a contact sensor or motion detector. I wasn't expecting any trouble, but it never hurt to be prepared.

Once the shelter was as secure as I could make it, I went into the bedroom and began reading the document Gabe had emailed me earlier. I didn't know what to expect when I opened it, figuring maybe it was some kind of journal, or memoir, or maybe a how-to manual for surviving the end of the world. What I found, however, was none of these things.

By the time I finished, I was more terrified than I had ever been in my life.

I was in a mild state of shock after the first time I read it, and had to retreat to the kitchen for a strong drink. Fortified by a little liquid courage, I sat back down and turned the pages to a section that Gabe had flagged as being especially important and carefully re-read it.

Summary of undead characteristics, and means of termination:

Until the Phage kills its victims, the subjects are conscious and aware of their surroundings. Infected persons who are near death generally suffer from severe fever, dementia, and convulsions. It is common for the infected to injure themselves in the throes of violent seizures. There does not seem to be any consistent amount of time that passes before the subject reanimates. Subjects may reanimate in as little as two minutes, or it may take as long as three days. Reanimation occurs one hundred percent of the time, unless an operative destroys the victim's brain.

Once reanimated, a revenant appears to have extremely limited motor function and cognitive abilities. They move in a shambling, uncoordinated manner, and do not appear to be capable of deliberate communication. They are, however, capable of making an unnerving moaning sound that invariably attracts other undead to their location. This does not appear to be intentional on the part of the revenants, but analysis is ongoing.

The undead can instinctively recognize any sound that indicates the presence of potential prey. Their range of detection varies somewhat, and is no better than what they were capable of when still alive, but the undead have an uncanny ability to triangulate sounds and follow them to their sources. If one finds the undead on his trail, he should stay quiet and hidden, and the undead will eventually wander off.

Revenants do not seem to possess anywhere near the olfactory capabilities of predatory animals such as dogs or large cats, but they are able to track scents over a limited distance if the trail is fresh and nothing else attracts the undead's attention. Revenants seem to hunt primarily by sound, utilizing smell and sight as secondary methods.

It should be emphasized that revenants are very easily distracted, and even if an undead is tracking your scent trail, any loud noise will draw them away from your location. This method of evasion can be utilized by simply throwing a rock, or some other object, in the opposite direction of one's position, provided that the undead cannot see or hear you. If the undead see or hear a potential victim, they will continue to pursue that person until they catch them, or are distracted (or destroyed).

The primary weakness of the undead, as it applies to one on one combat, is their lack of coordination and mobility. Even the fastest of them can only proceed at speeds comparable to a brisk walk. And although they are clumsy and ungainly, they have the ability to lunge quickly across very short distances. This usually occurs once the undead is within arm's reach of its intended victim, and can bring the revenant's snapping teeth dangerously close to its target. The undead do not experience pain or fear, and consequently do not tire, even during protracted periods of unarmed combat. They seem superhumanly strong because they simply do not get tired as a living person would, and can utilize one hundred percent of their body's strength capability at all times. This is impossible for a living person to accomplish due to fatigue, and the damage that vigorous exertion causes to living muscle tissue.

One can only permanently kill the undead by shutting off the creatures' brain function. Even beheading is not one hundred percent effective unless the brain stem itself is destroyed. The severed head of a revenant can still move its eyes and mouth, and will click its teeth together in an effort to bite anything that comes near it. Bullets fired directly into the brain are the fastest and most efficient method of dealing with the undead, but because the walking corpses are attracted to sound, shooting a revenant often leads to more of them converging on the area of the shot. It has been stated before, but bears repeating, that the undead are exceptionally good at triangulating and locating sources of sound. Neutralization by firearm should only be undertaken utilizing a silenced weapon, or as a last resort when faced with overwhelming numbers.

Melee weapons have varying degrees of effectiveness, depending on the individual weapon's characteristics and the skill of the user. Some commonly available items that have proven effective in the field are large hammers, crowbars, pick axes, fire axes, and hatchets. Other effective, albeit more difficult and risky means are detailed as follows, based on actual observed confrontations:

Knives:

These weapons can bring down a revenant, but require the wielder to engage the enemy at very close range. The danger posed by this method cannot be over-emphasized. The blade must be driven deep into the undead's brain, and often the weapon will become lodged in the skull of the attacker. The most effective means of dispatching revenants with a knife is to trip the undead and drive the knife upward into the base of the skull, thereby severing the brainstem, or to strike upward beneath the jaw, through the soft palate, and into the base of the brain. The latter method is especially effective with a bayonet fixed to the end of a rifle.

Swords:

Only one operative has ever attempted to use a sword against a revenant. Said operative was an expert martial artist, and a highly skilled swordsman. The first sword he utilized was a Japanese odachi, (a very large and heavy katana style sword) and so long as he had room to swing the massive weapon, it was very effective at beheading the undead, and severing their legs at the knee to reduce their mobility. At close range, however, the blade became useless, and the operative nearly found himself overwhelmed.

The next weapon he tried was an Iberian falcata. The blade was shorter than the odachi, but nearly equal in weight, and proved effective not only as a chopping weapon, but also at cleaving the skulls of the infected. With a strong, properly executed blow delivered at a forty- five degree angle to the top of the skull, the sword caused catastrophic damage to the revenant's brain without the blade lodging in the brain case. The weapon in question was custom designed, prohibitively expensive, and due to limited availability, will most likely see only limited use in further revenant engagements.

Spears:

A strong, heavy, long bladed spear, preferably with a narrow, spike-like profile, has proven very effective as an anti-revenant weapon. A quick, powerful thrust to the nasal cavity, under the soft palate, or the base of the skull will usually put the undead down permanently. Destroying the brain by stabbing the revenant through the eye is effective, but due to the small target area that the human eye presents, this technique is difficult to accomplish as quickly or as consistently as a strike to other, larger parts of the skull. Spears are mid-range weapons best used at a distance, and become ungainly and ineffective at close range.

Special notes:

-As a best practice, tactical situation permitting, it is usually easiest to destroy an infected person by tripping them, then destroying the brain while the infected is face down on the ground. Undead are extremely easy to trip. Simply holding a T or L-shaped obstacle in front of their ankles will usually result in a fall. Once down, the undead can be held to the ground with the same implement until dispatched by placing the restraining device across the back of the undead's neck and putting weight on it.

-The undead will doggedly follow prey so long as they remain within the revenants range of sensory perception. Revenants have been successfully destroyed by placing live bait on a high precipice out of reach of the undead, and simply letting them plunge down to their demise. The pitiful creatures will literally walk off the side of a cliff or tall building in an attempt to capture prey, further proving their lack of intelligence.

-Patterns of Movement: The undead do not seem to have any set pattern to their movement or behavior, other than that they are more active at night than during the day. Revenants do not seem to suffer any degradation of their tracking ability at night, most likely because they rely on sound and scent more

than on vision. If trapped in an area with a large infected
population, movement at night is strongly discouraged.
Revenants seem to instinctively attack and tear out the throats
of their victims, resulting in walking corpses that do not emit
the loud, gurgling moan typically associated with a ghoul
spotting its prey. Several times, operatives have been attacked
and killed by undead that they did not know were tracking them
due to limited visibility.

****

Gabe's clinical, detached writing method was powerfully at odds with his brooding, surly personality. It demonstrated a keen, calculating intelligence that I had caught a few glimpses of since I had known him. Not for the first time, it occurred to me that I didn't really know that much about the big man. But unlike before, I intended to find out.

Reading on, I found descriptions and illustrations of various group and individual tactics employed against the infected, as well as the relative success or failure of each one. It soon became clear that two or more people working together in a coordinated attack was far more effective than one person fighting alone. A long section of the journal detailed different types of firearms and ammunition used against the infected, as well as how each one performed in combat. Initially, Gabe's strike team tried using sniper rifles that fired powerful 7.62 mm and .338 Lapua magnum rounds. Their strategy was to keep at least one hundred meters away from the undead, relying on accuracy and long-range firepower to bring them down. The strategy was effective at first, but the noise from the loud rifles attracted large numbers of infected, and the team soon found themselves running low on ammo. Due to the heavy weight of the bullets, each operative carried less than three hundred rounds apiece. The team soon found themselves trapped on the roof of a poorly constructed schoolhouse, surrounded on all sides by the dead. They were forced to radio for a helicopter to rescue them, and had to make several return trips to eliminate the remaining infected.

Afterward, Gabe's team decided to use weapons that fired smaller rounds that allowed them to bring more ammo to the battlefield. Through trial and error, they determined that the optimum load-out was to have at least one operative carry a sniper rifle for long-range engagements, two to three riflemen armed with carbines that fired 5.56mm NATO rounds, and the remainder of the team utilizing submachine guns with high capacity magazines.

On a bet, one of the team members tried using a civilian .22 caliber version of the MP5 sub-machinegun. Everyone on the team, including the operative who brought the small rifle, was surprised at how effective it was at close range. The .22 rounds killed the undead from up to forty yards away, often getting the job done with a single trigger-pull. By picking his shots and staying on the move, the operative single-handedly wiped out a horde of more than a hundred infected. Afterward, .22 caliber carbines became a staple of eradication teams.

Despite their improving tactics, the strike teams saw heavy casualties and requested their employer start issuing suppressors for all of their firearms. At first, the executives were resistant, reasoning that drawing the infected with gunshots was critical to preventing their spread. They believed that keeping them in one place made them easier to wipe out. The teams argued that staying silent and drawing the infected where they wanted, when they wanted, was not only a more effective way to destroy them, but would also save lives.

Finally, the suits at Aegis caved, and on subsequent missions, the benefits of silenced weapons were immediately apparent. Prior to the issuance of suppressed firearms, the strike teams suffered an average of two casualties per mission. But with silenced firearms at their disposal, the casualty rates dropped to nearly zero. In light of that, Gabe's insistence on purchasing silencers for my guns suddenly made sense.

When I finished reading, it was only seven in the evening, but felt much later than that. Weariness had me yawning and rubbing at my eyes, and I wanted nothing more than to put a gun under my pillow and go to sleep. I ate a quick meal of re-heated leftovers, washed it down with a few bottles of Red

Hook, and double-checked the security system. Satisfied, I climbed into bed and quickly fell asleep.

The next morning, I woke up around seven and checked the laptop to make sure it was safe to go back in the house. Seeing that all was clear on the cameras, I went back in through the basement hatch, made a quick breakfast, and sat down in front of the television. I'm not usually a praying man, but before I hit the power button on the remote, I sent up a request that the situation in Georgia be stabilized, and the outbreak be under control.

My prayer, as usual, went unanswered.

The infection had completely overrun Atlanta and was spreading like wildfire into Florida and South Carolina along the interstate highway routes, and spreading to towns adjacent. Footage from helicopters showed traffic jams that spread for dozens of miles in both directions with hordes of undead moving amongst the stopped cars attacking anyone they found.

The President declared Southern Georgia a disaster area, and sent National Guard troops from all over the country to help. Unfortunately, because of the two wars still raging at the time, most of our troops were deployed halfway across the world in Iraq and Afghanistan. The President had not yet ordered troops to be withdrawn from the Middle East, but I had a feeling that might change if things got any worse.

I picked up my cell phone from its charger and called Gabe.

"Yeah, what's up?" He sounded groggy.

"Sorry to call you so early, but you need to see what's on the news," I said.

"Things any better than they were yesterday?"

"No, they're not. It looks like you were right about this thing being out of control. It's already spread to South Carolina, and will probably cross the Florida border by the end of the day."

"Fucking shit," he swore. "Those stupid bastards. How could they let this thing get loose?"

"I don't know, but it's headed our way." I spun the remote around on the coffee table and hesitated, knowing Gabe was not going to like my next question. "Listen man, I read that document you sent me yesterday, and it's got me thinking. Have you thought about maybe…I don't know, contacting the media, or someone in the military or something? The people fighting the infected down in Georgia don't seem to know what they're doing. If they learn what's in that manual, it might make a difference."

I heard Gabe breath a frustrated sigh. "Don't you think I've tried? There's only so much I can do, it's not as if I have the President or the goddamn Pentagon on speed dial. I left messages with some people who might be able to help, but I wouldn't bet my life on them getting the word out before it's too late. What about you? Had any trouble down there?"

"Nope. No problems yet. You manage to get any sleep last night?" I asked.

"I fell asleep at my desk around two in the morning and woke up about five minutes ago in a puddle of my own drool. My back is stiff as hell, and I got a four-alarm headache. Other than that, I'm just peachy."

I chuckled. "Alright man, I'll leave you to it. You get the chance, check out the news. I'll be home all today, so call me if you need anything, or think of anything else I should know."

"Just stay put for now. If things go south, hole up in your shelter until you're down to a week of food, like I told you before. When you get to that point, that's when you set out for Morganton. Things should have settled down some by then, and you should be able to get here quickly if you're careful. And by the way, did you really read all of that manual, or did you just skim over it? There's things in there you need to know."

"Scout's honor, man, I read the whole thing. Twice, actually. Is all that crazy shit you wrote about really true?"

"Every word of it. It's good that you've read it, but I want you to read it again, and again, and after you do that, read it again. Memorize as much of it as you can, especially the parts about how to fight the undead. Check your weapons, put a few rounds through them with the silencers on to make sure everything is in good working order, and then load every spare magazine you have for them. Keep at least a side arm and a couple of spare mags on you at all times. Got it?"

"Got it." I was silent a few seconds before continuing.

"Hey…what if this…what if it's really is the end of the world, man? I mean, I feel like I'm in a bad dream or something, I keep expecting to wake up. Every time I think about it, it's like I have a big ball of ice in my gut. I don't mind telling you that this whole situation has me scared shitless."

"I know what you mean," Gabe said. "I've lived with the knowledge that the Phage exists for over six years now, and the only advice I can give you is to stay strong. What we need to do is focus on survival. There's a storm coming our way, and we have to get ready for it. We'll deal with what happens after if we live long enough."

"Jesus…this is some craziness," I said. "I can't believe we're even having this conversation. I gotta get out of this house and do something to clear my head, or I'm going to lose my fucking mind. Stay in touch, alright?"

"Will do. Later." The line went dead.

I went back to the bedroom on the living compartment side of the underground shelter and unlocked a small safe in the floor of the closet. Inside the safe was a key ring with three keys on it, which I took to the supply unit. Unlocking the compartment marked WEAPONS, I opened the heavy steel door to reveal three metal shelves. The top shelf was flat, and held boxes of fragmentation and concussion grenades. The second rack held several rifles including two Heckler and Koch 416 assault rifles, an FN A3G sniper rifle, a Benelli semi-automatic shotgun, and a Bushmaster M-4 carbine. On the shelf below were several pistols including my personal favorite, a Kel-Tec PMR-30.

The Kel-Tec fires .22 magnum, its magazines hold thirty rounds each, and when fitted with a silencer, it makes very little noise. I attached a suppressor to the end of it, loaded a couple of spare magazines, and then grabbed one of the H&K rifles. With three magazines loaded for the carbine, I attached the pistol and all the spare ammo to a military issue load-bearing harness, and took everything topside for testing.

Picking up a few pinecones from the tree line behind the garage, I set them on an old wooden sawhorse from my storage shed, counted thirty steps backward, and thumbed off the safety. Normally I preferred optics, but I figured I should practice with the iron sights to stay proficient with them.

Lining up the apertures, I took a breath, let out half of it, and squeezed the trigger. My aim was true, and the pinecone went flipping up into the air. The military-grade suppressor fitted to the end of the barrel kept the report minimal, such that anyone standing more than a few yards away would only hear a muffled crack, and the clang of the next round loading. Sighting in again, I hit the next few targets in rapid succession and smiled a little as each one went spinning away. All the time I had spent at the range was finally paying off.

Satisfied with the carbine, I sat a few more pinecones atop the sawhorse and put a few rounds through the Kel-Tec at closer range. All of them except one flew away on the first shot, and I got the one I missed with a follow-up shot less than a second later. Good ol' double tap. After testing my two favorite guns, I took them back to the bunker and did the same test with the other carbine, my .22 pistol, and the sniper rifle. They were the only other weapons for which I had silencers available, figuring that if I ever actually had to fire the other weapons in anger, noise would probably be the least of my concerns.

Besides the Kel-Tec, I had a few other pistols in varying calibers, thousands of rounds of ammunition, and of course, the two boxes of grenades. Twenty of them were the high-explosive fragmentation variety, and the rest were concussion grenades. Gabe explained to me how to use each type, and the different tactical scenarios they were best suited for, but I had never actually tried them out. I had exactly zero experience using grenades, and did not want to blow myself up trying to learn a new skill. Where Gabe got them from, and why he decided to give them to me, I have not the faintest idea. And to be perfectly honest, the things scared the hell out of me.

If I were ever caught with them, I would be facing serious time in federal prison. As a result, about once a month I asked Gabriel to come take them away. He always refused, saying that I might need them someday, and as long as I kept my mouth shut, I had nothing to worry about from the law. I told him that if I ever got busted I was turning state's evidence against him. He had laughed at the time.

I don't think he realized that I wasn't joking.

I left the grenades in their boxes. Good old ballistic firearms would do just fine, thank you very much. No needs for explosives, at least not yet.

After cleaning the weapons I had fired, I loaded up a Sig Sauer 9mm pistol, holstered it on my belt, and then went back inside to catch up on events in Georgia. By then, the news media had figured out that the infected were not living people suffering from a virus that turned them into homicidal maniacs, but were something else entirely. CNN was the first outlet to report that the infected were actually walking corpses, and I watched as it happened.

A field reporter and his crew were riding in a Humvee toward the quarantine zone, tagging along with reinforcements from the Tennessee National Guard. They were about ten minutes away from the Army outpost closest to the fighting when the Humvee suddenly screeched to a halt, cutting the reporter cut off mid-sentence. The driver got out and started running toward an approaching column of vehicles, followed by a few other men in Army uniforms. The reporter and his crew followed as well.

Large plumes of smoke rose in the distance, and a long column of military vehicles were driving toward the news crew. They caught up with the soldiers as a captain saluted and began speaking with the commanding officer of the retreating soldiers, a tall, stony-faced colonel with a bloody bandage over his eye. The camera got within microphone range mid-conversation.

"...what's going on? Aren't you with the unit from Dalton, sir?" the Captain asked.

"Get your men turned around, Captain. Dalton is overrun. Our orders are to retreat back up I-75 and establish a perimeter on Battlefield Parkway. We have to stop the infection from making its way into Tennessee."

"But sir, I thought…"

"NOW Captain!" the Colonel shouted, pointing in the direction the younger man's column had come from. "Those damn things are right on our heels, we don't have time to chit-chat! Get that goddamn column turned around!"

The Captain snapped to attention. "Yes sir!"

He saluted again, then ran back to his Humvee. The reporter followed closely and put a microphone in the Captain's face.

"Captain Wilson, did I hear the Colonel correctly? Has the infection spread past Dalton? What happened to the people who live there?"

"I don't know, you heard as much as I did," he snapped.

The Captain motioned to one of his sergeants. "Get on the radio and let all the drivers know that we're heading back north. I want this column turned around, and I want it turned around now."

"Yes sir!" The sergeant snapped off a crisp salute and took off toward a large troop transport vehicle. The reporter kept trying to ask questions as the Captain and his driver got back in the vehicle.

"I don't have time to answer questions right now," Captain Wilson said. "Just get in the truck. We're leaving."

While the journalist and his people piled into the back of the Humvee, Wilson picked up a radio handset and began speaking with someone from the retreating unit. The lead reporter motioned to the rest of his crew for silence, holding a finger to his lips with one hand and pointing at the radio with the other. The cameraman leaned forward, trying to get the microphone closer to the conversation.

"...why are we retreating? I thought the infection was contained to the west. Over."

The radio crackled as the person on the other end replied, "Negative, sir, too many people with bites made it past the quarantine. They must have turned after they got past us. It only takes one infected person to start a whole new outbreak. Over."

"I don't understand, what bites are you talking about, is this thing spread by mosquitoes or something? Over."

"Negative, sir, the bites are from other people. That's how the infection spreads. The dead ones get up and go after the living. Over."

The Captain furrowed his brow in confusion. "Dead ones? What do you mean dead ones? Over."

"I mean dead people sir. The ones who die, whether from wounds or from the infection killing them, they get back up. I know this is hard to believe, but I'm telling you that they are walking dead people, sir. No bullshit, I've seen it for myself. We all have, and we've suffered heavy casualties from the damn things. Nothing seems to hurt 'em. I threw a grenade at a group of them, blew them to pieces, and the damn pieces started crawling for me. Freakiest shit I've ever seen. The only thing that kills them is a head shot. Over."

Captain Wilson paused for a moment, and exchanged an incredulous look with the sergeant driving the Humvee.

"Let me get this straight, you're saying that the infection brings dead people back to life, the dead attack living people, and that's how the disease spreads? Over."

"Yes sir, that's correct. Over."

"Is your commanding officer aware of what you just told me? Over."

"Yes sir, he's on the radio right now trying to get word out to all the squads about how to kill these things. You might want to let your men know to aim for the head when the fighting starts back up. Over."

"Could you get your CO on the radio? I need confirmation from him. Over."

"I can do that sir, but it might be a minute or two. He's pretty busy right now. Over."

"I'll wait, and Corporal, you had better not be fucking with me. Over."

"Affirmative. I'll get Colonel Jacobs on the line as soon as I can. Bravo One out."

The reporter remained silent for a moment, then picked up his microphone.

"Captain Wilson, did I hear correctly that the soldiers from the other unit think that this is a disease spread by the infected biting people?"

Wilson turned around and glared at the reporter. Evidently, he had forgotten that the news crew was sitting behind him.

"We haven't confirmed anything yet. I'm going to have to ask you to stop shooting until I can get more accurate information."

The reporter began to ask another question, but the sergeant in the driver's seat interrupted him.

"You heard the Captain. The camera goes off. Now. You ain't gonna like it if I have to do it for you."

The reporter began to protest, but the cameraman was a little smarter and turned off the camera. That sergeant was a big man, I wouldn't have argued with him either.

The report from the Tennessee National Guard convoy caused newsrooms and internet sites around the world to go completely ape-shit, touching off a massive media-generated panic. Reporters and bloggers seemed to grow nearly as hysterical as the people who took to the streets and sparked riots, which the news media devoured like candy and broadcast in as much gory detail as they could manage. Fox News showed footage of a church in Arizona where hundreds of people had gathered to listen to an unhinged reverend preaching from the bed of a pick-up truck.

"The end is nigh!" he ranted. "This is the time that was foretold in the book of Revelations! Repent! For as it says in the scripture: 'and the sea gave up the dead that were in it; and death and hell delivered up the dead that were in them!' The hell-mouth has opened! God has passed his judgment on this world! Repent, and beg mercy for your soul!"

I was about to turn the television off when the network cut back to the newsroom. They had received word that the White House was about to address the nation regarding the disaster in Atlanta, and a few minutes later, the broadcast cut to the President sitting behind a massive wooden desk in the oval office. He waited a few seconds, presumably to allow the nation to absorb his patriarchal demeanor, and then began to speak.

"My fellow Americans, by now most of you are aware of the tragic events unfolding in Georgia. I would like to start by reassuring all of you that every effort is being made by local, state, and federal authorities to contain the disaster, and our military leaders on the ground in affected areas have informed me that they expect order to be restored very soon.

For the people living in and near the affected regions, please remain calm and do not attempt to evacuate. Disaster relief workers need access to your areas, and if large numbers of people attempt to flee simultaneously, it could block roads and prevent aid from reaching those who need it. Please remain calm, stay in your homes, and wait for military and law enforcement personnel to restore order.

In the interest of public safety, I have authorized National Guard officers in the affected regions to have their troops arrest and detain anyone caught looting or otherwise violating the law. This is a temporary measure, and all those who have been granted police powers have been admonished to use this authority with the utmost restraint, and with regard for people's civil rights.

Additionally, military and medical personnel assisting with relief efforts in Georgia have provided us with more information regarding the cause of this tragedy. Now, much of what I am about to tell you may seem difficult to believe. I admit that I had a hard time believing it myself, until I saw the evidence. But this information has been verified by some of the best medical minds in the country, and let me assure you that everything you are about to hear is the truth.

Yesterday morning in Atlanta, there was an outbreak of an infectious disease that the Center for Disease Control has not yet been able to identify. While the origin of this disease remains unclear at this point, we do know how it spreads, and what its effects are.

Now, this information is of the utmost importance, and I must implore you to listen carefully. The disease in question spreads by direct physical contact, such as fluid transfer. At this time, it does not appear to be airborne, as most of the people who have been infected became so as a result of a bite wound received from another infected person. This disease initially causes flu-like symptoms that quickly deteriorate into convulsions, hallucinations, and eventually death. Now, as terrible as it is, what I have told you thus far is not the worst of what this disease is capable of.

After the infected person dies, the disease somehow reactivates the body's functions, and the person regains consciousness. For reasons we do not yet understand, the people who awaken from this stage of the disease become extremely aggressive, and exhibit psychotic, animalistic behavior. A person in this stage of infection will attack and attempt to bite any person who comes into contact with them.

Let me be clear: People suffering from the advanced stages of this disease are extremely dangerous, and should be avoided at all costs. If you see an infected person behaving in such a manner, please do not attempt to approach or subdue them. The disease renders its victims impervious to pain, and even severe injury will not deter them from attacking. They also seem to be incapable of communication, and will not differentiate between strangers, or family and friends. They will attack absolutely anyone that gets near them.

If you are attacked by a victim of the infection, please report to the authorities immediately. If you know of anyone who may be infected, please do not hesitate to turn them in to the authorities, even if it is a member of your own family. I know it will be difficult, but an infected family member must be reported, or else they run the risk of infecting the people around them.

When we have more details available, we will give additional updates. My staff and my press secretary will be working closely with the media to make information available to the public as soon it is obtained. In the meantime, I would ask that all Americans keep the people of Georgia in their thoughts, and in their prayers. After this broadcast, a list of organizations assisting with disaster relief efforts will be released, and I encourage all citizens of our great nation to do whatever you can to help. I believe in the strength, unity, and generosity of the American people, and I believe that we will all exercise wisdom and charity in this difficult time. Thank you, and may God bless America."

The message was shorter than I expected; the President's speeches were usually long winded. I figured he probably had a lot to do, and needed to get back to it. Wishing him luck, I picked up my cell phone and called Gabe. After several failed attempts, I finally got a ring.

"Did you see the President's address?" I asked when he picked up.

"Yeah, I saw that. I'm glad he's the one handling this, that last asshole we had couldn't find his dick with both hands and a flashlight," Gabe replied.

I wasn't sure if I agreed with him on that. My opinion of politicians in general was that they were all incompetent, lazy buffoons.

"You think they'll be able to get things under control?" I asked. "They know what they're up against now. That's good news, right?"

Gabe sounded dubious. "I don't know, man. I hope so, but I'm getting ready for the worst anyway. Knowing how bad the Phage can get, and stopping it, are two completely different animals. There must be thousands of infected out there now, and all it takes is one of them to start another outbreak. I don't think the military will have the manpower or the know-how to round them all up."

"I guess we'll just have to wait and see," I said. "I feel a little better knowing that the government isn't trying to feed the public a line of bullshit on this one. Honestly, anything but the truth would be more believable than what's really happening. From what I've seen on TV, people aren't taking the news very well..." I stopped, remembering something.

"Hey Gabe, I forgot, I need to call Vanessa. Is there anything else you need to tell me, just in case I can't get you back on the phone?"

"Everything you need to know is in that little manual I emailed you. Do what I said and memorize it. I think pretty soon that you're going to have plenty of time on your hands. If I don't talk to you again before the networks go down, good luck to you, Eric."

"Same to you, Gabe. Take care."

After hanging up with Gabe, I tried calling Vanessa, but it went straight to voice mail. A dozen futile attempts later, I finally gave up, resolving to try again later that night when the networks would be less busy. I hoped Vanessa had managed to convince her parents that what we discussed the day before was the truth. The footage airing on every TV station in the world certainly supported my story.

As I watched the news over the rest of the day, the situation in Georgia continued to get worse, and by the time I got too tired to keep my eyes open any longer, the outbreak had spread to South Carolina, Florida, and Tennessee. Police and military forces were being overwhelmed, hospitals filled up with patients and became the sites of new outbreaks, and the violence became so out of control that the President ordered FEMA to withdraw its people from the quarantine zones until the military could get a handle on things. I began to worry that Gabe was right, and that the government wouldn't be able to stop the outbreak.

I fell asleep on the couch, and by the time I woke up the next morning, the Phage had spread to Charlotte.

Chapter 5

Shelter in Place

The fall of Charlotte happened in much the same way as most other cities when the Phage reached them. No one could pinpoint exactly when or where the outbreak started, but it spread quickly, and soon engulfed the entire city. Local news networks provided coverage for the first few hours, but when it became clear that police and military forces could not halt the destruction, they cut their broadcasts and abandoned their headquarters. Roads and highways clogged with tens of thousands of cars as people tried to flee the city. Fires broke out all over town, followed by riots and looting.

News networks based in other cities continued to broadcast coverage of the carnage in Charlotte even after the undead completely overran the city. One broadcast showed three of the tallest buildings in downtown burning like gigantic torches over a ruined landscape. Hordes of infected wandered the streets looking for prey. Those who could not get out of the city either found a place to hide, or joined the ranks of the undead.

Not long after Charlotte went to hell in a hand-basket, Congress approved a motion by the President to declare martial law in all U.S. territory east of the Mississippi River. Canada and Mexico closed their borders. The President ordered the shutdown of all nuclear power plants in the area under martial law as a precautionary measure. It was probably the best decision he ever made. Unfortunately, for the nuclear plants in regions already overrun, shutdown was not an option.

The President also ordered all military forces deployed overseas to return to the US immediately, effectively abandoning the war in the Middle East. The various jihadist groups, and about a million of their friends, were dancing in the streets proclaiming victory over the "Great Satan" as U.S. troops scrambled to get back to American soil. The International news media went into a frenzy over the events in America, speculating wildly as to the implications of the disaster for the rest of the world. The stock market crashed to unrecoverable levels, and people all over the country began to panic. Mobs of frightened people converged on grocery stores, gun shops, and gas stations. Even in areas not yet hit by the Phage, chaos began to take hold.

Army troops were able to keep the nuclear plants near Charlotte and Raleigh safe long enough to shut them down, but the plant near the southern coast of North Carolina fell before government forces could reach it. I was relieved that I was not facing an imminent nuclear disaster, but after the nuclear and coal plants were abandoned, the entire city lost power.

As the outbreak consumed Charlotte, I tried at least a hundred times to call Gabe and Vanessa. The cell phone network in our area was completely non-functional, but the internet still worked. Gabe's computer connected to the web via a 3G card, and when the cell phone networks went down, so did his internet access. Vanessa should have been able to answer my emails, but for some reason she didn't. I began to fear the worst.

During the fall of my hometown, I spent my nights in the underground shelter, and my days in the house, in spite of Gabe's warning to stay underground. I monitored the spread of the Phage on television until the President declared martial law. After the power went off, so did my contact with the outside world. I was limited to keeping up with events by listening to the wind-up emergency radio I had bought almost a year ago. Thankfully, I had my solar panels and wind turbines, but I used electricity as sparingly as possible. The bank of batteries in my basement could store enough power to keep my appliances running for a day or so, but I turned off everything except my security system. I thought about using my gas-powered generator to keep the refrigerator in the bunker running, but decided against it. I took all of the perishables out of the bunker and had myself a hell of a cookout, then buried the rest.

I felt sure I was a good safe distance from the hordes of infected. My house was over ten miles northwest of Interstate 85, which cut straight across the northern boundary of the city. I lived in a sparsely populated area with over a mile of dense woodland separating me from my nearest neighbor. The road leading to my house was one of the multitudes of winding two lane routes that snaked across the Carolina piedmont. If you didn't know what to look for, you would never find where I lived without a GPS. My driveway was half a mile long and mostly hidden by surrounding foliage. I figured that the infected probably wouldn't find me in the middle of all that undeveloped forest.

I figured wrong.

One morning, eight days after the power went out, I was in my front yard using some water from a rain barrel to shave with, when I heard a loud metallic crunch. I had been in a couple of minor automobile accidents before, and I recognized the crunch as the sound of a car running into something. I rinsed the foam off my half-shaven face, grabbed my pistol, and got on my bicycle. I pedaled down my driveway out to the road. About two-hundred yards away, a blue Camry had run off the side of the road and hit a tree. The front end of the car was crushed in and partially wrapped around the tree's thick trunk. Steam hissed from the broken radiator, and green fluid poured out onto the ground beneath. I rode over to the car and looked into the driver's side window. I nearly fell off my bike when I saw who was inside.

It was Vanessa.

She was slumped over the steering wheel, and appeared unconscious. I pounded on the windshield, shouting for her to wake up as I pulled at the door handle. It was either locked or jammed shut from the impact, and I couldn't get it to open. I pulled my pistol from its holster, squatted down to make sure the shot would not hit Vanessa, and pulled the trigger. The window shattered inward as the bullet went through it.

I took my shirt off and used it to clear away broken glass from the driver's side window, then I reached in and unbuckled Vanessa's seat belt. She was completely limp as I pulled her out of the car and laid her down on the pavement. Her eyes were closed, and her clothes were soaked with blood.

"Holy shit, Vanessa, wake up."

I gently slapped her cheek trying to rouse her. No response. I leaned down and put my ear over her mouth and nose, listened for breathing. Nothing. My heart hammered in my chest as I checked her pulse. No pulse. Her heart was still. I was about to start CPR when I noticed the wound on her right shoulder. There was a patch of flesh torn away, revealing muscle and the white gleam of bone beneath. It was oval shaped.

Like a bite wound.

I stopped and stared for a moment, debating what to do. I remembered that the Phage spread by fluid transfer. Would I get infected if I gave her mouth to mouth?

"What if it wasn't an infected that bit her?" I said aloud to no one.

That didn't make any sense, who else would bite a chunk of flesh off someone? After another moment's hesitation, I remembered something from Gabriel's manual.

Reanimation occurs one hundred percent of the time, unless the victim's brain is destroyed.

I eased back until I was sitting down on the pavement. For a moment, my senses sharpened, and I was acutely aware of my surroundings. The wrecked radiator continued to hiss. Birds sang, small animals skittered through the undergrowth, and the wind gently rustled the limbs of the surrounding trees. A single strand of blood-soaked hair lay limp and tangled against Vanessa's pale cheek. I felt an urge to reach out and brush it aside. Everything that had occurred up to that point, I watched from afar. Detached, and disconnected. It all seemed unreal, like a bad dream.

Vanessa's corpse was not a dream. Vanessa's corpse was real, and it was lying on the ground in front of me. The Phage killed her.

I stood up and got back on my bike. I rode back up to my house, grabbed a sheet from the linen closet, and started up my pickup truck. After driving to the spot where I left Vanessa's body, I covered her with the sheet and gently placed her in the back of the truck. I drove the truck to my garage, got a shovel from the shed, and lifted Vanessa from the truck and set her on the ground. I pulled the sheet below her shoulders so that I could see her face clearly, then walked a few feet away and began to dig. After about two hours of work, I had dug a hole long enough to suffice and about three feet deep. I stuck the end of the shovel in the pile of dirt beside the hole, grabbed a folding chair from the shed, and sat down by Vanessa's body to wait. Just as the sun was beginning to descend behind the trees on the western side of my yard, Vanessa opened her eyes. Slowly, she began to sit up. The sheet slipped off her as she got to her feet.

I thought I was prepared. I thought that after everything I had seen on television, and everything I read in Gabriel's manual, that I would be able to deal with it.

I was wrong. Nothing prepares you for your first encounter with the undead.

I stared in horrid fascination as she got to her feet, and began to stagger toward me. Without realizing I was doing it, I stood up and leveled my pistol at her. Her face twisted into a mask of hunger and rage, and a gurgling, keening, predatory moan burst from her throat. Her fingers curved into claws as she reached toward me.

I backed away from her for a few steps, and then stopped. I felt something inside of my chest begin to burn. The thing that was once Vanessa continued to stalk me. I dropped into a shooting stance and took aim.

"I'm so sorry Vanessa."

I pulled the trigger.

The bullet hit her between the eyes, just above the bridge of her nose, and a red spray erupted from the back of her head. She shuddered for a moment, then collapsed, limp and lifeless. I lowered the gun, and placed it back in its holster. After wrapping Vanessa's body in the sheet, I put her in the grave and spent the next half hour shoveling dirt over top of her. After burying Vanessa, I got two buckets of water from the upstairs bathtub, as well as a bar of soap and my shaving kit, and went out into my back yard. I shaved off the rest of my beard, then I stripped naked and used the water to wash the sweat and dirt from my tired body. I needed the cleansing ritual to keep my mind off what I had just done.

I put my filthy clothes in the laundry bin and put on clean ones, then went down to my shelter to sleep. I was hungry, but I was too exhausted to eat. I sank down onto the bed and didn't get out of it for nearly twelve hours. The next morning, my shock wore off enough for me to begin thinking clearly about the previous day's events. The fact that Vanessa had wrecked near my driveway meant that she was deliberately coming to my house. After I thought about it, I remembered that the blue Camry was her father's car. She must have been with them when she was attacked. Or maybe she was attacked by them. I rode my bike out to the Camry to see if I could find anything to explain what happened to Vanessa.

Pools of radiator fluid and oil stained the ground beneath the engine. I brought my crowbar with me, and used it to pry the passenger's side door open. The interior of the car was clean, except for the blood, and I didn't find anything out of the ordinary. The glove box had an owner's manual and a street map, but nothing else. I reached over to the driver's side and popped the trunk. Inside the trunk was the backpack that I had bought Vanessa four months prior, and a twelve-gauge shotgun. I got the pack for her so that we could go hiking together. Vanessa was never one for the outdoors, and had never actually used it. Now, she never would.

The bag contained a change of clothes, toiletries, some canned food, and two boxes of deer slugs for the shotgun. I found her cell phone in one of the side pockets. I checked her call history, and my number was the last one she had dialed. My guess was that she had gone to her parent's house, something attacked her, and she fled in her father's car. Who attacked her, and what happened to her parents, would have to remain a mystery. I took the backpack and the shotgun back the house with me, figuring I could never have too many guns.

The next few weeks passed slowly. I never realized how much I relied on TV and computers for entertainment. I had enough electricity from my solar panels to run the laptop, and watched every DVD I owned twice. I practiced with some of the different swords in my collection, trying to decide which one would be best for dealing with any revenants that wandered onto my property. The broadswords and katanas were elegant, but were built to inflict trauma, not split skulls. I had a functional replica of a medieval war hammer that looked promising. It was big and heavy, and had good range, but was tiring to wield. I would be fine if I only had to deal with three or four undead, but any more than that, and I would need a lighter option.

Although Gabriel taught me a great deal about knife fighting, I knew little about using a sword in combat. I competed in fencing for a couple of years in junior high, but that was using foils. A full sized battle sword is a completely different weapon. I was sitting on my bed in the bunker one night, reading Gabriel's manual for the fiftieth time, when I got an idea. The next day I climbed into the attic and opened up a dusty chest with my old fencing gear in it. I pushed aside the gear and took out the small-sword that my father gave me when I was thirteen. It was his idea of a reward for winning a small fencing tournament. I honestly wasn't sure if I'd ever pulled it from its sheath.

I drew the sword out and took it outside for a few practice lunges. It was light and well balanced. I remembered that my father said it was made of 9260 high carbon spring steel, meaning that it was an alloy of silicon, carbon, iron, and a few other metals. The silicon makes the steel extremely tough and flexible, and is normally used to make heavy-duty springs.

I took a piece of cardboard out of the garage, drew a hundred or so quarter sized circles on it with a marker, and propped it up against the hedgerow in my front yard. I tried stabbing the little targets with lunges from a few feet away, but missed them by a mile. I thought about different ways to try to hit them, and realized that lunging was the problem. After all, the undead are not going to be using fancy footwork to dodge my sword. Why rush it? I stood sideways in a slight crouch, held the tip of the sword a few inches from the target, and quickly thrust it though the cardboard. After about fifteen minutes of practice, I was consistently hitting the small targets in rapid succession. I put the sword back in its sheath, and resolved to keep it with me, just in case. I used some old nylon water line to rig a sling so that I could carry the sword on my back.

Life went on for another few weeks, and I saw no sign of the walking dead. The broadcasts on my little radio ceased, but they lasted long enough for me to learn that the Phage had overrun the entire country. The President and a few other members of the Federal Government evacuated to a safe location. The military struggled valiantly, but there were just too many of the infected. Reports of military units retreating from overrun cities became more and more common. Just before the broadcasts ceased, the guys at NORAD were saying that the military had established a few safe zones in the rocky mountains, and that any survivors should try to make their way out to them. The rest of the country was left to fend for themselves. I didn't know for sure if the Phage had spread beyond North America, but I suspected that it had.

When I reached the point that I had about two weeks of food left, I decided that I needed to do some exploring. To do that, I would need to bring some gear with me. For weapons, I decided on the Kel-Tec .22 magnum, and one of the H&K assault rifles. I loaded some spare magazines onto a load-bearing harness, then put the guns and a couple of days' worth of food and water in my truck. I cranked the engine and sat in the driveway staring into the distance, trying to decide where to go. After a few minutes, I decided to drive to a housing development about ten miles south of my house. It was a straight shot, and I would easily be able to find my way home if anything happened to the truck. I loaded my bicycle into the bed of the truck as a precaution.

The road was clear during the drive. I saw no other cars, or any other type of movement, living or dead. I slowed as I neared the entrance to the neighborhood, not wanting to attract any attention. I pulled off to the side of the road to consult my street map. I didn't want to just drive straight in, as I had no idea what I would be walking into and I didn't want noise from the truck attracting the undead. After studying the layout of the streets surrounding the development, I decided to circle through the woods to the south on foot, and approach through the back yards at a cul-de-sac.

I strapped on the load-bearing harness with my pistol and spare ammo, and looped the carbine's tactical sling across my chest for quick access. Both the pistol and the rifle had silencers fitted to them, but I hoped I would not need to use them. My goal was to get in and get out, quick and quiet. I strapped a hiking pack that was empty except for a few items I thought I might need, and set out through the forest.

I had a small compass that I used to stay oriented southward. Every twenty yards or so I would stop and check my surroundings, ears straining, looking for any sign of movement. I hiked about half a mile toward my destination when I saw the first of the undead. It was staggering in my direction, occasionally cocking its head to the side as though trying to listen, and sniffing the air. It reminded me of my Uncle Roger's terrier when he was out hunting rodents.

I was fortunate to spot it before it homed in on me. It must have heard me walking through the thick carpet of dead leaves and pine needles on the ground. As quietly as I could, I crouched beside a tree in a shooting position. I peered through the rifle's reflex sights and waited for a clean shot. It took about two minutes before the ghoul rounded a thick stand of pines, presenting an unobstructed shot. The undead was a petite blond woman wearing a large t-shirt that hung halfway down her bare, filthy legs. Dried blood had turned the entire front of the shirt a dull rust color, and she was missing large chunks of flesh from her shoulders, face, and arms. Her left eye dangled from its optic nerve, swaying like a grotesque pendulum down her face. It took everything I had to resist the urge to cut and run. My heart pounded in my chest, and I struggled to fight off the panic that the sight of the undead roused in me.

Get it together, I thought. *The world is crawling with these things. I have to learn to face them. I have to stay calm. I have to think.*

After a few deep breaths, I took careful aim and fired. The round struck her in the forehead and she collapsed, shuddering as she fell. I knew that if one revenant was tracking me, then there could be more on the way. Even with the silencer, the assault rifle's report was audible from several yards away. I didn't want more undead to show up, and set off at a faster pace.

It took another ten minutes of trekking through the woods to reach the development. Just before emerging into the back yard of a large two-story house, I paused behind a bush at the edge of the tree line, and pulled a small pair of binoculars from my cargo pocket. I scanned the yards of the houses in front of me for movement.

The back yards were empty, but I could see at least a dozen infected, all wandering aimlessly around the front yards. Some of them simply stood still, a dull, vacant expression on their pale gray faces. I would need to be fast and quiet, or this could go very bad, very quickly. I slid the rifle backward and used a Velcro strap on the web gear to secure the barrel in place, and then drew the Kel-Tec from its holster. I had loaded the pistol's magazines with sub-sonic rounds to reduce noise if I had to shoot it. I attached a suppressor to the barrel and made ready to exit cover. I emerged from the woods in a crouch, pistol at the ready. I moved quickly toward the house closest to me, rolling my steps from the sides of my boots to reduce noise. Loud buzzing from thousands of cicadas in the surrounding pines drowned out the sound of my feet crossing the thick, overgrown lawn.

The house I approached had a tall wood-slat fence that surrounded the back yard. The gate stood open, and I paused for a moment as I stepped through it and crouched just inside the fence line. I listened for a minute or two, and didn't hear anything approaching. I got up and slowly crept toward the back door. It had a large multi-paned window on its upper half, and I peered through it looking for movement inside the house. Seeing none, I tried the doorknob. Locked. Awesome.

I took off my backpack and retrieved a roll of duct tape. I covered the glass in the windowpane closest to the door handle with tape and struck it sharply with the butt of the pistol. The glass broke with a dull crunch, and I cringed at the noise. I pulled aside the glass as quietly as I could and then reached through to unlock the door. I avoided the broken glass on the floor as I stepped through. The house was dark, with heavy shades drawn over the windows. The room I walked into was furnished with plush, comfortable-looking sofas and chairs and a massive coffee table. I guessed it was some kind of sitting room, probably used for entertaining neighbors and friends.

Steeling myself to continue, I took in a deep breath and immediately regretted it. The reek of death filled my sinuses, making my eyes water. I swallowed hard to avoid gagging, and raised my weapon. Gabe's manual said that the undead reek to high-heaven, and one could often smell them before they could be seen or heard. Again, I had to fight the urge to turn and run.

If there are any undead in here, I have to deal with them, I thought. *I've done it before, and I can do it again. I've come too far to turn back empty handed.*

I walked through the doorway and scanned the room beyond. The lower section of the house was open, a TV and couches on the right, and the kitchen on the left. A staircase near the front entrance led to the upper portion of the house. A long counter separated the kitchen from the living room. The house was spacious and richly decorated, with hardwood floors, granite counter-tops, and stainless steel appliances. The kitchen was my goal, but the smell of death grew stronger as I continued inside. I briefly considered going back out and trying another house, but decided against it. Everything had gone well so far, I might as well see it through.

I didn't want to be blindsided while stuffing cans in my pack, and I knew I was going to have to make some noise to get supplies from the kitchen. I needed to clear the house. I checked my pistol to make sure the safety was off and a round was in the chamber, then took a small flashlight from my pack and shined

101

it up the staircase. I didn't see any movement, and slowly proceeded upward, leaving the pack behind at the foot of the stairs. I turned the corner on a landing, climbed a few more stairs, and reached the top facing a long hallway. There were several closed doors on either side of the hall, behind which anything could be waiting. Fucking fantastic. I slowly crept down the hall, finger on the trigger and ready to fire. I remembered something Gabe had taught me, and shifted my stance so that I could quickly launch a front kick if needed.

I came to the first door and twisted the handle, pushed the door open, and took a step back, waiting. I listened to my heart hammer in my ears ten times, then edged my way in front of the door. Beyond the doorway was a tastefully decorated bedroom, probably a guest room. I stepped inside and checked the closet and under the bed. Nothing. I proceeded down the hall checking rooms as I went. I cleared an empty home office, a bathroom, a linen closet, and a bedroom converted into a home gym, complete with adjustable weight dumbbells, a treadmill, and a yoga mat. Evidently, the former residents were health conscious. The last doorway loomed before me, and the smell of death was strong enough to make me want to gag with every breath. I held my pistol at the ready, and threw the door open. The smell was nearly overwhelming. I had to take a few steps back and clench my jaw to keep from throwing up. I pulled the collar of my shirt over my nose and walked through the door, breathing as shallow as I could.

The smell emanated from two dead bodies lying on a king sized bed in the center of the room. They had obviously been dead for quite a while, and their bodies were crawling with maggots. Body fluids spread out in stinking pools that soaked the mattress beneath them. I reached out a hand and knocked twice on the door, figuring that if they were not completely dead then the noise would rouse them. When they didn't respond, I stepped further inside. The two bodies on the bed had been holding each other when they died. A large empty pill container stood on one of the night stands, next to a half empty glass of water. I picked up the pill bottle and read the label. Sleeping pills, and strong ones at that. They must have seen what was happing during the outbreak, and decided to check out rather than stick around for the show. I didn't blame them. Satisfied that the house was safe for the time being, I turned to go back downstairs. On my way out, I noticed a note on a small desk. I picked up the note and read it:

Brian and Cathy,

If you find this letter, please forgive us. We couldn't stand to watch the world die anymore. We love you, and we will see you again in a better place.

Love always,

Mom and Dad.

Tears stung my eyes as I placed the letter back on the table. I thought about my own parents, and was glad that fate had spared them from the horror of watching the world fall apart. I closed the door behind me as I left the room.

I went back downstairs to search the kitchen, but didn't bother with the refrigerator. Anything in there would be rotten, and the house smelled bad enough as it was. I searched the cupboard and a small pantry. They were both full of canned goods, dried pasta, and various other things. I picked out the food with the most nutritional value and stuffed as much of it as I could into my pack.

The pack was heavy, probably weighing over fifty pounds once it was full. I didn't expect to have much trouble carrying it. I am a shade over six feet tall, and back then I was a solid two-hundred and ten pounds. I was used to carrying heavy packs from all the hiking trips that Gabriel and I had taken over the years.

I went out the back door and crossed the lawn as quietly as I could. As I stepped through the back gate, I saw movement out of the corner of my eye. I turned to my left and saw an undead come around the corner of the fence line. I didn't wait for him to react, I raised my pistol and fired two rounds at his head. The first round skipped off the side of his skull, but the second caught him just above the eye, and he dropped.

I hurried to the tree line, and after a quick look at my compass, I headed back north toward my truck. I got about halfway there when I started seeing staggering figures roaming through the trees. They must have been in the forest when I came through before, and followed the sound of my boots crunching on the dry undergrowth. As I approached them, I saw several heads swivel in my direction. That damned horrible, hungry moan began to drift through the forest like an evil, intangible fog.

I knew that turning back was a bad idea, as the moaning would no doubt attract the ghouls wandering around in the housing development. I figured my only chance was to keep heading for the truck, maintain a fast pace, and drop any undead that got in my way. I had learned from Gabe's manual that a person's best ally against the undead, once detected by them, was speed. I broke into a slow trot, abandoning any pretense of stealth. I holstered my pistol and unfastened the barrel of my assault rifle. I flipped off the safety, and made sure the fire selector was set to semi-auto. No sense in wasting bullets on full auto when one shot will get the job done.

I kept up my pace until I got to within five yards of the nearest undead. I stopped long enough to level my rifle and fire. I missed it on the first shot, and dropped it on the second. I continued on this way, pausing only to reload or kill the undead that I couldn't avoid until I made it back to the road. As I emerged into the ankle high grass bordering the highway, I looked toward my truck and stopped short. At least a dozen undead surrounded it. I swore vehemently, and debated what to do. The moaning of the undead slowly pursuing me through the woods was getting louder. The ghouls surrounding my truck noticed me, and began to stagger in my direction. I knew I didn't have much time before being surrounded. I had no choice but to clear the undead away from my truck. I stepped onto the pavement, dropped my pack and kneeled down into a steady shooting position. I started with the nearest ones, and dropped the ghouls one by one. The last one was only about ten feet away when I put a bullet through his head. Just as I grabbed my pack to put it back on, several undead emerged from the tree line, and lurched toward me.

I dropped my rifle and let it hang from its tactical sling. I grabbed the pack with both hands and ran for the truck. I managed to put about thirty feet between me and the nearest corpse by the time I made it to the driver side door. I chucked the heavy pack into the bed of the truck and climbed into the cab. Thankfully, I left the keys in the ignition just in case I had to beat a hasty retreat. I cranked up the truck and did a wide U-turn, heading back the way I came from. My instincts screamed for me to floor it, but I knew that wasn't necessary. Even at low speed, the truck would quickly outdistance the undead. I kept my speed below thirty miles an hour and easily dodged a few ghouls that wandered out in front of me. I looked behind me, and saw at least forty or fifty corpses shambling after me as I pulled away.

After I got a mile or so away from the development, I saw no more of the undead. The road was clear all the way back home. I parked my truck in the garage, and took the pack with the newly acquired supplies down to the bunker. After arming my security system, I sat down at the kitchen table to clean my guns. As I worked, I mulled over the day's events, and realized that I had to think of new ways to gather supplies without drawing the undead to me. The truck was great, but it made too much noise. My theory that the undead would not find my house seemed to be correct. If they were close by, not only should I have seen some of them by now, but they would have been drawn to the sound of the truck. That meant I could use the truck to get close to a source of supplies, but would have to proceed on foot afterward.

I wrote down a few ideas, and then helped myself to some of the linguine and marinara sauce I had liberated that morning. Pasta is my favorite food in the whole, wide world, and my supply had run out a week earlier. I was craving it something fierce. After eating, I thought about Gabe, and wondered how he was making out up in Morganton. I also thought about my own situation, and began to have serious doubts about my long-term survival chances. The food I took from my scouting run, in addition to what I already had before, was enough to live on for three weeks. But then what? Go on another dangerous supply run? I had gotten lucky this time. If there had been any more undead around the truck when I reached it, I would have been forced to abandon it and flee on foot. How long would it take me to hike back there to retrieve it, if I even could? I could not stay at my house indefinitely. Sooner or later, I would have to leave and make my way north to Morganton. My best chance for survival lay in reaching Gabriel. Working together, our chances for survival would be far greater than trying to go at it alone.

Several months before the outbreak, at Gabe's insistence, I purchased a map of North Carolina and marked out several different routes leading to Morganton. On a good day, it was only an hour or so drive. If the roads were clear, I could be there tomorrow. If they weren't, I could use the map to find alternate routes. I went into the storage unit to inventory my supplies. It didn't take very long. As I stared at the pitifully empty shelves, I knew what I had to do. It was time to get on the road.

Chapter 6

It's dangerous business, walking out your front door.

I thought it would be easy. Just load up the truck, plot out a route, and enjoy the ride. It should have been nice and quiet. Maybe I would have to dodge the occasional undead, or broken down car, but no major obstacles, right?

Wrong.

But I'm getting ahead of myself.

The day after my nearly disastrous supply run, I loaded up the truck for the trip to Gabriel's place. I packed the rest of my food in a few boxes, as well as four ten-gallon Jerry cans of water. All of the clothing I brought fit into one large suitcase, and I only took the toughest and most durable stuff I owned. I brought all of my guns, grenades, and ammo except for the Bushmaster carbine, and the Sig .40 caliber pistol. I left the two guns and a few hundred rounds of ammo for each on my front porch. I unlocked my front door and taped a letter to it.

Dear whoever,

I'm leaving these guns behind with the hope that someone will find them and use them responsibly. Guns should be used to protect people, so don't do anything stupid with them. My house is yours for as long as you like. I won't be needing it anymore. There is a nice surprise waiting for you in the basement. Look behind the dryer. And yes, I paid a lot of money for it.

Enjoy.

Sincerely,

E.R.

P.S.- Please don't take my toolbox. I know it's big and pretty, but it was a gift. Lord willing, I'd like to come back for it someday.

After leaving a parting gift for whatever lucky soul found my house, I spent a good forty-five minutes wandering around my garage trying to figure out ways to bring as many of my tools as possible. I rearranged the gear in the truck's bed through at least ten permutations in an effort to create more space. By moving the suitcase into the passenger seat, I managed to fit a small toolbox, bolt cutters, my crowbar, a gasoline powered generator, and my arc welder. Maybe I would need them, maybe I wouldn't. It's a hard thing for a man to do, walking away from his tools.

Before leaving, I picked some flowers from the flowerbed in my front yard and laid them on top of Vanessa's grave. I knelt beside her resting place to pay my last respects. A wave of guilt came over me as I spoke to her for the last time.

"I'm sorry for what happened to you, Vanessa." I said to the cold ground. "I should have tried harder to get you to stay with me. If I had, you might still be alive, for what that's worth."

I looked up at the tree line, imaging the undead staggering around between the tall trees. My heart sank as I thought about what kind of world remained for those of us who survived the outbreak. What kind of future did we face? The cold weight of despair settled heavily on my mind.

"Then again, maybe you're the lucky one. Your suffering is over. I got the feeling mine is just getting started." I picked up a handful of earth from her grave and let it run slowly through my fingers.

"Rest easy, beautiful. I'll always remember you the way you were. If I can, I'll try to come back here some day and make a proper headstone for you. I hope you find peace wherever you are. This world ain't such a nice place anymore."

I stood up and fished my keys out of my pocket as I walked away. I drove the truck to the front of the house and got out to take one last look at my home. I am not ashamed to admit that I had a lump in my throat as I prepared to leave for the last time. This was my dream home. I spent a boatload of money having the place built, and I loved every square inch of it. As hard as it was, I knew that making my way north to Morganton and teaming up with Gabriel presented the best chance I had for long-term survival. I said one final goodbye, and got back in the truck.

The trip to Morganton was only supposed to take about an hour and a half. I had driven there at least a hundred times, and knew the way like the back of my hand. I left home at about ten in the morning, and I expected to be at Gabriel's before noon.

At noon, I was nowhere near Gabriel's place.

The trouble started as I headed south to get on highway 16. As I neared the town of Lucia, I saw increasing numbers of cars parked on the side of the road. Eventually, the cars became so dense that they blocked traffic completely in the southbound lane, and I had to drive on the wrong side of the road to make any progress. As I passed the cars, I looked inside them to see if there were any signs of the drivers. All but a few were empty, and the occupants of the ones that weren't thrashed and moaned as I drove by. After seeing a few of the undead trapped in their cars, I stopped looking. The sight of all those pathetic, hungry creatures trapped in a steel prison was just too unsettling.

I kept a slow pace on the hilly, winding two-lane road. As I crested a hill near a shopping center adjacent to a large suburban neighborhood, I saw why so many of the cars on the road were empty. There was a large horde of the undead milling aimlessly about the intersection to highway 16. The parking lot of the strip mall ahead of me, and the gas station to my left, were littered with corpses, both walking and non-walking. It looked like the local law enforcement had tried to set up a barricade in the intersection to stop the horde from reaching the houses just beyond the road. Several of the undead wore police uniforms. One of them clutched a pistol with the slide locked to the rear in its bloody fist. The cop must have emptied all of his ammo before succumbing to the horde. At least he went down fighting.

I slowed to a halt atop the hill and considered my next move. I couldn't drive down into the intersection without attracting the attention of several hundred undead. On the other hand, if I turned back I would have to find a safe place to consult my atlas and find an alternate route to 16 North. I watched the infected for a few moments and noticed that although there were a lot of them, they were fairly well spaced apart. If I moved quickly, and dodged as many as I could, I should be able to make it through them without getting stuck. I rolled up both of my windows and accelerated down the hill.

As I neared the intersection, the undead noticed my truck and dozens of vacant, bloody faces swiveled in my direction. I heard their moaning over the sound of the truck's engine, even though the windows were up. The sound was a catalyst that quickly had every corpse in shouting distance homing in on my truck and stumbling toward me as fast as their awkward legs could carry them. I sped up to get through the crowd before they could converge and block my path by sheer force of numbers.

I reached the first of them at over forty miles an hour and swerved off the road into the gas station parking lot to avoid a clump of six or seven infected. I circled around to my left and just barely missed taking my mirror off on an SUV parked in front of the fuel pump. I spun the steering wheel back to my right and stepped on the gas, shot through a gap between two large groups of undead, and swerved back onto the road. A loose skirmish line of walking dead stood between me and the highway. I feathered the brakes and slowed down to less than twenty miles an hour before I hit them. I cursed as I realized that I was going to have to take a few of them out to get clear. Thankfully, I had a large steel brush guard mounted to the front of the truck, and I hoped that it would bear the worst of the damage. If one of them punctured my radiator, I could be in serious trouble.

Slowing down turned out to be a good idea. The horde was too slow to react to me weaving through the main body of their number, and they had yet to converge on my truck. I was only going fifteen miles an hour when I hit the last of them. Two corpses bounced off the edges of the brush guard, and rolled ass-over-heels away from the truck. I hit a third one straight on and it fell directly beneath the front end. I felt it tumbling and thumping against the underside of the truck as I drove over it, and had to bite back a wave of nausea as I heard its bones crunch under my back tires. As I cleared the horde, I sped up and left them behind as fast as I dared to go. I came around a curve and breathed a sigh of relief when I saw a long stretch of clear road ahead of me. I slowed down and checked the rearview mirror. The horde was still stumbling in my direction, but I would soon be far ahead of them. I relaxed a bit and focused on driving for a few miles. Right as I was just beginning to think that the worst of the trouble was behind me, I ran into an even tighter spot than the one back at the intersection.

I came around a sharp corner on a steep downhill slope and damn near ran headlong into the back of a massive traffic pileup. I was going faster than I should have been, and only had an instant to react. I slammed on the brakes and skidded to a stop just inches away from the back bumper of a canary yellow H2.

I sat in the cab of my truck for a few moments willing my pulse to slow down, and looked at the carnage in front of me. A line of cars ran down the hill in both lanes, spilling from the road to the tree line on either side of the highway. I could see down the hill that the pileup spanned nearly a quarter of a mile to a bridge over a broad, swift running creek. The ground, where it wasn't covered with every make and model of automobile under the sun, was littered with corpses. I got out of my truck to investigate. It quickly became clear that there was no way I was getting around this little catastrophe.

I climbed up into the bed of the truck and onto the roof. I shaded my eyes with one hand as I tried to see what had caused the pileup. I made out the shape, and distinctive olive drab color, of military vehicles parked across the entrance to the bridge forming a makeshift barricade. I climbed down long enough to fish my binoculars out of a box and took another look at the bridge. The military vehicles parked across the entrance to the bridge were armored personnel carriers with machine gun turrets on their roofs. Large caliber bullet holes riddled the cars directly in front of the barricade, less than ten feet away.

A dead soldier lay motionless, draped over one of the gun turrets. A long streak of blood ran down the side of the APC beneath him. A waist-high pile of dead bodies carpeted the ground between the barricade and the foremost cars. Withering fire from the heavy machine guns had literally torn many of them apart. Severed limbs and streams of entrails lay strewn about the heaps of dead bodies. Some of them still moved, struggling and crawling through the pile. I lowered my binoculars and turned away. Sitting down on the roof of the truck, I clenched my jaw and swallowed hard against the bile that rose in my throat. I closed my eyes and tried to erase the image from my memory. For a moment, I focused so hard on not losing my shit that I forgot the danger I was in.

It was almost the death of me.

While I sat there with my eyes closed, an undead with its throat torn out staggered out of the woods and saw me sitting on the roof of my truck. I heard a rustling in the brush beside me and looked up just as the ghoul made it to the side of the truck and reached for me. Before I could react, it had an iron grip on the bottom half of my pants leg and gave a tremendous heave, pulling me from the roof down into the truck bed. The back of my head struck the roof as I fell, and spots exploded in my vision. I landed painfully on the boxes and tools piled beneath me. The infected opened its mouth wide and continued pulling on my leg, trying to bring my ankle within biting range.

The strength of the thing was incredible. The only reason it hadn't taken a bite out of me yet was because its left arm was severed at the elbow. It pulled my ass three feet with a single tug using only one arm. Normally, I would have been impressed, but at the time, I was so terrified that all I could do was let out a high-pitched girlish scream and flail around as the undead dragged me over my gear. I reached out with my arms, scrambling for purchase as the ghoul pulled my leg closer to its snapping jaws. My right hand closed on the handle of my crowbar as I thrashed and fought to get away from the horror in front of me.

The undead creature leaned forward and tried to bite down on my foot. I lunged upward with my other leg and turned so that the sole of my boot was the only thing in front of its mouth. The fucking bastard got my boot heel between its teeth and tore at it like a pit bull on a piece of rawhide. I kicked and pulled backward with my leg, but I couldn't get free of the creature's powerful grip. Adrenaline lent me a burst of desperately needed strength as I sat up and swung the crowbar at the thing's head. The blow landed solidly, but not hard enough to kill the ghoul tearing at my boot.

I hit it a couple more times and it finally released my boot from its jaws. Whether the blows from the crowbar distracted it, or it was trying to find something else to chew on, I'm not really sure. It still had my pants leg clutched in its one remaining hand. I turned the crowbar in my grip and put the hooked end under the ghoul's thumb. I gave it a hard tug and the creature's thumb pried loose from my jeans, giving me enough slack to finally pull myself free of its grip. It immediately reached out for me again, but I managed to avoid it by leaping backward and out of the truck bed. I turned halfway over as I fell and landed heavily on my side, grunting and cursing loudly when I hit.

As I struggled to my feet, the ghoul came around the back of the truck and reached out to grab me. I turned and ran around the front of the truck, scrambled over the back of the H2 I nearly ran into, and sprinted a few yards up the road to give myself enough time to assume a balanced fighting stance. Once I had some breathing distance, I hefted the crowbar like a baseball bat and circled around to the undead's left side as it stumbled forward. When it was just out of arm's reach, I stepped in and swung the crowbar with all my strength, aiming for its temple. The hook end of the heavy tool penetrated the ghoul's skull just behind the temple, and lodged several inches into its brain. It nearly pulled the crowbar from my grasp as it collapsed onto the pavement. I wrenched the bar free and bashed it several more times, screaming and cursing at the foul creature as I reduced its head to a pulped red mash.

After a minute or two of gruesome work, I stepped backward and leaned down with my hands on my knees, breathing hard. The wind shifted, bringing the scent of hundreds of dead bodies toward me, and I could no longer hold back my revulsion. I dropped the crowbar and heaved everything I had eaten that morning onto the highway. I went down to my knees and retched so hard I thought my ribs were going to break. After a few minutes of misery, the dry heaves subsided enough for me to pick up the crowbar and get back to my feet. I could hear rustling, crunching, and snapping as the undead in the woods along the highway wandered toward me. They must have heard the commotion from my fight with the rotten son of a bitch I had just killed.

I threw the crowbar into the back of the truck and hopped into the cab. I got the truck turned around and took off back the way I came. I drove two miles, far enough to get out of sight of the undead, and stopped in the middle of the road to plan my next move. Going north on 16, obviously, was not an option. The highway was the fastest route to get where I wanted to go, but there was no way to get around the pileup at the bridge. If I headed back the way I came, I would have to find my way through the horde at the intersection again. I was lucky to make it through the first time, I didn't think it was a good idea to tempt fate with a second try. For a few tense moments, I racked my brain trying to come up with ideas. I checked my mirrors to make sure there weren't any undead sneaking up on me, and saw nothing. That didn't necessarily mean there weren't any nearby. The foliage beside the highway was thick, and the road wound around sharp curves and traversed numerous hills. Sight distance was severely limited.

That gave me an idea.

If the undead I encountered earlier in the day had lost sight of me and couldn't hear me, then based on what I had observed to that point, and read in Gabe's manual, the infected should have lost interest by now and gone back to wandering aimlessly. Or whatever the hell it is they do when they're not munching on people. I vaguely remembered passing some small side roads and farm trails on my way to the bridge. If the undead weren't actively looking for me, I should be able to shoot down one of the smaller access roads and try to find another way to get on highway 16 north of the bridge. I put the truck back in gear and crept forward at less than twenty miles an hour so as not to miss any avenues of escape.

After driving about a mile and a half, I reached a gravel covered farm road that branched northward from the highway. I turned on to it and slowed the truck to a crawl to minimize noise and avoid kicking up too much dust. The narrow trail wound through several hundred yards of dense foliage before emerging into a clearing. The land on either side of the road opened up into huge soybean fields that spanned hundreds of acres in every direction. The plants stood thick and green in their long, orderly rows. A few months ago, they would have represented hundreds of thousands of dollars' worth of crop. Now, they were little more than a snack for the multitudes of deer that populated the area. I saw several Whitetail does and their young feasting on the ripe green pods, their long graceful necks raising their heads up as they watched me drive by. I hoped they kept their furry little heads on a swivel. It wouldn't go well for them if one of the infected caught them off guard. I had nearly just learned that lesson the hard way.

As I followed the dirt road, I resolved to myself never to let my guard down like that again. Those rotten things could be anywhere. Danger could quite literally be lurking around every corner. If I expected to survive, I would have to be more vigilant. The three months I spent at my isolated home, far removed from the worst of the horror wrought upon the rest of the country, had made me too careless.

After a few miles, I crested a low hill and spotted a large two-story house atop a hill in the distance. A few minutes later, I reached it and slowed to a halt in the gravel driveway. I left the truck running, and the transmission in drive for a few minutes, as I looked around for any sign of movement. Not seeing any, I studied the house more closely. It was a beautiful, stately home with a broad front porch, and a balcony that spanned the entire length of the second floor. The balcony formed a roof for the porch supported by long, fluted white columns. The place looked like something out of a civil war movie. A large, four-car detached garage stood off to one side of the house, and hundreds of tall, magnificent oak trees surrounded the overgrown yard. The house had obviously been there for a long time, and most likely belonged to whoever had planted all the soybean fields.

To my left, I saw a large wooden structure that looked like a barn with the front and back walls removed. Two large green combines were parked beneath it, as well as what appeared to be different types of equipment that could be attached to them. Judging by the tall grass growing around them, they hadn't been moved in a long time. If they had, the tractors would have crushed the grass leaving a visible trail to mark their path.

Not seeing any obvious danger, I shut off the truck and climbed out of the cab. I left the keys in the ignition just in case I needed to make a quick escape. I opened a plastic trunk that I had stowed most of my weapons in, and took out the Kel-Tec and one of the H&K assault rifles. I also took out my load-bearing harness and several extra magazines for the guns. I strapped on the harness and holstered the pistol. I put the extra ammo in pockets across the front of my waist for easy access, and slung the rifle's tactical sling over my shoulder. As an afterthought, I also took out my small-sword and strapped it to my back on its makeshift harness. I positioned it for a left-handed draw, and then did a quick inventory of my ammo.

Including the magazines already loaded into the guns, I had four spare mags for each firearm. That gave me a hundred and fifty for the rifle, and a hundred fifty for the pistol. I checked both weapons to make sure the safety was off, and that they had a round in the chamber. Even with all the hardware, I was still apprehensive about approaching the farmhouse. If someone was in there, they would almost certainly have noticed my presence by now. Although I couldn't see anything through the windows, they could just as easily be standing behind the door with a gun leveled at the entrance. Gabriel once told me that the cone shaped angle of fire presented by a doorway is called the Fatal Funnel in military and law enforcement circles. I did not relish the thought of catching a slug to the chest while breaking in.

I walked through knee-high grass to the steps and up onto the front porch. I held my rifle low, but kept my right hand on the handle in case I needed to bring it up quickly. I hesitated for a moment in front of the door, then raised my hand and knocked three times. Nothing happened. I knocked again, louder this time, and called out.

"Anybody home? Hello?"

My voice rang out loudly in the still, quiet air. It broke the silence so harshly that I actually startled myself. I listened for a few moments and still didn't hear anything from the other side of the door. I reached forward and tried the handle. It was unlocked, and I opened it slowly, peering inside as I did so.

"Hello? Is anyone in here? I'm coming inside, okay? If you have a weapon, please don't shoot. I'm not here to hurt you."

Tentatively, I stepped into the house. Closing the door behind me, I stood in the foyer for a few moments as my eyes adjusted to the gloom. I would have to remember to bring a flashlight next time. I took a few steps forward and winced as the hardwood floor groaned and creaked beneath my work boots. I went through a wide doorway into a sitting room filled with old, well-worn furniture. I called out again, but no one answered. I made my way through the lower floors of the house checking all the rooms I came to. In addition to the sitting room, there was a den with a flat screen TV and a DVD player, a large home office with cherry stained bookshelves and a massive oak desk, a bathroom, a wide, airy kitchen with windows that overlooked the back yard, and a large walk-in pantry. I debated raiding the kitchen, and decided I should check the rest of the house before taking anything. I walked up the staircase and made sure that my footsteps were loud and deliberate. If anyone was upstairs, I wanted them to know that I wasn't trying to sneak around, just in case all the shouting and knocking hadn't gotten the job done.

The upstairs consisted of four bedrooms, and what must have been a children's playroom. The playroom had a television and a video game console, as well as several toy boxes on low shelves. I found no evidence in any of the rooms that anyone had been there recently. A thin coating of dust covered everything in the house, and the closets and drawers in the bedrooms were missing most of the clothing in them. I went back downstairs to check the kitchen, and found that most of the shelves in the cupboard and pantry were empty. A few stray cans of food littered the ground, and a bag of flour lay burst open on the floor. I went down a narrow hallway from the kitchen that led to the back yard. The back door opened outward, and was hanging half open. Whoever lived here must have left in a hurry.

I walked out the back door and over to the detached garage. There was a door on the far side of the building, and I tried the handle. Locked. *That figures.* I thought. *Leave your house wide open, but lock your damn garage.* A man had definitely lived here. Only men are capable of that kind of obsessive protectiveness for cars and tools.

I figured that whoever this place belonged to must have left a long time ago, so I went back to the truck and got my crowbar. I used it to break open the door to the garage. Inside, I found an old, red work truck, a Ford Crown Victoria, and a Yamaha Rhino. One of the spaces was empty, save for tire marks and a few oil stains. A large workbench and numerous shelves lined the near wall, as well as a massive toolbox and an empty gun cabinet. The gun cabinet's glass door was open, and the drawer for storing ammo in the bottom was missing. I didn't see it laying around anywhere, so I guessed that whoever took it must have used it as a box to carry the ammo to the missing vehicle.

On a shelf above the workbench, I saw a large red gasoline container. I picked it up to see if it had anything in it. It was full. I picked up a can filled with greasy old bolts from underneath the workbench and dumped its contents out on the cement floor. I set the can on the bench and poured a little of the gasoline into it. The gasoline was mostly clear, meaning that it hadn't been sitting there long enough to go bad. The container held two gallons, so I decided to bring it along, just in case.

I went back to the house to search for anything useful. I took what little non-perishable food was still in the kitchen, and checked the rest of the house. I didn't find anything I might need on the ground floor, other than the little bit of food from the kitchen, so I proceeded upstairs. The bedrooms and playroom were more of the same, but in the office, just above a low bookshelf, I found a hand drawn map pinned to the sheetrock. I took it down from the wall and studied it.

In the center of the map were two lines labeled as highway sixteen. The long driveway that traversed the soybean fields was one of several lines that radiated out from a box representing the farmhouse. Most of the lines led to different parts of the property, but one of the lines led to a road whose name I recognized. If I followed that road north, it would take me around the bridge I ran into earlier that day, and onto highway 16. I couldn't believe my luck. If not for that map, God only knows how long I would have spent driving aimlessly around back roads trying to make my way north. Excited by my good fortune, I hurried back to the truck. I took off the small-sword and threw it in the back, then laid the load-bearing harness on top of my suitcase in the passenger seat. I propped the rifle up on the center console, and then drove across the front yard to the wood line and the trail marked on the map.

The trail was a rutted dirt road that would probably be impassable in a heavy rain. Thankfully, the last couple of weeks had been dry, and the road was in pretty good shape. I took it slow, not wanting to hit any potholes or risk running off the road. The road bent and twisted through the thick forest, the massive branches of the surrounding trees forming a dense canopy overhead. I was rounding a particularly sharp turn when I saw one of the infected standing in the middle of the trail facing away from me. Its head snapped around when it heard my truck behind it. It was about thirty yards away from me, and I briefly debated simply running it over. Deciding not to risk damaging the truck, I slowed to a stop. I grabbed the rifle as I stepped out and walked to within twenty yards of the walking corpse. It was wearing bib overalls and a t-shirt that had once been white, now stained brown with dried blood. There was a chunk of flesh missing from one of its arms, and it had gore smeared all over its mouth and chin. Decaying flesh crusted the creature's teeth turning them black. It raised its hands toward me and moaned loudly.

I leveled my rifle and put a round through its skull. The shot took off most of the top left portion of its skull, and the creature fell to the ground in a limp, bloody heap. I drove the truck closer to it and dragged it to the side of the trail. Reddish gray brain matter dribbled from its skull as I pulled it by its feet across the dirt. I clamped my teeth down and looked away, trying to keep from vomiting for the second time that day.

As I climbed back into the truck, I heard the sound of something crashing through the brush. I turned around, rifle at the ready, and saw another ghoul emerge from the forest about ten feet ahead of me. This one was an older female with most of her face gone. Flaps of loose, rotting skin dangled from her bare skull. Both of her eyes were missing, but she still knew what direction to stumble in to get me.

I took a knee, and a deep breath, and put a bullet between the empty sockets where her eyes used to be. Even as the corpse collapsed, I heard more of them tearing through the undergrowth as they homed in on me. I left her body beside the trail and got back in the truck. As I pulled away, dozens of undead emerged onto the path behind me, and I had to dodge a couple that wandered out onto the road ahead. I sped up and cursed as I drove away. For creatures that can only move at a walking pace, they sure as hell got to me quick. They must have been close by already to hear the first undead moan as he saw me. Or maybe they heard the muted report from the rifle. But why were there so many of them this far out into the boonies? Could they have come all this way from the small towns and housing developments that dotted this part of the county? I needed to rethink my view of these things.

Until then, I thought that they pretty much stayed in one place, maybe wandering around in circles or something. From what I had witnessed that day, it was evident that they actually roamed long distances in search of food. I wondered if there was any method to their way of travel, or if they just stumbled in whatever direction they happened to be facing when the local food supply ran out. Were these things capable of any kind of cognitive reasoning? If they were, that could mean trouble. Big trouble.

A few miles later the trail ended and I turned northeast on a two lane road. It was good to be back on asphalt. Dirt roads do not make for a smooth ride, especially when you have a few hundred pounds of gear in the back of your truck. In about ten minutes, I was back on highway 16, two miles north of the bridge where that walking pus-sack had tried to take a bite out of me. The highway was clear for the time it took me to reach a side road that cut over to highway 273. I reached the outskirts of the small town of Lucia, and turned left onto Alexis Lucia road. Things got a bit tense when I drove through the center of town and a few hundred undead noticed me, but I managed to zip through before they could converge. Once I got a couple of miles out of town, I didn't see any more undead.

The way was clear until I reached highway 27 north near another small town called Alexis. I knew that the road I was on ran through the center of town, and between the two fire stations, a gas station, restaurants, and the strip mall on that stretch of road, there were likely to be a large number of undead. I topped a hill near the intersection of Alexis Lucia road and 27 North, and stopped the truck to take a look at what I was heading into. I climbed on top of the truck and peered into the shallow valley ahead through my binoculars. Sure enough, it was just as congested with undead as Lucia had been. As I was scanning the street, I heard a faint, distant cracking sound.

"Was that a gunshot?" I said.

A few seconds later, I heard it again. And again. I scanned around looking for the source of the sound. After a minute or two of searching, I spotted the shooter. A man was standing on the roof of a Burger King, surrounded by undead, and firing into the mass of corpses around him with a bolt-action rifle. From the sound of it, I guessed that it was a .22 magnum. A massive black duffel bag lay on the roof at his feet. As I watched, he worked the weapon's bolt and fired another shot into the crowd. A corpse dropped to the ground, but it was like swatting mosquitoes in a swarm. I doubted that he would have enough bullets on him to dispose of all the ghouls converging on the restaurant. From this distance, I doubted that he could see or hear me. The crowd of undead was growing larger by the second, and corpses were staggering toward him from every direction. Every damn ghoul in town seemed to be on its way to Burger King, and they were not ordering Whoppers.

I lowered the binoculars and debated what to do. On one hand, the distraction could work in my favor. While Mr.

Dumbass down there was picking shots, I could skirt around the edge of town and be gone before any undead knew I was there. But if I did that, I would have to live with this man's death on my conscience. I was determined to survive, but in that moment, I realized that I did not want to survive at the cost of my humanity. Even here, at the end of all things, I still thought of myself as a good person who would not leave someone to die at the hands of the infected if I had the means to help. I had to do something.

I got back in the truck and drove toward the town, formulating a plan as I went. The first thing I needed to do was to get the man with the rifle to notice me. If he ran low on ammo, there was a very real chance that he might turn the gun on himself to avoid dying of dehydration on top of the restaurant. He probably did not realize that if he just hunkered down in the middle of the roof out of sight of the ghouls, stayed quiet, and waited a little while, they would eventually lose interest and wander off. It might take a few hours, but it beat the hell out of the alternative.

I drove to within about two hundred yards of the restaurant and stopped in the middle of an intersection. Most of the undead that I first spotted milling around the town square had by then packed into a moaning, struggling ring around the Burger King. The smell of the heaving mass of dead flesh was almost overwhelming. To give you an idea of how bad the undead smell, take a dead rat, soak it in a toilet full of diarrhea, put it in a bag, let it sit in the hot sun for a couple of days, then stick your nose in and take a big whiff. That would be about one tenth as bad as the horde in front of me smelled. I was amazed that the poor dumb bastard on the roof had not lost his guts throwing up.

I got out of the truck and climbed onto the roof of the cab. I brought my rifle with me and took off the suppressor. I waited until the stranded man was between shots before firing a round into the air. The noise got his attention, but the undead didn't seem to notice. They were too intent on the walking meal shooting at them from above. There was a loud crash as the press of dead flesh became too heavy for the restaurant's front windows, and they collapsed inward. The guy on the roof raised a hand in the air and waved to me. I waved back and cupped my hands in front of my face.

"Can you hear me!" I shouted.

Rather than yell back he gave me a thumbs-up.

"Go to the middle of the roof. Lay down. Don't make any noise." I yelled.

He gave me another thumbs-up and did as I asked.

"I must be out of my fucking mind," I muttered.

I turned the truck around and pointed it down the street back the way I came. A few of the undead in the crowd noticed and started staggering toward me. I climbed up into the truck's bed and sat down on the roof. I leveled the rifle and started taking pot shots. To my credit, I managed to drop a ghoul with almost every shot, but a few of them went wide. I got through about twenty rounds before I had the undivided attention of a very large, very hungry audience. Once I was certain that all of the undead were coming my way, I got down off the truck and put the silencer back on the barrel. I took out the nearly empty magazine and popped in a full one.

I put the truck in gear, rolled up both of the windows, and waited until the first rank of the horde was within ten feet of me. I took my foot off the break and let the truck creep forward. I didn't even need to touch the gas, the engine idling was enough to stay in front of the undead. The street in front of me was long and flat, and I led them to the end of it a quarter mile away. I checked the rear view mirror to make sure that they were all still behind me, then accelerated and turned right into the parking lot of an auto parts store. The parking lot adjoined several others, and I used it to double back behind the horde.

I got back onto the street, and after dodging a few stragglers, I drove straight for the Burger King. It took only a few seconds to get there, and as I arrived I saw the man who had been on the roof emerge from behind the restaurant carrying the big duffel bag. Whatever was in it must have been heavy, because he was bent almost double under its weight. I wondered what could be in there that was valuable enough for the crazy bastard to risk his life for it. I rolled down the window and unlocked the passenger side door. The man heaved the duffel back into the back of the truck and came around to the passenger side. I slid my load-bearing harness down onto the floorboard beneath me.

"Take the suitcase and throw it in the back," I said.

He nodded and pulled it out with a grunt of effort. He set it in the back and took a moment to make sure it was wedged in tightly. Apparently satisfied, he got in the truck and closed his door.

"Head north," he said, pointing down the road ahead of us. "I know a place where we'll be safe."

Figuring that introductions would have to wait, I pulled out of the parking lot and drove north on highway 27.

Chapter 7

The Compound

We drove north for about three miles until the man beside me pointed to a road that turned off to the right.

"Turn up here. We're close now."

"Close to what?" I asked.

"To what passes for home these days."

I glanced over at him to read his expression, but he faced away from me staring out the window. I slowed the truck to a stop just before reaching the road he indicated.

"Why are we stopping?" he asked.

"You're welcome." I replied.

He gave me a sidelong glance for a moment, then realized what I meant and looked down, flushing a bit.

"Yeah, I guess I have been kind of quiet. Thanks for helping me. I didn't mean any disrespect, it's just…" he seemed to struggle with what to say next.

"Hey, it's cool, don't worry about it." I said, making a dismissive gesture. "What's this safe place you mentioned?"

"There's an abandoned textile mill about two miles down the road here. I'm one of thirty six survivors that have holed up there in an old warehouse. It's defensible, there aren't a lot of creeps around, and we have plenty of food. You're more than welcome to come and stay with us."

He looked up and I finally got a good look at his face. He had a thick brown beard, and obviously had not had a haircut in a long time. His hair was a shade lighter than his beard, and he had large brown eyes that would have looked effeminate if not for his broad nose and strong, square jaw. He was wearing Army surplus battle fatigues and combat boots similar to mine. I could tell that he was a little taller than me, and probably had about forty pounds more muscle than I did. His neck was nearly as big around as his head, and he had big, thick hands with long fingers. His arms were significantly larger than mine, and they strained the fabric of his bush jacket.

"Actually, I'm headed north to try and find a friend of mine, but I don't mind giving you a ride home. How did you come to be down in Alexis anyway? And by 'creep', do you mean one of the infected?" I asked.

"Yeah, that's what we've started calling them. My wife gets the credit for coining the term. To answer your first question, every week or so a few of us go out on trips to look for supplies. Two others went north to find food, and I volunteered to go south to Alexis."

"Why go to Alexis alone? Why didn't you go with the other two?"

"They're after food, and I'm after ammo. I knew there was a gun store not far from the Burger King where you found me. The old man who ran the place was a survival nut, and kept a ton of guns and ammunition in a cellar under the building. We're starting to run low on ammo at the compound, so I figured I'd get as much as I could and bring it back."

"Judging by the mess I found you in, I'm guessing something went wrong."

His expression darkened, and he nodded.

"I'd be happy to tell you about it once we get to the warehouse. I hate to be a pain, but do you think we could get moving? I'd really like to get back. My wife is probably worried sick by now," he said.

I looked around to see if any undead were approaching, and didn't see any. That didn't mean they weren't nearby.

"Yeah, that's probably a good idea." I put the truck in gear and turned down the road to the right. We rode in silence until we got close to a service road with a dilapidated sign that read "ARCONN TEXTILES" in faded letters on a filthy, pitted white background.

"Turn in here. It's around the other side of the factory," he said.

I figured as much, but kept silent as I turned in. I followed the service road around the massive building that once housed a thriving business, and approached a wide, squat warehouse about fifty yards behind the factory.

The warehouse was large, but not as big as many I had seen. It was seventy or more yards long, and fifty yards wide. For all of its area, it was only about two stories tall, giving it a strangely squashed appearance. A large blue shipping container sat against the front of the building, and the top couple of feet of a steel garage door were visible above it. A wooden scaffold stood on the side of the warehouse nearest to us with a winding staircase that led to the building's roof. I could see three people on top of it, one of them looking at us through the scope of a hunting rifle. I hoped he kept his finger off the trigger.

"Pull around the back, that's where the entrance is."

I did as he said, and stopped in front of a heavy steel door. My passenger got out and waved to the man on the roof with the hunting rifle. He lowered his weapon and waved back, then turned and made his way down the scaffold. I got out of the truck as my passenger walked around the truck toward the entrance. He stopped in front of me and held out a hand.

"I'm Ethan Thompson, by the way," he said.

"Eric Riordan." I shook his hand.

"And this is Bill Cooper," he said, pointing to the man with the rifle walking toward us.

Bill looked to be in his late fifties or early sixties, and wore the same kind of Army surplus fatigues as Ethan. He was about five-foot nine, medium build, and wore a flat brimmed straw hat that detracted from the military look his clothing suggested. His beard was mostly white, and he had bright, intelligent blue eyes that regarded me with mild suspicion. He stopped a few feet from me and looked at Ethan.

"You have a good hunt?" he asked.

I noticed that although his rifle was lowered, he held it in a way that allowed him to level it quickly if he needed to. I suddenly wished I had grabbed my pistol before getting out of the truck.

"Clear all the way," Ethan replied.

I looked at him in confusion for a moment trying to figure out what the hell he was talking about, and then it dawned on me that they had just exchanged some kind of code. Bill slung his rifle over his shoulder and approached me with his hand out, smiling.

"Pleased to meet you sir. You'll have to excuse the frosty reception, we don't get many visitors here."

"Yeah, looks like it," I replied.

I glanced up to the roof of the warehouse and noticed the other two guards standing on the edge of the building watching us. Bill followed my line of sight and waved a hand at them.

"Go on now, you two can gossip later," he shouted, smiling.

He had the thick, resonant Southern accent common amongst older generations native to the region. The guards reluctantly turned away and went back to their patrols. Bill pushed his hat up from his eyes and regarded me for a moment.

"You don't look too bad, son. Last folks that come around were mighty hungry looking." He let the comment hang in the air.

"Yeah, well, my house is pretty isolated. I hunkered down and waited out the worst of the outbreak. I managed to stay fed by raiding abandoned houses, but pickings were getting pretty slim back my way."

It wasn't a complete lie, but I didn't feel comfortable telling these people everything just yet. My grandmother, who grew up during the Great Depression, once told me that desperation makes demons of us all. I didn't know how desperate these people might be, and it didn't make sense to take chances.

"And where might your way be?" Bill asked.

"Just north of Charlotte, about twenty miles southwest of Lake Norman."

Again, not a complete lie, but Bill seemed to sense that I wasn't telling him everything.

"You run into any trouble on the way up here?"

I was getting a little tired of playing twenty questions with this old man. I had just rescued one of his friends, and wanted nothing more than to be on my way. I was about to say as much when Ethan defused the situation.

"Bill, you're being rude. This man just saved my life, at great risk to his own, and asked for nothing in return. He's got his own food and equipment, he's not here for ours. He was just giving me a ride back to the compound."

Bill glared at Ethan, but the younger man met his gaze with an even stare. Bill looked away first, glancing down for a moment, then looking back up at me. He seemed tired all of a sudden, and I could see the apology in his expression.

"I'm sorry if I seem impolite. The last folks who came through tried to steal from us. It didn't end very well, for them or for us. You look like you're doing okay, so I guess you ain't gonna try to steal from us. If you was the bad kind, I doubt you would have stopped to help a stranger." He made a gesture toward Ethan, who had visibly relaxed.

"I reckon I better get back on watch, then. Don't want Donna and Jake getting themselves in trouble." Bill tipped his hat to Ethan and me, and ambled back over to the scaffold.

"Sorry about that," Ethan said. "Bill is kind of the leader here. He took it hard when we lost a couple of folks not long ago. Been real serious about security ever since then."

"What happened?" I asked.

Ethan frowned and shook his head.

"I'm not the best person to answer that question. I was on a supply run when it all went down. Why don't you come inside, I'll introduce you to some of the folks."

"I appreciate the offer, but I really need to get going. I'm trying to get to a friend's house before sundown," I replied.

"Which way you headed? Me and the other scouts have ranged pretty far afield, maybe I can tell you where the trouble spots are. It's the least I can offer, considering what you did for me today."

I debated for a moment whether I should tell him or not. Gabriel wouldn't want anyone knowing how to get to his cabin, but on the other hand, Ethan might have valuable information about the road ahead. He seemed like an honest enough guy, and he could just as easily have told Bill to put a bullet in my head and taken all of my stuff. I decided to trust him, for the time being. I motioned for Ethan to follow me and walked back over to the truck. I took my atlas out from the center console and opened it to the route I had marked out earlier in the day.

"I'm planning on heading this way north up to Morganton. You know of any trouble up that way?" I asked.

"Uh, yeah, a little bit," Ethan said as he studied the map. He pointed to one of the towns along the route.

"The Army sent some troops out from Fort Bragg to set up a safe zone here at Iron Station, and here at the Lincolnton Regional Airport. Both were overrun. If you try driving through that way, you'll never make it. The roads are choked with abandoned vehicles, and the place is swarming with creeps. You're going to have to take back roads northeast past highway 73, all the way up to 150. From there you can cut back west and pick up your route just north of Bolger City."

"Shit," I swore. That would add several hours to the trip at the low speeds I would need to drive to ensure a safe journey.

"What about north and west of Bolger City? Any trouble out that way?" I asked.

Ethan shook his head. "I don't know. I've been north as far as 150, but I haven't been near Bolger City since before the dead started walking. I can plot you a clear route to the highway, but I don't know what you'll be up against once you head back west. Sorry."

I waved off his apology.

"No, you've been a big help. I'm glad I didn't have to find out about Iron Station the hard way. At least now I have an idea of what I'm up against."

I closed the atlas and tossed it back into the passenger seat. I leaned against the side of the truck and crossed my arms over my chest, sighing in frustration. Right then, my stomach decided to groan loudly, and I remembered that it had been nearly five hours since I had eaten last. Ethan heard it and chuckled.

"Listen, man, you saved my ass today and I owe you one. There's no way you're going to make it to Morganton before sundown. Why don't you stay the night with us? We've got plenty of food, and my wife is a pretty good cook. The folks in the compound would be glad to hear some news from the outside. We even have a place to take a shower set up, warm water and everything. Trust me, you ain't gonna find a nicer place to sleep anywhere within a day's drive," he said.

I thought about it for a minute, and realized he was right. I was hungry, and tired, and drenched with sweat from the day's events. A warm meal, a shower, and a good night's sleep sounded pretty appealing. Gabriel had waited this long, what was one more day?

"Yeah, what the hell," I said. "I might as well get some rest. God knows what's waiting for me between here and Morganton."

I reached into the bed of the truck and started to pull out my sleeping bag and toiletry kit, but Ethan stopped me.

"Instead of lugging all this shit inside, how about I get a forklift and move that shipping container. You can just drive your truck in," he said.

I shot him a suspicious glance.

"Why would I need to park my truck inside?" I asked.

Ethan laughed and shook his head, then raised a hand and pointed to the western sky.

"Because there's a storm rolling in, and I would hate to see your fancy tools get all wet."

I looked where he was pointing, and sure enough, there was a massive thunderhead moving in our direction.

"Uh…right," I said, embarrassed.

Ethan laughed again and clapped me on the shoulder.

"Drive her around front, partner. I'll get the container moved for you."

I drove the truck back around to the front of the warehouse and waited while Ethan climbed into a forklift parked under a makeshift carport. He drove the forklift around to the near side of the container, used the fork to lift it off the ground a few feet, and pushed it forward. I noticed there were two wheels welded to the other side of the container. Clever design, that. The undead wouldn't be able to move the heavy container in the direction needed to get in, but the forklift could move it with ease if they needed to drive something inside. Like many forklifts, the one Ethan drove ran on propane. I guessed that they must have a stockpile of canisters somewhere.

Once the container was far enough out of the way, Ethan lowered it and climbed down from the forklift. He walked over to the rolling steel door and slapped it with his hand three times in rapid succession.

"Earl, open the gate!" he shouted.

A moment later, the gate slowly started to rise. I could hear the sound of a chain being drawn through a pulley, and after a minute or two, the door was high enough to drive my truck through. A massive man with dark ebony skin and a shiny bald head stepped out and waved for me to drive in. I pulled forward and drove into the gloom of the warehouse. The large black man motioned for me to follow him, and I parked the truck beside a long row of shelves laden with all manner of containers. By the time I got out of the truck, Ethan had moved the blue shipping container back into place. The man who I assumed must be Earl walked back over to the garage door and pulled the chain to lower it. When it reached the concrete floor, he used two large padlocks to secure the door to irons rings set into the cement.

Once the door was secure, he made his way back over to where I stood beside the truck. He held out a hand big enough to swat condors out of the sky, and grinned broadly, his brilliant white teeth standing out in contrast to his dark skin.

"How you doin'. Name's Earl," he said, his voice surprisingly high-pitched for a man his size.

"Eric Riordan, nice to meet you," I replied as I shook his massive, calloused hand.

Just as I suspected, he was strong enough to crush bricks. Something popped in one of my knuckles as he gave it a firm squeeze. He noticed my pained expression and quickly released my hand, his smile fading a bit.

"Sorry bout that. Don't know my own strength sometimes. Hope I didn't hurt you."

I flexed my fingers, and everything seemed to be in good working order.

"No problem, I'm fine." I gestured at the massive expanse of the warehouse.

"Nice place you got here."

"Yeah, it ain't too bad. Long as you don't mind livin' in a big-ass cave."

I laughed at that one. "I guess it beats the alternative, right?" I replied.

"Yeah, I guess it does at that. How bout I give you the grand tour?"

"Sounds good, lead the way."

The big man turned and walked toward the other end of the warehouse. On both sides of us, there were stacks of crates and boxes, some of it on shelves and some of it sitting on the bare concrete. Most of the stuff on my right, near where I parked the truck, looked like food and other dry goods. On the left were large stacks of various types of lumber, as well as metal sheets, long square bars that I recognized as raw metal stock for machining, and more barrels than I could count at a glance.

Ahead of us, beyond the storage area, were what looked like wooden shacks built against the warehouse walls. As we drew closer to them, I noticed that the shacks varied in size. Some covered close to eight-hundred square feet, and others were smaller and seemed to be made for only one or two people. There were twenty shacks in all, with plenty of room on the warehouse floor for more.

Earl jerked a thumb behind him at the massive piles of supplies.

"Back there is just storage. We got all kinds of stuff over there, and we bring in more all the time. If we ever run out of room in here, there's plenty more storage space on the factory floor. Most of the production equipment got pulled out of there back when the plant shut down, so it's mostly just empty space now. We keep the living quarters in here on account of its easier to keep the creeps out."

I looked around the expanse of the warehouse. Now that my eyes had adjusted to the gloom, I noted that most of the light in the place filtered in from windows near the ceiling. All of the shacks had what looked like metal pipes that extended from their roofs to the windows less than ten feet above them. I figured they were set up to vent heat and smoke from cooking fires. Some of the shacks had candles burning in glass holders.

"Yeah, I guess this place is kind of a fortress. How do you light it up at night?" I asked.

"Candles, mostly. Bill makes sure everybody uses those glass candleholders when we burn em. Says it's too easy for a fire to break out, everything being made of wood and all."

"About that, what's with the shacks? Seems like there should be plenty of room for everyone. Why not just lay out cots and avoid the fire hazard?"

"We did that, at first. Then folks started arguing bout what belongs to who, complaining about people snoring at night, some of the couples got to hurting for some alone time, things like that. Bill said we should build partitions to give everybody some privacy. Turned out to be a good idea, most of the arguing died off since then. Bill's a good man for thinking up ideas."

We reached the far half of the warehouse and I saw that each of the shacks had names spray-painted on their fronts in a variety of different colors. Bill's was one of the smaller ones, about the size of a single bedroom. As I began to study some of the artwork and decorations that adorned the outsides of the shacks, the steel door at the far wall opened and Ethan stepped inside, closing the door behind him and sliding a steel bar in place to secure it. The door opened inward, and anything trying to get inside would have to be strong enough to break through the steel barrier. Smart.

Ethan took a moment to look around, saw me walking toward him, and made his way over.

"You parked down by the rolling door?" he asked me.

"Yeah, why?"

"I need to get that bag out of your truck."

I had completely forgotten about the heavy duffel bag Ethan brought with him during our escape from the besieged Burger King.

"Oh, yeah," I said. "What the hell is in that thing? It looks like it weighs a ton."

"Nah, just about two hundred or so pounds," he replied, grinning.

"Right, so what's in it?"

"The most valuable commodity on the face of the Earth, my friend. Ammo, and lots of it."

A few of the people who had been milling about perked up when he said that. A tall young man and a pretty girl with dyed blond hair that had grown several inches of brown roots approached.

"Dude, did I hear you say you got ammo? 'Cause that would make my fucking week," the tall guy asked.

Ethan beamed. "Yup, round everybody up, and call Bill down from the roof. I'm gonna start parceling it out. And as for you little lady," he said, playfully punching at the young girl's arm, "I got a gun that you ought to be able to handle just fine."

"Whatever, douchebag. The only gun I care about handling is Justin's," she said, sliding an arm around the young man's waist.

Ethan turned to say something to me, but right as he was about to speak a door to one of the shacks slammed open and a gorgeous redhead came storming out marching straight for Ethan. She carried a baby that couldn't have been more than a year old on one hip. Ethan's expression immediately became serious and he raised his hands in a placating gesture.

"Alright, Andrea, calm down..."

"Don't you tell me to calm down, damn it! What the hell is wrong with you? Where have you been? Are you trying to give me a heart attack, you thick-skulled idiot? I've been worried sick about you."

She punctuated each sentence with a poorly aimed slap that deflected off the side of Ethan's arms as he backpedaled away from the woman. The baby, finding the whole situation immensely entertaining, laughed uproariously and flapped his little arms in glee. I couldn't help but smile. Here was a big, strapping man getting the riot act read to him by a little redhead with a baby on her hip. Classic.

"Baby, calm down! I'm fine, everything is fine. I got the ammo we needed. Can you stop hitting me for a minute?"

Finally, he caught the woman's arm not holding a baby by the wrist, and brought her close in a tight hug. She struggled for a moment, then buried her head in his chest and clutched him tightly. Her shoulders hitched, and she began to sob. Ethan looked as though he felt like the world's biggest shitheel, and muttered soothing words to her, stroking her long hair and holding her against him. The baby babbled and reached his little arms up toward Ethan. He took the baby and held him in one arm as he consoled his wife with the other. The people gathered around, me included, stopped smiling. Everyone suddenly seemed to find the ground at their feet acutely fascinating.

"You can't scare me like that," Andrea said between racking sobs. "I thought you weren't coming back. You can't leave us alone."

"I'm not, baby. I'm right here, I'm not going anywhere."

The baby seemed to miss the gravity of the moment, and babbled happily as he tugged at Ethan's beard. Ethan winced, and pulled his head away.

"Come on babe, come see what I got for you."

Andrea released her hold on Ethan, and used the bottom of his shirt to dry her eyes. She regained some of her composure and reached for the baby.

"It better be good for you to scare me like this, or your ass is gonna be sleeping on the roof."

Ethan smiled. His grin had an infectious, endearing quality to it. I decided that it must be pretty hard not to like the guy.

"It's good, honey. Hang out here for a minute, I'll be right back."

Ethan turned away and walked to the storage area. As he left to get the ammo, Andrea noticed me, and she stiffened in surprise.

"Hi, I'm Eric," I said, giving a little wave.

Andrea flushed, and walked forward, offering me a hand.

"Hi, Andrea Thompson. I'm sorry about all of that. It's just been really stressful lately, with everything that's happened..."

"Yeah, I know what you mean." I shook her hand and gave her what I hoped was a reassuring smile. It must have worked, because she smiled back.

"And who is this little fella?" I asked, holding a hand out toward the baby. He reached for it and gave a high-pitched squawk when he got my index finger in his little fist.

"This is Aiden. Say hi Aiden." She took his hand from around my finger and mimicked a wave with it. The baby turned to his mother and gave her a sloppy, open mouthed baby kiss on the side of her face. Andrea giggled, and wiped slobber from her cheek.

"He's a bit of a mess, just like his father."

"I'm guessing Ethan is your husband?" I said.

"Yes, that's right. I assume you met him out on the road?"

"Yeah, something like that," I responded, looking toward the far end of the compound where Ethan was pulling the bag out of my truck. Her smile faltered, and her brow furrowed slightly in confusion.

Before she got a chance to ask any questions, Ethan came back with the duffel bag on a rolling cart. By that time, more people had gathered around to see what was going on.

The folks inside the warehouse ran the gamut of ages, ethnicities, and gender. There were four or five old timers, fifteen or so adults anywhere from twenty to fifty-five years of age, and a handful of children. A few of the children were teenagers, but the rest looked twelve or younger. Earl, who had somehow managed to stay quietly in the background during Ethan and Andrea's theatrics, helped Ethan lift the bag from the cart. A crowd gathered round as the two men opened the bag and started taking out boxes of ammunition and a few guns. Ethan had retrieved the .22 magnum rifle from the back of my truck and wore it strapped across his back. Earl stood up and addressed the crowd, holding out his arms and calling for order.

"Alright everybody, back up and chill out for a minute. We gonna divide this up and everybody gonna get what they need."

"You heard the man." A voice called out from behind the crowd. I turned and saw Bill push his way to the front. Justin had let him in, and was securing the steel door.

"Go get your weapons and lay them out in front of your shelter. Earl and Justin will make an inventory of who needs what, and Ethan and I will make sure everything gets distributed accordingly. Go on now, you're holding up work."

He waved his arms in a shooing gesture at the crowd. There were a few grumbles, but everyone did as they were asked. It seemed that the people here really did look up to Bill. Andrea switched the baby to her other arm and stooped down to plant a kiss on Ethan's cheek.

"You know what we need, I'm going to go finish feeding Aiden," she said.

Ethan nodded. "Okay, I'll be in shortly. Just got to get this stuff handed out."

He reached out and gave Andrea's hand a squeeze before going back to work. Andrea turned and went back into her shack.

Earl knelt down to help Ethan sort the ammo. There were at least a couple of thousand rounds in numerous calibers. Justin and Bill pitched in, and they quickly had the boxes sorted by caliber into several piles. Ethan also pulled a few handguns and four rifles out of the bag. One of the rifles was a .270 hunting rifle, and the other three I recognized as civilian model SCAR 16 semi-automatic assault rifles. Prior to the end of the world, that would have been about ten thousand dollars worth of hardware. Bill's eyes widened as he looked at the weapons.

"Ethan, where the hell did you get all this stuff? Not that I'm complaining, mind you," Bill said.

Ethan stopped working for a moment and stared at the ground.

"It's a bit of a long story Bill. If it's all the same, I'd rather just tell it once, after dinner." Ethan looked up, his expression somber. Bill nodded, and Ethan went back to sorting ammo. I tapped Bill on the shoulder to get his attention.

"Anything I can do to help?" I asked. "I don't like standing around while everyone else is working. Makes me feel lazy."

Bill pointed at the people taking weapons out of their shacks and laying them out in front of their doors.

"You can go with Earl and Justin and take inventory of the ammo everybody needs, and make sure all of those weapons are safe and cleared. You know how to do that?"

I nodded. "Yep. I'm on it."

I met Earl and Justin in front of the shack closest to the entrance. It was one of the larger ones, and four people stood in front of it. Two were adults, a man and a woman, and the other two were teenagers. Earl had a pencil and a piece of paper and Justin squatted down in front of the weapons rattling off their ammunition types. Earl glanced up, and offered me a pencil and a small notepad from one of his cargo pockets.

"You mind going across the way and starting on that side? If we finish up over here we'll come help you out," he said.

"Sure, no problem," I replied.

I went across the warehouse to the opposite row of shacks and introduced myself to the resident of the shelter nearest the far end. It was a small one, about the same size as Bill's, and the man in front of it was a short, middle-aged fellow with close-cropped gray hair and a strong build.

"Hi, Eric Riordan, nice to meet you." I offered a hand.

"Rick Farrell. You must be new here." He gave a slight smile, and I noted the strength of his grip as he shook my hand.

"Just passing through actually, thought I might lend a hand while I'm here," I said.

"Well, we can use all the help we can get. What can I do for you?" he replied.

"Bill needs me to inventory the guns and what ammo they use, and make sure they're all safe and clear."

"Well mine should be easy then." He pointed at his feet, and I recognized the rifle as a Ruger Mini 14 tactical.

"Nice choice," I said. "Simple, rugged, easy to shoot. My grandpa had one, used it for varmint hunting."

"Yeah, well, beggars can't be choosers. I took this thing off a guy's corpse when I ran out of ammo for my twelve gauge.

Wish I still had the shotgun, but I bent the barrel busting open a creep's head. This thing shoots .223, and it's safe and clear already."

I wrote down the man's name, his rifle, and the ammo it used.

"Cool, thanks. Nice to meet you, Rick."

Rick nodded and I continued down the line. I took a moment to introduce myself to the people at each shelter as I went. Most were friendly enough and seemed genuinely glad to see me, but a few were tense, and glared at me with suspicion clearly written in their eyes. I was polite to each of them, not wanting to start any trouble. After ten minutes or so, Earl and Justin finished their inventory and helped me with the last few people on my side of the warehouse.

I walked back over to Bill and Ethan, who were inspecting the new firearms. I handed my list to Bill, who pulled a pair of reading glasses out of his breast pocket and peered down his nose at the piece of paper. Justin came over with his list and handed it to Ethan. After a few moments, Bill took off the glasses and called out to the other survivors.

"Anyone who doesn't have a firearm, come on up."

Four people approached, three of them women. Bill pointed at the rifles and pistols on the ground.

"Them two assault rifles are going to be for folks on guard duty, and that third one is Ethan's. Call it a finder's fee. You can take your pick from the rest, including that hunting rifle. Any of you ever hunt?"

The lone male of the group, a portly man who looked to be in his mid-thirties, raised a hand.

"I go deer hunting every fall in South Carolina. Well, I used to at least." The man looked down as he spoke.

Bill nodded solemnly, and offered the man the rifle and several boxes of ammunition.

"These should last you awhile, Greg. We got more if you need it, just let us know."

The man muttered a subdued thanks, and walked away. The three women examined the pistols, asking Ethan's opinion on which one they should choose.

"They're all nine-millimeter," he said. "They all shoot the shame bullet, so just try to find one that feels alright when you aim it."

After a few more moments of hefting the various guns, each lady settled on one, and Ethan gave them all two hundred rounds and a spare magazine for each weapon.

Bill again turned and addressed the people standing in front of their shacks.

"Alright, now that everybody has at least one weapon, we're going to start passing out ammo. I'll call your name, then you come over and we'll give you a few hundred rounds. The rest will go into the gun locker. If you need more, just let me or one of the other three deputies know so we can keep track of how much we have left. Ya'll know the gun locker ain't locked, but that ain't a license to go crazy and use up ammo we can't afford to lose."

I turned to Ethan, a skeptical look on my face. "Did I just hear him call you guys 'deputies'?"

Ethan nodded. "Yeah, I'll explain later."

Bill began calling out names, and one by one, Ethan gave them a few hundred rounds for their various guns. In spite of the variety of firearms on display by the compound's residents, the range of calibers was fairly narrow. It made sense, really, considering that most guns are chambered for a few popular types of ammo. Ethan had plenty of bullets for all of them.

After everyone's name had been called, Bill thanked everyone for cooperating and asked for volunteers to help pass out food for the evening meal. Several people raised their hands, and followed Bill to the other side of the building. I turned to Ethan, who was loading ammo back onto the rolling cart. It looked like only about a third of what he brought back with him was distributed.

"Looks like you made everyone's day," I remarked.

Ethan smiled and nodded. "I bet so. Folks were starting to worry about the lack of ammunition around here. Having a loaded gun next to you makes sleeping at night a little easier these days."

"How did you know what kinds of ammunition to bring back?"

Ethan shrugged. "I got eyes. I just paid attention to what everybody carried around and made sure to pick up the most common kinds. This here," he said, patting a pile of .223 boxes, "is just a sample. There's a shitload more where this came from. We just have to find a way to get it out of Alexis without getting eaten alive."

The blond girl with the two-toned hair I met earlier came over and sat down by Justin, who was helping Ethan load boxes onto the cart. Ethan stood up, took the .22 magnum rifle off his back, and held it out to the girl.

"This should work pretty well for you. It shoots a small bullet, but it has good penetrating power out to eighty yards or more. It even has a halfway decent scope on it. Let me know if you need help learning to shoot it."

Ethan placed several boxes of ammunition beside the girl, and loaded the rest onto the cart. The girl looked the rifle over, worked the bolt, and brought the stock to her shoulder to peer through the sight.

"So who's the new guy?" she asked as she lowered the rifle.

"The new guy is Eric, and he can hear you," I said, glowering at her.

"Don't mind her," Ethan said. "She's all bark and no bite."

The girl slapped Ethan on the leg. He ignored it, and continued his work.

"I'm Emily, and this is my boyfriend Justin," she said.

She laid a delicate hand on the young man's shoulder. She looked up at me, and I noticed that she had green eyes set in a pretty, heart shaped face. She wore a t-shirt with a heavy metal band's logo emblazoned across the front, and a pair of threadbare jeans. She was exactly the kind of girl I would have gone for in high school and college.

"Nice to meet you Emily. And you too, Justin. How do you folks know Ethan here?"

Justin spoke up, "He saved both of our asses getting out of Charlotte. We wouldn't be alive if not for him."

Justin's voice, and the look in his eyes, conveyed a maturity and seriousness that seemed out of place given his boyish exterior. He couldn't have been more than nineteen, if he was a day. Emily looked barely legal for a guy his age to be shacking up with.

Ethan, meanwhile, flushed beneath his beard and waved off the compliment.

"I did what anybody would have. You two don't owe me anything."

"Plenty of people saw us on top of that bus, and not a damn one stopped to help. Nobody except you and your father," Justin replied.

Ethan looked up, a pained expression on his face. Justin met his gaze and laid a sympathetic hand on his shoulder.

"I know, man, I know. He might still be out there, we don't know anything for sure," he said.

Ethan nodded and got up to haul the ammunition back to the other side of the compound. Justin watched him walk away, his expression somber. Emily wrapped her arms around his waist and he hugged her back.

"He'll be okay, he just needs some time," she said.

"His old man was a tough one. If anybody could have survived that mess, it would be him," Justin replied.

"Did you know his father?" I asked.

Justin turned to me and shook his head.

"Just stories that Ethan told us. He sounds like a tough old bastard, though. Taught Ethan most everything he knows.

Anybody who can raise a man like that is someone who knows how to fight, and how to survive."

"So what happened? Why isn't he here?"

"That's a long story, and one best told over a warm meal," Justin said. "Come on, man, I can hear your stomach growling from here. Let's get you some food."

The rumbling in my belly again became distracting, and I decided that satisfying my curiosity about the people of the compound could wait until I had some food on my stomach. Just as I was about to follow Justin to his shack, Ethan returned from stowing the spare ammunition. He walked over to me and patted Justin on his shoulder.

"Hate to deny you company, bud, but this guy saved my life today. He's earned himself some of Andrea's cooking."

Both Emily and Justin's eyes widened.

"What do you mean, he saved your life?" Emily asked, stepping in front of Ethan. "What happened?"

"It's a long story, and if you guys come over for dinner, I'd be happy to tell you about it."

Justin gave me a glance that held a combination of respect and curiosity, then took Emily by the hand and led her away. The young woman protested, clearly not happy about Ethan's admission.

"Don't worry about them," Ethan said. "They worry too much."

I followed Ethan to his shack, which was one of the larger ones, at about six hundred square feet. Inside, it looked like a small one bedroom apartment. There was a Coleman stove on a table beneath a makeshift range hood, which connected to a pipe that extended through the ceiling. It was warmer in the shed than outside on the compound floor. Andrea came from the lone bedroom and held a single finger to her lips.

"Baby's sleeping," she whispered as she pulled a heavy burlap cloth across the door.

Ethan motioned to a couch and a couple of comfortable looking chairs that, along with a large coffee table, took up most of the near half of the room. Looking around the shack, I could tell that it wasn't built to be a sturdy barrier, but only a rough partition to provide some privacy. It was constructed of two-by-fours and plywood, and the cinder block wall of the warehouse comprised the far wall. Everything around me was exposed wood with no insulation or drywall. Two candles burning in glass containers on the coffee table provided the room's only illumination.

Ethan sat down on the couch, and I took a seat in a chair across the table from him. Andrea opened a cardboard box beside the Coleman stove and started pulling out boxes and cans.

"Is mac-and-cheese with kidney beans and corned beef hash okay, guys?" she asked, keeping her voice low.

"I could eat just about anything right now. Whatever you want to make is fine by me," I said.

Andrea stacked a few items beside the stove and filled a pot with water from a small plastic barrel beside the kitchen table. A spice rack stood to the left of the camp stove, and she picked a few spices and dried herbs from the racks.

"It might be simple fare, but that lady can make miracles happen with even the most simple ingredients," Ethan said, gazing lovingly at his wife.

"Honestly, I could eat roast snake and grilled frog legs right about now," I replied.

"That won't be necessary, at least not yet," Andrea said as she set the water to boil on the stove and started opening the cans.

There was a knock at the crude front door, which was simply a sheet of plywood hung on three hinges with a latch to hold it closed from the inside. Ethan got up to open it, and Justin and Emily came inside. Justin waved at Andrea.

"Hi. I hope we're not interrupting anything."

"Oh no, sweetheart, come on in. You two want some dinner?"

"We'd love some," Emily said as she crossed over to Andrea and gave the other woman a warm hug.

"Didn't Bill say something about preparing the evening meal?" I asked. "Does everyone here cook indoors, or is there like a little mess hall or something?"

"A little bit of both," Justin replied. "Most folks bring out folding tables and eat in the open area between the partitions. We call that the common area. It's usually pretty simple stuff, and not nearly as good as what Andrea puts together, but it's nice to sit down as a community and have people to talk to."

I nodded. It was easy enough to understand how being surrounded by flesh-eating ghouls might make a person long for some friendly company. Justin's words reminded me of something Ethan mentioned earlier.

"Hey, didn't you tell me there were two other people out scouting with you?" I asked him.

"Yes, but they may not be back for a few days yet. They've set up a relay system that allows them to bring supplies back in large shipments, at least as long as the available gasoline holds up."

Emily looked quizzically at Ethan. "What do you mean? There's plenty of gas out there. We just have to siphon it out."

"Gasoline expires," I said. "It doesn't stay volatile forever. It usually goes inert after about nine months or so, unless you put an additive in it to preserve it. Even then, under ideal conditions, you might get a few years out of it at most. Whatever work you need to do that requires a gasoline powered motor, you better get it done in the next six months or so. After that, gasoline supplies will become increasingly unreliable."

Emily stared at me for a moment, then turned back to Ethan pointed a thumb in my direction.

"Is all that shit he just said true?"

Ethan laughed. "Yes, it is, and he said it a heck of a lot better than I could have. That's why we're working so hard to stockpile supplies as quickly as we can. Once the gasoline goes bad, we're back to pulling carts."

"So what do we do when that happens?"

Ethan shrugged. "The best we can I guess. If we play our cards right, and store up the right materials, we can build a sustainable community that doesn't rely on gasoline."

"How do we do that?" Emily asked.

Ethan gave her a look of mock condescension. "Since when do you care about planning and logistics?"

Emily slapped him on the arm. "Don't make fun of me, I'm serious. How are we going to survive without machines?"

Ethan heaved a sigh. "That's a simple question with a very complicated and uncertain answer. For now, we plan as best we can and make do with what we have. No sense borrowing trouble from tomorrow." He gave her a gentle pat on the shoulder and led her to the little sitting room with Justin and I in tow.

"Anyone fancy a little wine?" Andrea asked.

Even Emily perked up at the mention of wine. A chorus of affirmatives went up from the gathered company, myself included. Andrea fished around in one of several cardboard boxes stacked in the little kitchen and produced three bottles of a decent pinot noir. She uncorked one of them and poured the rich red liquid into clear plastic party glasses.

"Sorry folks, but we left the good crystal in Charlotte," She said. Her comment elicited a round of rueful chuckles from the assembled guests. I didn't get it, but I smiled anyway as Andrea passed them around. Justin raised his cup in the air.

"To living to see another day," he said.

Everyone agreed, and we clinked the plastic cups as best we could. I sipped the wine, and sat back in my chair.

"So, Ethan." I said. "Why don't you tell me how you ended up down in Alexis stranded on the roof of a Burger King?" I asked.

In unison, everyone's heads first swiveled toward me, then toward Ethan, almost as if they had rehearsed it.

Andrea gave Ethan a piercing glare, cocked her head to the side, and placed one petite fist on her hip. "Yeah, honey, why don't you tell us about that?"

Ethan squirmed a little under her scrutiny and shot me an irritated glance. I smiled my best guileless smile, and took another sip of my wine. Emily did her best to rescue him.

"How about this, why don't you tell us how you came to be here," she said, giving me a hard glare.

"Three reasons," I responded, counting off on my fingers. "Number one, the stories are related. Two, this guy owes me one for helping him out today, and three, he already promised to explain it all over dinner. I made no such promise."

"Well, dinner ain't here yet, but I suppose you're right," Ethan said. "I did promise, and I owe you for helping me today."

That last part wasn't necessarily true, but he didn't need to know that just yet. I planned to share what I knew about fighting the undead with these people, assuming they didn't turn out to be meth-smoking cannibals or something, but I would do it when I was damn well good and ready. For the moment, I wanted information.

"Go on," Andrea said, making a twirling motion with one hand. "Tell us where you been the last two days."

"Two days?" I asked. "You were stuck in Alexis for two days?"

"Yes, I was," he said, heaving an irritated sigh. "And if everyone will pipe down for a minute I'll explain everything."

Ethan tossed back the rest of his wine, picked up the bottle from the coffee table to fill it back up, then leaned back on the couch for a moment, his gaze distant. Uneasy silence filled the room for the space of a few heartbeats. The storm that Ethan had pointed out to me earlier rolled in, and rain began to beat on the roof of the warehouse. The first peals of thunder rumbled as Ethan began to speak.

"Okay," he said. "Here's what happened."

Chapter 8

Ethan's Story

"When ammunition started running low, I talked to Bill about putting together a team to get a new supply from a gun shop over in Alexis. He wouldn't hear of it. He said that there were less dangerous places to look, and we should exhaust those sources first before risking anyone on a supply run to an infested town. I railed, argued, begged, and bullied, but Bill wouldn't change his mind. Finally, I told him he might be the leader, but I still have the freedom to make my own decisions, and I was going to try it alone. He tried to talk me out of it, of course, but my mind was made up.

I set out early Monday morning at the same time Cody and Stan went north to gather supplies. I wanted to bring back as much ammo as possible, so I brought the biggest duffel bag I could find and set out for Alexis on a bicycle. My plan was to ride the bike close to town and leave it at the bottom of a hill, out of sight of the creeps. After that, I planned to approach on foot and circle around behind the main part of town on highway 27. There is a steep hill less than a quarter mile from the back entrance to a gun shop that I knew would have plenty of ammunition.

I figured that I could use the woods for cover until I reached the hill, slip down nice and quiet, and get into the back entrance before the creeps spotted me. Once inside, I could fill up the bag with as much ammo as I could carry, go back up the hill, and make my way back to the bicycle. Once there, I would cache the ammo and head back for more. After I had staged as much as daylight would allow, I was going to ride back to town and use one of our vehicles to retrieve it."

I raised a hand. "Uh, why not just drive a car to the bottom of the hill? I mean, why bother with a bike in the first place?"

"Noise," Ethan replied. "The sound of the car, even from that distance, would attract the creeps. I've seen it for myself. In order for my plan to work, I had to avoid alerting them. I needed time to make several trips back and forth to the gun shop. If I staged the ammo by the side of the road nice and quiet, the noise from the car wouldn't matter. I could be there and gone before the creeps would have time to do anything about it."

"That part makes sense," I said. "It's the rest of your plan that I find fault with."

"We can go over that later, in detail if you like, but for right now let me go on with the story."

"By all means." I gestured for him to continue.

"After leaving the bike, I made my way to the hill behind the gun shop and down to the fence at the bottom. Everything was going fine. I brought a pair of metal snips with me and cut a hole in the fence big enough to walk through. I made it to the back door of the gun shop without incident. The door was locked, but I was expecting that, and brought a pry-bar with me. What I didn't expect, was the shop owner still being in the damn store. He must have heard me trying to force the door open, and set up a welcome for me."

"Alan was still there?" Andrea asked, a horrified look on her face.

Ethan nodded. "I was prying the door open when all of a sudden I heard the lock turn. I stopped for a second, and started backing away. Next thing I know, the door slams open and Alan McMurray is standing there with a shotgun pointed at my head. I shouted 'Don't shoot! I'm alive!' or something like that. Thank God he recognized me when he opened the door. He lowered the gun and asked me what I wanted, and I told him I was there to search for ammo. He motioned me inside and locked the door behind us.

'Where the hell did you come from?' he says. I told him about the compound here, and asked him to come back with me. Alan didn't want to go at first; he had survived the last three months by staying out of sight in the basement. He had at least another year's worth of food, and didn't want to take any chances by leaving. After arguing with him for about ten minutes, I convinced him to at least come and see the place, and if he didn't want to stay, then I would personally escort him back to the gun shop. Finally, he agreed.

I pulled the duffel bag out of my waistband and unfolded it on the floor. 'What's that for?' Alan asks me. I told him it was to bring ammunition back to the compound with me. He asked me how I planned on paying for it, considering that everything in the store was his property. I told him he could have his pick of any supplies we had at the compound once we returned. All of a sudden, Alan goes ape-shit.

He points his gun at me and starts accusing me of being a thief. 'I know what you're doing!' he says. 'You gonna take me back somewhere and kill me! Then you gonna come take my property! I ain't gonna let you! Get out! Get out now or I'll shoot ya!'.

I tried to tell him he was wrong, I didn't mean him any harm, I was just trying to help him. He wouldn't hear it. He just kept telling me to leave and threatening to kill me. He backs up to the door and unlocks it, all the while pointing his gun at me and not looking at the door.

He opens the door and there are at least seven or eight creeps standing on the other side. Alan is still howling like a mad man at me, and before I could do or say anything, the one closest to the door grabs him and takes a bite out of his neck. Alan rears up and pulls the trigger on the shotgun, putting a load of buckshot in the ceiling. The damn creeps start spilling through the door, falling on him. The only weapon I brought with me was a hatchet."

Ethan stopped for a moment. He lowered his face into his hands and rubbed at his forehead. Andrea sat down beside him and placed an arm around his shoulders.

"I'm so sorry honey, I had no idea. I feel so awful, I shouldn't have yelled at you."

Ethan sat up and kissed his wife on the forehead. "It's okay babe, you didn't know. I would have been pissed at me too."

Tears shone in her eyes as she looked at her husband. Ethan held her delicate jaw in one big hand and gave her a gentle kiss. She wrapped her arms around his neck and hugged him.

"You don't have to tell us the rest, you're home safe and that's all that matters," she said.

"It's okay, I don't mind. I made a promise, I intend to keep it."

Suddenly, I regretted pushing Ethan on the subject. I had no idea things had gone so badly for him.

"Hey, it's cool man, I've heard enough. You don't need to say anything else on my account," I said.

Ethan was thoughtful for a moment.

"You know, I think I want to say it. Just so I'm not the only one who knows about it, you know? My old man said you have to talk about things like this."

Andrea stood up from the couch and kissed Ethan on the cheek.

"The water is boiling, I'm going to get started on dinner," she said.

"Thanks babe," Ethan replied. "You guys okay if I go on?" he asked Emily, Justin and me.

We all agreed and encouraged him to continue.

"So all these creeps are beating down the door, and three things go through my head at the same time. Number one: why were all these fuckers waiting outside the door? Number two: why did Alan go all crazy on me like that? Number three: fuck me running, I have to get that goddamn door shut.

I pull my hatchet out from my belt and slam it into the head of the closest creep, who happens to be tearing out Alan's throat. I try to pull it out, but the damn thing is stuck. Alan is

154

fighting and kicking this whole time, but can't do anything to get them off of him. After a second or two, I give up on the hatchet and pick up the shotgun he dropped when they pulled him to the ground. I put double-ought buckshot through the heads of five more creeps before I run out of ammo. There were still two more of them, and I could hear moaning from outside the door. More were on the way.

I looked around for a weapon, and the only thing I saw of immediate use was a display case full of tomahawks. I broke the glass with the shotgun and grabbed two of them. I turn around and the last two creeps stop taking bites out of Alan and look up at me. Alan is dead, and there is blood and gore all over the place, both from him and from the five creeps whose brains I splattered all over the wall. The stink was incredible. I ran at the first one and buried a tomahawk in its skull before it had a chance to do anything other than hiss. The second one reaches out and grabs me by the pants leg. Let me tell you guys something, don't ever let those things grab you, because they are strong as a motherfucker.

So anyway, the thing grabs me and I try to pull away. I can't get loose, it just holds on and starts lunging forward, trying to take a bite out of my leg. I turn the last tomahawk sideways and jam it in the things mouth, pushing it away from me. We just stood like that for a minute, straining at each other. I can hear the moaning outside getting louder, footsteps are crunching in the gravel not ten feet away. I let go of the tomahawk with one hand and reach down for the one stuck in the other creep's head. After a few seconds of wrenching it around, I manage to get it free and promptly cave in the skull of the one holding my leg.

Right as it hits the ground, I see two more about to come through the door. I jump over the pile of bodies and slam the door shut in their faces. I turn the knob to set the dead bolt and stagger away. As I'm going backward, I trip over one of the bodies behind me. I hit my ass on the floor, then slip in a puddle of blood as I'm trying to stand up. Finally, I get to my feet, and I can see more of the damn things at the front window pounding and pushing on it, trying to get in. I figured the only chance I had of surviving the day is to head down to the basement and pray for daylight, so to speak."

"Can I ask a question?" I said.

"Shoot," Ethan replied.

"How did you and your wife know the guy who owned the store? I mean, you two lived in Charlotte, right? Alexis is a bit of a drive from there."

"He was a friend of my father's," Andrea called over her shoulder as she stirred something in a pot. "They served together in Vietnam. Used to go skeet shooting together."

I nodded. "Sorry to hear about what happened to him. Were you guys close?"

"Not especially," Ethan replied. "I met him a few times when he came over to Andrea's parents' place. Seemed like a nice enough guy, if a bit odd. Had some funny political ideas, conspiracy theories and such. I always figured he was just a harmless old kook. He might have threatened to kill me, but nobody deserves what happened to him."

Ethan leaned forward, his hands clasped in front of him, his expression grim and tight.

"I can't help but feel responsible for his death," he said. "If I hadn't come into his store that morning, he'd probably still be alive."

"Don't you start that shit," Andrea scolded from the kitchen, pointing at Ethan with a wooden spoon. "The only thing that got Alan killed was Alan. If he had acted like a reasonable human being, instead of like a paranoid, delusional asshole, then he would be sitting next to you on that couch enjoying our hospitality."

Andrea put down the spoon and knelt down in front of Ethan, holding his hands in hers.

"Besides, he pointed a gun at my husband and threatened to kill him," she said, a fierce light in her bright blue eyes. "Nobody threatens my family. Nobody."

With that, she kissed Ethan on one of his big knuckles and went back into the kitchen to finish dinner. Ethan stared after her for a moment, a strange expression on his face.

"Anyway," he continued, "I go down into the basement and bolt the door. I spend a few seconds looking for a light switch, and finally I hit a chain hanging down from the ceiling with my head. I give it a tug, the light comes on, and it's like, hoooolyyyyy shit." Ethan made a sweeping gesture with his arms.

"The basement is more than twice the size of the store upstairs. He must have knocked down the wall between his store and the one next door. The place had to be at least four thousand square feet. Every square inch of space is packed with shelves full of food, ammo, guns, gear—you name it, the shit is probably down there. If the ATF had ever raided the place, they would have gone nuts. A third of the guns down there are illegal as hell. Some of them even have silencers, if you can believe it."

I perked up when he said that. Could Alan have known? After all, even Gabriel didn't know how far back the conspiracy to cover up the Phage went. Maybe he knew something about it. My musings were interrupted when Justin jumped out of his chair and began playfully slapping Ethan about his head and shoulders.

"Duuuude! Do you know what that means!" he shouted.

Andrea stepped in from the kitchen and cracked him on the back of his leg with a wooden spoon. The happy, elated look immediately left his face as he collapsed into his chair, hissing in agony. Andrea reached under his leg and rubbed the offended area while Emily hid a poorly concealed smirk behind one hand.

"Now Justin, I'm sorry I had to do that, but I can't have you waking the baby," she said.

"Right, sorry about that. I just got excited, is all." He relaxed as the sting of the blow faded.

Ethan, meanwhile, stared at his friend in mute sympathy. When he continued, his voice was noticeably quieter.

"Right, so I take a tour of the place, and there is enough hardware down there to outfit a fucking army. The problem is, how do I get it all past the creeps without ending up on the dinner menu?"

"What all was down there?" Emily asked.

"Guns, bullets, bullets, and more bullets. Grenades, knives, food, a curiously large collection of porn, and three grocery store pallets full of toilet paper."

Justin and Emily exclaimed at the same time.

"Toilet paper!" cried Emily.

"Porn!" shouted Justin.

Andrea stepped into the room, brandishing her wooden spoon. Everyone immediately went quiet. All in attendance, myself included, stayed still and silent until the pretty, freckle-faced threat went back into the kitchen to stir the macaroni and cheese.

"So how did you get out of there?" Justin asked.

"I knew I couldn't go back upstairs, and I figured the big steel security door at the basement entrance would be strong enough to hold off the creeps if they tried to bust in. The only thing left for me to do was wait, so that's what I did. I ate some canned food, loaded up one of the assault rifles and set it by the door to make me feel better, and spent a couple of hours digging through Alan's stuff looking for anything interesting. Finally, I find a bottle of Jim Beam and a couple of clean glasses. I took the booze into a far corner of the room, stacked as much crap between me and the door as I could, and sat down to rest with a couple thousand rounds of ammo, a good rifle, and a bottle of Kentucky's finest."

Andrea stepped into the room. "Dinners ready, y'all mind eating around the coffee table?" she asked.

The aromas from the little kitchen had been growing increasingly appetizing, and we were all eager to eat. Andrea mixed the macaroni and cheese with a little dried basil and onion powder, put a sprinkle of cumin in the corned beef hash, and salted the kidney beans to perfection. I never would have believed that such a simple meal could taste so good. Maybe it had something to do with the fact that I was hungry enough to eat the ass-end of a cape buffalo. Either way, the meal was thoroughly enjoyed by all. After everyone finished eating, Ethan helped Andrea wash the dishes in a plastic tub, then Andrea opened another bottle of wine.

"So what happened after you barricaded yourself in the basement?" Emily asked, as Andrea poured another round of pinot.

"I poured myself a few fingers of whiskey, ate some canned spaghetti and meatballs, and eventually fell asleep. The next morning when I woke up, I could hear thumping and moaning coming from upstairs. I figured they must have broken the windows at the front of the store. I wanted to get out of there, but I had no way of knowing how many of those things I'd be facing if I opened the basement door. Even with all the ammunition down there, I didn't favor my chances if I had to shoot my way out.

I spent that day and night in the basement reading old paperbacks and eating Alan's food. The next morning, the noise from upstairs had stopped. I loaded a pistol and opened the basement door. I didn't see anything on the stairs, so I crept up into the store real quiet. I looked around as much as I could without walking in front of the windows, but the only thing I saw was what was left of Alan's corpse and the creeps I killed the day before. There wasn't much left of Alan. The bastards that broke the windows worked him over pretty bad."

Ethan was silent for a moment before continuing. Andrea refilled everyone's wine, and took Ethan's hand into her own as she sat down next to him. I was starting to get a little buzz from the alcohol.

"So I lay down on the floor," Ethan continued, "and low crawl over to where I left the duffel bag. I take it with me back down to the basement and fill it with as many boxes of bullets as I can carry. As it turns out, I can carry a lot."

Andrea smiled at that, and shifted closer to Ethan. He placed an arm around her shoulders as she laid her head on his broad chest.

"Yeah, yeah, you're all super gorilla big-balls retarded monkey strong. You'll have to excuse me if I don't swoon," Justin joked. "So what happened next?"

Ethan chuckled, and gave his young friend a one-finger salute.

"After I filled the bag with the ammo and a few guns, I carried it up the stairs and did another low crawl to the door, pushing the bag in front of me. I nabbed the .22 magnum rifle I gave to Emily from one of the shelves at the back of the store, then set to work moving the dead creeps out of the way so I could get the damn door open. Finally, I get it open and check the parking lot. It looked clear, so I drag the duffel bag outside and take a look around. I didn't see any creeps, and I couldn't hear any nearby.

I couldn't go back up the hill the way I came because the bag was too heavy. There was no way I could get it to the top without making a lot of noise. I picked it up and started making my way back to the highway one building at a time, staying quiet and out of sight. I could see the creeps wandering around the main road that went through the center of town, but there weren't any near where I was going. I was about a hundred yards from freedom when everything went to shit.

I came around a corner and stumbled over some broken concrete. Normally, it wouldn't have been a big deal, but because I had over two hundred pounds of gear on my back, I overbalanced and fell over. I hit a trashcan as I went down and knocked it over. It clatters to the ground, and makes a hell of a racket. So much for being quiet. As I get to my feet and pick up the bag, about five hundred or so creeps start moaning and stumbling in my direction. I gave up on stealth and just started running. I made it to the parking lot of the Burger King, but the highway was crawling with the dead.

There was no way I would make it through, there were just too many of them. At this point, I'm starting to panic a little, because there is no way forward, and a huge horde of creeps is following behind me. I look around, and I see an old work truck in the parking lot with an extendable ladder lashed to the roof rack. That gave me an idea. I run over to the truck, get the ladder, and use it to climb on top of the Burger King."

"You carried a two hundred pound bag of bullets up a ladder?" I asked.

"Yes," Ethan replied. "It wasn't easy, and honestly, if not for the adrenaline pumping through my veins at the time, I'm not sure I could have done it. Somehow I got it up there, though, and none too soon. I pulled the ladder up after me just as the creeps arrived. After a minute or two, the whole damn parking lot is swarming with dead people. I was safe for the moment, but I was also trapped. The only option I had was to use the weapons I brought with me to thin out the herd. I figured that if I put enough of them down, I could open up an avenue of escape. I started shooting them, one by one, but for every one I put down, two more took its place. I had no idea that many people lived in Alexis before the outbreak.

Right as I'm starting to wonder if I have enough ammo to put them all down, this crazy guy in a silver pickup truck comes along and starts shooting the creeps. He yells out to me to get down and stay quiet, then he draws them away from me with his truck. He gets to the end of the street and doubles back, I carried the duffel bag to the truck, and we got the hell out of dodge." Ethan grinned at me as he concluded his story.

Andrea looked at me for a moment, then stood up and came around the coffee table. She reached down and gently took the empty wine cup from my hand before setting it on the table.

"Could you please stand up for a second?" She asks.

"Uh…sure," I replied.

I rose to my feet, a little unsteady from the wine, and Andrea wrapped her arms around my neck in a fierce, surprisingly strong hug. I awkwardly hugged her back, not quite sure how to react.

"Thank you," She whispered in my ear. She gave me a peck on the cheek before releasing the hug and taking my hands in to hers.

"You risked your life to help my husband. If you ever need anything from us, anything at all, all you have to do is ask."

"Really, it wasn't that big of a deal," I said. Everyone was looking at me and smiling. I felt a little embarrassed by the attention.

"Saving someone's life is always a big deal. Especially when that person is my husband," Andrea replied, staring at me with a steady, blue-eyed gaze. She really was quite lovely. Ethan was a lucky man. Andrea squeezed my hands one last time before sitting back down beside her husband.

"Can I give you a refill?" she asked, opening up the third bottle of wine.

I smiled and sat back down. "Please, that would great."

"So what's your story?" Emily asked me.

"What do you mean?" I said.

"How did you find Ethan?"

"Oh, right. I had stopped my truck on top of a hill that overlooked the highway, and I was using a pair of binoculars to try and find a way through without stirring up the undead. All of a sudden, I hear gunshots in the distance. I looked around with the bino's and spotted this guy on a roof," I said, gesturing toward Ethan.

"So rather than use the commotion as a distraction to get through town unscathed, you risked your life to help an armed stranger," Andrea said, smiling a little.

I stared at her for a moment, startled. She had just said exactly what was going through my mind when I spotted Ethan. Her smile widened at my surprise.

"Don't worry, sweetie, I would have been thinking the same thing," she said.

"You're a sharp one, Andrea. Remind me not to get on your bad side."

I saluted her with my cup and drained the last of my wine. I had a warm, buzzy feeling in my head. Andrea picked up the wine bottle and held it out to me. I held out my cup while she refilled hit.

"So how did you survive the outbreak?" Emily asked me.

I looked at her for a moment, then stared down at my wine, swirling it around in the cup.

"If it's all the same, I'd rather not talk about it right now."

Emily opened her mouth to say something else, but Andrea cut her off.

"That's fine Eric. I know it's hard, dealing with everything that's happened."

I nodded in reply, still staring into my wine. The room went silent as everyone brooded over where they were, and what had they lost. Justin broke the silence by clapping his hands together and leaning forward.

"Well, I don't know about you guys, but in my opinion, hard times are best dealt with by imbibing of large amounts of alcohol. I'll be back in a minute," he said as he stood up and left the room. Andrea poured everyone else more wine, and a minute or two later, Justin came into the room with a bottle of Casadores tequila.

"Oh, no you didn't," Emily said, laughing.

"You sure you want to drink the hard stuff after all that wine?" Andrea asked.

"Why the hell not?" I said. "If it's the end of the world, then I, for one, intend to have a little fun before I go."

"Fuck yeah, that's what I like to hear." Justin said, clapping me on the shoulder.

Andrea frowned. "Alright, fine, but keep the noise down. If you wake up the baby, I'll bust that bottle over your head."

Justin, Emily, and I took a couple of shots, but Ethan and Andrea declined. The two teenagers started pawing at each other as they got drunk, and the conversation shifted to other topics. Ethan and Andrea finished off the last bottle of wine. Ethan stifled a yawn with one big hand, and stretched his arms over his head. The storm outside was in full swing. Thunder rumbled and boomed outside as rain lashed the building. I hoped that whoever was on guard duty had a poncho or something.

Andrea slid forward on the couch and collected all the empty cups.

"I'm getting tired, I think I'm going to turn in," she said.

Ethan stood up and took off his bush jacket. "I'm not far behind you, I just need to talk to Eric about a couple of things." He said.

Andrea took the cups and empty wine bottles into the kitchen and put them in a black plastic trash bag. On her way to the bedroom, she sat down in Ethan's lap and gave her husband a less than gentle, and much less than chaste, kiss.

"I've missed you. Don't stay up too late."

Ethan's eyes burned like torches as he watched his wife saunter into the bedroom, swaying her hips and casting a teasing glance back over her shoulder. Emily, meanwhile, was staring hard at Justin and chewing on her bottom lip.

"You know, maybe I should grab my bedroll and get some sleep," I said.

"Yeah, I guess we can talk in the morning," Ethan said, then got up and went into the bedroom after Andrea.

Justin stood up and offered me a hand.

"It's nice to meet you Eric. Thanks for helping Ethan today. I don't know what would happen to this place without him," he said. I shook his hand and nodded in reply.

"Come on," Emily said, dragging him toward the door. "I'm drunk and horny. Let's go."

I waved at them as they left. I heard a feminine giggle come from the bedroom, and the creak of bedsprings. I was about to leave when I noticed the bottle of tequila still sitting on the coffee table. I grabbed it as I left and shut the door behind me. Hopefully, Justin wouldn't miss it. If he did, maybe I could find something to trade him in exchange.

As I emerged out into the common area, Bill and a few others were cleaning up the remnants of the evening meal. I waved at them, and as I turned to walk to my truck, Earl waved at me from in front of one of the shacks. He was sitting in an Adirondack chair with a tin cup in one hand. There was an empty chair beside him, so I walked over.

"Mind if I join you for a spell?"

"Hell no, long as you don't mind sharing some o' that liquor," he said, smiling.

I sat down and held the bottle out to Earl. He tossed back the rest of whatever was in his cup, and filled it with a generous amount of booze before handing the bottle back to me. I took a pull from the bottle and set it on the ground between us, wincing as the liquor burned me on the way down. Earl sniffed at the tequila.

"Shit, you even brought the good stuff. I'm getting to like you, man."

"Yeah, well thank Justin. It's his bottle. I, ah, procured it while he was otherwise occupied."

Earl laughed. "Justin and Emily seem to be occupied a lot here lately. I'll be sure to thank him in the morning."

Earl took a long drink from his cup and sat back in his chair.

"So how did all these people come to be here?" I asked. "I mean, did you all get here together, or what?"

"Most of us did, yeah. After the disease hit Charlotte, there were a lot of people trying to get out of town. Problem was, there ain't but a few major highways that lead away from the city. I-77 was a parking lot, and 85 wasn't any better. Most of the folks you see here, we all lived in the same neighborhood. Ethan's daddy, Nathan, was the president of our homeowners association. Real nice guy, if he liked you. Real hardass if he didn't. Most people he didn't like were assholes anyway, so me and him got along real good.

He called a meeting the day after the outbreak in Atlanta. What folks were still left in the neighborhood all showed up. Old Nate told us that the outbreak was heading our way, and if we wanted to survive, we needed to work together. He said he knew a place we could go, but it was up north a ways, and we would have to get there on foot. The roads around our neighborhood were so clogged up you couldn't ride a bicycle on 'em. Most everybody was willing, but a few thought we should stay and stick it out. Ol' Nate gave em a mean-eyed glare and told them they were a bunch of damn fools. 'Fine, stay here and die.' He says, 'I'm getting the rest of these people out of here.'"

Earl chuckled briefly, then his smile faded and he was distant for a few moments.

"I sure miss that old bastard. We could sure as hell use him now."

"So what happened next?" I asked.

Earl looked up and sighed.

"Nate sent us home to pack up as much food and clothing as we could carry, and told everybody to be ready to go by morning. He wanted to leave at nine o'clock sharp, and he wanted everybody who had a weapon to bring it with them. The next morning, the outbreak had reached Charlotte, and half the damn city was on fire. The sky was an ugly shade of orange, and ashes fell down like snow. Everything was covered in it. None of that seemed to faze Nate, though. He went around checking on people, and making sure everybody had what they needed. There were forty-four of us when we left. A week later, when we finally managed to reach this place, we were down to thirty."

"Jesus," I said. "You lost fourteen people on the way here?"

"Yeah, and we counted ourselves lucky not to have lost more. Nate got separated from us as we crossed over I-85 getting out of town. That's where we lost most of them. Too many damn creeps, and not enough bullets. Nate and Ethan left the group to try and help a couple of kids trapped on top of a bus. Nate put me and Bill in charge, and told us to go on ahead. I thought Andrea was gonna burst a blood vessel or something, she was screaming so loud. Ethan gave his baby to Rick, and told me to carry Andrea across the highway."

"Seriously?" I asked.

"Yeah, and she gave me one hell of an ass whooping, let me tell you. That little girl was kicking, and screaming, and biting like crazy. Damn near clawed my eyes out, but I got her across safe. We spent the rest of the day on the run, and made camp in the loft of a barn that Bill spotted not far from the road we were on. Ethan got back to us just before sundown, and he had Justin and Emily with him. I asked him what happened to his old man, and he said they got separated. He wasn't sure if Nate made it out or not. I never seen Andrea cry like that, before or since."

Earl shook his head, and reached down to grab the tequila. He poured a little more into his cup and handed me the bottle. I took another pull and coughed a little. I had a pretty good buzz going by then, and my eyelids were getting heavy. I opened my eyes when Earl started talking again.

"A few weeks later, I was out looking for supplies with Justin, when we spotted some folks on the road ahead of us. It was a couple and two kids. The father damn near shot us when we caught up to them. I talked them down, and once we convinced them that we didn't mean any harm, I gave them some food and offered to lead them back here to the compound. They came with us and been here ever since. Not long after that, Rick and Greg were scouting around and ran into four more folks, bunch of college kids, that managed to escape the city. They were starving and scared, and when Rick brought them in and gave them all food, they huddled up into a little ball on the floor holding each other and crying."

"Wow. That's crazy," I said.

"This whole damn world done gone crazy," Earl replied. "I remember choking up a little bit when we brought them kids in. A month or so later, three of them wound up dead."

"What happened?"

"They got fed, and comfortable, and decided that this place wasn't where they wanted to be anymore. Well, three of 'em anyway. I guess they figured they would be better off on their own. One of them was this little rat-faced weasel named Arthur that didn't get along with Bill too good. He didn't want to pitch in on things like guard duty, or waste pickup. Always argued with everybody, saying we didn't need sentries. 'That's why we have walls.' He used to say.

Bill finally got tired of his shit, and told him if he didn't like the rules, he could take his chances out on the road. The kid backed down, but I didn't like the look that came across his face once Bill turned his back. I knew he was planning something, I just didn't know what. I said as much to Bill, and he told me to keep an eye on the boy. Couple of days later, Rick gets off watch and wakes him up for his shift. For once, the little shit doesn't complain, and Rick knows something is up. He gets Bill, and they go outside like they gonna do a perimeter check. Soon as they get out of sight, Arthur and one of the guys on watch with him climb down and sneak back into the compound. It's real early in the morning, and most folks are asleep.

They raid the gun locker, then put a bunch of food into some boxes, and run it out to one of our vehicles. The one on the roof is keeping watch. After six or seven trips, they get in the truck and the third one comes down from the roof. What they didn't figure on was Bill disconnecting all the batteries for the trucks."

"No shit. So Bill set them up?" I said.

"Sure did. He comes around the corner with Rick and a couple others. They all got guns trained on the truck and he tells them to get out. They know they're caught, but they don't move. Bill starts talking to them, trying to get them to come out. 'Don't you think it's funny, you three being put on watch at the same time?' he says. The boys start talking to each other, and get all agitated. Finally, they get out of the truck, but Arthur pulls his gun and goes to point it at Bill.

Bill doesn't hesitate, he pops the kid in the chest with that hunting rifle of his. The other two freak out and pull their guns. Everybody's so freaked out about Bill shooting Arthur, that they don't realize the boys done drew down on them until they start shooting. Bill and Rick shoot them, but not before they hit two of the guys that came out with them. Their names were John and Gil. They was both gut shot."

"Dear God," I said.

Earl drained the rest of the tequila from his cup, and stared into it for a while. He picked up the tequila, and shook the bottle.

"Ain't much left, you mind if I kill it?" he asked.

"Go ahead, dude. It's all yours." After a story like that, I couldn't very well deny the man a stiff drink.

"It took 'em both a long time to die. They was in a lot of pain. Andrea, Ethan and Bill are the only ones with medical training, and they did what they could to help, but without proper medical equipment there wasn't much they could do. Bill took it really hard. I swear he must have aged ten years in three days. He blamed himself for what happened, and wanted to step down as sheriff. Ethan and a few of the others talked him out of it."

"Sheriff?" I asked. I remembered Bill referring to Ethan, Earl, and Justin as deputies.

"Yeah, not long after everyone got here, we had a meeting. Ethan and a couple others figured we needed to lay down some rules, and decide who was going to be in charge. We held an election, and Bill got elected. The first rule he put to a vote was calling his position sheriff, and giving him the authority to name deputies to help maintain order. He figured making the position a form of law enforcement would keep things simpler."

I nodded, and stifled a yawn.

"Well, that explains a lot," I said.

Earl stood up from his chair and knocked back the last of the tequila.

"I'm gonna hit the sack. See you in the morning. Thanks for the booze," he said as he went into his shack.

I got up and stumbled to my truck. I fished out my bedroll and laid it out on the concrete floor, stripped off my shirt, pants and boots, and laid down in my sleeping bag. I soon drifted off into a deep, dreamless sleep.

Chapter 9

Hangover

The next morning, I woke up with a headache and an awful taste in my mouth. I opened one eye and looked around me, disoriented. It took me a few seconds to remember where I was, and why I was not at home in my bed. I threw off the sleeping bag, and slowly got to my feet. I looked around for my clothes, which I had left in a pile next to my truck the night before, but they were gone. Just as I was about to start cursing, I noticed a white five-gallon bucket next to my sleeping bag with a note taped to it. I picked up the note and read it.

Good morning gorgeous,

Andrea sent me over to give you this bucket and get your dirty clothes. The folks on laundry duty this morning will wash them and dry them for you. If you need to do any business, or wash up, use the bucket and then take it outside to one of the blue barrels. That's where we keep all the waste water.

Oh, by the way, I peeked under the cover. Not bad.

xoxo

-Stacy

Great. I thought. Now I have an admirer. I hope she's cute, at least.

After relieving myself in the bucket, I opened my suitcase and took out a pair of mesh shorts, a t-shirt, and a pair of flip-flops. After getting dressed, I dug out my mess kit and set a jerry can full of water on the ground next to my truck. I used the water to brush my teeth, then splashed some of it on my face and rubbed it on my head. After using the truck's rear-view mirror to comb my hair, I got three ibuprofen tablets from my first aid kit and washed them down with a canteen full of water. There was a scratchy growth of beard on my face, but I didn't feel like going through the trouble of shaving it off. I opened a box of food and wolfed down some Vienna wieners and a can of ravioli. Breakfast of champions.

With some food on my stomach, I felt a little more human and got to work straightening out my gear. I put away my sleeping bag and moved my suitcase back to the passenger seat. I checked the equipment on my load-bearing vest and reloaded the empty magazines. The guns didn't look too much the worse for wear, but I cleaned them anyway. Better safe than sorry.

After tending to my weapons, I walked over to the common area to see if I could scare up some fuel for my truck. The compound was humming with activity. More than half of the people living there roamed back and forth carrying out one task or another, while others simply lounged about as though they were enjoying a day off from work. Ethan and Andrea were out in front of their shack with little Aiden. Justin and Emily sat in lawn chairs watching them. Ethan was reading a manual on how to clean his new SCAR rifle, and Andrea had Aiden by his little hands balancing him as he walked around. Evidently, he found vertical locomotion immensely entertaining, and giggled with the kind of unrestrained enthusiasm reserved only for small children.

"Come on Aiden, you're doing so good!" Andrea said, as she held his hands and shuffled backward.

"I told you, babe, three months tops and that little man is walking," Ethan remarked as he pulled the upper and lower portions of the rifle apart. He had stripped down to his waist due to the heat in the building, and large slabs of muscle rippled under his skin as he moved around.

"Look who decided to rejoin the land of the living," Emily shouted to me, smiling.

I gave a half-hearted wave, and took a chair from a stack next to the little shelter. I sat down next to Justin as he offered me a bottle of water. I took it from him and stopped, staring at the bottle in surprise.

"This is cold," I said.

Justin nodded. "There's a big pond nearby. We put the bottles in nets, and sink them to the bottom overnight. The water down there is cold, and it chills the bottles."

I opened the bottle and took a long drink. It was hot inside the compound, and the cold water felt wonderful. I held the bottle up to my temples, my ears, and the back of my neck.

"Dude, you have no idea how good this feels right now," I said.

"Yes I do," Justin replied. "I had a bit of a hangover myself this morning. By the way, fuck you very much for drinking my tequila." He shot me a look of mock anger and nudged me in the shoulder with his elbow.

"Yeah, well, I had help. Besides, you didn't seem too interested in it." I shot Emily a meaningful glance. She laughed, and flicked some water at me.

"You're just jealous. Everybody else here got laid last night."

I thought about Vanessa, and looked down, my smile fading. Emily realized the sting her words had inflicted and came over to kneel down in front of me, taking one of my hands in hers.

"Hey, I'm sorry. I didn't mean anything by that, I was just kidding. I'm an idiot sometimes, I shouldn't have said that."

I looked up and patted her on the back of her hand.

"It's okay, I'm not mad at you. It's just…"

"You lost someone to the infection, didn't you," Andrea said, picking up Aiden as she did so.

I shrugged. "Hasn't everyone?"

"Good point," she said, nodding.

"Look guys, I didn't come over here to ruin the good mood. Emily, we're cool. Andrea, go back to playing with the baby. Ethan, put a shirt on for crying out loud, you're making me feel

173

like less of a man." My last comment elicited a round of laughter.

Ethan responded by standing up and making a show of flexing his rather impressive physique. Emily and Andrea whooped and applauded. A third voice joined in, and I turned around to see who it was. A pretty brunette approached and startled me by laying a hand on my shoulder. She looked down at me with a pair of soft brown eyes and smiled.

"I was hoping you'd be walking around in those little boxer briefs." She said, her southern accent rich and sweet as honey.

I smiled in return. "You must be Stacy."

"Guilty as charged." She said as she took a chair from the same stack as I had, and sat down next to me.

"How you feeling this morning?" She asked.

"I've been better, and I've been worse," I said. "Thanks for the bucket. It came in handy."

She laughed with a rich, velvety voice.

"I thought it might. Your clothes are being dried as we speak."

"I appreciate that. Ethan, didn't you mention something about a shower yesterday?" I said.

"Oh yeah, I forgot about that. Stacy, you mind giving him a hand?" Ethan replied, grinning.

"Absolutely not." She winked at me and stood up, holding out a hand. "Come on, handsome, let's get you cleaned up."

I took her hand and followed her outside. It had been quite a while since the last time I held hands with a pretty girl, and I have to admit that my heart beat a little faster as we walked. Stacy led me out of the warehouse and around to the side of the building closest to the abandoned factory. Crude graffiti covered the factory's back wall, and all of the windows had long ago been broken out. Birds hopped and flapped in the empty panes, calling back and forth to one another.

The shower area stood between the factory and the compound. It hadn't been there the day before, so it must have been set up that morning. The showers consisted of several large, black plastic bladders mounted on wooden tripods eight feet off the ground. Thin wooden partitions surrounded each shower to provide privacy. A short hose with a plastic shower nozzle jutted from the bottom of the bladders, and as we came closer, I recognized them as camping showers. I remembered seeing them advertised in a magazine for outdoors enthusiasts. The black plastic absorbed heat from the sun and warmed the water within the bladder. Each bladder held five gallons, and were collapsible for easy storage when not in use.

A stack of clean towels sat on a bench beside the showers. All of the showers were in use, and a young man with a stepladder and a five-gallon bucket stood ready to take water from one of several barrels and refill the showers once their occupants were finished. I looked around, and noticed that there were four guards on duty around the perimeter. Two of them were carrying the SCAR rifles that Ethan brought in the day before with the kind of casual competency that I have always associated with police and the military. The other two guards I recognized as Greg and Rick. Greg carried the hunting rifle Bill had given him the day before, and Rick had his Mini 14.

"I've already met Greg and Rick over there," I said to Stacy, "But who are those two with the big guns?"

"The blond guy is Cody Starnes and the older one is Stan Walters. They were both SWAT with CMPD before everything happened. They've been out gathering supplies the last couple of days, and they didn't get back until this morning. Don't worry, they're nice guys. I'll introduce you later."

I nodded and grabbed a towel from the table. Stacy pointed to a couple of boxes sitting against the nearest partition.

"There's shampoo and soap in those boxes. Ethan found a load of the stuff in a hotel a few miles up the road from here. Think you'll need anything else?" she asked.

"I wouldn't mind some company," I replied jokingly.

Stacy smirked, and hit my arm with a half-hearted slap.

"No problem, I'll go get Cody. I think you're just about his type."

I laughed and held up my hands. "No, no thanks. I'll be fine on my own, thank you very much."

A man stepped out of one of the showers with a towel wrapped around him and went behind another set of partitions to put his clothes on.

"Looks like you're up." Stacy gave me a swat on the backside.

I watched her walk back around the building admiring the way she filled out her shorts. Just before she turned the corner, she glanced back in my direction, saw me watching her, and gave a little wave.

"I know the scenery is nice, but you're the last one getting a shower this morning, and I need to get this place cleaned up. Sorry to rush you."

I turned around and faced the young man with the bucket and the stepladder. I was expecting him to be irritated, but instead he merely looked tired and a bit sunburned. He was a few years younger than me, and had the loose skin and sunken features of someone who had recently endured rapid weight loss. A few shallow pockmarks lined his cheeks, and he wore a pair of thick glasses. I wondered if he was one of the college kids Earl had told me about the night before.

"Sorry about that. Can't blame me though, know what I mean?"

His face brightened slightly into a weary, haunted smile.

"No, I guess I can't. Stacy is pretty hot."

I held out a hand. "Eric Riordan, nice to meet you."

"Noah Salinger. Likewise," he said as he shook my hand. "Seriously though, I have to break down the showers and get everything moved back inside before ten-thirty. Use this one on the end. I'll leave enough walls up for you to get showered and dressed."

"Thanks. I'll give you a hand as soon as I'm done," I said.

"I should be most of the way finished by then, but I appreciate the offer."

He turned and walked to the other end of the showers where a large blue lumber cart like the kind used in home improvement stores stood. He started taking apart the partitions and loading them onto the cart. I watched for a moment, then grabbed some soap and water and stepped into the nearest shower stall. I hung my clothes over the top of the stall and turned an orange lever at the bottom of the bladder to let water flow through the nozzle. The water was warm, and it felt wonderful on my grimy skin.

The shower made me feel, and smell, immensely better. You know you stink pretty bad when you can actually smell yourself. I put my clothes back on and walked back around to where I last saw Noah. True to his word, most of the shower's partitions, tripods, and bladders were already loaded onto two carts.

"Jeez. You work fast," I said.

Noah gave another one of his grim smiles.

"I designed the walls to fit together by hand, no fasteners necessary. You just fit the pieces together and let gravity do the work. They're super easy to put together and take down."

I watched him take apart the last stall. He emptied the water from the bladder into a barrel, and put it on the cart with the other bladders. The tripod was actually three four-by-fours, each post had a large nail jutting from one side. Bungee cords wrapped around the boards under the nails and held them together. A flat piece of plywood with a foot long two-by-four nailed to the center of it formed the platform upon which the bladder rested. The two-by-four rested between the tall supports and held the plywood steady. The partitions around the shower itself were thin pieces of wood paneling that slid into slotted boards braced by more plywood. It took Noah all of about forty-five seconds to break the shower stall down and load it onto the carts. I had to admit, it was a clever design.

"If you want to help, you can wheel one of these carts back inside," he said.

I nodded and grabbed the one with the heavier looking load. Noah went ahead of me and parked his cart in front of the blue shipping container that covered the front entrance. He trotted over to the same forklift Ethan had used the day before and moved the container, then slapped the door three times and called out.

"It's Noah. I'm bringing the showers back in."

The door slowly rolled up and Stacy stood on the other side. She smiled when she saw me.

"Damn, you just got here and somebody already put you to work," she said.

I laughed and pushed the cart inside. Noah directed me where to park it and thanked me before walking off to move the shipping container back in place. Stacy lowered the door and locked it, then sauntered back over to me.

"You look a damn sight better. It's amazing how much better being clean makes you feel, ain't it?" she said.

"God, you're not kidding. I feel like a new man."

I walked over to the bed of my truck and took out a shaving kit. Stacy followed behind me and walked a lap around the big gray Tundra.

"You've got quite a bit of stuff in this thing. What's it all for?" She asked.

"I'm not sure yet, but I'll let you know when I find out."

I grabbed a folding camping stool from the truck's bed and set it down on the floor. I did not want to get shaving cream all over my clean shirt, so I took it off and threw it into the cab through the passenger side window. Honestly, I didn't think anything of it at the time, but Stacy noticed and whistled at me.

"'Bout damn time, I was wondering if the front was as nice as the back." She stepped in front of me and ran a hand over my abdomen.

"Looks like you've done a few sit-ups."

She stared at my mid-section for a moment then looked me in the eyes, her full lips slightly parted. She was standing very close, and the touch of her fingertips made me break out in goose bumps. The effect was not lost on Stacy and she stepped closer, only an inch or two away. My heart started pounding in my chest, and I had a strong urge to lean down and kiss her. Just as I was about to lose my will to resist, Stacy stepped away, winking at me.

"I'd love to stick around, but I got work to do. You staying the night, or are you still planning on heading out today?" she asked.

My hot blood quickly cooled down, and the gears of my brain started to turn again. How did she know I was leaving today? I had just met her that morning, and I hadn't mentioned anything about my plans to drive to Morganton.

"You must have been talking to Ethan," I said.

"Yeah, I had breakfast with him and Andrea this morning. He told me about what happened yesterday. You did a good thing stopping to help him. It's nice to see there's still at least one decent guy in the world."

Her teasing smile went away, replaced by an expression of sincere respect. I felt myself flush a little, and shrugged.

"I'm just glad I was there to help. Ethan seems like a good man."

"The best." She said. "A lot of people around here owe him their lives. We would all probably be dead if not for him and his father."

Stacy walked around the truck and picked up a small tool bag from one of the numerous shelves.

"I promised to help my dad make a bed frame today. It only took me the last three months, but I finally convinced him to stop sleeping on the concrete."

"Have I met your father yet?" I asked.

"Yes, I believe you met Bill yesterday."

I felt my eyes go wide with surprise. Stacy laughed. "Don't worry sweetie, I take after my momma. I didn't figure you'd see a resemblance."

She turned, still laughing, and walked to the common area. I shook off my surprise, and when her buttocks was too far away to properly admire, I sat down on my stool and poured some water in a metal bowl. I spent the next few minutes shaving off my beard stubble and pondering my next move. I still needed to see about getting some gas for the truck, and I needed to talk to Ethan about plotting a route around the disaster at Iron Station. If the roads were as bad as he said they were, I had no desire to tackle that particular obstacle head on. I decided that my policy for dealing with the undead was going to be stealth, evasion, and speed. After the encounters of the previous day, it had become painfully clear to me how dangerous engaging the undead in a fight really was, even with a suppressed firearm. One on one they weren't much, but their advantage lay in numbers—something they had plenty of.

I wiped off the last of the shaving cream, rinsed my face with a handful of water, and dried off with the same towel I had taken from the showers outside. After putting my shirt back on, I walked back to the common area. Ethan had put his rifle back together, and worked the charging handle a few times to make sure it operated smoothly. I didn't see Andrea, and figured that she must be inside the shack with the baby. Emily and Justin were busy painting a beach themed mural on the side of their little shelter. I took a seat beside where Ethan sat cross-legged on the floor.

"How do you like your new toy?" I asked.

Ethan hefted the rifle and peered down the barrel. "This thing is fucking sweet. I've wanted one since I first heard about them, but they were too expensive. EMT's don't make that much money."

"Is that what you did before the outbreak?" I asked.

Ethan nodded. "That's how I met Andrea. She was an ER nurse at Presbyterian Hospital. Bill worked there too."

"What did he do?"

"Heart surgeon. Guy was fucking loaded too. Had a patent on some kind of heart pill that made a gazillion dollars." Ethan turned to me and winked. "I believe you met his daughter just a little bit ago."

"Yeah, she already let me in on that one." I smiled as I thought of her. Ethan looked a bit crestfallen.

"Oh. Damn it all, I wanted to see the look on your face when you found out."

I patted him on the shoulder. "Life is full of little disappointments."

Ethan chuckled and spent a few more moments admiring his rifle. Three magazines lay on the ground next to him beside a pile of .223 cartridges. By their length, I could tell that they were thirty round mags. That gave Ethan ninety rounds close at hand, if needed. Ethan noticed me looking and gestured at my truck.

"After Andrea and I finished with our, ah, festivities last night, I took a look in the bed of your truck. That's some serious hardware you've got there." He looked up at me expectantly.

"So you snooped around in my shit while I was passed out drunk?" I gave him a hard stare. If he noticed, he did a good job of hiding it.

"Call it due diligence. You are a stranger here, after all," he said.

I felt my temper begin to rise a bit. "Really? Is that a fact? After I save your ass, and you invite me over for dinner, and your wife tells me how grateful she is that I saved your life, and your friends thank me for helping you, and I meet your little boy, after all that, I'm a fucking stranger here? Good to know."

A few people passing nearby stopped to look at us. I ignored them as I stared Ethan down. After a moment, he looked away, his jaw working as he nodded.

"I suppose I deserved that. Look, I didn't mean any offense. Not everybody here is as trusting as I am. I just had to check to make sure you weren't going to put the community at risk. I have a responsibility to these people."

He looked back up at me, his expression pleading and resolute at the same time. I felt my anger begin to subside.

"You know Ethan, you really shouldn't play poker. Ever. You wear your heart on your face every time you talk."

I broke into a smile as I said it, and the tension between us evaporated. Ethan laughed and shrugged.

"That might explain why Andrea always kicks my ass at cards."

He picked up the rifle and slapped in a clip, then pulled back the charging handle and chambered a round. After double-checking to make sure the safety was on, he got up from the floor and sat down in the lawn chair next to me. He laid the rifle across his lap and ran one hand across the collapsible stock.

"What I brought in yesterday was a good score, but there are too many of those damn things out there. It won't last. We need more ammo." He glanced up at me, and I had a pretty good idea what he was thinking.

"Right. So, after your whole John Wayne cowboy thing backfired, and you damn near got yourself killed, you started thinking and recognized the giant, gaping holes in your plan. A strong willed guy like you doesn't let a silly little thing like almost getting killed keep him down, so you come up with a new plan. I'm guessing this is the part where you tell me how I fit into it?" I said.

"Yeah, something like that." Ethan gave me one of his damned infectious grins.

I figured the conversation could go one of two ways. I could agree, and most likely wind up risking my life again, or I could refuse to help, get in my truck, and drive away. I knew beyond doubt that the latter path would lead to me feeling like a cold-hearted bastard, and forever wondering what became of the poor folks at the abandoned factory just north of Alexis. Right as I was thinking that, Stacy walked by with a basket of laundry and winked at me as she passed. She had a thin sheen of sweat on her tanned skin, and her hair was slightly mussed. She looked good enough to eat.

Never underestimate the power of the male libido when it comes to influencing decisions.

"Well shit," I said, heaving a frustrated sigh. "In for a penny, in for a pound. What's your plan, big guy?"

Ethan's grin broadened, and he set the rifle on the ground beside him.

"How about we start by you telling me what I did wrong?" he said, leaning his elbows on his knees and clasping his hands in front of him.

"Well, for starters, you went out alone. Never take those things on by yourself if you can help it." I replied.

Ethan nodded and gestured for me to continue.

"Second, you didn't bring enough firepower. Hatchets are good for chopping down saplings, not fighting revenants."

Ethan's expression became quizzical.

"Revenants?" he asked.

"Yeah, it's an old Latin word for the ghosts that come back to haunt the living, or something like that."

Ethan raised his eyebrows and nodded. "Well, it sounds more scientific than 'creeps', I guess."

"Anyway," I continued, "you just don't take on that many infected without some serious firepower at your disposal. You need something that fires a light round, and carries a high-capacity magazine."

Ethan picked up the SCAR with one massive arm and gave a cheesy, fake smile as he pointed at it.

"Done," he said.

I shook my head and smiled in spite of myself. "That's a great weapon, but it's loud. You need something quieter."

"You mean like one of those two illegal HK 416's in the back of your truck, with the illegal silencers on them?" he asked.

"Yes, exactly like that." My smile faded, and I glared at him in genuine irritation.

Ethan put the SCAR down, and held out his hands in a conciliatory gesture.

"Sorry, I couldn't help but notice. Not that the rule of law matters anymore. As much as I'd like to know how you got those things, I'm more concerned with how we can use them to help keep the people of this compound safe."

"Well, like you said, there's two of them. And I do have silencers for both." I leaned forward, resting my chin in one hand as I pondered.

"Now just so you know," I said, "the suppressors don't get rid of all the noise from the shot. The action of the chamber is still audible, and the crack of the bullets is still pretty loud. It's just not as loud as without the suppressor. It's not like in the movies where a silenced gun makes a little science-fiction laser sound."

Ethan nodded. "I figured as much. Those suppressors look like military grade equipment. What about the pistols? That Kel-Tec must be pretty quiet with that big-assed can on it."

"How much of my shit did you search through?" I asked.

Ethan gave me a level stare. "Enough to know that you aren't a threat to this compound, and that you must be one extraordinarily resourceful son of a bitch."

I narrowed my eyes at him. "My mother was a wonderful person, thank you very much."

Ethan laughed. "Sorry, man. Just an expression."

I dismissed the comment with a wave, and went back to considering what tactical advantages we might have against the undead.

"Did you notice the Sig Mosquito?" I asked.

"Yeah, I did. You got more than one of those?"

"No. Just the one. The Kel-Tec is louder, but not terribly so."

"Alright, bearing all that in mind, what plan of action would you recommend so that we can get what we need from Alexis."

I sat back in my chair and thought for a few moments.

"First thing we need is a diversion. Something to draw all the undead away from town long enough for us to do what we need to do."

Ethan nodded. "Agreed. Stealth ain't gonna cut it. There's just too damn many of the things."

"Right," I said, "so we set up a diversion, then we get every available vehicle down to the gun shop shit-hot-quick, and load them up with as much gear as they can carry."

Ethan sat back in his chair, frowning. "We have enough vehicles, and enough people to drive them, to get everything out in two, maybe three trips tops. The problem is keeping the undead away long enough to do it. Got any ideas on that front?" he asked.

I frowned and sat forward again. After a minute or two of mulling it over, I thought I might have an idea, but it would require help from the people of the compound.

"We need to get Bill onboard with this," I said, making a gesture to encompass the warehouse around us. "We need him to rally these folks together. Otherwise, this plan is dead in the water."

Ethan nodded. "I agree. Problem is, Bill will never agree to this if we don't present him with some kind of a reasonably workable plan. What kind of diversion did you have in mind?"

"You said the creeps can hear the trucks from a couple hundred yards away, right? What we do is use a few trucks to grab their attention, and get them to follow, then split up and divide the horde into smaller groups. We plot routes for each driver to follow so that they can double back and reach the compound without getting cornered."

Ethan considered my plan for a moment, and slowly started nodding.

"You know what? I think that might just work."

"Well it's settled then," I said. "Now all we have to do is get Bill on board."

"Get Bill on board with what?"

Ethan and I both jumped a little, and I turned to see Stacy standing behind us with her hands on her hips.

"Ethan, what kind of shenanigans are you up to now?" she said.

"No shenanigans, I promise. This time we have a real plan," he replied.

"What do you mean 'we'? Did you sucker Eric here into going along with you?"

"Actually," I said, "he didn't sucker me into anything. It's my plan."

"Oh. Well, in that case, let's hear what you got." Stacy pulled up a chair and sat down next to me, close enough to be somewhat distracting.

Ethan frowned at her, but stayed quiet. I explained my plan to Stacy.

"That actually sounds like it might work," she said. "We just have to get a few other folks to buy in on it. How many people do you figure we'll need?"

"Three to run the distraction, two to take care of any stragglers, and as many as can be mustered to ferry gear back from the store," I said.

"I can probably convince Earl and Justin to help me pull off the diversion." Ethan said. "Cody and Stan can handle any undead that don't wander off. I'm pretty sure they won't be too hard to get on board. If Bill agrees to help us, a lot of people will most likely volunteer to drive the moving trucks."

"Well, it looks like we need to find Bill and see what he thinks." I said.

Stacy stood up and laid a hand on my shoulder. "Leave that one to me. I'll send him by when he gets off watch. In the meantime, I have laundry to do."

Stacy walked away, and Ethan got up to go get a map. He came back a minute later, and we spent an hour or so pouring over the map, plotting routes for the diversion drivers to follow. Right as we finalized what roads the drivers would take, Andrea stepped out of the front door of her little home with Aiden riding along on one hip.

"Baby, can you take him, please? He just woke up, and I need to rest a little while longer." She said.

Her eyes were puffy, and her long, straight red hair hung down in loose tangles. Aiden, on the other hand, seemed in good spirits. He smiled and made a weird sounding gurgle-shriek when he saw his father. He reached his little arms out toward the big man and babbled something similar to 'da-da' as Ethan took him from his wife.

"I got him babe, you go get some rest." Ethan leaned down and kissed her cheek. Andrea reached out and squeezed him around the waist for a moment before mumbling a vague thanks and going back inside her shack.

"Is she okay?" I asked after Andrea closed the door behind her.

"She's fine, she just works too hard is all. She was feeling last night's wine when she got up this morning. Little man here woke her up just after sunup."

Ethan wiggled a fingertip against the baby's belly. The little fellow squirmed and giggled as he pushed at his father's hand.

"You're a ticklish wittle baby aren't you? Yes you are." Ethan kissed the little boy on the head and sat down in the chair with him, issuing forth a steady stream of baby talk as he played with his son.

I smiled as I watched and wondered what kind of future waited for little Aiden. I looked around me at the people hustling to and fro, carrying out one task or another. It seemed like there was plenty of work to do, between cleaning, organizing, taking inventory, and building things to make life inside the confines of the warehouse more livable. There was something about it all, in light of everything that had happened in the last three months, that inspired a sense of hope.

Even here, in the worst of times, people were trying to live their lives. The world outside the warehouse was crawling with horrible flesh-eating monsters, but these people were still trying to make a home for themselves, trying to move forward. I felt a strong surge of respect and admiration for Ethan and the people around me, and a cold wave of despair as I pondered what had been lost. So many lives, just wiped out. Gone. All the hard work, inventiveness, and effort, all the life stories, families, and everything people spent their lives building. All of it swept away in an irresistible surge of destruction that left only ashes and broken lives in its wake.

I shook my head to ward off those thoughts. My mind had been wondering into that territory more and more often lately, and it always led to the same conclusion—there was no going back. The world as I knew it was over. My comfortable, quiet, easy life was a thing of the past. From here on out, it was going to be a daily struggle for survival. The sooner I got used to that idea, the better.

My dark thoughts were interrupted by the clang of the bar across the steel door being raised as Bill and the other four men on watch with him came into the warehouse. Three other people waited for them by the door. Cody and Stan turned over their SCAR rifles, somewhat reluctantly, to two of the people taking over the watch. The third one had an M1A battle-rifle strapped across his back, and a military style vest with several spare magazines hanging from the front of it. He gave a contemptuous snort at the two high-tech weapons as the oncoming watch looked them over. I figured he must be one of those gun purists that despise the smaller 5.56 and .223 rounds fired by most modern assault rifles.

After they finished turning over the watch, the four men walked toward Ethan's shack. Bill stopped in front of where Ethan and I sat, and the other four men fanned out behind him. He looked over his shoulder and made a gesture in my direction.

"Everybody, this here is Eric. He just got here yesterday. Eric, I believe you met Greg and Rick already, these other two yahoos are Cody and Stan." He smiled as he said it, and the two big police officers stepped forward to shake hands. I stood up from my chair and offered them each a hand in turn.

"Hi nice to meet you," I said.

Stan's expression was stern, but not unfriendly, as I shook his hand. He was a little taller than me, and rivaled Ethan for muscle mass. He had salt-and-pepper hair, and a thick mustache covered his upper lip. If not for the crew-cut, he would have looked like a gunslinger out of the old west. Cody was much younger, probably not any older than me, and favored me with a warm, friendly smile.

"Nice to meet you Eric," he said. "Been a while since we had any cute single guys around here."

I stiffened a bit and stared for a moment, not quite sure how to respond to that one. Cody released the handshake, and his smile faded into an irritated frown.

"Damn. Another straight-y," he said.

Stan let out a short bark of laughter.

"Told you so. Pay up." He held out one hand, and Cody glared at him for a moment before reaching in a cargo pocket and handing him a pack of hard candies. Stan opened them and offered me one.

"You helped me win 'em. Want some?"

I laughed, awkwardly. "Uh…no, I'm good. Thanks anyway."

Stan shrugged. "Suit yourself."

He smirked at Cody before popping one of the little red candies into his mouth.

"I'm going to go home and enjoy these. Talk to you folks later." He called over his shoulder.

"Yeah, I hope they rot out your teeth dickhead," Cody muttered, then turned and stalked back to the other side of the warehouse.

Rick's shoulders bounced in a silent laugh as he watched Cody walk away.

"I think you broke his heart," he said.

The others broke out in laughter, including Ethan. I gave them all an irritated glare and sat back down in my chair.

"I'm glad I could be here to amuse you."

"Aw, come on. Don't be like that," Bill said. "Cody's a good man, but he's the only gay guy here. I think he's getting right lonesome. He was swearing up and down to me and Stan today that you were homosexual."

My frown deepened. "What the hell would make him think that?"

"I don't know. Wishful thinking maybe?" Ethan said, smiling. He affected a thick, drawling southern accent.

"You got to admit, you is mighty purty."

That brought on another round of laughs at my expense from the men gathered around us. I shook my head and pointed a finger at Ethan.

"Don't get any ideas, Romeo. You're a married man," I said.

Ethan sat back in his chair and leaned Aiden's back against his chest as he motioned to the stack of lawn chairs standing nearby. The baby occupied himself by chewing on his hands as he reclined.

"Why don't you fellas sit a spell. Eric and I got something we need to run by you guys," Ethan said, turning serious.

Bill and the other two men grabbed chairs and sat down in a semi-circle across from Ethan and me.

"Stacy came to talk to me today. Said you fella's had some kind of a plan to get more supplies from Alexis," Bill said. "Ethan, we've been over this before. It's just too dangerous, we can't risk it. Besides, we don't have enough firepower to clear out all the creeps, even with what you brought back yesterday."

"We may not have to," Ethan replied. "Eric here seems to know an awful lot about fighting these things. He came up with a plan that might just work without us having to use up too many resources."

Ethan looked at me and gestured toward Bill. "Tell 'em Eric."

I laid out the plan the same as I had described it to Stacy. Bill put a hand to his chin and seemed to think about it for a moment or two.

"How do you know the creeps will follow you? What if they don't? If the distraction doesn't work, we could wind up in a heap of trouble," he said.

"They'll follow, don't worry about that. Ethan has seen evidence of that for himself." I nodded in Ethan's direction, and he related the story to Bill and the others about how he became stranded in Alexis, and his subsequent rescue.

"I'm telling you Bill, I watched those damn things follow him for at least a quarter mile," he said as he finished his story. "When he turned back around to pick me up, they turned around with him and started coming back in our direction. Damnedest thing I've ever seen."

Bill stood up from his chair and began pacing around. His expression had brightened, and his body language became more animated as he thought over the plan.

"You know Eric, if you're right about these things, and we can use your diversion strategy effectively and consistently, this changes everything. We might actually be able to go on the offensive against the creeps, instead of skulking around in small groups scavenging supplies wherever the hell we manage to find them," he said.

"I got a question," Greg said, one hand raised in the air. "How the hell do you know so much about the creeps? We've been trying to fight these things for months, and we're barely holding our own. How did you become such a creep-killing expert?"

The group went silent, and stared at me expectantly. I looked down at the ground, and considered how to respond.

"I could tell you, but I doubt you would believe me."

"Son, you'd be amazed what I can believe these days," Bill said. "Let's hear it."

I clasped my hands together for a moment, then ran them over my face.

"It all started when I met a man named Gabriel Garrett…"

I laid it out for them. Everything. I left nothing out, not even the part about buying all the illegal weapons. I told them about everything that happened to me, all the way up to where I ran into Ethan. When I finished, everyone was silent and stared at me with a mixture of shock and disbelief. I couldn't help but laugh at them.

"I said you wouldn't believe me."

It was strangely cathartic, spilling all of my secrets. The burden felt a little lighter for having shared it.

"It's not that I don't believe you," Bill said. "It's just that we've all been speculating since the outbreak started about what caused all of this. Now here you sit, solving the mystery for all of us. A damn bacteriophage did all of this?"

Rick shook his head. "Unbelievable," he muttered.

"So the fucking government knew about the Phage before the outbreak? How could they let something like this happen?" Ethan's voice shook with anger as he spoke.

"Listen guys, I don't have any answers. I'm not sure that anyone left alive does. Regardless of how this all started, we are where we are. The problems sitting in front of us are not going to go away on their own. Now is the time to take action." I said and stood up. "I need to go get something out of my truck, I'll be right back."

I walked over to my truck and dug out Gabriel's manual. I brought it back over to Ethan's shack and handed it to Bill.

"Everything you need to know about how to fight the undead is in there. Do you have the necessary equipment to make copies?" I asked.

"Yeah, we have a whole bunch of computer equipment around here somewhere. I'll get Justin to fire it up and make copies. Rick, do you mind fetching Justin and help him set up one of the generators?"

"No problem." Rick stood up and walked toward Justin's shack. Greg stood up as well and slung his rifle across his back.

"I know where all the computer equipment is. We have a couple of boxes of paper in the storage area, I'll give Justin a hand getting everything set up." Bill nodded and Greg set off toward the other side of the warehouse.

"Well, looks like I have some reading to do," Bill said as he stood up. He stared at the binder in his hands for a long moment before looking up at me and offering me a hand.

"I tell you what, if everything you've said is true, and we really can pull off this plan of yours, I'll give you my blessing to date my daughter."

I smiled and shook his hand. "Sir, you have yourself a deal."

Chapter 10

Logistics

Justin set up a laptop and printer on a folding table, and plugged them into a gasoline-powered generator. He scanned Gabriel's manual and printed ten copies, then placed each copy in a separate binder. Meanwhile, Bill sent Ethan around to let everyone know that he was calling a meeting. Work continued as word spread, but I could hear people talking to each other, speculating as to what the meeting was about. I caught quite a few people giving me curious stares and whispering to one another. I helped Stacy clear some space in the middle of the common area and arrange enough lawn chairs so that everyone would have a place to sit. We placed five chairs in front for Bill and the other compound leaders. When we finished, Bill came over to me and motioned for me to lean down so that he could whisper something.

"Sit up front when the meeting starts, I want you to be able to answer questions after I call the meeting to order," he said in a low voice.

I nodded and clapped him on the shoulder to let him know I understood. I wasn't sure what kind of reaction to expect, being that I had arrived there less than twenty four hours ago, and had already caused quite a stir. I had some serious reservations about whether my fellow survivors would believe me when I told them what I knew about the Phage.

Work around the compound slowly ground to a halt as people wandered over in two's and three's to the assembled chairs and took their seats. Andrea woke up at some point and pulled herself together enough to attend the meeting with little Aiden dozing against her shoulder. She sat next to Emily and

Stacy, and the two women filled her in on everything that happened while she was asleep. After everyone had taken a seat, Ethan, Earl and Justin sat down in the row of chairs facing the crowd. I took a seat next to Earl, and he gave me a little wink as I sat down.

"You just all kinds of trouble, ain't you?" he said, smirking.

I shrugged, and gave him a rueful smile. "Trouble seems to be finding me more and more often here lately."

Bill stepped in front of the crowd with me and his deputies seated behind him.

"Alright, everyone, if it's alright with you all, I'd like to get the meeting started."

Bill waited for the small side conversations to subside. He had a small smile on his face, and looked every bit the grandfatherly patron.

"As you're all aware, we have a visitor that's been with us since yesterday. Quite a few of you have already had the chance to meet him. For those of you who haven't, this gentleman," he stepped aside and motioned toward me, "is Eric Riordan. He found our good friend Ethan in a spot of trouble down in Alexis yesterday, and was kind enough to stop and help him out."

As he spoke, most of the audience switched their attention from Bill and stared at me. I started to sweat a little under the scrutiny. I've never been much of a public speaker, and I hate being in front of crowds. The situation reminded me of every bad dream I had as a kid about standing in front of a classroom wearing nothing but my underwear.

"Mr. Riordan has some information that he would like to share with all of us," he continued, "and I believe we finally have a workable plan to retrieve some very badly needed supplies from Alexis."

Bill turned around and motioned for me to approach. I almost froze up for a second, but managed to get my feet underneath me and walk a few shaky steps to stand next to the old surgeon.

"Mr. Riordan, would you be so kind as to relate to these folks what you told me earlier today? Folks, please, if you have any questions, hold them until Mr. Riordan opens the floor." Bill gestured toward the people seated in front of me, and then sat down in the chair I vacated.

I hadn't been expecting to give a speech, but there was nothing for it at that point, so I launched into it. It took me about half an hour to give an abbreviated version of how I came to meet Gabriel, and how I learned about the Reanimation Phage. When I concluded the story, I was facing thirty-two stunned, disbelieving faces. The silence lasted almost long enough to be awkward, but thankfully, Bill got up and stood beside me, giving me a little pat on the shoulder.

"I'd like to go ahead and open up the floor to questions. Please raise your hand and wait to be recognized," he said.

The man I had seen earlier in the day carrying the M1A rifle was the first to raise his hand. I pointed to him, and he stood up.

"At the risk of sounding ungrateful," he said, "do you think you might be able to provide some kind of proof to back up what you're saying? That's quite a story you just told."

Now that I could get a close look at him, I saw that he was about five-foot ten, with longish hair a similar sandy blonde color to my own, and he had a lean frame with sinewy, whipcord muscles. His eyes were a piercing hazel that was almost yellow, and he regarded me with no small amount of suspicion.

"I don't have any proof other than my word," I replied. "I gave Bill a copy of a document that my friend Gabriel sent me which details, in depth, how to fight the undead. Gabriel had a lot of experience in that area. His advice is the only reason I'm still alive today."

"And what exactly do you want in return for all this free information?" the yellow-eyed man asked. "Do you expect us all to believe that you're just trying to help us out of the kindness of your heart?"

Bill glared, but yellow-eyes ignored him. I bristled somewhat at his tone, but I understood his suspicion.

"Actually I do," I replied. "And to answer your first question, I'm not asking anyone for anything. I have my own weapons, equipment, and food, and I don't need to take anything from anyone here. I helped Ethan yesterday because he is a living, breathing human being. Living people are a pretty damned rare commodity these days, in case you hadn't noticed."

Yellow-eyes glared at me for a moment longer, and then slowly took his seat. He didn't ask any more questions, but his suspicious gaze never left me for the rest of the meeting. The rest of the questions were less hostile in nature. Everyone wanted to know how the Reanimation Phage works, and I got a lot of frustrated sighs and shaking heads when I told them that I didn't know. Bill was kind enough to explain in basic terms what a bacteriophage is and how it can spread. Unfortunately, he did not have any more of a clue than I did as to how the infection could bring a dead human back to a life. I was beginning to get the impression that I had created more questions than I could answer, when an attractive young black woman raised her hand and stood up when I recognized her.

"I appreciate you telling us all of this, Mr. Riordan, but what difference does it make at this point? I mean, we're all still holed up here in an old warehouse, except now we know a little bit more about those things trying to kill us."

The young woman left her seat and walked to the front of the assembly to stand in front of me. She was almost as tall as me, and moved with the kind of casual grace one sees in dancers and professional athletes. Her body was lean and fit, and she had mocha colored skin pulled tight over strong muscle. Rather than continue talking to me, she turned and addressed the crowd.

"We can spend all day wondering why this has happened, or we can find a way to take advantage of the information this man has brought us. I, for one, am tired of sitting around and being scared. I'm tired of waiting for the axe to drop. I'm tired of wondering what will happen to all of us when we run out of places to scavenge supplies. If this guy knows a way to take the fight to the creeps, then I'm all ears."

Her last comment was received with a few encouraging comments, and some nodding heads. The woman turned around and gave me a little nod before taking her seat.

"Thank you very much, Jessica," Bill said. "That brings us to the next part of our meeting, assuming no one has any further questions…?"

Bill paused for a moment, and when no one raised a hand, he continued.

"Alright then. Mr. Riordan here has been working with Ethan to come up with a plan to clear the infected out of Alexis long enough for us to round up some supplies. Ethan, Eric, if you would be so kind as to explain your plan."

Ethan stood up to join me, and Bill took a seat as we laid out our plan to the compound's residents. There were a few questions about why the undead behaved the way that they did, but I didn't have any answers for them.

"Listen," I said, "you don't need to understand solid-state electronics to turn on your television. You don't need an advanced degree in mechanical engineering to drive a car. We might not understand why these walking dead people do what they do, but we know that they are predictable. If you read the manual Bill is going to be passing around later, you'll see that it describes what all of you have probably seen for yourselves by now. These things are deadly, but they're also slow and stupid. We, on the other hand, are fast and smart. They outnumber us by an astronomical margin, but if we plan ahead and work together, we can beat them because we know what they are going to do before they do it."

It took some time, and a lot of repeating the same things over and over again, but eventually we managed to get most everyone on board. A few who were on the fence gave in when Bill stated that he thought our plan was sound, and that he would personally step in to lend a hand. Bill told the assembled residents that he didn't expect all of them to support the plan. He understood that they were taking a hell of a risk by trusting my information, but he asked that they do what they could to help those who were taking part in the operation.

When it was clear that the plan was popular with enough people to make it practicable, Bill called an end to the meeting and asked those who wished to participate to remain behind so that we could begin working out the details. Surprisingly, yellow-eyes was one of them. His suspicion of me had clearly not waned during the course of the meeting, and he continued to stare me down at every opportunity. I was starting to get a little tired of his nonsense, and found myself glaring back. I'm not normally the belligerent type, but I'm not a coward either. Push me, and I push back.

Bill motioned everyone to gather round.

"Alright, we need to decide who's doing what. First things first, who wants to drive the diversion vehicles?" he said.

Several people raised their hands, including me. Bill seemed a bit surprised that I volunteered.

"You sure, son? Seems like you should be more on the planning side of things," he said.

"I have my own truck, and I can handle myself just fine. I'd rather be in charge of the diversion team," I replied.

"Or maybe you just want to be able to get the hell out of dodge if things go south?" Yellow-eyes said.

I walked over to him and got about an inch away from his face.

"I don't know what your fucking problem is, asshole, but I've had as much of your crap as I'm going to put up with. You got a problem with me? Do something about it."

A faint smile tugged at the corner his mouth, and his yellow gaze narrowed. He was a couple of inches shorter than me, and I outweighed him by at least twenty pounds. The guy in front of me did not seem worried. Either he had some training of his own, or he thought I was all bluster. I tensed for him to move. As soon as he did, I planned to lunge in for a takedown and follow up with a little ground-and-pound. Nothing will humble a man quite like a few hard elbows across the bridge of his nose. A few tense seconds went by before I felt a hand on my shoulder.

"Eric, calm down. Steve, knock it off. This is the last thing we need right now," Bill said in a firm voice.

Yellow-eyes, or Steve I guess, stayed still for a moment more before he took a step back, still smirking. He took his time about it to make sure I knew he was not intimidated. I didn't give a flying lump of monkey shit if he was intimidated or not. Even the most confident man in the world can still get his ass kicked.

I relaxed and took a deep breath, never taking my eyes off the creepy bastard in front of me. After taking a step away to show everyone that I was back under control, I turned to Bill and nodded to him by way of apology. Ethan shot Steve a reproachful glare and stepped in front of him.

"I don't know what's gotten into you Steve, but this man saved my life. If you have a problem with him, you have a problem with me. Got it?" he said.

"I got no quarrel with you Ethan, I know you're a good man," Steve said. "I just wonder if it's smart for us to trust this guy so quickly. We don't know anything about him."

"I know he risked his life to help me, and he's willing to do it again to help a bunch of strangers," Ethan said, putting his hands on his hips.

Steve turned his head to stare at me again, then looked back to Ethan.

"Alright, man. We do this your way for now, but I suggest we keep a close eye on this guy," he said.

I held my temper in check and stifled the urge to confront him again, figuring it would do little to help the situation. Ethan glared at Steve, then turned away and dismissed him with a wave of his hand.

"If this is how you're going to be, Steve, we don't need you. Take a walk."

Steve seemed to deflate a bit. He looked around for support, and found only irritated faces. After a moment, he rolled his eyes and threw his hands up in defeat.

"Fine. We trust the new guy. Let me tell you something though," he pointed a finger at me, "you try to screw us like that last bunch did, and you will regret it."

"If I wanted to hurt you people," I replied, "I could have done it a dozen times by now. Maybe you didn't hear me the first time. I'm trying to help."

I was careful to keep any hint of anger out of my voice. Steve fixed a glare at me for another moment, and then turned to Bill.

"Alright then, chief. How are we doing this?"

We spent the rest of the afternoon planning the diversion. We decided to use three vehicles to lure the creeps (damn it, they had me saying it) away from the main part of town. Each vehicle would have two people assigned to it with one as a driver, and the other as a gunner. We would approach on Highway 27 and draw the undead south away from town, splitting up when we reached the furthest intersection from the gun shop. Each team chose a route to follow and circle back on once the hordes were a good distance away. Steve insisted that each team also plot out a few alternate routes, just in case anything went wrong. I didn't like the prick, but I had to admit that he had a good point.

The teams consisted of Ethan and I, Steve and Rick, and Earl agreed to drive the third vehicle with Justin in the back. Cody and Stan had managed to liberate a dozen walkie-talkies, complete with chargers, from an abandoned police station a few weeks earlier. We agreed on channels to maintain communication during the drive, and set the radios to charge using one of the compound's generators. Once the diversion team had their ducks in a row, Bill and I had a meeting with the people driving the cargo vehicles.

I learned that the compound had two moving trucks, a large church van that could seat fourteen people, and three pickup trucks. Justin and Rick volunteered to head out early in the morning to requisition two more abandoned cars to use for the diversion. Bill agreed to the idea, saying that it would be best if they could use the vehicles they already had to haul supplies. The moving trucks could hold a lot of gear, and the church van could haul workers to load them with supplies.

"You sure you don't want to go out with Justin and Rick to get another car?" Bill asked me at one point. "We could have somebody drive your truck and get this done a little quicker."

I shook my head. "No way man, nobody drives my truck but me. Besides, I trust my Tundra. If I am going to be running away from a horde of the infected, I want to know beyond doubt that my wheels aren't going to break down on me. Dig?"

Bill nodded and held up his hands. "Hey, no harm in asking, right?"

Once we laid out all the plans, everyone went back to work on the compound's daily duties. There was a new energy and excitement in the air as everyone went about their tasks. Not having anything to contribute for the moment, I went back over to my truck to get something to eat. It was late afternoon by the time I sat down on my little camp stool and opened up an MRE. The military rations weren't the tastiest thing in the world, but they had plenty of calories and neat little bottles of Tabasco sauce. Pretty much anything tastes better with a little hot sauce on it.

I finished my meal and heated up some water to make a cup of tea. I looked up from my little stove and noticed Steve walking toward me. I made no overtly aggressive movements, but I did gather my feet beneath me and lean my weight just a bit forward in case I had to stand up quickly. I put one hand on the cup and moved it around over the chafing fuel. If it came to it, I could splash the scalding water in his face as a distraction. I regretted not having a weapon within arm's reach, and I made a mental note not to make that mistake again.

Steve stopped a few feet away from me and sat down cross-legged on the concrete. He regarded me for a few moments without speaking, his expression blank. I glanced at him to let him know I wasn't impressed, then went back to making my tea.

"Something on your mind?" I asked, not looking up.

"You really would have done it, wouldn't you?" he said.

"Done what?"

"Fought me."

I looked up at him for a second or two, then took the tea bag out of my cup and tossed in a bucket. "If you had made a twitch, I would have stomped a mud-hole in your chest."

"You would have tried," Steve said.

I looked up at him, and he was smiling. Unlike the infuriating smirk he showed me earlier in the day, this expression seemed be from genuine amusement. I frowned at him.

"You sure do talk a tough game, you scrawny bastard. If you ever decide you're man enough, you know where to find me. Now, unless you have anything else to waste my time with, I would appreciate it if you could kindly fuck off, and let me finish my tea."

I sat back on the stool and leaned against the side of my truck, sipping at the hot liquid. Steve's smile faded. After a moment, he nodded to himself and stood up to walk away. There was definitely something strange about that guy. Not many dudes are willing to brawl outside their weight class unless they are either complete idiots, or highly confident in their abilities. I would have to keep an eye on Steve, and a weapon near at hand, if it came down to it.

After finishing my tea, I felt like some company, and walked over to the common area to look for Stacy. I found her sitting at a picnic table with Bill and a few other people talking over cups of instant coffee. There wasn't any room to sit at the table, so I kept on walking toward Ethan and Andrea's shack, making sure to catch her eye and wave as I walked past. Her face brightened when she noticed me, and she favored me with a little wink. So far, my chances looked pretty good.

I knocked on Ethan's door, taking care not to be too loud just in case the baby was sleeping. Andrea opened the door and welcomed me inside. Ethan was sitting on the couch with one of those U-shaped baby pillows across his lap. Aiden sprawled across it drinking from a bottle, his eyes slowly opening and closing as he drifted closer to sleep. I sat and watched them until the little guy's hands went limp and he lost his grip on the bottle. Ethan was ready and caught it, holding it for the baby while he continued to drink.

"Does he drink even when he's asleep?" I whispered.

"Yeah," Ethan replied, "it's like a reflex or something."

Aiden stretched his pudgy arms over his head, and heaved a small, contented sigh. I wondered how much innocence and simple beauty was left in the world. How long would it be before Aiden's bright little eyes became sunken and haunted, like the eyes of everyone else in the compound? How many parents out there lost their babies to the infection? How many children lost their parents? How many whole families were wiped out? As bad as it sounds, I didn't envy Ethan his position. I couldn't imagine the fear and worry that must plague him every day as he struggled to protect his family.

"You can't let it get to you," Ethan said.

I was so fixated on the baby that I didn't notice Ethan looking at me. He wore a ghost of a smile as he looked down and ran a big hand over his son's soft hair.

"How do you do it?" I asked.

Ethan shrugged. "Easy. I don't have a choice. I give up, my son dies. My wife dies. I will not let that happen. Come what may, my family will live."

Andrea stood up from her chair and kissed her husband on the forehead.

"Let me put him to bed sweetie," she said, gently.

Ethan sat the bottle down on the coffee table and, somewhat reluctantly, gave Aiden to his wife. She cuddled the little man close to her and took him into the bedroom.

"We have some work to do tomorrow," Ethan said. "I figure we spend a day getting everything ready, and then head out early Saturday morning. With any luck, we can clear out Alan's shop and get everything back here before noon."

"With any luck," I said, shaking my head. "Seems like the world is running mighty short on luck these days."

"We're still alive, aren't we?" Ethan replied.

"Yeah, I guess we are."

Andrea walked back in the room and placed a hand on my shoulder.

"Did you eat anything yet?" she asked.

"Yeah, I did, thanks."

She nodded and sat down on the couch next to Ethan.

"I hear you had a little run-in with Steve today," she said.

I winced at the memory. I had actually managed to put it out of my mind while enjoying a peaceful moment with Ethan and the baby.

"Yes. I did. Fucker pushed my buttons a few too many times. I let him know I wasn't impressed."

"He's a good man, Eric, he's just a little paranoid. His brother was one of the people who got shot when Arthur and his cronies tried to steal from the compound."

My eyebrows went up. "Holy shit," I said. "Man, that's tough. What were their names again? The two guys who got shot?"

"John McCray and Gil Steed. Good men, both," Ethan said.

"Which one was Steve's brother?"

"John," Andrea replied. "Ever since his brother died, Steve just hasn't been the same. He's been distant and angry, and he snaps at anyone who tries to talk to him. He still pulls his weight around the compound as far as work and guard duties go, but other than that he just wants to be left alone."

"So what was John like?" I asked.

"Young, about our age," Ethan replied. "He was a full ten years younger than Steve. We stood guard duty together pretty often, and he told me all about his life to pass the time. Their old man was a useless drunk who skipped out on them when Steve was thirteen, and Steve spent most of his life helping raise his brother. When he turned eighteen, he joined the Army and sent nearly every dime he made back home to his mother. He made it up through the ranks pretty quick, and after his first tour, he applied for Special Forces training. Served with the Green Berets for a few years before the war broke out in '01. He did a tour in Afghanistan and two in Iraq. He got out of the military and went to work as a civilian firearms instructor out in Arizona. He just happened to be in town visiting his family when the outbreak happened. John and his mother bought a house in our neighborhood about three years ago. Barbara saved most of the money Steve sent her over the years, and what she didn't use to put John through college, she saved to buy a house. John lived with his mother, but unlike a lot of guys his age, it wasn't out of laziness. He had a good job in the IT department at one of the big bank headquarters in Charlotte. His mother had some health problems that made it difficult for her to work, so John got her on his health insurance and made sure that all the bills got paid. Steve came around whenever his work schedule allowed to make sure they were doing okay. As much as John always looked up to Steve, Steve was the one who was the most proud. John grew up in a rough neighborhood. At least until he was about fourteen, anyway. By that point, Steve was sending enough money for them to move into an apartment in a better neighborhood. He grew up without a father, and because his mother worked two jobs and was hardly ever home, he didn't have a lot of supervision or guidance. Most kids in a situation like that will find all kinds of ways to get themselves in trouble, but John didn't do that. He kept away from drugs and gangs, and he worked hard in school. He even managed to earn himself a partial academic scholarship at UNC Chapel Hill. He got a master's degree in computer science in just five years, and then moved back to Charlotte to take care of his mother."

"Sounds like he was a good man," I said.

"He was. He always said he wished he could have followed in his brother's footsteps and joined the Army. Steve just laughed at him when he said things like that. Told him he was too smart to serve in the military. When the outbreak hit, they were with us when we left our neighborhood. They helped fight our way to I-85.

Man, that place was a nightmare. It was swarming with undead. The military was shooting at anything that moved, and there were thousands of people trying to get away from the city. My father and I kept everyone hidden in the basement of an abandoned office building until the military fell back. We didn't even make it to the highway before the creeps saw us and started swarming in our direction. Our only choice was to keep moving and shoot our way through. We lost a lot of people then, and Steve's mother was one of them. They got cut off from the rest us, and no one could get around to them to help them. Steve opened up with that big battle-rifle of his and told John to get their mother clear. John tries to get going, but one of the infected reaches out from a car window and grabs Barbara by the arm. The infected was just a little girl, and Barbara was so stunned that she didn't try to fight it off until after it bit her. John turns around a second too late, and blows the thing's head off with a pistol. I lost track of what happened to them after that, I was too busy busting heads with my fire axe."

Ethan went silent and stared into space. Andrea took up the story.

"Ethan and his father saw Emily and Justin trapped on top of a bus surrounded by the infected. They sent the rest of us ahead and went over to help."

I smiled at Andrea. "Yeah, Earl told me about that."

She flushed and looked down for a moment. Ethan chuckled and ran a hand over her shoulder.

"I may have been a little upset at the time," she said.

"Upset? Is that what you were? Considering the scratches and bruises on Earl when I found you guys that night, you were a little more than upset," Ethan said, smiling.

Andrea rolled her eyes. "Yes, and I have apologized to Earl many times for that. He has made it clear to me that he has no hard feelings, so unless you would like to have a little taste of what he got, I would suggest that you stop bringing it up."

Ethan laughed and held up his hands. "Fine, fine, sorry I mentioned it."

"Okay, I have a couple of questions," I said. "First, what happened with Emily and Justin?"

"They were on their own trying to get across I-85 the same as us. The Army was sending out broadcasts that they had established a safe zone at Iron Station. The two of them were trying make their way up there with a few others, when they were surrounded by infected while trying to cross the highway. Justin managed to climb on top of a big pickup truck and scrambled on top of a bus. He pulled Emily up after him, and they were stuck there for two days. Hundreds of people made it across the highway within sight of them, but no one would stop to help. At least that was what they told me afterward.

My father and I saw the two of them waving to us and crying out for help. Even from a distance, I could tell they were in bad shape. We were most of the way to the road by then. Now, what you need to understand is, crossing the highway itself wasn't the problem. If you could make it to the tops of the cars, you stood a pretty good chance of getting across. The problem was making it that far. There were thousands of cars, on and off the road, crashed, smashed, and stuck in rows for as far as the eye could see. Half the cars on the highway were on fire, and the military, who we thought were gone, showed up in attack helicopters and started strafing the highway. I don't know what they thought they were going to accomplish. There were thousands of infected out there."

Ethan stopped speaking for a moment and shook his head, his face grim as he relived the memory.

"Anyway, when my father and I saw the two kids trapped up there we knew we had to do something. I was out of ammo for my pistol, so I used a fire axe I took from a dead firefighter.

As it turns out, the thing works pretty well for putting down creeps, especially the spiked part on the back.

My dad had an M4 and about a gazillion rounds for it. He cleared the way to the bus, and I covered his back with the fire axe. Dad laid down fire as I helped the two kids get down from the roof. A fuck load of creeps had surrounded us, so we climbed on top of the cars and started running from roof to roof. Dad was a crack shot with that little rifle and he kept the infected from getting too close. We were doing okay for a little while, until Emily slipped on the roof of an Escalade and sprained her ankle pretty bad.

I had to help Justin carry her, so I couldn't swing the axe. The way ahead of us was swarming with undead. Dad got on top of a city utility truck and told us to make a bee-line for the other side of the highway. He pulled sniper duty on the creeps while the three of us got clear of the highway. Once we were about thirty yards from the nearest undead I turned around to see if Dad was following us. He was up to his knees in creeps, firing into them as fast as he could, but there were too many of them. He saw me start to run in his direction and put a bullet in the ground right at my feet. He hollered at me to get the hell out of there, and then turned and ran across the cars in the other direction. That was the last I saw of him."

Ethan's expression grew tighter and more pained as he spoke. By the time he finished, he was talking through clenched teeth. He wrung his big hands in front of him. The muscles in his forearms twisted and bunched like thick cables under his skin. Andrea leaned over and put an arm around his shoulders, as he sat forward and put his elbows on his knees.

"I should have followed him. I should have done something."

"Sweetie, it's not your fault. Your father did an incredibly brave thing, and so did you. We don't even know for sure that something happened to him," Andrea said.

"Then why hasn't he shown up yet? I mean, he was the one that came up with the idea to come here in the first place. He knew where we were going."

The two of them were silent for a long moment. Andrea looked lost for anything to say. I leaned forward and put a hand on Ethan's shoulder.

"We've all lost people we love. If your father gave his life to save yours, then I'm willing to bet he wouldn't have had it any other way. Beating yourself up isn't going to do you, or anyone else, a damn bit of good. You have a family, and a community that needs you. Don't lose sight of that," I said.

Ethan looked up at me and nodded.

"You're right, you're right. It's just hard, you know? Not knowing."

"I lost my parents too, about five years ago. I know how you feel, and I wish I could tell you it gets easier, but it doesn't. You just learn to accept it, and you move on with your life," I said.

Ethan heaved a sigh, and ran a hand through his hair.

"I think I'm going to go lay down. I'll see you in the morning, Eric."

Ethan stood up and walked into his bedroom without looking at either Andrea or I. Andrea was a bit misty eyed, and looked for all the world like a sad, delicate little woman. She sat with her back ramrod straight, her fingers working at the hem of a pillow in her lap, fidgeting and uncomfortable. I wanted to stand up and give her a hug, but I didn't for fear that the gesture would be unwanted. After a few awkward moments, I stood up and turned to leave.

"Thanks for all your hospitality, Andrea, I really do appreciate it. It's been a long time since I had a chance to make any new friends. I count you and Ethan among the best people I've ever been lucky enough to meet."

Andrea looked up and me and smiled. She seemed to relax somewhat.

"That's very kind of you, Eric. I'm grateful to you for helping Ethan, and for offering to help all the other folks around here. You're a stronger man than you know."

I flushed at the sincere intensity of her blue-eyed gaze. Her words had an effect on me that is difficult to describe. I felt inspired, sad, hopeful, and some powerful, determined, fearsome thing that I can't put a name to, all at the same time. Most of all, I felt appreciated. It's nice to know that there is at least one good person out there in the world that thinks you're worth a damn. Very nice indeed. I wiped at my face as I walked out the door to the common area. Damned dust getting in my eyes again.

I wandered back over to the picnic table where I had seen Stacy earlier. She was still sitting there along with the fit young woman who had spoken in my defense earlier at the meeting. They sat across the table from one another, leaning forward and conversing in low tones. Stacy noticed me and smiled. The woman in front of her stood and offered me a strong, long fingered hand.

"Hi. Jessica Robinson, nice to meet you," she said.

I could not help but notice her soft, slightly almond shaped eyes and her surprisingly strong grip. She stood nearly eye-to-eye with me, and lithe muscles rippled beneath her flawless mocha skin. She was obviously strong, but it was an alluring, feminine kind of strength.

"Nice to meet you ma'am. Thank you for speaking up for me today, that was very kind of you, I appreciate it," I said.

"You can thank me by delivering on your promises," she replied.

"I intend to do so. Barring incident, of course."

Jessica released my hand and stepped away from the table.

"I'll be seeing you tomorrow, kids. We got a lot of work to do, so don't stay up too late."

She smiled teasingly at Stacy, who blushed up to the tips of her ears even as she gracefully gestured for me to sit down across from her.

"So what brings you over my way, handsome?" she asked, giving me a sideways smile.

"Just looking for some friendly company, I guess," I said as I sat down across from her. We were silent for a moment looking at one another, neither of us quite knowing what to say.

"Big day tomorrow, huh?" Stacy asked, breaking the awkward silence.

I nodded. "We're not heading out until the day after tomorrow, but we have a lot of preparations to make in the mean time. Are you coming with us?"

"No, a few of us will stay behind to look after the children. Andrea will be on guard duty for the supply run, and she asked me to look after Aiden while she's gone."

I raised an eyebrow at that.

"I have to admit, that surprises me. I would have figured she'd want to stay close to her son."

"She does, but she's a damn good shooter, and the folks doing the supply run will need every marksman that they can get. Markswoman. Whatever. Andrea can do everyone a lot more good by protecting the people gathering supplies than she can by sitting around here babysitting."

"Where did Andrea learn to shoot? I thought she was a nurse," I said.

"Ethan's father taught her. They used to compete in some kind of firearms competition. I think she called it 'Three-Gun' or something like that. She dropped a lot of creeps on the way out here, until she ran out of bullets."

"Wow. I never would have guessed. What about Ethan? Can he shoot too?"

Stacy laughed. "I've seen him shoot pretty well with a pistol. I'm not sure how good he is with a rifle, but I can tell you for certain that he is hell-on-wheels with a fire axe."

"Well, let's hope he doesn't have to demonstrate that particular skill. If all goes well, we should be able to take what the compound needs without a shot fired, or an axe swung, for that matter.

"So what do you get out of all this?" Stacy asked. "I mean, are you planning to stay here? Is that why you're helping?"

Maybe it was my imagination, but I thought I heard a note of hopefulness in her tone. I thought about it for a second, and I really did not know what I planned to do at that point. The people at the compound seemed to have a good thing going, and staying there didn't seem like such a bad idea. On the other hand, I was worried about Gabriel, and I still felt the need to find him.

"I don't know," I said, shrugging. "It just seems like the right thing to do."

Stacy opened her mouth to say something else when gunfire erupted from the roof of the warehouse. A few seconds later a bell began ringing loudly. The compound's residents, most of whom were in their respective shelters winding down for the evening, came pouring out their doors and gathered in the common area, weapons in hand. Ethan stepped out of his shack with his SCAR rifle in one hand, and a big fire axe with an orange and black fiberglass handle in the other.

"Everyone take up defensive positions!" he shouted over the commotion.

"Hold up, Ethan, I'll be right back!" I shouted as I sprinted toward my truck.

I grabbed my load-bearing harness and one of my rifles, strapped it on as quickly as I could, and ran back to the other side of the warehouse. I was still wearing shorts and flip-flops, and cursed myself for not changing into something more practical earlier in the day. The flimsy sandals impeded my running, so I kicked them off and went barefoot. I must have looked ridiculous in tactical gear while dressed like a guy getting ready to spend a day at the beach.

Bill, Earl, and Justin came out, and in a few short moments they had organized the startled crowd into two fire teams. One of them ran to the side of the warehouse with the rolling door and set up a field of fire to cover it. The other group fanned out in a semi-circle around the steel entrance closest to the common area. Cody, Stan, Steve, and Ethan stacked up on one side of the entrance, while a man I hadn't met yet covered the entrance with a shotgun. Ethan had set the handle of his axe into a makeshift sling, and held his SCAR at the ready. Steve was in front with his M1A as the point man. I caught up to them and took up position beside Ethan.

"What are we doing?" I asked.

"We're getting ready to clear the entrance and help the guys up on the roof. You see anything dead coming at you when we open the door, put it down, and then make your way to the scaffold. Try not to shoot any of us while you're at it."

Ethan stopped for a moment, and looked down at my feet. "Dude, where are your shoes?"

"Sorry. I didn't have time to put them on," I replied, not quite sure why I was apologizing.

Ethan chuckled and shook his head. "Well, watch your step then, and stay close to me."

"Get ready to move!" Steve shouted from the front.

He was in a half crouch, leaning forward into his rifle with the front sight slightly below his line of vision. I dropped into a similar stance that Gabriel taught me, and readied myself to go out the door. Steve lifted the bar across the door and pulled it open. The man with the shotgun moved forward and checked as much as he could see without stepping out of the warehouse.

"Clear to thirty yards, check your corners," he shouted.

I tried to call to mind everything Gabriel ever taught me about close-quarters tactics as Steve moved forward and stepped out the door to the left. Cody followed close behind and branched off to the right. Stan went out and followed Steve. I stayed behind Ethan as we exited, being careful to exercise muzzle discipline (AKA not pointing my gun at the guy in front of me) as I moved.

Ethan turned to the right and I followed him. The sky above was overcast, but the light still stung my eyes after the gloom of the warehouse. I blinked a couple of times to clear my vision and looked around as I ran. Cracked and crumbling pavement covered the ground behind the warehouse for fifty yards, and then turned into a field of overgrown weeds that terminated at a tree line about thirty yards further away. At least three dozen infected stood in the open space between the warehouse and the trees with dozens more stumbling out of the woods behind them.

"Holy shit," I muttered.

Steve and Cody opened up with their rifles, dropping an infected with each shot. Steve's powerful battle-rifle blew the undeads' heads apart in a black and gray plume of rotten gore every time he pulled the trigger. The roar of the big gun was deafening. Stan and Ethan began firing in front of us, and I realized that I had stopped moving to watch Steve and Cody. I turned and hurried to Ethan's side and crouched into a firing stance. Stan and Ethan were picking off targets as soon as they got to within twenty yards. I flipped of the safety and chambered a round, then lined up the red dot on my optical sights with an infected forehead and began firing.

The sights on my gun allowed me to shoot with both eyes open, and the suppressor made the H&K much quieter than the unsuppressed rifles the other defenders carried. The staccato chatter of gunfire drowned out my ability to hear anything other than rifles unloading hot lead into the walking corpses around us. I'm not sure how many undead I put down, I missed a few shots in all the commotion, but I know I used up one magazine and more than half of another before Steve called a cease fire.

"That's enough, get to the roof," he ordered.

We all turned and sprinted toward the wooden spiral staircase and clambered to the top. My adrenaline pump was going full blast, and I was slightly winded by the time I got onto the roof. A man and two women that I recognized from the meeting earlier in the day were busy picking off the infected. The two women sat near the edge of the building and fired .22 rifles at the undead. The man had a scoped AR15 on a bipod, and fired from the prone position. Every time he pulled the trigger, a revenant hit the ground. The two women took out anything that he did not have time to pick off, letting the creatures get to within twenty meters before firing. At close range, the little rifles that the women used were very accurate and effective, but there were too many undead emerging from the surrounding forest for them to be able to shoot them all. Steve ordered the four of us to spread out and pick an area to defend. I moved to the far side of the wall closest to the tree line, and Ethan took up position twenty feet to my right.

"Take care of anything that comes from that direction," he said pointing diagonally away from the warehouse's northeastern corner. "I'll take out anything from the closest part of the wood line."

I nodded and sat down into a shooting position. I kicked myself mentally for not fixing a bipod to my rifle's lower rail, and took a few deep breaths to slow my heartbeat. I ignored the loud bangs and cracks of gunfire around me, and focused on controlling my breathing. I looked around to see what angles of fire the other defenders were controlling, and mentally drew two lines radiating from the corner of the warehouse all the way to the tree line. I spent the next few minutes firing on anything that wandered into my territory. It was strange, but there was something very Zen-like about clearing my mind and focusing only on hitting the next target.

Line up the dot, aim a little high, crack.

Line up the dot, aim a little high, crack.

Over and over again, until my rifle was empty. I took out the empty magazine, set it aside, and loaded a fresh one. The cycle began again until the next time I had to reload. By the time I got to my last clip, I could feel heat from the barrel radiating out through the four-sided shroud. I was down to just ten rounds when I dropped the last infected within my field of fire. I looked around, and most of the other defenders had either stopped shooting, or were picking off the last few stragglers.

"Cease fire!" Steve called. There were only five undead left, and I didn't see any more coming out of the tree line.

"We'll take out the rest by hand," he said, and motioned for Ethan to follow him.

Ethan slung his rifle over his shoulders and unlimbered his fire axe. I followed the two men down the staircase, and when we reached the bottom, Steve turned and pointed a finger at me.

"Not you," he said. "Ethan and I will take care of these assholes."

"I don't remember asking for your fucking permission," I said, as I walked past him.

I drew my pistol as I approached the last few infected. They were spread out pretty far, with at least twenty yards between them. I jogged over to the two farthest from the warehouse and took aim with the Kel-Tec. The gun bucked in my hand twice, and the revenants fell down, twitching for a moment before going still. Steve had fixed a bayonet to the end of his M1A, and drove it through the eye socket of an infected after knocking it to the ground with a perfectly executed reverse foot sweep. Ethan dispatched his two by casually planting the spike end of his fire axe in the tops of their skulls, and booting them away with a powerful front kick. The three of us spent a few minutes checking around to make sure no more were coming, and then made our way back to the warehouse.

"You shoot pretty good," Ethan said to me as we neared the entrance.

"I've had a lot of practice," I replied.

The fight seemed to have improved Steve's spirits, and he even smiled a little as he approached us.

"Pretty nice little bit of fun, eh buddy?" he gave Ethan a light punch on the shoulder.

Ethan nodded and gave him a grim smile, "Yeah, well, the fun part is over. We need to get a clean-up crew together and get rid of all these corpses. Must be nearly four hundred of the damn things."

"What do you think brought them all out here?" Stan said, approaching us from the other side of the warehouse.

Ethan shrugged. "I don't know. Got any theories, Eric?"

I frowned, and considered the question for a moment before responding.

"I can't say for certain, but I think these things might have some kind of herd mentality. It would explain why I keep seeing them moving in hordes."

Ethan frowned, and Steve's smile faltered.

"That is not a comforting thought," Ethan said.

"We should head inside and let everyone know it's clear," Cody chimed in.

Ethan agreed, and knocked three times on the steel door.

"It's Ethan, you can give the all clear."

I heard the sound of the bar being lifted, and the man with the shotgun opened the door.

"Any casualties?" he asked.

"Not unless you count those bastards." Ethan pointed a thumb behind him at the piles of dead bodies.

The five of us walked through the door back into the compound. It took a moment for my vision to adjust to the gloom, and my ears were still ringing from all the gunfire. Bill and Andrea looked all of us over, and asked us to give them our clothes. Andrea used the wooden partitions from the showers to set up a screen for us while we disrobed. We gave our clothes to Stacy and a few others over the top of the screen so that they could wash and sterilize them. Bill brought us buckets of water and bars of soap, and ordered us to scrub ourselves down.

"Before you go get dressed, I need to check each of you for any traces of infected blood or tissue," he said at one point, with clinical detachment.

I used up most of the little bar of soap cleaning myself, and sponged water from the bucket to rinse off. Bill looked me over, pausing when he saw my feet.

"Did you go out there barefoot?" he asked, frowning.

"Yes, I did. And before you start, I know that was a stupid thing to do. It won't happen again." Bill glared at me for a moment, then nodded and checked my feet.

"I don't see any cuts or scrapes. You got lucky."

He dismissed me with a wave and motioned for Ethan to step forward. Noah Salinger stood at the edge of the partition and handed me a towel. I dried off quickly and turned to walk back to my truck with the towel around my waist.

"Hey, Eric. These belong to you," Noah said, holding out my sandals.

"Right, thanks man. I appreciate it."

Noah nodded as I put on my sandals and walked back to my truck. I put on a pair of Army surplus BDU pants, boots, and a t-shirt. I was lacing up my boots when I noticed Stacy approaching.

"Busy day, huh?" she said as she sat down on the concrete in front of me.

"Yeah, little bit."

"You okay?"

I laughed a little at the question. "Of course. Why wouldn't I be?"

A half smile turned up one corner of her mouth as she shook her head at me.

"You're not just acting tough, are you? You really mean it."

"I'm not really interested in being tough, so I guess I do."

"I thought all guys wanted to be tough."

I laughed again. "Not this one. I'd rather be smart than tough any day of the week."

Stacy's smile widened, and it was like the sun coming out from behind the clouds.

"You planning on sleeping out here tonight?" she asked.

"Yeah, after I get done helping dispose of the bodies outside."

"I have a better idea," she said as she stood up and offered me a hand.

"How about you come over to my place, and we spend the night together. Let the others take care of the bodies."

I felt my blood heat up immediately. Stacy saw me flush, and stepped closer to me. I took her hand and followed her to her little shelter. It consisted of a bed, a chest of drawers, and a bar suspended between two walls that did the job of a closet.

"Welcome to my home. It's not much, but…well, it's not much." She smiled as she held her arms up to encompass the room.

I responded by sliding an arm around her waist and pulling her close. Her arms wound around my neck as she stood on her toes and kissed me. She did an amazingly thorough job, and wrapped her legs around me as I lifted her up. We spent the rest of the evening in her little bed venting all of the stress, worry, tension and fear that we had both kept pent up inside of us for the last three months. When we were spent, we fell asleep with our naked bodies entwined around one another.

As I drifted off to sleep, I let myself relax for the first time in months, and simply enjoyed the feeling of holding a beautiful woman in my arms.

Chapter 11

Planning Phase

I woke up the next day when Stacy stirred and got out of bed. It was dark in the little shack, but I could make out her beautiful, naked form as she put her clothes on.

"Where are you rushing off to?" I asked.

She smiled and sat down on the edge of the bed after she finished dressing.

"There's a lot of work to do today. You've gone and stirred yourself up a hornet's nest."

She ran a hand through my hair and down my face. It felt wonderful. I took her hand in mine and kissed it.

"Do we have to get up so early? Come back to bed for a little while."

I smiled and reached up to pull her close to me. She caught my hands and playfully pushed them down against my chest.

"No way, mister. As tempting as it might be, I will not be drawn into a bout of morning sex. Not when we have so much to do."

Her smile faded a bit, and she stared intently at me for a long moment before she leaned down and gave me a soft, gentle kiss.

"There are a lot of people out there who will be risking their lives because of you. I care about those people, and I expect you not to let them down. Can I count on you for that, Eric?"

Her words dispelled my blissful reverie like a thin fog under the noonday sun. A sharp spear of anxiety pierced my stomach, and for the first time it occurred to me just how much I was asking the people outside Stacy's door to count on me. If I was wrong, if I made a miscalculation or a mistake, then people would die and it would be on my head. To call the thought of leading people to their deaths worrisome would be to understate the sentiment by a profound degree. I sat up in Stacy's bed and took a deep breath before responding.

"You're right. We have work to do."

I stood up and picked my clothes up off the ground. Stacy regarded me for a moment with a strange look in her eyes. I was dressed in less than a minute, and Stacy and I stepped into the early morning light filtering down through the windows. Several people, including Ethan, were already up and moving. Justin and Rick stood near the gun locker dressed in combat fatigues. They were loading spare magazines for their weapons and stuffing them into the pockets of tactical vests. Rick had his Mini 14 and a pistol on his hip. Justin had a Kel-Tec SU16 rifle.

Stacy stopped me by taking my hand and gently turning me around.

"I'm going to go help get breakfast ready. I'll come get you when it's time to eat."

"Thanks. I'm going to see what I can do for the diversion team," I replied.

Stacy put a hand on my chest and stood on her toes. I gave her a kiss and a brief hug before she turned to help some of the other women set up tables. I turned and walked over to Justin and Rick.

"Looks like things are going pretty well between you two," Justin said with a smirk.

"So far. What are you guys getting into today?" I said.

Justin looked at me for a moment longer, and when it became clear that I nothing to say about Stacy, he shrugged and went back to work loading magazines for his rifle.

"That the only gun you have?" I asked him.

"Yeah, but it's a pretty good one. It's light and it's reliable, albeit not quite as accurate as an AR."

"You have a pistol?"

"I could take one of the nine millimeters, but honestly I prefer not to carry the extra weight."

"Stay here a minute, I have something for you."

Justin looked quizzically at me as I turned and walked over to my truck. I retrieved my Sig Mosquito and the sound suppressor for it, as well as four extra magazines and a holster. I went back to the gun locker and handed it to him.

"This will fit in the holster with the silencer on it, but you need to make sure you have plenty of room to draw it with that thing attached. Each clip only holds ten rounds, so make them count. You can get skull penetration reliably out to about ten yards. Beyond that, no promises."

"Sweet. Thanks dude," Justin said as he looped the holster into his belt.

"You can thank me by making damn sure you bring it back, and don't damage that suppressor. It's the only one I have for that gun," I replied.

"No problem," Justin replied, smiling.

I turned to Rick. "You okay with the Ruger, or do you want one of my HK's?"

"Hell, if you're offering, I'll take one. You got one of those fancy silencers for it too?"

"Yep. Hang out, I'll be right back."

I went back to my truck, got one of the carbines and some spare magazines, and gave them to Rick. He thanked me, and I helped him load the magazines before showing him how to operate the rifle. Between the rifle's silencer and red-dot sight, I felt a lot better about his chances if he had to slug it out with the infected. Not that I have a problem with the Mini-14, it is a good rifle, but it was not designed for stealth, and the HK is much more accurate at long range.

I put Rick's rifle in my truck for safekeeping (and as collateral for my HK) before walking over to where Ethan and Bill sat pouring over a map on a small table. I was a bit apprehensive about speaking to Bill. I did not know if he had heard about me spending the night with his daughter, and I wasn't quite sure how he might react when he found out. Avoiding him, as nice as it sounded, was not an option if I was going to help plan tomorrows activities. My mother used to tell me that it is better to face a problem head on, than to live in fear of it. Good advice, that.

Ethan noticed me first, and motioned for me to have a seat next to him.

"You're just in time, we got some questions about the creeps we need answered," he said.

Bill looked up, and his eyes crinkled at the corners as he smiled at me. "Just so you know, I heard about you and Stacy."

I stopped in my tracks with my hand a few inches from the back of the chair I was about to pull out. My surprise must have registered on my face, because both Bill and Ethan laughed at me. Loudly.

"It's okay, Eric," Bill said. "Stacy is a grown woman, and I trust her judgment. Besides, she's a red-blooded human being, the same as anybody else. What she does in the privacy of her own bedroom is her business."

"Um…thanks," I said, and sat down across from him.

Andrea walked up to the table with Aiden on her hip and a cup of coffee in one hand. The baby made a noise that sounded like he was saying "hooo, hooo" when he saw his father and leaned toward him with his little arms outstretched. Ethan smiled broadly and took the baby from Andrea as she sat the coffee down on the table far enough away that the baby could not reach it.

"How's my little man," Ethan said as he held the baby up and nuzzled his belly. Aiden giggled and pushed at his father's head. Ethan turned to me and held the baby out.

"You mind holding him for a minute while I put down some coffee?" he asked.

"Uh, no, not at all."

I could count on one hand the number of times in my entire life that I had held a small child, and my nervousness must have showed. Andrea smiled and moved to stand over my shoulder. I took Aiden and sat him down on the table in front of me, holding the baby awkwardly. Aiden grinned at me and reached out to grab my face. One little hand landed on my cheekbone and squeezed. I leaned back and turned my face away. Aiden kicked his little feet and laughed.

"I think he likes you," Andrea said.

Aiden picked that moment to raise both hands high over his head and shout, "Dab, dab, daaaaab," before leaning forward and smacking me soundly in the forehead with both hands. The kid hit surprisingly hard. I winced, irritated for all of about half a second, and then the baby laughed uproariously. He looked ridiculous with drool running down his chin and four tiny little teeth poking through his gums. I smiled at him in spite of myself. Everyone at the table, meanwhile, was leaning over and trying not to fall on the ground as they laughed at me. Andrea rescued me from any further assaults by taking Aiden and planting him back on her hip

"I'm sorry Eric, I shouldn't laugh at that," she said, still laughing.

"It's okay. He's just a baby," I replied.

A moment later, she regained her composure and offered to bring Bill and me a cup of coffee. We both accepted.

"Where do you guys get coffee from? That stuff goes bad in like a week. I wouldn't have thought it would still be around," I said.

"The vacuum sealed stuff stays good for forever and a day, as long as its stays sealed," Bill said.

I nodded. I hadn't thought of that. Some people who knew me before the outbreak thought that I did not like coffee. That is not true, I actually like coffee. I just stopped drinking it when I went to work as a financial analyst after college. The job was stressful enough by itself without caffeine nervousness making it worse. I switched to tea a few months after taking the job, and never looked back. Considering the amount of work I had ahead of me that day, a strong cup of Joe did not seem like such a bad idea. I took Andrea up on her offer, and started fielding questions for Bill and Ethan as she left to go get it.

We spent the next hour pouring over maps checking and rechecking the routes the diversion teams would take. Ethan knew the area well, and came up with some alternate routes to follow should the need arise. I volunteered my truck to lead the way into town. The heavy-duty brush guard on the front could plow a path through the infected, hopefully without damaging the engine. Not long after we finished deciding on the diversion routes, Stacy came over to the table to let us know that breakfast was ready. The three of us walked over to the common area and ate with the other compound residents. A few people were on watch, and a handful of others had elected to eat alone. I learned a few more names, and I also learned that Jessica Robinson was Earl's wife. The two of them made an unusual looking couple, Jessica being lean and athletic, and Earl being a massive mountain of a man. As we talked, I learned that Earl had worked as a diesel mechanic before the outbreak, and Jessica was a personal trainer. Jessica served a stint in the Marines before moving back home to Charlotte three years ago and meeting Earl.

After breakfast, I spent the rest of the day in meetings with Bill and other members of the community. At three in the afternoon, we called another meeting, and went over every aspect of the plan in detail with everyone who was going to be participating. We planned to make the assault in three phases.

Phase 1: The diversion vehicles, led by my truck, would make their way through the center of town and distract the undead. Once we had led them out of sight, we would radio back to the compound, and Bill would lead the retrieval crew to the gun shop.

Phase 2: With the undead diverted, Cody and Stan would enter town first as designated marksmen and clean up any stragglers that didn't leave with the rest of the horde. When the way was safe, they would radio Bill to bring forward the rest of the crew and start loading the trucks.

Phase 3: Once the vehicles were loaded with as much as they could carry (which would be a lot, considering the size of the moving trucks) the retrieval crew would radio to the diversion team to return to the compound and take the supplies back as quickly as possible.

I suggested to Bill that after his crew unloaded the trucks, time permitting, they should return to town and see if they could scavenge any other supplies that might be useful. Once the undead were led away from town, it was unlikely that they would be quick to return, if they ever came back at all. Bill considered it, and said he might try it if everything went well on the first trip.

We spent the rest of the day making sure everyone knew their roles, checking the radios to ensure that they functioned properly, and scrounging up fuel for all of the vehicles. Just before sundown, Justin and Rick returned in two commandeered pickup trucks. When I heard that they were back, I went outside to greet them. Earl had already raised the rolling door, and Bill moved the big, blue cargo container with a forklift. Both trucks were full size F150s. When they pulled up next to the compound, I noticed that the beds of both trucks were nearly overflowing with cargo. I walked up to the truck Justin was driving and leaned an elbow against the driver side window.

"Where on Earth did you get all this stuff," I said, gesturing at the supplies.

Justin grinned. "We took it from a housing development not far from here. The place was crawling with undead when we found it, but we managed to set up a little trap for the bastards, thanks to those nice weapons you gave us this morning."

Justin got out of the truck and lowered the tailgate. Rick pulled to a stop behind him and got out of his truck. He walked up to me and clapped me on the shoulder.

"Man, that rifle you gave me is something else, I tell you what. I must have dropped two hundred creeps with this thing today," he said, patting the HK. "Justin over there was like Annie freakin' Oakley with that little pistol."

Bill overheard the conversation and came over to stand beside me.

"Whoa, whoa, hold up a minute. What did you two get yourselves into today?" he asked.

"We'll tell you all about it once we get inside. Both of us are hungry and thirsty, and we need to get all these supplies stowed before nightfall," Justin replied.

Bill looked like he might argue for a moment, but relented.

"Fine, get a work detail together and get everything inside. I'll have Earl check these here trucks out."

Bill grabbed a case of bottled water and carried it back into the compound. Several other people came out and helped bring everything inside. Justin and Rick had scored a large amount of non-perishable food, sets of cookware and kitchen knives, clothes, shoes, toys for the compound's children, a few dozen boxes of ammunition, and several more guns. Most of the weapons were pistols of varying calibers, but there were also a couple of AK-47s. I picked up one of the Russian assault rifles and inspected it. It was functional, and looked nearly brand new.

"Where the hell did you find these things?" I asked Justin.

"One of the houses we raided," he replied. "Whoever owned the place must have been a drug dealer or something. These rifles were illegal as hell before the outbreak; they can shoot full auto. That's not all though, check this out."

Justin removed a few items from the top of a large wooden box with a lock on the front, and strained as he moved it to the tailgate. It made a loud rasping sound as it slid across the painted metal. Whatever was in it was very heavy. Justin looked at me and grinned.

"I think I remember seeing a pair of bolt cutters in your truck," he said.

"I'm on it."

I retrieved the tool and handed it to Justin. He placed the hardened pincers over the padlock and squeezed the handles together. After a few seconds of effort, the lock gave way and Justin removed it from the latch. He paused and looked over his shoulder at me for a moment.

"If this is what I think it is, then I am about to be a very happy boy."

"Open it, dude. Let's see what we got," I said.

Justin opened the lid, and we both stared for a moment at what was in the case.

Inside were neatly stacked boxes of 7.62x39mm ammunition, each box containing twenty rounds. I took one of the boxes out to measure its depth, and counted the length and width of the other boxes in the crate. After a quick bit of mental math, I let out a low whistle.

"Looks like you've got about two thousand rounds here," I said.

Justin nodded. "I believe it. This will definitely come in handy. High five," he said, holding up one hand.

I slapped it, and went over to the gun locker to get a rolling cart. We loaded the crate on the cart and stashed most of the ammo in the locker. Justin also took a canvas bag from the back of his truck that contained twenty spare magazines. Justin and Rick divided them up and spent the better part of the next hour loading them. They were as excited as a couple of teenagers on prom night over their new weapons.

The rest of the community sorted the other supplies and distributed them where they were needed most. I marveled at Bill's leadership. Not a single argument or disagreement broke out over who should get what. Bill simply directed the two women sorting the supplies where to take them, and nobody seemed to have a problem with it. I was beginning to understand why these people looked up to him the way they did.

I was sitting with Justin and Rick in front of the gun case when Bill walked over to us carrying a folding chair. He sat down in it and fixed the two men with an expectant stare.

"So. Gentlemen. What happened?" he asked.

Justin turned to Rick and pointed a finger at him. Rick shook his head and pointed back at Justin. Justin shrugged, and turned back to Bill.

"After we left this morning, we headed north on 27 and made our way toward a housing development that we knew still had plenty of vehicles in it. The place used to be pretty nice before the outbreak, and a lot of the people living there tried to stay rather than run. We were halfway hoping to find some survivors there."

Justin looked down for a moment and shook his head.

"Anyway, we've been planning to raid the place for a while now, but we couldn't think of a good way to do it until today."

Justin drew my Sig Mosquito from its holster and handed it to Bill.

"Eric let me borrow this neat little pistol here, and it gave me an idea."

Bill looked over the little weapon, unscrewing the suppressor and peering through it.

"Impressive. You have some nice gear, Eric."

I thanked him, and held out my hand for the pistol. Bill handed it to me, and Justin gave me my holster and spare magazines. I looked at Rick.

"You mind giving me my rifle back?" I asked, smiling.

Rick chuckled. "Damn, I was hoping you'd forget."

He picked up the rifle and set it down next to me, along with the spare clips. I motioned for Justin to continue with his story.

"Most of the community is surrounded by a brick fence, but some parts of it aren't. Those places have natural barriers, like steep wooded hills and such. The entrance to the community is an automatic rolling metal gate. The HOA used to give everybody who lived there a remote control to open it. When we found it a couple of months back, the gate was standing wide open. Rick and I shut it and locked it, figuring it would be better to keep the undead locked up in there rather than take a chance on them wandering out."

"Good thinking," Bill said.

"When we got there this morning, the gate was still locked, and I could see at least a couple of hundred creeps still walking around inside. There is a water tower on a hill not far from the community, so Rick and I climbed it to do a little recon. We counted seventy-five houses, and at least three-or-four-hundred creeps. Between the two of us, we had three-hundred rounds for the rifles, and a brick of ammo for the .22 pistol. We figured that as long as there were less than eight-hundred creeps down there, we could take all of them out. The problem was getting to them. If we came through the front gate, we wouldn't last ten seconds. We needed to get in nice and quiet and get on the roof of one of the houses. From there, we could just attract them to us and take them down one by one."

"And if you didn't, then you would be stuck on a roof and surrounded by the undead until you died of dehydration," Bill said.

"Not necessarily," I chimed in. "If the undead can't see, smell, or hear you, then after a few hours they forget what they were after and wander off. Their poor, rotten brains don't seem to have very much in the way of short term memory."

Everyone stared at me for a moment.

"I did not know that," Justin said. "I'll have to keep that in mind."

"Are you sure that's true?" Bill asked.

"My friend Gabriel was pretty sure about it when he wrote that manual I gave you. I have no reason to doubt him," I said.

"I really need to read that thing…" Bill muttered.

"Right. So anyway," Justin continued, "we figured that with the silencers on our weapons, we could get where we needed to go without alerting too many of the infected. We made our way around to the eastern side of the neighborhood as quietly as we could until we spotted a steep section of hill that butted up to a break in the fence. We made our way to the hill and slipped down it into the neighborhood. No sooner do we get past the fence than do we see four creeps just a few feet away. I dropped them with the .22 before they had a chance to start groaning. That gun makes less noise than a mouse fart.

We worked our way to one of the houses near the center of the neighborhood, killing a few more creeps along the way. We broke into the house and went upstairs to the second floor where two windows opened up onto the roof of the first floor. The spot was perfect. Rick and I sat down in the windowsills and yelled at the poor dumb fuckers until the whole neighborhood was stumbling over. When there were enough of them bunched up in front of us to make for easy shooting, we opened up with the rifles.

It took about ten minutes of shooting to use up all of the rifle cartridges. There was a small hill of undead in front of the porch that the others actually climbed onto. Their ugly little faces were just above the edge of the roof, and it made killing the rest of them that much easier. I took my time and picked my shots, while Rick reloaded the spare clips for me. I had to stop every fifty rounds or so to let the pistol cool down, so it took me better than three hours to kill the rest of them."

"You didn't do that with the suppressor on, did you?" I asked.

"No, I took it off before then. No sense putting wear and tear on it unnecessarily," Justin replied.

I nodded, and he continued with his story.

"All together, I figure we probably killed more than six hundred of the things. Once that was done, we climbed down and went out the back door to start searching the neighborhood. The first house we went to, we could hear a couple of creeps moaning behind the front door. We get up to the door, and the things spot us through the window and start beating at the glass. One of them breaks through and starts trying to crawl out the window. I put them down with the pistol, and we searched the house. We found those two trucks together in the garage, must have been a his-and-hers deal or something. The keys were on a table by the front door. We took the trucks around the neighborhood and loaded up the most useful stuff we could scavenge. A couple of the other houses still had some infected in them, but we put them down without any trouble. If you just stand outside the door and make noise, they come right to you. Makes it easy.

One of the houses we search, I'm upstairs raiding the kitchen and Rick calls up to me from the basement. I go down there, and Rick has the two AK's and a big box of what could only be ammunition. We damn near threw our backs out loading that crate into the truck, but it was worth the effort."

Justin reached down and patted the AK leaning against his chair affectionately.

"The best part of all this is, we only raided about a dozen houses. There are still plenty more to search."

Justin leaned back with a satisfied smile on his face as he finished his story. Bill appeared lost in thought for a few moments before responding.

"That's good news, guys. Once we finish with this business tomorrow, I want you to take me, Ethan and Earl out there to check the place out."

"I know that look, Bill," Rick said. "You got something cooking up in that head of yours?"

Bill gave an enigmatic smile. "Maybe I do, Rick. Maybe I do."

"Well, this has all been very interesting," I said, "but you two are going to be on the diversion team tomorrow. We need to get you up to speed on the plan."

"Right you are," Bill said. "Earl is checking the trucks as we speak. Assuming they're in good enough shape to be of service tomorrow, the two of you will be riding in them through a horde of the infected. I suggest you sit down with Eric and hash out the details."

I nodded to Bill as he got up and folded his chair. The old doctor ambled off toward his shack, and I motioned for Justin and Rick to follow me to Ethan's shelter. I knocked on his door, and when Andrea answered, I told her that we needed to speak with Ethan. The big, bearded man came outside a moment later and joined us at a picnic table nearby. I had Ethan show them the route they would be following, and all of the alternate routes available to them. As we spoke it grew dark outside, and Rick had to light a few candles so that we could see the maps. When we finished with the briefing, I bid the other men a good night and walked over to Stacy's little shelter. She was sitting out front in a plastic Adirondack chair and sipping from a mug of apple cider.

"Where did you get that?" I asked, pointing at the cider as I pulled up a chair and sat down next to her.

"I pilfered it from Justin and Rick's haul today."

I raised an eyebrow. "Really?"

She smiled, her full lips parting slightly. "No. They brought in a couple of gallon jugs of the stuff. It still had the tamper seals on it, so we figured it would be safe to drink. There was enough for everybody."

"There any left?" I asked. I really like apple cider.

"No, this is the last of it. Sorry."

I shrugged. "No worries."

I leaned back in the chair and stretched my legs out in front of me. There was a candle burning in a jar on a small table to Stacy's right. The firelight framed her in orange and gold, accentuating the graceful curves of her face. She was almost painfully beautiful in that light. I reached out and laid my hand over hers on the arm of her chair. She turned her head toward me and smiled.

"Busy day, huh?" she asked.

"You're not kidding. What time is it? I haven't even looked."

Stacy held her watch over the candle. "A quarter after nine."

"Really? I thought it was later than that."

"Well, we got up at six-thirty this morning. You've been going non-stop since then," she said.

"Yeah, and I'm feeling it. I'm exhausted."

"How tired are you, exactly?"

I turned to look at her, and a playful smile tugged at one corner of her mouth. She raised her eyebrows twice and winked at me. I couldn't help but laugh at her.

"I think I have a little left in the tank," I said.

"Good. I'd like you to try for an encore of last night's performance, if you up to it."

I answered by standing and sweeping her up out of her chair. She let out a surprised squeak as I picked her up, and playfully slapped me on the chest. I carried her into her shack and kicked the door shut behind us. The rest of the evening was equally, if not more pleasant than the one before. As I fell asleep, I sincerely hoped that all the noise didn't wake anyone up. Stacy got a bit loud for a while there.

Chapter 12

Last Minute Changes

I woke up early the next morning to the sound of the rolling door going up at the other end of the warehouse. Stacy and I extricated ourselves from one another and got dressed. We stepped out into the dim light of the warehouse and held hands as we walked across to the storage area. The compound was a hive of activity. Excited voices filled the air as people checked weapons, cleared space on shelves, and packed up food and water to bring with them to town. The other members of the diversion team were already gearing up beside the gun locker. I started to head toward them when Stacy tugged on my arm and turned me around.

"I'm going to go help make breakfast for the children. Come see me before you leave, okay?" She said.

"Sure. Save me a plate, will you?"

She smiled and stood on her toes with her face upturned. I gave her a kiss and a long hug before letting her go. She was warm, and her arms felt good around my neck.

The guys at the gun locker watched us part ways. They exchanged a round of elbow nudging and meaningful glances as I approached. They all wore old-fashioned Army surplus combat fatigues and tactical vests, except for Earl. He wore a pair of grease-stained coveralls with his name embroidered over the breast pocket. I guess whatever surplus store they had raided didn't have anything in Earl's size. Ethan smiled and clapped me on the shoulder by way of greeting when I reached him.

"Glad you decided to join us. I was beginning to wonder if I should go and knock on Stacy's door, everything is just about ready to go," he said.

"Yeah, well, better late than never. Any of you guys seen Bill around?" I replied.

Justin pointed out the rolling door. "He's out with a couple of other guys checking the moving trucks."

"Okay. I'm going to suit up and see about calling a final meeting to get everyone organized before we head out. Can one of you guys check the radios?"

"Already done," Steve said. "They all have a full charge. We just need to suit up and get our ducks in a row, and we'll be ready to roll out."

His expression and tone were neutral, and I appreciated that he was behaving like a professional. In his combat gear, Steve looked every bit like the elite soldier he had been before the outbreak. He was clean-shaven, and had even managed to get a haircut at some point during the previous night. He looked several years younger with his hair clipped short and without the five o'clock shadow.

"Great. Looks like you guys are on top of things," I said, nodding to Steve. "I'll be ready to go in about ten minutes. Have you all eaten yet?"

"Yeah, we ate earlier," Ethan replied. "You should get something before we leave. It's going to be a long day."

I nodded. "I'll do that. It probably wouldn't be a bad idea for all of us to bring some spare food and water, just in case."

"Already got it covered," Justin said. "Emily is packing three days' worth of food and water into rucksacks and putting them in the diversion vehicles."

"Alright then, I'll see you in a few minutes."

I turned and walked over to my truck and took a pair of cargo pants, a white t-shirt, and a bush jacket out of my suitcase. I put them on, along with a pair of sturdy leather combat boots, and buckled on my load-bearing harness. I loaded five spare magazines each for my pistol and rifle, and put them in pouches on the harness. After grabbing my small-sword and its makeshift sling, I set the weapons aside and started unloading the truck.

I stacked all of my weapons and ammunition to one side of the truck, and set everything else on the ground behind it. The red plastic gasoline container I took from the abandoned farmhouse a few days ago was one of the first items I picked up, and I poured all of its contents into the truck's gas tank.

I couldn't believe it had only been three days since I left home. It felt like much longer than that. In that short amount of time, I had managed to find a group of survivors, befriend a few of them, make one enemy, get drunk, and I had even managed to get laid.

Twice.

Now I was about to take part in a dangerous assault on a town overrun with infected, and risk my life trying to help a bunch of people that I barely knew.

Why was I doing this? What did I stand to gain?

The gas can emptied, and I set it down with the rest of my gear. As I sorted through my weapons, I thought about why I wanted to help the compound. I honestly did not know why I felt compelled to do something for these people, but compelled I was. Maybe it was not about what I stood to gain, but about what all these poor, beleaguered people stood to lose. They had managed to create a bastion of safety and sanity in a world gone completely mad. In the face of the worst disaster ever to strike the human race, these folks were still working and trying to build something. They were willing to fight to ensure that they had a future.

I wondered what I would have done if the people here had decided not to raid Alexis. Would I still have stayed? Would I have tried to help Ethan come up with another plan?

No. Probably not.

I would have thanked them for their hospitality, apologized to Ethan, packed up my gear, and gotten back on the road. I was thankful things had not gone down that way. What really made the difference for most people here was when Bill threw his support behind me. He weighed the risks against the rewards, and decided it was worth taking the chance. Even Steve, who liked me about as much as I like rat shit in my chicken soup, was willing to put aside our differences to help his fellow survivors. If these people were willing to trust me, and to put their faith in me, then what kind of man would I be if I did not try to help them?

Not much of one, that's for sure.

After making sure all unnecessary items were out of my truck, I dragged my box of weapons, and the two boxes of grenades, back to the open part of the storage area. Bill came back into the building while I was doing so, and I waved him over.

"What can I do for you, Eric?" he asked as he approached.

"I have a few things here that might be of use today," I replied.

"Let's see what you've got."

I opened the plastic trunk and took out all of my weapons. When I opened the boxes of grenades, Bills eyes went wide with surprise.

"Good Lord in the morning, where the hell did you get those things?" he asked, staring at the explosives.

"Would you believe they were a gift from a friend of mine?"

"You get these from that Gabriel fella you were talking about earlier?"

"Yes, I did. I honestly don't like these things, I've never tried to use a grenade before. Is there anyone here who might be able to do something useful with them?" I asked.

Bill took a deep breath and rubbed a hand across his forehead.

"Well, I imagine that Steve could use them. There are a couple of other folks here who served in the military, maybe they could too. I'm not sure how good of an idea it is to put these things in untrained hands."

242

"I couldn't agree more. That's exactly why I'm not taking any of them with me. Tell you what, let's call a meeting and see if there is anybody here who can think of something to do with a big box of grenades."

Bill nodded. "Good idea. We need to settle these folks down and make sure the plan is clear to everyone before we get started."

Bill climbed up on a crate and called for everyone's attention. In a few moments, a small knot of excited, anxious people stood in front of him and listened as he gave final orders for the day's mission. He answered a few questions, clarified some instructions, and then motioned for everyone to follow him over to my pile of weapons. I had laid the rifles and pistols out on a blanket, and the two boxes of grenades stood open to the crowd. The sight of the impressive arsenal earned me more than a few suspicious stares from the good people of the compound.

"Does anyone here other than Steve have any military experience?" Bill asked.

Jessica, Rick, and surprisingly, Noah Salinger raised their hands.

"What branch did you serve in, and what did you do?" Bill said.

Rick spoke up first. "Army. I was a tank mechanic, but I was also a good rifleman."

Bill nodded and pointed at Jessica. "Jess, I already know about you. What about you, Noah?"

"I served in the Navy for four years. I was a gas-turbine electrician, but I also volunteered for my ship's security force. I can handle a pistol and a shotgun pretty well, but I don't have a lot of experience with rifles. We didn't use them very much."

"Alright, good to know. Any of you ever been trained on how to use grenades?"

Rick and Jessica gave affirmatives, but Noah shook his head.

"I'm afraid not, Bill. Grenades are too destructive to use on ships. You never know if you might hit a fuel line or something," he said.

"Cody, Stan, what about you two?" Bill asked.

The two former police officers looked at each other and shrugged ruefully. "Sorry, Bill. Police generally try to avoid blowing things up," Cody said.

"I can use them," Steve said as he walked up to the boxes. "Jess, Rick, come and take what you want. I'll bring the rest with me."

Steve looked at the diversion crew and smiled, his yellowish eyes gleaming with mischief.

"Change of plans guys. I'm riding with Eric."

I wasn't sure if I liked the sound of that.

Bill asked if anyone else had any questions, and when no one spoke up, he called an end to the meeting.

"Alright, the diversion crew will head out shortly. Everybody else, get to your stations and be ready. If anyone wants to swap out weapons, now is the time to do it."

I stood by my weapons and waited for people to come over. I figured a few of them might want to borrow some of my guns. I handed out all of my pistols except the Kel-Tec, and Greg traded out his hunting rifle for my Benelli shotgun. Jess and Rick took three fragmentation grenades each, and Steve placed the rest of them in the back of my truck. He also picked up my sniper rifle and a couple of boxes of ammunition for it.

"What are you planning to do with that?" I asked him as he propped the rifle up in the passenger's side of the truck.

"Never hurts to have options," he replied.

I thought about pressing him on the subject, but decided against it. If the Green Beret wanted to bring a sniper rifle, then I was not going to argue with him. He was certainly qualified to use it.

I gave my other suppressor-equipped HK rifle to Stan, and told him to act as primary gunner. Cody was his backup just in case he had more targets than he could handle. I gave Cody the Sig Mosquito and the silencer for it, figuring that if they both had stealth on their side, then their chances of survival were much greater. Making sure that the town was clear of undead was going to be dangerous work for the two SWAT officers. I also gave them plenty of ammunition, and all the spare magazines that they could carry. Stan gave his SCAR to Jessica, who only had a 9mm pistol. She grinned as she looked it over.

"Hell yeah, it's nice to finally have some firepower," she said as she raised the rifle to peer through its sights.

"That thing looks good on you, lady," a woman's voice shouted from behind me.

I turned around and saw Ethan, Andrea and Stacy walking toward us. Andrea carried her husband's SCAR on a tactical sling. Ethan wore a pistol on his belt, and his fire axe rested on one broad shoulder. He had another, smaller axe tucked into his gun belt. Stacy held Aiden on one hip and carried a heaping plate of food with the other. My stomach growled when I saw breakfast coming my way.

When they reached us, Stacy handed me the plate as I leaned down to kiss her. Just as our lips met, Aiden took the opportunity to smack me on the side of my face with one grubby little hand. I flinched, and nearly dropped my plate. I straightened up and glared at the wee offender, who laughed maniacally and reached out toward me clasping and unclasping his fingers.

"He wants you to hold him," Stacy said, and smiled as she held the baby out to me.

I handed her my food and took the little guy from her. He smiled and babbled something incoherent at me. It was uncanny how much he looked like his father. He had the remains of his breakfast smeared on his chubby cheeks, and I couldn't help but laugh at him. He was a cute little fellow.

"Wish us luck today, okay buddy?" I said, and tickled him under one arm.

He giggled, and leaned into my shoulder. I gently stroked his soft hair a couple of times, and kissed him on his little baby head before handing him back to Stacy.

"You coming with us today, Andrea?" I asked.

"No. I'm just walking around with this gun because it makes me look so damn sexy," she replied.

Ethan grinned and smacked her on the rear end. "Damn right it does."

Andrea shot him an irritated glance. I pointed at the SCAR with one hand, and at Ethan with the other.

"I thought this was your rifle."

"It is, but Andrea is a better shot than I am. I prefer the direct approach," he said, patting the haft of his axe. "If things get hairy, I still have my trusty Glock."

I shrugged and took my breakfast back from Stacy.

"Okay. Whatever works for you guys. I'm going to go put some food on my stomach before we head out. See you in a little bit."

I gave Stacy another kiss, taking my time about it and ignoring the baby.

"Wanna sit with me while I eat?" I asked her.

"Sure, let's go over to your truck."

I walked back over to the Tundra and set my plate on the tailgate before taking the box of grenades and setting them on the ground. Stacy eyed the little bombs, and gave me an appraising look.

"That is some seriously dangerous stuff you have there. Where did you get those things? What are you going to do with a bunch of grenades?"

I sighed and shook my head. "My friend Gabriel gave them to me. Don't ask me why, I have no idea. I figured they might come in handy today."

I sat down on the tailgate and Stacy put Aiden down in the bed of the truck. He immediately started crawling around and making little cooing sounds as he explored the large metal box he found himself in. I turned and put my back against the sidewall so that I could watch the little guy. Stacy sat down next to me and ran one soft hand over my calf muscle. I picked up my food and dug in with gusto. I had not realized how hungry I was until I started eating. I pulled a canteen from my harness and washed down the rice and beans with lukewarm water.

"How are you feeling?" She asked me.

I looked away from the baby and saw concern in her beautiful brown eyes. I smiled and shrugged.

"I'm not afraid, if that's what you mean. I'm not really excited either. This is just something I have to do. I'm not looking forward to it, but it needs to get done. I don't know if that makes any sense."

Stacy smiled and brushed an errant eyelash off my face. "You know, me and a few of the other girls have been talking about you. We all wonder what you did before…you know…everything. I think you were an FBI agent or something."

My hand stopped mid-way up to my mouth with a spoonful of beans. I stared at her for a moment.

"Really?" I laughed a little, and shook my head. "I sorry to disappoint you, but I was just a regular guy. I never worked in law enforcement, or served in the military. In fact, the only job I ever had before the outbreak was as a financial analyst. I'm not exactly the Rambo type."

Stacy's brow furrowed, and she leaned back with a disbelieving expression.

"Are you serious? Just the other day you went out with Steve and the other guys when that bunch of creeps attacked. Ethan said you killed close to a hundred infected all by yourself. Where did you learn to fight like that?"

I opened my mouth to tell her about Gabriel teaching me how to fight when something occurred to me and I stopped short.

Let me take a moment here to bring up something that I haven't mentioned yet.

Ever since the large horde of infected attacked the compound, I had been feeling a nagging sense of unease nibbling at the back of my mind. Every couple of hours I would think about it, trying to figure out what it was that bothered me, only to wave if off like an annoying housefly. I had the same feeling that I used to get when I would walk out of the house to go to the grocery store and realize that I had neglected to grab my wallet, or when I would forget where I had left my keys. There was some important fact about the attack that should have been immediately obvious to me, but for some reason I was failing to see it. While talking to Stacy, something clicked in my mind, and I realized what it was. In his manual, Gabriel wrote about how the undead will follow any potential prey until they become distracted, or find something else to chase. I remember thinking, what if they aren't distracted? What if they don't find something else to chase?

The answer to that question was now painfully obvious to me. If they are not distracted, they keep marching toward the last source of food they detected until something else comes along to draw them away. If they do not find something else to chase, then they will follow the direction that their last potential meal ran away in for…well, until something stops them. The undead that tried to swarm the compound were not just a random assortment of infected marching in unison under the influence of a herd mentality. They were following a source of prey.

They were following me.

But that didn't mesh with what Gabriel had written about them. Did he miss something? Did I miss something? Why the sudden change in behavior? How fast could these ghouls move? A mile an hour? Less, even? The compound was several miles northeast of Alexis. Save for the stretch of road that leads there, the way to the compound consists of steep hills and dense forest. I imagined the path that the undead would have taken to reach the abandoned textile mill, and I understood why it took them so long to get there. Stacy stared at me for a long moment whilst I pondered. Eventually, she waved a hand in front of my face and leaned down to look me in the eye.

"Helloooo. Eric? Earth to Eric? What's going on, sweetie? You look like you just saw a ghost."

I shook my head to clear it, and focused on Stacy.

"I think I know why that horde attacked the other day."

Stacy's eyebrows went up. "Okay. Do you want to tell me about it?"

"They were following me. Well, both of us actually. Me and Ethan, I mean. I lured the undead to the other end of the street, and then doubled back to pick up Ethan. The infected were following me at a distance when we escaped. They must have trekked through the woods for two days to get here."

"Okay, I think I actually managed to follow that, but what difference does it make now? I mean, you and the other guys killed them all, right?"

"Yeah, we did, but that doesn't mean that it won't happen again. I'll talk to your father about it. We'll have to be more careful going forward, maybe take some extra precautions."

I put my half-eaten plate down on the tailgate and frowned. Aiden crawled over and tried to grab a handful of rice. Stacy picked him up before he could, and put him in her lap.

"Eric, are you sure you're okay?" she asked, placing a finger under my chin and turning my face up to hers.

"Yeah, I'm fine. I'm just trying to make sense of all this. I wonder if some of what Gabriel taught me about the undead might not be completely accurate. But why would what he observed about the infected be different from what they're doing now?"

"I don't know. Maybe they're learning?" Stacy said.

I looked her in the eye. "Let's hope not. If those things can learn, then we are all in deep shit."

"They can't learn."

I looked over Stacy's shoulder to see Steve standing behind her. The guy was stealthy, I never even heard him approach.

"They're dead. Their brains are dead. Anything they do is just instinct," he said.

Stacy turned and glared irritably at Steve. "And what would you know about it, exactly?"

"I've been talking to Bill. He's got some theories on how the infection works."

"What did he say?" I asked, interested.

Steve's gaze switched from Stacy to me. It was weird watching his attention shift. His entire body remained still, with no subtle shift of his balance, or turn of his neck. The only thing that moved was his eyes. He reminded me of a lion watching its prey through a stand of tall grass.

"He thinks the contagion can re-sequence DNA. He says that most of human DNA is just filler material, and with the right manipulation it can be made to do some pretty crazy things."

"Does he think the Phage could be man-made?" I asked.

Steve shrugged. "He seems to think it's possible. You should probably ask him about it sometime. In the meantime, we need to get moving."

I nodded, and handed the rest of my uneaten food to Stacy. "Alright then, let's make this shit happen."

I put the box of grenades back into the truck while Stacy took Aiden and handed him off to Emily. Emily gave me a smile and a wave, and I waved back. Stacy came back over to me, wrapped her arms around my neck, and squeezed.

"Be careful out there," she said.

"Count on it," I replied, and smiled down at her.

I gave her one last kiss, and then let her go so that I could meet the other members of the diversion team at the gun locker. When I got there, Earl was hugging Jessica, and Ethan was sharing a few whispered words with Andrea. The petite woman had slung the SCAR around to her back, and Ethan's fire axe leaned against the wall behind him. I couldn't imagine what they must be feeling, knowing that the most important person in their lives would be in danger, and that they would be unable to reach one another if they got into trouble.

I stayed quiet until the couples said their goodbyes. When Jessica and Andrea went back outside to wait in their trucks, I waved everyone over for a few last words. I noticed that Justin and Rick were carrying their new AK-47s, and had enough ammunition strapped to them to start a small war. I sincerely hoped that they wouldn't need it.

"Alright guys, small change of plans. Ethan, I need you to ride with Rick. Steve is with me in the lead truck. Steve, you want to tell us what you have planned?"

Steve stepped forward and placed his hands on his hips. "Once we get the horde moving, before we break up and split directions, I want Eric to double back to the same parking lot he used when he rescued Ethan the other day. The other two trucks will pull away, and I'll use these grenades to thin out the infected as much as possible. We'll radio back to Cody and Stan once we're clear to come in and sweep the town, just like we planned before."

Justin raised his hand, a single finger pointing upward. "Uh, Steve, do you really think that's a good idea? I mean, what if you drop a grenade or something? I don't think it's worth the risk."

Steve reached over and placed a hand on Justin's shoulder.

"I appreciate your concern, buddy, but I know what I'm doing. As long as Eric drives where I tell him to, everything will be fine."

I must admit that I was feeling a few doubts myself, but once a thing is decided its best just to see it done.

"Alright, anyone have any other questions before we get started?" I asked.

Justin still looked dubious, but no one said anything.

"Great. Do a final weapons check, and get to your trucks. We leave in five minutes," I said.

I walked back to my truck with Steve in tow. I looked over my rifle, and made sure that the safety was on, and that there was a round in the chamber. I did the same with my pistol, and placed it back in its holster. Once I had the guns squared away, I slung my small-sword across my back and adjusted it so that I could get into and out of the truck if I needed to. As an afterthought, I buckled a combat knife onto the chest strap of my load-bearing harness with the handle pointed downward.

I practiced drawing it a couple of times while Steve did a final check of his gear. Now that I was up close to it, I realized that his M1A was actually a Scout Squad version. The Scout Squad has a shorter barrel than a standard M1A, and Steve had placed a red-dot sight on the rifle's forward mounted rail. There was a twenty round clip already in the gun, and Steve had nine more of them in pouches across the middle of his tactical vest. He also had a model 1911 pistol in a holster on his right thigh, and he wore a small assault pack on his back.

When you've done as much hiking as I have, you can judge how heavy a backpack is by how it hangs against its wearer. Judging by the tension on the straps against Steve's shoulders, I was thinking that he was probably carrying at least twenty pounds of extra ammunition. Bullets were the only thing I could think of that could pack that much weight into such a small space, and still be worth bringing along. My own equipment was much lighter because the ammunition for my HK was much smaller than what Steve used in his battle-rifle. I had just as many spare rounds as he did, but at about a third of the weight. His gun might hit harder, but mine could hit more often and do it without beating my shoulder to a pulp. We weren't going after Iraqi insurgents, after all. We were going after walking corpses. Any fighting we were going to do would probably happen at less than a hundred meters. My rifle was plenty accurate, and plenty deadly, at that range.

When Steve finished checking his gear, he nodded to me and jumped nimbly over the side of my truck and into the back. An impressive feat, considering that he had at least forty pounds of equipment on him. I realized his guns were his only weapons, and got a crowbar from my pile of equipment behind the truck. He cocked an eyebrow at me when I held it out to him.

"Bludgeons don't run out of bullets. Keep it just in case," I said.

Steve seemed to think about it for a second, then gave a slight nod and took the crowbar from me. While he threaded it through the loops on his pack, I wedged my rifle up in the center console and climbed into the truck. The engine rumbled to life on the first turn of the key, just as it always did, and I drove out of the warehouse and into the bright early morning sunlight. I parked it in front of the two Silverado's that Earl and Ethan would be driving, and got out to have a quick word with both of them. After they reassured me that they were ready to go, I walked over to Bill who was a few yards away with the folks who would drive the moving trucks. Cody and Stan stood nearby beside a white work truck, and they both gave me a mock salute as I passed. Bill smiled at us and shook his head.

"You all ready to go, son?" he asked.

"As ready as we're going to get, anyway. Wish us luck." I reached out a hand, and Bill shook it.

"Good luck then. Keep me posted on the radio. If things go south, you get those guys the hell out of there, understood?"

I looked Bill in the eye and nodded. "Count on it."

I turned and walked back to my truck. Steve was sitting on the roof with his rifle across his lap. His face was impassive, and his gaze rested on the people gathered behind me.

"You want to ride up front until we get there?" I asked.

He shook his head. "Nope. I'm fine back here, just take it easy and try not to throw me out onto the road."

I nodded and climbed into the cab. A few seconds later, I pulled out of the factory parking lot and turned onto the narrow two-lane leading back toward highway 27. The other two trucks followed close behind me. It wasn't until we were actually on the road that I began to feel apprehensive. This was it. If things went wrong, I might not live to see another day. Worse, I might end up as one of the undead. I could not help but wonder if I was leading these men to their deaths. After a few moments of doubt, I shook my head to clear it and focused on driving. The time for doubts had passed. Now was the time for action. The reasons were no longer important, I had decided on a course of action and I was committed to seeing it through.

A few minutes later, we crested the last hill that stood between our little convoy and the overrun town. The throngs of undead looked significantly thinner than the last time I was there. I fervently hoped that it was a good sign, but I could not ignore the hard knot of tension forming in my gut. I slowed my truck to a stop, and the drivers behind me followed suit. After rolling down the window, I shouted to the other drivers.

"Everbody stay close until we get to the far intersection, then split up. Don't worry about Steve and I, just carry out your part of the plan. Radio for help if you get in trouble. Everyone ready?"

The other five men shouted agreement and gave me thumbs-up signals. I rolled up the window, took a deep breath, and eased off the brake.

Time to go to work.

Chapter 13

When a Plan Comes Together

I drove down the hill and checked my rearview mirror. The second truck let me get a hundred yards or so ahead and then accelerated to follow me. I was still a good quarter mile away from the main part of town, but I could already see infected heads whipping around in our direction. I realized that we would not have very long before they surrounded us, even though there seemed to be fewer undead. I increased my speed, and radioed back to the other trucks to do the same.

I reached the bottom of the hill and angled the wheel to dodge the first few infected stumbling toward us. Once I was past them, I slowed down to about twenty miles an hour and let the corpses bounce off my truck's brush guard. I checked my rear view mirror again, and I saw that I was cutting a wide swath through the undead that the vehicles behind me were driving through. The walking dead swarmed in to fill the space in our wake, but not quickly enough to trap us. I felt a fierce grin cross my face as I realized that our plan was working.

It only took me a couple of minutes to plow my way to the other end of town. The truck bounced around as the undead fell beneath the wheels. Thankfully, the sound of the infected moaning at us drowned out the crunch of crushed bones and the squelch of ruptured organs beneath the truck's tires. The undead poured toward us like floodwaters, emerging from every crack, crevice, alley, and building that we passed. When I was close to a hundred yards from the intersection where we planned to split up, I gunned the engine and put some distance between my truck and the horde. Steve slid into the side of the truck and cursed as I turned the steering wheel sharply to my right and ducked into the parking lot of the auto parts store at the end of the street. I slowed to a crawl, and watched as the other two trucks reduced speed to allow the mass of infected to catch up to them.

With the other two trucks safely out of his line of fire, Steve hopped down from the back of the truck and leveled his rifle. The big gun roared, fire erupting from the end of its barrel as he tore into the ranks of revenants staggering after us. His marksmanship was amazing. The horde was at least a hundred yards behind us, but he still managed to drop an infected with each and every shot. Even though Steve did his best to thin their ranks, revenants were joining the horde faster than he could put them down. The bastards were literally coming out of the woodwork.

I realized why there seemed to be fewer infected in town than the last time I was here. It seemed that they had wandered away in search of other prey, and the sound of vehicles and gunfire was bringing them back by the hundreds. I checked around us to make sure that nothing would sneak up on Steve, and sure enough, I saw at least a dozen undead emerging from the woods to my left. They were coming at us from every direction, but most of them seemed to have funneled into the narrow road to follow the diversion trucks. I rolled down the driver side window and took aim with my rifle. The silencer kept the report from blowing out my eardrums as I dropped the walking meat sacks, focusing on the ones closest to us. It was obvious that we could not stay where we were.

"We need to get moving, if we stay here we'll be surrounded," I shouted over my shoulder to Steve.

Steve gave me a thumbs-up, and fired off three more shots before climbing into the back of the truck. I let off the brakes and slowly drove through the adjoining parking lots to keep the undead at bay as the horde got to within twenty yards of us. The other two trucks had reached the intersection and split off in separate directions. I pulled around behind the building to my left to stay out of sight. Steve grabbed the box of grenades and stepped down onto the pavement.

"Steve! What the hell are you doing?" I said as I put the truck in park.

Steve was grinning like a mad man, and he had a wild, savage gleam in his eyes.

"Come on. I have an idea. Bring the sniper rifle with you."

I spat a vehement curse, and climbed out of the truck. Steve was already heading off toward one of the buildings nearby. I grabbed the sniper rifle, slung it over my back, and stuffed the boxes of ammunition into the cargo pockets on my pants. I trotted after Steve, and fervently hoped that he was not about to get both of us killed with whatever hare-brained stunt he was planning. When I reached him, he was using my crowbar to break a pad lock from an iron grate that covered a service ladder. We were behind what had once been a restaurant.

"What the fuck are we doing Steve? If you want to get me killed, just be a man and shoot me already." I hissed.

"Quit whining, you'll see what I'm doing in a minute. Help me break this damn lock." He replied.

Steve levered the crowbar against a steel support bar, and both of us grabbed hold and pulled downward. After a few seconds of red-faced straining, the cheap padlock broke and we nearly fell on our asses. Steve opened the iron grate door and pulled a bundle of parachute cord out of his back pocket. He bent down, looped the cord through the grenade box handles, and tied a slipknot at the end. He climbed the ladder and let the cord spool out behind him. I kept my rifle at the ready, and scanned the area behind us for any undead. The buildings on either side of us were a police station and a bank, and they both protruded farther toward the wood line than the little restaurant did. We were in a U-shaped bend between them, which limited my line of sight. I heard Steve snap his fingers several times above me, and I turned to look at him.

"Come on up." He said.

I climbed the ladder as quickly as I could. Steve stepped to the edge of the roof and pulled the box of grenades up with the para-cord. I squatted down and low-crawled to the edge of the building closest to the street. The building had a false front that rose up three feet from the end of the roof. It gave us good concealment to hide behind. I poked my head up over it and peered southward. The other two trucks were still slowly proceeding out of town with a large crowd of infected following close behind. Ethan and Justin were standing in the trucks waving their arms and shouting obscenities at the infected to keep their attention. It looked like the diversion was working.

So far, so good.

I turned around to see what Steve was doing. He crouched low and carried the box of grenades over to where I lay.

"How's your throwing arm?" he asked, still grinning like a lunatic.

I shook my head and looked back down to the other end of the road. The center of the infected horde was ten yards past the building where we were hiding. All of their attention was riveted to the meals-on-wheels leading them out of town. Steve took a grenade out of the box and handed it to me.

"You know how to use one of these?" he asked.

I almost said no, but then I remembered that Gabriel had taught me how to use them. Grenades are pretty simple, really. Pull the pin, release the spoon, and throw the green ball of metal at the thing that you want to blow up. Take cover, wait for the explosion, and repeat as necessary. Steve didn't wait for me, he pulled the pin and hurled his grenade directly into the center of the horde. I watched in horrid fascination as the little bomb detonated, sending a sphere of gore, blood, and severed limbs flying into the air. Before realizing what I was doing, I pulled the pin on my own grenade and did the same thing.

The undead following the trucks barely seemed to notice. They couldn't tell which direction the bombs were coming from, and didn't seem to care. I wondered if there was enough cognitive capacity left in their rotten brains for them to grasp what was happening to them. Steve put the box of grenades between us, and we lobbed bomb after bomb into the tightly packed mob of revenants. At some point, I realized that the both of us were giggling and snickering like a couple of schoolboys every time a grenade tore a hole in their ranks. As I did my grisly work, I vaguely wondered if I had the same crazed smile on my face that Steve did.

"Dude, this is so fucking freaky," I said, struggling to hold back a bout of hysterical laughter.

"I know. I don't know why I think it's so funny when they blow up like that." Steve laughed as he tossed another grenade.

When we had thrown all but five of the grenades, Steve tapped me on the shoulder and pointed at the sniper rifle slung across my back. I took it off and handed it to him, as well as the boxes of cartridges. Steve came up to a kneeling position and propped the sniper rifle on top of the false front. He flipped the lens covers off the scope and peered through it at the horde that was slowly moving away from us.

"How well does the suppressor on this thing work?" he asked.

"Pretty good," I replied. "Let them get a hundred yards or so away before you open up. They shouldn't be able to triangulate us from that range."

Steve cast me a quizzical glance "What do you mean 'triangulate us'?"

"The infected have some kind of weird ability that enhances their hearing. Didn't you read a copy of that manual Bill passed around?"

"No, I haven't gotten around to it yet." Steve turned back to the scope and sighted through it.

"Well, you should. Assuming we get out of this alive, that is."

Steve smiled as he swiveled the barrel from target to target.

"You worry too much. If worse comes to worse, we can shoot our way out of here."

"I'd rather it not come to that," I said.

We waited for a few minutes while the diversion trucks put some distance between our position and the horde. The grenades had not done as much damage as I had hoped they would. We had taken out a total of maybe twenty or thirty infected. More than twice that number were blown apart or knocked down by the blasts, but were still not out of

259

commission. Several of them dragged shattered legs or stumps of ragged, bloody torsos behind them as they crawled in pursuit of the horde. I tapped Steve on the shoulder and pointed to them.

"Take the crippled ones out first, they're the most dangerous."

"How do you figure?" Steve asked, looking up from the scope.

"They're low to the ground. The folks coming behind us might not see them. All it takes is one bite on the leg, and its game over," I replied.

Steve thought about it for a moment, then nodded in agreement. He shifted his aim, and started eliminating the crawlers. If his accuracy was impressive with a battle-rifle, then his work with the sniper rig was nearly superhuman. He went from target to target, painting the asphalt with their brains faster than I would have been able to from close range with my HK. The speed at which he could sight in and fire was quite a thing to behold.

While Steve went to work killing the infected, it occurred to me that I must have undergone some kind of drastic psychological change over the last few months. Before the outbreak, the sight of all that bloody carnage would have had me spewing my guts out. After everything I had seen and been through, even in that short amount of time, I had become inured to the sight of guts and gore. I wondered what else about me was going to change in the days to come. Steve interrupted my thoughts by touching me on the arm.

"Come on, let's get to the truck and radio the sweep team."

I stood up into a crouch and surveyed as much of the town as I could see. Steve had dispatched all of the crawlers, and I didn't see any infected coming in our direction. The horde had split into two groups, and the closest of them were just disappearing over the hills to the south of us. Steve clipped the last five grenades to his tactical vest and slung the sniper rifle over his back. We left the empty grenade box on the roof and climbed down the ladder to the street below.

Steve switched to his M1A as I brought up my rifle and scanned around. We moved to the edge of the building to our right and checked both directions. The way was clear. We double-timed it to the truck and climbed in the cab. I picked up the radio and pressed the button to talk.

"This is Eric, everybody check in, over."

Rick and Earl both responded at the same time. I told Rick to go first, and for God's sake say 'over' when he was finished. Rick advised that he and Ethan were half a mile from town and would stay on the road for another two miles before doubling back. Earl gave a similar report. I was relieved to hear that the divided hordes were following the diversion team just like we had planned. I asked if they needed any assistance from us, and both drivers declined. I looked at Steve, and he shrugged.

"I know we planned for three trucks, but it looks like two is getting the job done just fine. Let's just radio the sweep team, and help them clear the town."

I agreed and keyed the radio. Once I had Cody and Stan inbound, I drove the truck back onto the main highway and waited for them in the Burger King parking lot. The undead that Ethan and I had shot were still strewn about the pavement, maggot ridden and rotting in the hot sun. The smell was terrible. Now that the fighting had died down, scores of vultures returned to feast on the dead flesh littering the highway. There must have been more than a hundred dead bodies, and pieces of bodies, in varying states of decay.

When Stan and Cody arrived, I got out of the truck and walked over to greet them. Stan was driving, and Cody stood in the back bracing himself against the roof. When Stan slowed his vehicle to a halt, Cody hopped down and surveyed the carnage around us.

"Jesus Christ," he whispered.

His eyes went wide when he stepped out onto the highway and saw the mass of rotting corpses scattered down the road.

"We have to do something about all those dead bodies," Cody said.

Stan got out of the truck and walked over to stand beside Cody. The normally stoic police officer paled noticeably as he took in the horror that had befallen Alexis. The ground in front of every building glittered with broken glass. Shattered windows gaped at us like empty eye sockets. Swarms of flies buzzed from corpse to corpse, and scattered before the flapping wings of vultures that tore bloody strips from the dead bodies. Burned out shells of buildings tottered at dangerous angles, threatening to fall at the slightest touch. Waist-high grass and weeds choked the ground where the concrete and pavement didn't cover it. Even those places had the beginnings of plants and trees sprouting up between the cracks, potholes, and crevices that no one was coming to repair.

"Come on guys," I said. "Cody's right, let's see if we can use the trucks to clear out all these corpses."

Cody and Stan nodded slowly. Steve motioned toward the strip mall down the road from us. "There's a hardware store over there. Let's search it for something we can use to move the bodies."

"Good thinking. You guys take up firing positions outside the door, and I'll see if I can draw out any creeps in there," I said.

We walked over and formed a firing line in front of the store. Steve covered the door, while Cody and Stan watched our flanks. I took my crowbar from Steve and used it to bang loudly on the steel frame around the entrance. I peered through dusty glass into the dark interior looking for movement, and cursed myself for not remembering to bring a flashlight. After a minute or two went by with no sign of movement from inside, I tried to use the crowbar to break the lock. It was too strong. Stan suggested that I try breaking the hinges instead. After straining, grunting, and cursing, I finally managed to pry the door open. We stood outside and waited for a few moments. No undead appeared, so we went inside. I waited outside and guarded the exit while the other three cleared the hardware store. They did not find any infected inside, but they did find several large boxes of heavy blue tarps. I opened one of the boxes and nodded in satisfaction.

"These will do nicely. I'll pull my truck around," I said.

Stan and I were the biggest and physically strongest of the group, so we handled moving the bodies. I found a box of shop towels in the hardware store, and we tied them around our faces to ward off some of the stench as we worked. Cody and Steve kept watch as Stan and I rolled the bodies onto the tarps and dragged them into the middle of the highway. I could tell Stan was having a hard time keeping his revulsion in check. He struggled on manfully until one of the bodies we picked up fell apart. The leg Stan was pulling on came away at the hip with a crunch and a horrid sucking sound. The body fell to the ground, and its swollen stomach burst open spilling putrid entrails out onto the pavement. Stan dropped the leg, ran a few steps away, and heaved his guts out onto the ground. I didn't blame him, I almost lost it myself.

We spent the better part of an hour clearing buildings and dragging corpses out into the street. Once we had used up all of the tarps, I hitched them to my truck's winch by the anchor loops, and dragged them onto a wide lawn behind a small church at the southern end of town. Stan rode shotgun and helped me roll the bodies onto the grass. Once the first batch was clear, we folded the tarps up and put them in the back of the truck. Stan and I sat down on the tailgate for a few minutes to drink some water and catch our breath.

"Any particular reason you chose a church yard to dump the bodies?" Stan asked.

"It just seemed fitting," I said. "If we can't give them a proper burial, the least we can do is let them return to the Earth on hallowed ground."

Stan's face grew pensive, and he was silent for a while.

"Do you still believe in God?" he asked, staring out across the ruined town.

I shrugged. "I don't know. Before the outbreak I would have said yes, but now…"

Stan nodded. We got up and went back to work moving the dead. While clearing the storeroom of a Laundromat, Stan nearly got jumped by a couple of infected. Cody put them down with my Sig .22. They were a man and a woman, and both of them looked to be in their mid-thirties. They were both Asian, and I guessed that they owned the place before the outbreak. The woman had only a bite mark on one arm, but the man was missing most of his face, throat, and left shoulder. They must have barricaded themselves into the storeroom after the woman became infected. Sometime after that, she turned and went after the man trapped inside with her. They spent the next three months locked up together, unable to get out of the room. Stan checked their hands, and noticed that they wore matching wedding bands. I think he had tears in his eyes as he stood up, but I didn't say anything. I knew how he felt.

The last place we cleared was Alan McMurray's gun store. The scene was laid out exactly as Ethan had described it. I understood what Ethan meant when he said that the undead worked Alan over pretty badly. There wasn't much left on the bones, and what we found was scattered around the room in pieces.

We were a tired, sweat drenched, somber group of men by the time I radioed for Bill to bring in the moving trucks. The four of us climbed into the back of my Tundra and sat silently on the sidewalls as we waited for the others to arrive. Rick and Earl radioed in to let us know that they had ditched the creeps following them and were making their way back to town. Earl led his group of infected over the edge of a steep hill that descended into a creek. Rick drove his truck into a big cornfield and used a farm trail to get back to the road, leaving the horde behind. Even if the infected turned and pursued them back to town, it would be days before they reached us, being as far away as they were.

Bill arrived in short order with a caravan of vehicles behind him. Their first stop was the gun store. It took them two hours and three trips back and forth to the compound to empty all the supplies from the basement. I could only guess at how long it took Alan to stockpile everything he kept down there. There were five entire pallets of 5.56mm military grade ammunition. Each pallet consisted of eighty thousand rounds. I thought Steve's eyes were going to pop out of his head when he saw them. Old Alan must have had a hard-on for AR-15 rifles, because there were enough of them down there to give one to all of the survivors, and still have a few left over. Steve suggested to Bill that he let him start training the others to use the weapons as soon as possible.

I helped load the supplies onto the trucks, and I was amazed at the volume and variety of weapons we found. There were hunting rifles in every caliber imaginable, shotguns, pistols, AK-47's, M1A's (much to Steve's delight), and we even found five Barrett .50 caliber sniper rifles. There was much more, but I lost track of it after a while. In addition to the massive amount of 5.56mm ammo, there were thousands of rounds in more calibers than I could count. The guns and ammo by themselves would have been worth the trip, but they were just the beginning of what we found. There was enough food down there for a man to survive on for several years. Once divided amongst the survivors it would only last for a few months, but it was nice to know that no one would be going hungry any time soon.

Once we had cleaned out Alan's shop, we spent the rest of the day pillaging any building that did not look like it was about to collapse. The two diversion teams returned midway through the afternoon and received a warm welcome. Bill was practically jumping up and down with excitement. His mood was contagious, and all of the survivors were in high spirits. Every time I turned around someone was offering a handshake, or giving me a pat on the back. My esteem amongst the other survivors seemed to increase dramatically once it was clear that my plan had worked. I shrugged off the gratitude, and pointed out the fact that I really hadn't done very much.

Andrea stayed close to me throughout the afternoon, and I was grateful for her presence. I smelled horrible after handling all those corpses, but she did not seem to mind. After six long hours of work, Bill called a halt and ordered everyone to pack up and head back to the compound. There were a few complaints at that, as there were still many buildings yet to search, but Bill reminded them that the town wasn't going anywhere. They could come back for the rest later.

The people who stayed behind at the compound had been kind enough to set up showers for us. Bill gave the diversion and sweep teams first go at them. Once we cleaned up, Bill and Andrea looked us over for any signs of infection. They gave us all a clean bill of health. Stacy brought me a change of clothes from my suitcase, and hugged me tightly as she gave them to me.

"I can't tell you how happy I am right now," she said.

I laughed and put my hands around her pretty face. She leaned in and I kissed her soft, warm lips. When I stepped back, her beautiful brown eyes smoldered.

"I don't care how tired you are. You come to me after you get something to eat. Got it?"

I smiled and hugged her again. "Yes, ma'am."

Dinner that night was mac and cheese, pinto beans, cornbread, and grilled Spam. It was one of the best damn meals I've ever eaten in my entire life. It is amazing how much better food tastes after a hard day's work.

Chapter 14

Decisions

Me, and a dozen or so other people, spent a few days running back and forth to Alexis collecting supplies. We stripped the place bare, and wound up with so much stuff that we ran out of space in the warehouse to store it. Bill had to assign a team to start clearing the factory floor. Ethan organized a task group of seven people to inventory everything we brought in. When we finally sorted and counted everything, the compound had enough food put by to last at least an entire year. They also had a large inventory of weapons, and more than five-hundred thousand rounds of ammunition.

A few days after our first raid, Bill caught up with me during breakfast. I was sitting at a picnic table with Stacy, Ethan, and Andrea. Bill made small talk during the meal, and when everyone got up to go about the day's work, the old surgeon asked if he could have a word with me in private. I agreed and followed him to the roof of the warehouse. Bill told the people on watch to take a break, and after they had gone back inside, Bill walked over to the eastern side of the roof. The air already smelled of burning flesh from the furnace in the factory. Work teams were still incinerating the remains of the four hundred or so infected that attacked the compound a little over a week ago.

"So how are things going between you and Stacy?" he asked.

I frowned, and looked down at the tarred roof between my feet. "I was wondering when you were going to get around to this."

Bill half turned to look at me. "She is my daughter, after all. She's the only family I have left. I don't think I'm stepping out of line by asking what your intentions are."

I thought about it for a moment, and finally shook my head. "I don't know, Bill. She's beautiful, intelligent, kind, and she has a great sense of humor. Stacy is everything a man can ask for in a woman."

"But..." Bill said.

"I had plans before I came here," I replied.

"Your friend, Gabriel."

I nodded. "I promised him I would find him once things settled down."

"And you still feel the need to satisfy that promise?"

"I do. Then again, I can't help but see that we have a good thing going here. We have plenty of supplies, and its safe here. Well, as safe as any place can be, I guess."

"I understand that you are in a difficult position. Just do me one favor, Eric." Bill stepped close to me and laid a hand on my shoulder. "Be good to my Stacy. She's suffered a lot. Don't hurt her any more than she's already been hurt."

I looked him in his watery blue eyes for a moment before responding. "I promise to try. You never know how these things will turn out."

Bill smiled and patted my shoulder. "Fair enough."

He turned and walked back to the edge of the roof. The sun was cresting over the green hills in the distance. There was a slight chill in the air, and a low fog lingered over the treetops. It was early October, but the weather stays warm in North Carolina well into the fall.

"I want you to know how grateful I am for everything that you've done for us," he said, gazing off into the distance.

"I'm just glad I could help," I replied.

"You're a good man, Eric. You did a good thing for all of us here. Come what may, don't ever forget that."

I nodded, and smiled. "Thanks, Bill. I appreciate that."

The dark cloud hanging over Steve since the death of his brother seemed to lift in the weeks after the raid. Steve and I were not exactly friends, but we had a decent working relationship. We respected each other, and Steve began stepping up his efforts to train the other survivors. He set up some targets and instructed everyone, including the children old enough to handle a rifle, in the proper way to shoot. He insisted that everyone learn using iron sights, and issued optics to those who proved themselves the most proficient. I volunteered to pitch in on the training where I could. My marksmanship was good, but Steve's was superior. I told Steve about my years of martial arts training, and he and I sparred a few rounds to see what I could do. Steve was good, but I managed to impress him by getting the better of him in most bouts. He had me teach classes to the other survivors twice a day.

Bill assigned Justin a full time job as the compound's armorer. There was so much ordnance to keep track of that Bill felt it necessary to put someone in charge of it all. Justin turned out to be a great choice for the job. He was smart, mature beyond his years, and he had a good eye for detail. Justin got some more good news a couple of weeks later.

Emily was pregnant.

She confided in Andrea not long after I arrived that she had missed her period. She and Justin were not particularly careful about things, and she had a strong suspicion that she was carrying a baby. One of the businesses in Alexis that we raided was a pharmacy, and Andrea quietly procured a couple of home pregnancy tests. Emily used them on separate days, and Bill confirmed that she was most likely six weeks along. At first, she was mortified. She broke down in tears and told Bill about how she got drunk on wine and tequila the first night I was here. The old doctor reassured her that one bout of drinking was not likely to do any permanent damage, especially considering how young she was. He told her to take care of herself, avoid caffeine and alcohol, and let him know if she had any problems.

Justin took the news pretty well. He became much more attentive and concerned for Emily once Bill confirmed that she was carrying his child. I have to admit to being worried for her as well. Modern medicine was a thing of the past. Having a doctor and a nurse around improved her chances, but bearing a child is a risky proposition under the best of circumstances. I suggested to Bill that he choose a few bright prospects to pass on some of his medical knowledge to. For all we knew, he could be the last living medical doctor on the face of the Earth. He took my advice and started classes with a few students the following week.

I wish I could say that my relationship with Stacy deepened, but it didn't. I kept busy most days between combat training, scouting for supplies, and guard duty. I still came to her bed most nights, but our lovemaking no longer had the hot, heady rush one feels in a new relationship. It was just an emotional release for the two of us. We both put on a brave face for the other survivors, but deep down inside, we were hurting. We spoke less and less to one another as the weeks went by. I noticed that she spent more and more time with Noah Salinger, and I decided that I was okay with that. Noah was a nice guy.

I also decided that it would be time for me to go soon. I was waiting for something, but I was not quite sure what it was. My last two weeks at the compound were what cinched it for me. The housing development that Justin and Rick discovered became our focus after we stripped Alexis of anything that might be remotely useful. It took a lot of effort to clear out all the corpses in the development, but we managed to get it done. Greg and a few others started working on ways that they could better secure the neighborhood's perimeter and start moving some of the families into homes there. Ethan and Andrea were thrilled with the idea of having an actual house to live in, and not just a shack on the warehouse floor. Aiden was starting to walk, and I imagined him toddling around in a well-tended yard. It was a nice thought.

Unfortunately, we were not the only ones who had eyes on the neighborhood.

Steve spotted the trouble first. One day while he and I were doing an assessment of the security fence around the development, we noticed signs of other people having been there recently. Steve found footprints, broken twigs, and other indications that I never would have spotted on my own. It was obvious that it was not the kind of clumsy, aimless trail that the undead leave behind. Steve and I carefully followed the tracks as silently as we could, weapons at the ready. We found the ashes of several small campfires, discarded cans, empty water bottles, and human excrement a few hundred yards beyond the fence line. Steve carefully examined each camp that we found. He estimated that at least nine people had been there less than three days ago.

"Well that begs an obvious question," I said. "Where did they come from?"

"And how long have they been watching this place?" Steve added.

We were silent for a long moment in the shadow of the tall pines, maybe hoping that the ashes and garbage might produce some answers. We told Bill about what we found and suggested that he call a meeting. Bill agreed, and the next day we detailed everything we saw to the other survivors. There was a lot of back and forth, and conflicting opinions about how we should handle it. Bill suggested that Steve, Cody, and Stan conduct an investigation and see what they could find out. I volunteered to go with them. That seemed to make everyone happy. We were to track the other survivors and attempt to make contact with them, then find out if they were interested in joining the community. At least that is what we told everyone.

Our real purpose was to assess the threat that this new group posed to us. The campsites we found gave the people using them a good vantage point from which to watch the housing development. They had clearly been there long enough to notice us working among the houses below, clearing out dead bodies. We figured that if they were friendly, they most likely would have tried to make contact by now. Steve guessed that they probably were trying to determine our strength. Maybe they wanted the development for themselves. That didn't make much sense to me, considering that there was ample room for hundreds of people to live there, but I never underestimate the human capacity for stupidity.

We outfitted ourselves with camouflage battle fatigues, and Steve showed us how to use face paint to conceal our exposed skin. He gave us some pointers on moving quietly through dense foliage, and we spent a few hours practicing out in the woods. We were not skilled woodsmen by any stretch of the imagination, but we didn't sound like bull elephants either. The trick was to use the natural sounds of the forest to mask your movements, move slowly, watch where you step, and not walk at a steady pace. Easier said than done.

Since stealth was our goal, we only took weapons with suppressors. We found a few M4 rifles that were equipped with them from when we raided Alan's gun shop. Cody and Steve each took one, and I gave Stan my other H&K carbine. I brought my Kel-Tec and loaned Steve the sniper rifle. Cody took the Sig Mosquito. We did not have any other pistols with silencers, so Stan and Steve brought .45 caliber handguns with them. They promised not to use them unless they had no other choice. Steve fitted some good quality optics to the M4's, and I gave Stan my other red-dot sight. After a few rounds of discussion, we decided that Steve would function as both point man and, if necessary, as sniper. Cody would be our designated hitter if we encountered any undead. The Sig was the quietest gun we had, and if possible we would use it exclusively to kill any infected we came across. Stan and I were riflemen, and we would open fire only if Cody and Steve ran into something they couldn't handle on their own.

The radios we used had headsets that plugged directly into the handset, and a toggle switch that connected to an earpiece. They allowed us to communicate quietly and effectively, even when out of sight of one another. The four of us brought assault packs with food, extra ammo, first aid kits, water, and spare batteries for the radios. We each loaded ten thirty-round magazines, one in our rifles, and the other nine on our tactical vests. I still preferred my load-bearing harness, but the MOLLE gear let me carry more ammo. Steve had a pair of military issue night vision goggles that he brought along. I thought about asking him where he got them, but decided against it. What difference did it make?

The night before we left, we spent a couple of hours studying maps of the housing development and discussing the terrain around it. We wanted to make sure that everyone knew the lay of the land, and established a couple of different rally points in case we got separated. Our first rally point was the water tower that Justin and Rick discovered. If that was a no-go, then we would meet at an abandoned gas station a half mile north of the development. If all else failed, we agreed to retreat back to the compound. Steve and I got together with Bill, and discussed beefing up security around the compound. After he agreed to do so, we called it a night.

We set out well before dawn the next day. Steve used his night vision goggles and his radio to guide us through the dense forest. We could talk to each other by simply pressing a button on the cord connecting the earpiece to the handset. Push to talk, release to listen. Easy. We reached the housing development under cover of darkness, and Steve set each of us up near the security fence where we had a wide field of view. He took a little time to help us conceal ourselves into the landscape before moving on. When all three of us were in position, he set out to do a little reconnaissance.

"Everybody stay alert, and stay quiet. Make sure your rifles have a round chambered and safeties off. Keep your eyes open, and report anything unusual. Cody, be ready to move if anyone spots a creep. Radio check at five minute intervals. Any questions?" Steve asked.

No one responded.

"Okay. If I run into a situation where I can't send a radio check, I'll just key the mike three times, so keep your ears open."

Everything Steve said were things we had gone over the day before, but it made him feel better to say it. I spent the next couple of hours trying not to move around too much or let my mind wander off. I tried not to think about my rapidly filling bladder, or the bugs that buzzed and crawled around my face. I marked time on my wristwatch, and checked in every five minutes. The only movement I saw was tree squirrels, birds, and a small herd of deer that wandered by about a hundred yards to the south. Steve had positioned my post so that my back was facing east. I felt the sun warming my back as it rose above the horizon. Sunlight filtered through the pine and oak boughs above me, dappling the forest floor with scattered patches of golden light. I was just about to initiate another radio check when I heard my earpiece click three times. I clicked once in response, just like we had planned. There was a ten-second delay, and another click. That one was Cody. Another ten seconds, and another click from Stan.

From here on out, we would check in by keying the talk button on the handset until Steve gave the all clear. I hoped the batteries would hold up. Another hour went by before we heard from Steve. My bladder was a burning ball of pain in my mid-section, and my stomach was growling for food when he finally checked in.

"This is Steve," he said in a low, hushed voice. "Proceed to second rally point. Move slow and quiet. Maintain comms with each other, but do it quietly. We have company. I think they are well away from you, but don't take any chances. If I'm not at the rally point in an hour, bug out and head back for the compound."

We all gave a quick affirmative, and I started making my way to the backup rally point. I moved low and slow, making as little noise as possible. I found a thick tangle of kudzu that covered a copse of dead pine trees, and hunkered down behind it. It made good cover, and I used the opportunity to take a much-needed piss. With my bladder empty, it was a lot easier to concentrate on controlling my movements. My stomach was growling something fierce, so I dug a protein bar out of my cargo pocket and washed it down with water from my canteen. I could deal with the hunger, but I did not want noise from my groaning stomach to give away my position.

I didn't run into any trouble on my way to the gas station. I keyed my radio and asked if anyone else was there yet. Cody was hiding behind the tree line a few yards behind the building. Stan was still inbound and estimated it would be fifteen minutes before he got there. I stuck to the woods, and Cody guided me to his position over the radio. I spotted him sitting behind a large fallen oak tree, sweeping the road and the parking lot through the scope on his M4. I gave a low whistle, and he turned toward me. I held my hand down at knee level and waved it a few times. Cody spotted it and motioned me forward.

I low crawled slowly to where he sat, and kept my head down behind the tree. Cody had everything beyond the tree line covered, so I put my back against the massive log and watched our flanks. Stan arrived not long after, and he and I crawled away from Cody's position to try and get a better view of our surroundings. We made it to the top of a low hill not far away, and used Stan's binoculars to scan the surrounding forest.

"So what do you think is happening with Steve?" he asked.

"I don't know, but he definitely found our friends from the neighborhood," I replied. "There must be some problem with the water tower. We were only supposed to come here if the tower was compromised."

"I'm thinking our new friends found the tower and are using it for themselves," Stan said.

"You're probably right. Not much we can do about it right now, though. I'm going to head over to that hollow to the north," I said, and pointed. Stan nodded. "Cody has a good spot, and you should be fine up here. If I can get up there, we'll have a three way crossfire set up for anybody with bad intentions. We can use optics to watch each other's backs."

Stan covered me, and I made my way to the hollow. I climbed about halfway up one of the hillsides, and took position behind a massive boulder jutting upward from the ground. I had a good view of Stan's position, and I could cover anyone stupid enough to skyline themselves over the ridge to my left. Cody could see me and watch out for anyone coming over the hill behind me. Being spread out as we were, even if one of us got blindsided, the other two could back him up. Once we all settled in, it simply became a matter of waiting.

Half an hour went by. It was silent save for the sounds of the forest. I was accustomed to the buzz of cicadas, the chirp of sparrows and marlins, and the rustling of pine branches overhead. I could pick out noises not made by the woods, or the creatures living in it. My hackles went up when I heard a faint, droning hum in the far distance to the northwest. The gas station was directly in front of me, and the noise was approaching from my right, heading southeast. It was definitely a vehicle, and it sounded like it was going to pass by right in front of me. The nearest road to us was over a mile away, and judging by the increasing rumble, the car had not turned down it.

Within a minute, I saw a pickup truck crest the hilltop less than half a mile from where I sat. A painted camouflage motif covered the exterior. It had an array of lights across the roof and thick roll cage bars slanting between the cab and the bed. A brush guard similar to the one on my own truck covered the grill, and the body floated nearly a foot above the wheels on a high lift kit. Huge swamp tires with thick, deep treads beat a rapid staccato thrum across the pavement as it approached. Three men stood in the back hanging on to the roll cage with the barrels of assault rifles protruding over their shoulders. From my vantage, I could make out the outline of the driver, and another person in the passenger seat.

"We have five people inbound," I said into the radio. "At least three are packing heat, so assume they all are. Stay quiet, stay out of sight. Over."

Stan and Cody gave short affirmatives, and I watched the truck begin to slow down. The annoying roar from the tires lowered in pitch until individual slaps of rubber on tar echoed into the hills. With all that damned noise, these idiots were ringing a dinner bell for any infected within a half mile radius. As they pulled closer, I noticed a sixth person in the bed of the truck. Someone had bound him hand and foot, and he appeared to be unconscious.

"Oh shit, please tell me that is not Steve," I mumbled.

The truck rolled to a halt between the pumps under the gas station awning. I slowly pulled a small pair of binoculars out of my tactical vest and peered at the person in the back of the truck. It wasn't Steve. His hair was black, matted and filthy. Steve has sandy blond hair almost the same color as my own. My instincts were warning me that something was not right about this, but the reasonable part of my brain was telling me not to jump to conclusions. Anyone possessing an ounce of desire for self-preservation would be carrying a weapon these days, and the men in the truck might have had a good reason for restraining the individual in the back. I tried to get a better look at him, but he had his back to me. Just as I was about to radio Cody and Stan, I heard the mike click.

"This is Steve, how copy? Over."

About fucking time. I thought.

"Eric here, loud and clear," I said in a low voice.

Cody and Stan responded by keying the radio three times. The gunmen probably couldn't hear them from where they were, but the two SWAT officers weren't taking any chances.

The other two people inside the cab got out with rifles clutched in their fists. The driver had a pistol holstered on his right hip.

"Eric, Stan, I have your positions. Cody, I'm guessing you're behind the gas station in my blind spot. Give me one click for every ten yards you estimate between you and the pumps. Over."

My earpiece clicked four times. I approved of his estimate.

"Cody, do you have a visual on all five hostiles? Click once for yes, twice for no. Over."

I heard two clicks.

There was a pause. Steve probably took a moment to say something four lettered and colorful. In the ensuing silence, the word 'hostiles' echoed in my mind. Steve must have known something we didn't. He had also managed to spot Stan and me, even though we were both well hidden in the thick undergrowth. Impressive.

"Steve, Eric. How do we know they're hostile? Over."

"Trust me. I'll explain later. We need to take these bastards out. Don't shoot the driver, he's the one with a pistol on his hip, and the tall guy in jean shorts, hiking boots, and a baseball cap. I'll take those two personally, I want at least one of them alive. Cody, you take the one with the denim jacket sitting on the yellow barrier. Stan, the fucktard with the ponytail is yours. Eric, you take the one still standing in the back of the truck. Aim high, I don't want you to hit the hostage. Everyone clear?"

I hesitated for a moment. I was first in line to respond, and I knew nothing would happen until I did. I had never killed a living person before. I knew it was a possibility when I volunteered to come along on this foray, but the concept of shooting a man and actually doing it are two very different things.

"Steve, are you sure about this?" I asked. "If you're wrong, then we are about to be murderers. Over."

"I'm sure," Steve responded immediately. "These assholes are a bunch of sick fucks. We have to help the guy they have tied up. They're going to torture him and kill him. Eric, we are out of time, these guys won't be stopped for long."

The men below were moving boxes and small crates into the back of the truck. It looked like they were using the abandoned gas station as a supply depot. The man Steve told me to cover jumped down out of the back and took a large gas can from one of the others. He turned it upside down and started pouring into the fuel tank. I raised my rifle and drew a bead on his heart. I was only a little over a hundred yards away from him, and I was confident I could make the shot.

"You better be right. I'm ready. Over."

"Good. Cody, Stan, one click yes, two no. You ready?"

One click for yes. A delay, one click for yes.

"Fire on my mark. Ready…mark."

I squeezed the trigger. The bullet hit my target in the center of his chest and slightly to the right, straight through the heart. There was a nearly comical look of surprise on his face as he looked down at the bloodstain blossoming from a hole in his chest. The bullet must have missed his spine on the way out because he remained standing. A couple of seconds later, the blood in his brain began to run out of oxygen, and he collapsed to the ground dropping the gas can as he fell. The silencer did its job. The man I killed never heard the shot that ended his life.

Off to my left, the man who drove the truck into the gas station screamed when his right elbow disintegrated. For about a second and a half, the man standing beside him gaped at his wounded companion as he clutched his arm before Steve fired again and took his scrawny arm off at the shoulder. He stood frozen, a look of shock and disbelief etched on his face as he looked at the blood pumping rhythmically from the stump where his arm used to be. A second later his left leg gave out as his knee exploded and he collapsed like a rag doll, screaming in agony.

The man sitting on the yellow traffic barrier slumped to the ground when most of the top half of his cranium exploded courtesy of Cody's marksmanship. Stan's target jerked twice and fell down dead as two 5.56mm rounds ripped through his chest. It was all over in less than three seconds.

"Converge now. Move!" Steve ordered over the radio.

We emerged from our hiding places and sprinted toward the gas station. Steve emerged from the woods on the other side of the road from me, only about fifty yards away. I was watching that direction, and I never saw him moving into position. I was suddenly very glad that the former Green Beret was on our side.

I reached the fallen men a few seconds behind Cody and Steve. Stan was farther away, and it was another ten seconds or so before he arrived. Three of the men in front of me lay in dark, expanding pools of blood. Two of them were still, but the one I shot twitched spasmodically in his death throes. One of the two men that Steve shot, the one with a missing arm and a raw, bloody tangle where his knee used to be, was screaming like a banshee and begging for help. The other one had slumped down against the side of the camouflage truck. His face was pale from blood loss, and his lower left arm was hanging on by a strip of flesh and a prayer. He had taken off his belt and tied it around his bicep as a makeshift tourniquet. I had to give the guy credit, even though he was severely wounded and surrounded by enemies, he was still thinking.

Cody and Stan wore grim expressions. Killing people outright went against everything they had once stood for as police officers. It was obvious that they were not happy with this situation. Neither was I, for that matter. I hoped for Steve's sake that he had a very good reason for asking us to shoot these men, otherwise there was going to be hell to pay.

Steve slid the sniper rifle around to his back as he knelt down in front of the man leaning against the truck.

"Where are the others?" He asked.

The man looked up at Steve with raw hatred. He looked to be in his mid-forties, bald, with a heavy gut protruding over his legs.

"Go fuck yourself," he said with a thick, drawling accent.

Steve stood up and stepped forward, delivering a swift kick to the wreckage of the man's arm. He cried out and clutched his tourniquet, spewing a stream of curses at Steve.

"Wrong answer," Steve said, his voice flat. "I can do this all day buddy. I'm not even warmed up yet. Let's try this again. Where...are...the...others?"

Steve punctuated each word of his last sentence with a little kick to the man's ruined elbow. He flinched and hissed at each one.

"I ain't tellin' you shit. Just fucking shoot me and get it over with, you cocksuckin' faggot."

Steve responded by unsheathing his combat knife, grabbing one of the man's legs, and casually severing his Achilles tendon. The wounded man let forth a high-pitched squeal of agony. He fell over onto his side sobbing from the pain. Steve kneeled down and grabbed the man's other ankle. His blade bit into his skin just barely enough to draw blood.

"You're going to die. Nothing can save you from that. The only thing you can control right now is whether you die quickly, or slowly. Personally, I hope you pick slow. It's no less than you deserve."

Steve's yellowish eyes were empty and cold, like a hungry reptile. His face was completely devoid of any hint of expression. This man could kill and torture someone with as much effort as it took me to tie my shoes. I looked at Cody and Stan, and they were both edging away nervously. Steve ignored us and focused on the poor dumb bastard in front of him. I realized that the other wounded man had stopped screaming and looked over at him. He was unconscious. I couldn't tell if he was still breathing or not.

"Okay, okay, I'll tell you, just don't cut me again, please."

He laid his head down on the ground against the concrete, crying like a baby. Steve looked almost disappointed. I shivered.

"I'm listening," Steve said, not taking the knife away from the man's leg.

"We holed up at an old farm a few miles north of here, just off Randleman Road."

"How many?"

"There were sixteen of us."

"Including these assholes?"

The man nodded quickly, teeth bared against the pain in his arm and leg. He was breathing heavily, and his skin was as white as bleached bone. Violent shivers seized him, and he broke out in a cold sweat. He was going into shock.

"Give me directions," Steve said.

The man did, nearly losing consciousness at the end. Steve put his knife back in its sheath and took a few steps back before raising his rifle and painting the concrete with the man's brains. I jumped when the rifle emitted a muffled crack. Sunlight glinted off the brass casing as it spun through the air and landed on the ground in a chorus of pings.

"What the fuck, Steve?" I said.

He rounded on me and I took an involuntary step backward. I almost brought my H&K level with him, but managed to stop myself. Steve stood stock still, glaring and gripping his rifle. Stan and Cody edged a few steps closer, looping fingers over their triggers. I let my rifle hang from its sling and held my hands up, palms out.

"Look, man, I just killed a guy on your say so. Maybe that's not a big deal for you, but it is for me. I just want to know what's going on," I said.

The intensity of Steve's glare lessened, and he seemed to withdraw into himself. The nervous tension in the air abated. Steve turned away from me and looked at the ground. Stan and Cody relaxed and took their hands off the grips of their rifles.

"I promise, I'll explain everything. Right now we need to check on the guy in the back of the truck," he said.

I realized that I had forgotten about him in the midst of all the bloodshed. I looked at Stan and Cody, and we rushed to climb into the truck. The hostage was lying on his left side. His face was bruised and bleeding, his hair filthy and matted with blood. I drew my knife and cut the rope binding his feet. Stan stepped around me and did the same for the man's arms. His hands had gone purple from blood constriction under the tightly knotted bonds. He groaned and began to stir as Stan rolled him onto his back. One of his eyes was swollen shut, but the other began to flutter open.

"Hey, buddy, can you hear me?" Stan asked, placing one hand on the man's chest and shaking him.

He let out a rasping croak and began to thrash weakly.

"Hey, easy there. Calm down man, we're not going to hurt you. Settle down, okay? Everything is okay now, we're here to help."

His panic faded at the sound of Stan's calm voice. He stared blearily up through his one good eye. He croaked a couple more times, and finally reached up a shaking hand to point at my canteen. I pulled it from my belt and helped Stan sit the man up. He grimaced and moaned when we got him upright against the back of the truck's cab. I held the canteen up to his lips and slowly poured the liquid into his mouth. He gulped it thirstily, and beckoned for more. We had to give him a little more than half a quart before he was able to speak.

"Sir, can you talk?" Stan asked, falling into cop mode.

"Yeah, I can," he rasped.

"Can you tell me what happened to you? How did you end up with these men?" Stan said.

The man's one working eye widened and he began struggling to stand up.

"Marissa! They still have Marissa. I have to go back and find her," he shouted.

"Whoa, whoa, buddy. Don't try to stand up yet, you might have a concussion." Cody stepped in and pushed the man back down. "Tell us what happened, and we'll try to help you. Who is Marissa?"

"My sister," the man said. "Those fuckers took her. They caught us while we were out looking for food. They put her in a different truck and headed out toward the old Greely place."

"I know where they are," Steve said, as he stepped next to the truck. "I'm going to go and find them. If your sister is still alive, I'll bring her back. Do you know anything else about the men that took you?"

The man shook his head. "No. They showed up a few weeks ago, I don't know where they came from. They holed up at an old farm not far from my sister's house. We were careful not to let them know we were around, at least until today. I spotted them one morning not long after they got here taking a woman into a barn. She was screaming and fighting, and the sons of bitches were laughing at her. I think there were others in there with her, but I'm not sure. Marissa and I have been hoping that they would go away eventually, so we stayed put. I told her I would protect her if they ever found us."

He broke off, his voice choked. Anger bloomed in my chest. It was bad enough that the dead were walking, but now people were taking advantage of the lawlessness left in the wake of the outbreak to victimize other survivors. You have to be a pretty fucking low form of life to kidnap and rape when there is nothing but sorrow and destruction around you. My hand tightened on the grip of my rifle. I looked up to Stan and Cody. Judging by their expressions, they felt the same way.

"Mount up. We're going after them," Steve said.

We took a minute to drag the bodies behind the gas station, out of sight. If any others came by, we did not want them to see their buddies lying in pools of their own blood. The other man that Steve wounded had no pulse when I checked him. He must have bled out. I considered it a better death than what he deserved. Cody checked our new friend's wounds, and although he had been badly beaten, there was nothing life threatening.

"What's your name?" Cody asked him when he finished looking him over.

"Robert. Robert Gorman. Who are you?"

"I'm Cody Starnes. That's Stan, Eric, and Steve," he said, pointing at each of us in turn.

"Not to sound ungrateful, but how did you find me? It looks like you ambushed these guys," Robert asked.

"We can talk about that later," Steve interjected. He was standing by the driver side door of the truck. "I want to find those fuckers before nightfall. We need to get moving."

We all nodded in agreement and got in the truck. Stan rode up front with Steve, and I climbed in the back with Cody. I took an SKS rifle from the man that I killed and gave it to Robert, admonishing him not to shoot it unless he had no other choice. I wanted him to be able to defend himself, but I did not want the sound of gunfire giving away our position.

It took us fifteen minutes to drive within a mile of the farmhouse where the others were hiding. Steve hid the truck in a clearing, and we proceeded ahead on foot. Robert moved with the soft, quiet tread of an experienced hunter as he led us to the edge of a tree line that bordered the farm. The place must have been nice, once. A white, two-story colonial sat on the edge of a wide field of grass that swayed gently in the afternoon breeze. It was nestled in a small valley between two large hills. The fields extended for a dozen or so acres around the farmhouse, surrounded by dense forest. There was a dilapidated red barn about a hundred yards away. A thick chain and padlock held the double doors shut.

We stopped halfway up a hill where the fields ended, maybe two hundred yards from the barn. Our position gave us a clear view of the house and everything around it. There was definitely someone home. An SUV and a large pickup truck sat in the driveway, and through my binoculars, I could make out movement through the windows.

"What do you say, Steve? How do you want to do this?" I asked.

He stared intently at the farmhouse for a moment before responding. "We wait for nightfall. Until then, we spread out and stay out of sight. Once the sun goes down, we can use the grass for cover to get close to them. Sooner or later, they'll go to sleep, and that's when we hit them."

I nodded. "Sounds like a plan. Robert, you okay man?"

He clenched his swollen jaw and practically hummed with tension. "They have my sister down there." He said.

"Look, I know you want to get her back, but we won't be doing her any good if we get ourselves killed," I replied. "They outnumber us, but we have the element of surprise. Steve is a Green Beret, he knows what he is doing."

Robert looked at me for a moment, then nodded. "Okay. I owe you guys for helping me, so we do this your way."

"Everybody spread out," Steve said. "I want twenty yard intervals. Stay low, stay quiet, keep your eyes peeled. Cody, watch our backs for undead. Use the Sig if necessary. Everybody clear?"

We all agreed and fell back into the cover of the forest as we fanned out across the hill. Once I was in a good hiding spot, I dug a protein bar out of a cargo pocket and took my time eating it. I was tired and hungry, and I wanted very badly to be anywhere but where I was. I thought of Stacy's warm, comfortable bed and sighed. With luck, I could sleep there tomorrow night, instead of hunkered down in the dirt trying not to think about an imminent firefight. My mind turned back to the ambush at the gas station.

I had killed a man.

Granted, the bastard probably deserved to die, but I was the one who had done the job. I understood, then, what Gabriel meant when he talked about what it felt like to pull the trigger on someone. The guilt and the uncertainty. Did shooting that man make me a murderer? I thought about it for a while, and eventually just shook my head. What difference did it make? The entire country was dead. Maybe even the entire world. The only thing left to do was survive, and try to help other people along the way. Even if that meant dealing with people like the evil bastards down in the valley below.

Soon, the sun would go down. Soon, there would be a reckoning.

Chapter 15

The Thin Veneer of Civilization

We waited.

The sun went down.

"Stay alert." Steve told us over the radio. "Hold positions. I'm going to recon the house. Maintain radio silence until I say otherwise. Out."

Great. More waiting, I thought.

But there was nothing for it, so I waited. The pale blue night sky faded to full black as the stars wheeled overhead. The temperature dropped, and I did my best not to shiver in the chill autumn air. Two more hours passed. I must have dozed off at some point, because the radio woke me up.

"All positions, radio check."

"Loud and clear," I whispered.

"Where the hell have you been?" Cody asked.

"Ditto," Stan said.

"Listen up, and hold the fucking questions. There are people being held captive in the barn. At least three women and one man, maybe more. Don't let any shots go toward the barn if you can help it. There were two sentries on patrol, but I already took care of them. The rest are in the house. I've got the back covered, and I want you four to approach from the front of the house. Spread out ten yards apart in a skirmish line. I'm going to set fire to the house on this side, and try to flush them out to you. Stay low until they come out. Kill anything carrying a gun, and take the rest prisoner if you can. I don't know for certain if there are any hostages in the house, so don't shoot the place up. Everybody clear?"

We gave affirmatives, and I slowly eased up from my hide. I took a moment to stretch and check my weapons, then began working my way toward the farm house in a low crouch. My eyes had adjusted to the darkness, and I could see well enough by moonlight to watch my step. I managed not to break any twigs or trip on anything loud until I reached the tree line. I low crawled slowly through the tall grass the way Gabriel once taught me on a hunting trip in Kentucky. If I moved quietly enough to fool a buck, I could probably do the same to a person. It took me nearly half an hour to reach the edge of the field. The grass in front of me was shorter, and I had a clear view of the house and the barn. I could hear the faint sounds of rustling grass as Cody moved into position on my right. I couldn't tell where Stan and Robert were.

"Status?" Steve asked.

I keyed my radio. "In position, over."

"Ready to go," Cody said.

"Been waiting for you guys," Stan said. "Robert is with me. Cody, I'm twenty yards to your right, over."

"I'm going to start the fireworks," Steve said. "Be ready."

This time I had remembered to bring a tactical light and a bipod, both of which I had mounted on my HK's quad rail. I extended the bipod and sighted in on the door. Lying in the prone position would make my shots more accurate, but I would have less room to maneuver for running targets. I looked over to Cody's position, and he had come up to one knee with his weight on his back leg in a seated firing stance.

Two crashes from the other side of the house echoed out into the still night. Bright yellow light seared the night sky as the roof burst into flame. Black smoke roiled up into the air, illuminated in reds and oranges by the flames beneath. Less than a minute later, a tall man with a rifle clenched in his fist ripped open the front door and stumbled out, bent over and coughing. Smoke rolled out the front door behind him. I let him get halfway down the steps on the front porch before I hit him with a double tap center of mass. He clutched his chest and pitched forward onto the ground. He dropped his rifle, and it clattered down the steps next to him. Several more men poured out behind him. The two in the lead tripped over their cohort's dead body and fell down the porch. The ones behind them leaped over the tangled pile of bodies and spread out, brandishing weapons.

"Don't move!" Stan shouted. "You're under arrest!"

The men responded by lifting their weapons and firing in his general direction. The three of us with suppressed rifles opened up and began cutting the gunmen down. I heard Robert's SKS roar as he sent hot lead at the men who had abducted his sister. Three of them curled up on the ground with their hands over their heads shouting for us not to shoot them. I counted five dead, and the three soon-to-be prisoners. That left one asshole unaccounted for.

"Anyone left in the house, come out with your hands up!" Stan shouted.

After a few seconds, a short, rotund man with a bald head and a short beard crawled out of the house on all fours. I kept my rifle trained on him while Stan shouted instructions. In a few moments, we had all four of our prisoners lined up facing the house kneeling in the dirt with their hands clasped on top of their heads.

"Steve, how you doing? Over," I said over the radio.

"I'm clearing the house. Be out in a minute," he responded.

I thought about going in to help him, but decided against it. The flames on the roof were spreading rapidly. The fire consuming the house grew steadily brighter, casting an angry ring of writhing shadows around it. A tense minute went by before Steve radioed to us again.

"I'm coming out. I have a victim with me, check your fire."

Steve emerged from the smoke filled doorway. He half carried and half dragged a young woman with a blanket wrapped around her shoulders. Cuts and bruises covered her bare legs and feet where they were visible. She wept and clung tightly to Steve as he brought her over to us and sat her down on the lawn. Steve knelt down beside the distraught girl and put an arm around her shoulders.

"Listen, you're safe now," he said in a gentle voice. "No one else is going to hurt you. These men are here to help you. I have to go and check on the others in the barn. Do you know if there is a guard in there?"

"No, I don't think so," the girl said between sobs. "Please stay with me, don't leave me here."

The girl clutched Steve's arm and looked at him with desperate, terrified eyes. I walked over to them and kneeled down in front of her.

"Hey, my name is Eric. I'm going to stay with you, okay? Steve here has to go help the others."

Steve gave me a grateful nod, and stood up from beside the girl. I sat down beside her and pulled her close, keeping my free hand on my rifle. Steve motioned to Stan and Robert, and the three of them set off toward the barn. Cody covered our prisoners while I tried to console the poor frightened girl. She shivered under my arm as I held her. I could feel her petite, frail little bones against the skin of her shoulders. She had bruises around both of her eyes and a split lower lip. A cold anger began to burn inside me as I stared at the prisoners who captured her. They looked terrified, and they were right to be. Wide, bloodshot eyes gaped at me in the firelight. The fat one was the first to speak up.

"Listen, man, I didn't touch her. I didn't touch any of them, okay? I'm only with these guys because-"

"Shut up." I told him.

"Look I'm telling you-"

"SHUT THE FUCK UP!" I yelled, coming up to one knee and leveling my rifle at him. Cody took a step forward and swung the toe of his boot into the bastard's kidney. He emitted a choked hiss and clutched his back.

"Hands up, fucker," Cody said, nudging the man in the back of the head with his rifle. He grimaced in pain as he complied.

The girl beside me moaned in fear and curled up into a little ball, hands clutching the blanket around her. I sat back down and put an arm around her. I spent a few minutes saying soft, comforting words to her and holding her close. She relaxed a bit and laid her head on my shoulders as she cried into my bush jacket. It was not long before Steve returned with the other hostages. Robert carried a woman who I assumed to be his sister in his arms. He gently laid her on the ground and knelt down beside her. She had long brown hair, and her face was bruised and bloody. Robert had wrapped a bloody sheet around her naked, battered body.

The other victims could walk under their own power, barely. There were three women and one man. All four of them bore scores of bruises and small lacerations. One of the women sobbed silently and clutched her arm to her side. As badly as the women had been used, the man was the worst off. Sharp cheekbones jutted out over gaunt hollows above his jaw. He had several large hematomas on his forehead beneath lank, matted hair. A broken nose angled down the middle of his face in three directions, and one of his eyes had completely swelled shut. He looked monstrous in the light of the burning house. My throat tightened, and I looked away.

"What are you going to do with us?" The woman with the broken arm asked. Her voice shook, and her eyes were fearful. It made me want to cry for her. Steve tried to place a reassuring hand on her shoulder, but she flinched and cringed away. Steve held his hand up and took a step away.

"The first thing we need to do is get you medical attention. We have a doctor and medical supplies at our compound," Steve said.

As he spoke, I head a faint moan carried on the wind. And then another, and another, growing louder. I sat up and cupped a hand to my ear.

"Steve. You hear that?" I asked.

Steve turned and raised his NVG's.

"Shit. Creeps, less than two hundred yards out, coming across the field. Lots of them. We need to move."

I cursed and got to my feet. "We have to get these people to the truck," I said.

Steve pointed at the four prisoners with his rifle and motioned to Stan and Cody. "Zip-tie those fuckers and bring them with us."

The two former policemen quickly zip-tied the prisoner's hands behind their backs and bound them together with a length of Steve's parachute cord. Robert held his SKS level with the men's heads as Cody tied their bindings.

"Give me a fucking excuse you cocksuckers. One reason, just one goddamn reason. I dare you. I motherfucking double dare you," Robert said, his eyes blazing. The prisoners looked down, afraid to meet his gaze.

We had everyone up and ready to move as the first walking corpse appeared at the edge of the fire light. Flames engulfed the house behind us, and a large section of the roof collapsed into the inferno as we began to move away. Robert carried his sister in his arms. Her head lolled to one side as he walked. I hadn't noticed before that she was unconscious. Not good.

As we set off across the field back toward the forest, Steve put on his NVG's and began to pick off the infected that got too close. I clicked on my tactical light and lit up the ground in front of us with a bright penetrating beam from the LED's. The powerful little flashlight gave me good visibility for ten yards ahead. I was as good as ringing a dinner bell for the creeps, but I had no choice. The massive conflagration consuming the farmhouse had ruined everyone's night vision, and without any light to see by, we would be stumbling blind through a forest infested with the undead. Luckily, Stan and Cody had thought to bring flashlights as well. They guided the victims and prisoners over the uneven terrain behind me. Steve fired off a few rounds into the darkness before he made his way back over to us.

"Eric, you got point?" he asked.

"I got it, cover our rear. Stan, you and Cody keep our flanks clear." I rounded on the zip-tied prisoners marching behind me single file. "As for you fuckers, if you even think about running and I'll shoot you in the legs and leave your sorry asses for the infected."

They blinked and cringed away from the harsh glare of my tactical light. We made our way as quickly as we could across the field and into the forest. Trees and undergrowth made it difficult to spot the undead in the dark gloom. Several times, I had to send multiple rounds at infected before getting a head shot. Judging by the sounds erupting from the surrounding forest, the infected were closing in on us in spite of the efforts of our shooters to keep them away. I drew my pistol and handed it to the man with the badly beaten face.

"Here take this. If any infected get too close, put a bullet in their head. The safety is off, and there is a round in the chamber. You have thirty rounds, so make them count. Remember," I said pointing a finger between my eyes. "Head shots only. Anything else, and it's your ass." The man nodded and took the pistol.

"And watch where you point that thing," I added.

I stepped around a tree and damn near got tackled by a ghoul emerging from a thick patch of thorn bushes. I managed to bring my rifle up between us and hold him back. My barrel was too low to shoot him in the head. The thought flashed through my mind that body mechanics are body mechanics, regardless of whether you are alive or dead. I released the fore-end of my rifle and pushed against the revenant's throat with my left hand while hooking my right leg between his and executing a textbook inside reap. The combined push-pull effect caused the infected to stumble over backward and fall on its ass. The rotten fucker hissed at me and bared its black teeth as I leveled my rifle and put a bullet through its head. I raised the carbine and swept the forest ahead. It looked clear as far as I could see, so I continued on and signaled for the others to follow.

It took us nearly an hour to make our desperate, exhausted way back to the road. Groaning, shambling shapes weaved inexorably through the pitch-black night behind us in relentless pursuit. If it were just the other shooters and I, we could have made it in half the time. The man to whom I had loaned my pistol used nearly an entire magazine keeping the creeps away from the women behind him. The poor girls were having a hard time of it due to their injuries. The one with the broken arm, and the young girl I had tried to comfort, wailed in fear every time a gun fired too close to them. I wanted to turn around and hold them, and tell them everything would be okay. They sounded so afraid. I pushed the thought out of my head and focused on getting back to the truck stashed nearby.

We urged everyone into a slow jog down the dark road. My flashlight illuminated the way ahead much better once we cleared the oppressive forest. A ghoul staggered out onto the road ahead of me and half jogged in my direction. She had been a middle-aged Hispanic woman in life, but death had turned her into a hideous, blood-drenched abomination. Something had torn her lips away, and exposed white bone shined grotesquely through savaged skin and muscle tissue under the moonlight. Black ichor covered her teeth, and a rotten, shredded tongue roiled around in her mouth. I didn't want to stop long enough to line up a shot, so I took four running steps and put all my weight into a front kick that launched her head over heels backwards. She came to a rolling stop head down in a ditch, thrashing and struggling to get up. I threw the kick so hard that I knocked myself over. Strong hands gripped me under the arms and hauled me to my feet. I turned around and saw the poor man with the beaten face that I had given my pistol to. He flashed a broken-toothed smile and patted me on the shoulder. I nodded by way of thanks, and kept moving.

The horde of infected must have numbered a least a hundred or more, despite the several dozen we put down with our guns. I had to reload twice, and was more than halfway through a third magazine before we reached the clearing where Steve stashed the truck. He fished the keys out from beneath the driver's seat and hopped in. Stan and Cody loaded the prisoners and rescues in the back. I hopped into the passenger seat after helping Robert lay his sister down in the bed. The freed victims threw all of the assorted junk out to make room for themselves. Stan made the prisoners curl up into balls and pack in tightly toward the truck's cab. Steve threw the truck into gear, and kicked up dirt and gravel as he brought the vehicle around and bounced across the field back to the road. Once he put some distance between us and the horde, he reduced speed and followed the winding hill country road back to the compound.

The guards on duty at the compound sounded the alarm as our vehicle approached. It was late at night, and all that they could see was the headlights of a large truck coming toward them. As we got close, Steve turned off the lights and pulled up next to the warehouse with his window down.

"Don't shoot. It's Steve," he called out.

Bill came out with Ethan and Earl in tow. Ethan took the people we rescued inside to treat their wounds and get some food into them. As if being horrifically traumatized wasn't bad enough, they were severely dehydrated and suffering from malnourishment. We kept the prisoners outside. Steve and I spent a few minutes in terse, hushed conversation with Bill about what to do with them.

"There is a lot to talk about Bill," Steve said. "These guys were doing terrible things. I think they might be the reason that we haven't found any other survivors in so long."

"So what do you want to do with them?" he asked.

"For right now, we give them food and water and confine them under guard in the factory," Steve responded. "Tomorrow, we ask the people they kidnapped what we should do about them."

Bill paled at that, and nodded slowly. He had seen the terrible condition those poor people were in. Whatever they decided to do with the bastards that hurt them was not going to be pretty.

I helped Steve and a few others secure the prisoners on the factory floor. We found some chains and padlocks, and used them to manacle the sick fucks to iron rings in the concrete that once supported factory equipment. Justin and Rick volunteered to take the first watch so that the four of us who went out that morning could get some rest.

"Watch them close," I told Justin. "Don't let them talk, or do anything else but sit there. These fuckers are dangerous, and if you give them half a chance, they will kill you to get away."

"What did they do to those people you brought in?" he asked, his boyish face stiff with anger.

"Long story short, they beat, raped, and brutalized them. Tomorrow, we will find out everything that happened. For now, we keep these bastards on lock-down until we can decide how to deal with them."

"I vote we just put a bullet in their heads and have done with it," Justin said.

"Judging by what I've seen tonight, that might be too good for them. We'll see what their victims have to say about it tomorrow."

The four of us who captured the marauders and rescued their victims, along with Bill, Ethan, and Andrea, divided our time the next day between debriefing the victims and interrogating the evil pieces of shit that captured them. Stan and Cody turned out to be invaluable. They both had experience interrogating suspects, and suggested how we should go about getting their story out of them. We started with the fat bald one, since he seemed to be the weakest. Steve and I took him away from the others, forced him to strip down to his underwear, and chained him to a tree a few miles from the factory.

"You and I are going to have a little chat," Steve said, standing in front of the man. "I'm going to ask you questions, and you are going to answer them completely and honestly. Are we clear?"

The man tried to nod, but the chain around his forehead prevented it.

"Yeah, whatever you want man. Just don't hurt me," he said. Even though it was cool that morning, sweat ran down the man's fat, jiggling hide in long rivulets. Steve smiled. He looked like a hungry crocodile, and about as cold-blooded.

"Let's start with your name."

"Don. Don Grable."

"Okay Don, how did you come to be a part of that little ensemble you were with?"

"We used to work together at the water treatment plant. When the infection spread out of Atlanta, we all got together and said we would work together to survive if it reached us. We didn't think it would really happen, but it did. A couple of the guys who had families went north to Iron Station where the military was trying to set up a safe zone. Only one of them came back, and he lost his wife and kids to the infected. The rest of us holed up at Jack's place out in the country for a while, until we started to run low on food. That was when the trouble started."

"And what trouble was that?" I asked.

"And which one of you is Jack?" Steve added.

"Jack is dead. He was one of the guys you killed at the farm."

"Too bad for him," I deadpanned. "Back to my question. What trouble?"

"We…we were getting desperate. We were starting to fight over food. Jack caught a guy trying to take some stuff and run off one night while the rest of us were asleep. He…uh…stopped him."

"You mean he killed him," Steve said.

"Yeah. Fuck, man, Jack was crazy. He always had a screw loose, but it wasn't until then that I started to realize how fucked up he really was."

"Explain," Steve said.

"Well, that night when he caught him, he didn't kill him right away. He shot him in the foot so he couldn't run off, and gathered the rest of us around him. He had Ray tied up. He was bleeding all over the place and begging for help. Ray was our friend and all, but we were pretty pissed at him for trying to steal from us. We felt betrayed you know? Jack gave this speech about it being the end of the world, and survival of the fittest, and shit like that. I didn't pay much attention to most of it, except the part where he told us that the only way we were going to survive was to stick together. That part kind of made sense. He said that Ray was a traitor for trying to run off with our food. He was leaving us to die, and that he didn't deserve any mercy from us."

The man stopped talking for a moment as his gaze became distant. Steve snapped his fingers in front of his face. The man jerked, and swiveled his eyes back to us.

"What happened then?"

"He…he shot him. Right in the head. Right there in front of us. Something changed then, in all of us. It was like, some kind of ceremony or something. We just quit giving a shit about anything. We didn't have any women with us, so when we found some…we…did things to them."

"Like beating and raping them?" I asked. "Starving them? Terrorizing them?"

The man nodded as much as his bindings allowed him to and closed his eyes. Tears slid down his sweaty cheeks as he squeezed his eyes shut.

"Fuck, man, I never wanted any of this. Jack always knew what to say to keep people on his side, no matter what he did. After a while, it was like everybody started to enjoy it. Not having any rules, not having anybody to answer to. We could do whatever we wanted, take whatever we wanted. Nobody could stop us. It felt…good. Powerful. We didn't have to bust our asses for shit pay in a stinking sewer any more. Jack always talked about some fucker named Darwin and how we were apex predators, and all kinds of crazy shit. The other guys bought into it. I wasn't so sure, but I was scared to piss the others off, so I went along."

"Why didn't you just leave?" Steve asked. "Why stay, if you disagreed with what they were doing."

"Because of the infected, man," Don wailed. "There are so goddamn many of them. There's no way I could survive on my own. Hell, even with sixteen of us, we were having a hard time keeping them away. We kept having to move from one place to another. About the time we settled in somewhere, the damn infected would come around and we had to run away. That's why we were…"

He stopped talking, stammering as if realizing he had said too much.

"That's why you were what?" Steve said.

"That's…that's why we were staying in that farm house. It looked safe."

Steve smiled that creepy-ass smile of his and reached into his pocket. He pulled out a sixteen-penny nail and held it up for Don to see before taking a step back and kicking a fist sized rock up out of the dirt.

"Don, up until now you have been doing pretty well. That being said, I know a lie when I hear one. Now in order to avoid any unpleasantness, I'm going to ask you that question again, and this time you are going to tell me the truth. What were you doing to protect yourselves from the undead?"

"What do you mean? We were staying at that farm. It was out in the middle of nowhere, we didn't think…"

Don trailed off as Steve approached him. Steve put the tip of the nail against Don's shoulder and held the rock a few inches above it.

"Let's try that one more time, Don. What were you planning?"

"I don't know what-"

His words turned into a scream when Steve cracked the rock against the nail and drove it an inch into Don's shoulder. Steve stepped back as the man writhed against his chains and sobbed in pain.

"That was just a taste, Don. Just a taste. If you don't start telling me the truth, you are going to get the whole fucking menu. What were you and your asshole buddies planning?"

"We...we needed a place with a wall. Something we could reinforce. A couple of us found that housing development, and some people were already there." Don gasped between sobs. "Jack wanted us to watch you guys and figure out how many of you there were."

Steve nodded, then reached up and ripped the nail out of Don's shoulder. He screamed again, and sagged against his bindings.

"Let me see if I can sum this up for you, since you seem to be having a little difficulty," Steve said. "You and those other sons of bitches saw us clearing the dead out of that neighborhood, and decided to hang back while we did the hard work. I'm guessing you followed some of the workers back to the compound, and realized that you were outnumbered. Somebody goes back to your buddy Jack, and tells him that there is this big group of people with lots of food and weapons just waiting to be murdered and robbed. Jack gets stars in his eyes, and starts coming up with ways to take us out and steal all of our shit. How am I doing so far?"

Don said nothing. He just hung there, crying like a baby. Steve continued on, his voice growing in volume.

"You know what else I think? I don't believe for one second that you were an unwilling participant. A fat tub of shit like you, you've probably never had a piece of ass in your life that wasn't drugged, or making you pay for it. I bet every time somebody brought in some poor helpless girl who was terrified and begging for her life, you jumped to the front of the line to get your tiny little dick wet, didn't you? Well I hope you enjoyed it, you worthless hog-fat motherfucker. 'Cause that was the last thing that you will feel for the rest of your very fucking short life that will not be agonizing pain."

Steve turned to me, his face a mask of disgust. "Help me get this piece of shit down."

Don sobbed, and begged, and apologized as we loaded him into the back of the truck, trussed up like an animal. His pleas fell on deaf ears. We took him back to the compound and dumped him on the floor next to his buddies. Any hint of hope or defiance went out of them like air out of a balloon when they saw Don's bloated, sobbing carcass slap the concrete in front of them. We took the rest out to the same tree, one by one, and got roughly the same story out of every one of them. They all tried to make it sound like they were the victims, that they did not have a choice, they only did it because they were scared. I didn't really give a shit. They did it. I had spent all the previous night listening to Andrea try to comfort the victims. Listening to them cry. Thanking Andrea for feeding them. They were so hungry, so thirsty. It had been days since they had eaten. Since they were given water. Please don't let them take us again…

Bill and Ethan finished with the victims by four in the afternoon. Ethan looked like he was ready to rip the prisoners apart with his bare hands. Bill just looked sad, and very tired. Robert was with Andrea and Stacy. His sister was not doing well at all. Bill had done everything he could for her, but her internal injuries were extensive and severe. Bill just didn't have the equipment he needed to operate. Robert's ruined face went still when Bill gave him the bad news that Marissa probably would not last the night. He nodded, and walked slowly and carefully back to where his sister lay, as though he might shatter if he stepped too hard.

Two of other victims were doing better. A few meals, some clean water, and a little medical treatment had done wonders for them. The man and one of the women were effusive with their thanks. They were the marauders most recent acquisition. Fortunately for them, they had not been used quite as hard as the victims captured before them. The other two women were silent, speaking only when asked a question, or offered food. Their glassy eyes stared off into an unfathomable distance while they sat listless on the ground. I felt so sorry for them. If I had thought I could do anything to comfort them I would have, but there just wasn't anyone home to talk to by that point.

Bill called a meeting. Steve explained to everyone what happened the previous day. After setting the rest of the team up in surveillance positions, he made his way to the marauder's camp near the housing development. They had returned sometime the previous night, and Steve watched them through a scope when Robert and his sister happened by. They were talking loud enough for the marauders to hear them from their camp. Robert and Marissa were on the other side of a ridge from the marauders and did not see them until after the bastards were already on top of them. The cold-blooded shits took them prisoner at gunpoint. Once they had them tied up, Steve crept closer to listen in on their conversation. They were taking the girl back to the abandoned farm, and they were planning to have some sport with Robert. Their idea of sport was tying a man up to a tree, firing a few shots in the air, and watching from a distance while the infected tore them apart. Apparently, they had done this more than once.

The leader, Jack, explained to Robert and his sister exactly what was going to happen to them, and then ordered four of his men to go with him to the gas station to pick up supplies. It was just dumb luck that we had planned to use the same gas station as a rally point and were able to set up the ambush.

Two of the marauders took Marissa back to the farm. We found out from the other victims that they made the captives watch while she was gang raped. One of them got too close to her mouth, and she bit a piece of his face off. I would have cheered for her, except for the fact that the man she bit flew into a rage and nearly beat her to death on the spot. He only stopped because one of the other rapists puller him off of her. He did not do this out of pity. He simply had not taken his turn yet. He did his business while Marissa was unconscious, the sick fuck. As the meeting went on, I felt less and less bad about killing them.

It took everyone by surprise when Steve told them that the marauders had been watching us for some time, and were trying to work out a way to attack us. That little bit of news caused the blood to drain from quite a few faces. At the end of the meeting, Bill informed everyone that he was going to ask the victims what they wanted to do with the surviving marauders. That night, Bill sat down with the victims and spoke with them for a long time. Robert was the one that finally came up with their sentence. I turns out that Robert was a firm believer in an eye for an eye and a tooth for a tooth.

We drove them out to a secluded spot, and cut down a tree. Steve drove anchors into the ground on both sides of it and tied the prisoners down. One of the victims, the petite teenager that Steve rescued from the fire at the farmhouse, asked us to cut their clothes off them. We complied. When we finished, Steve set a small black duffel bag on the ground, and gave Robert a radio with instructions to call us if there was any trouble. Then we walked away.

It was not long before the screaming started.

I'm not sure what they did to them, but they were at it for a while. After they had taken their pound of flesh (literally), Robert called us back over on the radio. I almost lost my lunch when I saw the prisoners. The thing that made their condition so terrible was not necessarily what their victims did to them, but the fact that they were still alive. The victim's revenge wasn't complete, however. Robert whispered something to Steve, and Steve nodded. He pulled his pistol out and fired a few rounds into the air, then told everyone to back off up a hill nearby. We got about fifty yards away and hunkered down behind an old fallen pine near the top of the hill. The road where we parked our vehicles was close by, just in case we needed to bug out. We sat down and waited.

I think the prisoners were begging us to help them, or maybe kill them. It was hard to tell, considering that none of them had a tongue in their heads. They really started crooning when the infected showed up. I didn't stay to watch the rest. They may have deserved it, but I already had enough nightmare material to last a lifetime. Listening to the screams was bad enough. A few endless minutes passed while I sat motionless in the cab of my truck. The screaming stopped, and I heard four muted cracks. I decided to let Steve keep my sniper rifle. I didn't want it after that. The others came back to the trucks soon thereafter, and we rode back to the compound in silence.

That night, as I lay in Stacy's bed trying not to think about the last couple of days, I heard three loud reports in rapid succession. Coils of dread wrapped around my gut as I grabbed a rifle and rushed outside the compound to see what happened.

It was Robert and two of the other victims. The two women with the thousand-yard stares, the silent ones. The three of them lay on the ground in a rough triangle, each of them clutching a pistol in one blood-spattered hand. Under what was left of their heads, black pools of blood expanded outward reflecting the silver moonlight. The guards on the roof came down and told us what they saw. The victims came outside, and walked about thirty yards from the warehouse. The guards didn't think anything of it, as people often left the compound in the early evening to enjoy the cool fall air.

"Man, I expected them to walk around the factory, or sit down and talk or something. Next thing I know, they all pull out guns. The guy, he says 'On the count of three...' and when he gets to three, bang. I tried yelling at them, but they acted like they didn't hear. I swear to God, I couldn't do anything to stop them," One of the guards said.

"It's alright," Bill reassured him. "Go on back inside. I'll get volunteers to take the watch."

Ethan walked over and stood next to me. He huddled inside a wool jacket in the cold, and stared at the bodies.

"Why do you think they came all the way out here?" he asked.

"I'm guessing they didn't want a stray bullet to hit anyone inside the warehouse," I replied.

Ethan turned away and went back inside.

I sat down and cried.

The next morning, we gave them a proper burial, and Bill said a few words over them. We found a note in Robert's shirt pocket.

Everyone should get to choose when and how they leave this ruined world. We have seen too much. Hurt too much. There is no hope for us. Nothing left. We just want it to be over with. We know how hard you fought to save us, and we hope that you take comfort in the knowledge that you spared us a great deal of suffering. You gave us our revenge. You gave us a choice. You are good people.

We are so sorry.

Thank you for everything.

I understood. God help me, I understood.

I began preparing to leave the day after we buried the victims. I loaded all my gear back into the truck, and found some gasoline to put in the tank. I did not go to Stacy's bed that night. I laid out my bedroll and settled into it. Stacy came out of her little shack just before eleven that night and climbed into my sleeping bag. I held her for a little while.

"We're over, aren't we," She said.

"I care about you, Stacy." I replied.

"Do you love me?"

Four little words. But they have so much power, don't they?

"I'm not in love with you, but I do love you. Does that make any sense?" I said.

"Yeah, it does. I...I feel the same way." She rolled over and looked me in the eye.

"You are a good man. I'm so sorry for what you have been through in the last few weeks. I'm very happy that we have...well...whatever it is that we are. I'm glad for it. I just wish..."

"I know," I said.

Stacy smiled, and we kissed. She rolled over and I held her close as we fell asleep.

The next day, everything changed.

Justin was on watch that morning. The kid has sharp eyes, and he saw the vehicles winding their way down through the hills in the early morning sun. Because of our location, we had little time to react. Not that it would have done us much good if our visitors had turned out to be hostile.

A small convoy of several different types of vehicles rumbled and crunched down the narrow service road leading behind the factory. I recognized two Bradley fighting vehicles, two armored personnel carriers (APC's), two Humvee's, and a large deuce-and-a-half cargo truck with the back covered in olive drab canvas. Green, brown, and black paint coated their sides in the distinctive pattern of US military vehicles. A man in the lead Bradley climbed down and turned to face the convoy. He held a radio up to his mouth and said a few words into it before passing it to someone in his Bradley. Afterward, he stepped into view and made a show of putting his weapons down on the ground in front of him. He stepped over his rifle, pistol, and what looked from a distance like a long-handled hatchet, and approached the warehouse with his hands in the air.

The fact that any one of his Bradley fighting vehicles could have leveled our little fortress with a minimum of effort spoke volumes about his intentions. Even still, Bill was apprehensive, and asked Steve and I to engage the military men. I could tell he hated doing it, but a leader has to be willing to make the hard decisions. I did what he asked, and so did Steve.

We went out unarmed. We figured that a couple of rifles, one way or the other, were not going to affect the outcome of the situation. With all the badass hardware they had, resistance would not last long if they decided to break bad on us. Steve wore a pair of old BDU's that still bore his insignia that he had kept around for sentimental reasons after the war. He looked legit in my book, but what the hell did I know? Steve assured me that anyone who served in the Army would know his rank and occupation with a scant glance at his uniform. I took his word on faith.

We met the leader of this new group in front of the warehouse. He stood a little taller than me, and had several days growth of beard on his face. His uniform sagged on his frame somewhat. I wondered if he was there to look for food, as Steve began speaking with him.

"I'm Sergeant First Class Steven McCray. This is Eric Riordan. What can we do for you gentlemen?" he asked.

"Lieutenant Clay Jonas, formerly of the 82nd Airborne, now serving with the First Reconnaissance Expeditionary Command. We're on patrol out of the Fort Bragg Safe Zone, looking for survivors."

"I've never heard of your unit, Lieutenant, and at the risk of being rude, you look a little old to be a butter-bar," Steve said, eyeing the officer skeptically.

Lieutenant Jonas surprised me by laughing at Steve's comment. "I imagine I do. I haven't been an officer for very long, I got a field commission about two months ago. As for hearing of my unit, I would honestly be mighty surprised if you had. We haven't been around for very long. The President ordered our creation back about a month ago. We're not all Army, either. Got some marine's, and even a few airmen back there. Pickings are slim for recruits these days, so we take whatever we can get."

My eyebrows went up. "The President is still alive?" I said.

Lt. Jonas nodded. "The President, his family, the Joint Chiefs of Staff, the VP, and the Speaker of the House all managed to get to a safe location in Colorado. We have enough satellites up and running to stay in contact with them."

"You said Fort Bragg is a safe zone?" Steve asked.

"Yes, we managed to secure it before the Outbreak reached it. It wasn't easy though, we had to fight like hell to keep the infected out. We took a lot of casualties. A few other units have managed to do the same thing out west. It has only been in the last six weeks that things have settled down enough for us to start patrolling for survivors."

"How many have you found?" I asked.

Lt. Jonas sighed and shook his head. "Not many, unfortunately. And not all those that we found have been what you might call 'friendly'."

Steve and I exchanged a look.

"Well it sounds like we have a lot to talk about, Lieutenant," I said. "Do your men need anything? Food, water, medical attention?"

The Lieutenant perked up. "Actually, we do have a couple of wounded. A couple of guys ran into a booby trap a few days ago, and their legs got pretty torn up. Do you have a doctor around?"

"We do. I'll go back to camp and let them know we have wounded coming in. We can also prepare some space for your soldiers to rest for a while, and put a meal together. How many should we expect?"

"Twenty four, including myself. We have our own supplies though, I don't want to impose."

"No trouble at all, Lieutenant," I replied.

"While we get everything ready," Steve interjected, "you might want to keep your men here until we have a chance to talk to the others. These people here have been through a lot lately, and they're kind of jumpy. We wouldn't want any accidents."

Lt. Jonas nodded. "Understood. Honestly, these guys behind me are a little jumpy themselves. The last group we found didn't exactly roll out the red carpet for us. I'll talk to them and make sure they mind their manners while we're here."

Steve and I shook hands with him, and set off back to the compound.

"What do you think?" I asked Steve in a low voice as we walked.

"He's definitely legit Army. I don't know if I believe all that stuff about a safe zone, and the President."

"Well, if they wanted to kill us, they could have done it already. I don't think we have much of a choice but to trust them, at least for right now."

We walked into an anxious crowd of people as we entered the warehouse. Bill called a quick meeting, and we told them everything we had learned so far. There were a lot of skeptical faces, but the overall mood was hopeful. The possibility of receiving help from the military seemed to energize most of the survivors. Bill, Andrea, and Ethan started gathering medical supplies to treat the wounded soldiers. Everyone else went to work clearing space for the soldiers to sleep, and preparing a meal for everyone.

Steve and I went back outside to give Lt. Jonas the all clear. He ordered his men to advance and park their vehicles in the cracked and broken parking lot behind the factory. They formed their Bradley Fighting Vehicles, APC's, and Humvees into a circle. The supply truck parked outside the circle, and soldiers began unloading thin steel plates with metal rings welded to their sides. Upon closer inspection, I saw that all of the vehicles had modifications that looked recently made. Steel grates covered each vehicle's windows, and they had steel rings welded onto the sides. Lt. Jonas' men used chains and bolt clamps to fasten the steel plates to the gaps between the vehicles. After they secured the plates, they unloaded tangled cylinders of welded re-bar and laid them out in a circle several feet beyond the makeshift wall.

"That's a pretty clever design," I commented to the Lieutenant.

He smiled. "Yeah, it is. My twelve year old son came up with it."

I raised an eyebrow at him. "No shit?"

"No shit. It works great, too. We can stand on top of the vehicles and take out the infected as they gather round. Those pieces of cut up re-bar are called trippers. I'll give you one guess what they do."

"I'm guessing the undead aren't smart enough to just step over them."

Jonas smirked. "Nope."

Jonas wasn't lying when he said they had their own supplies. They had enough MRE's to last them a month, and more than a hundred thousand rounds of ammunition for their M4 rifles. Most of the soldiers also carried some kind of hand held weapon with them. Hatchets and axes seemed to be popular choices. One guy carried a long handled pick-axe with one of the spikes cut off in a handmade harness on his back. They had spare parts for the vehicles, spare tires, and they even had spare guns. The cannons on the Bradley's were not just for show, either. They had plenty of ordnance for them. I sincerely hoped these guys really were who they said they were. If they decided to make trouble for us, well…it would be over quickly, at least.

Ethan came outside and made his way over to Lt. Jonas and me. His expression was troubled, but he was polite as he greeted the soldiers.

"I understand you have wounded?" he asked a group of men standing near the supply truck.

"Yes sir," one of them replied. He was a short, stocky private with dark brown skin. He looked Somoan, or maybe Hawaiian. His nametag read 'Maiuna'.

"They're on stretchers in the back of the truck. Where do you want us to move them?" he said.

"Bring them over to the other side of the warehouse and take them in through the back door. We already have operating tables set up. What kinds of wounds are we dealing with?"

"Some asshole set up a homemade claymore on a tripwire. It was loaded with nails and bolts and shit. Their legs are in bad shape."

Ethan nodded, and climbed into the truck to help the soldiers bring out their wounded comrades. When they came out, I saw that someone had cut their pants away, and their legs were swathed in bloody field dressings. Both men ground their teeth and did their best not to scream as their fellow soldiers passed them hand-over-hand down to the troops waiting on the ground. Ethan helped carry one of them inside the warehouse. I wanted to follow them and try to help, but decided to stay put. I did not have very much medical training beyond first aid and CPR, and I figured that I would probably just get in the way.

"Is your doctor any good?" Lt. Jonas asked as his men were carried to the warehouse.

I shrugged. "He used to be a heart surgeon. We also have an ER nurse with us. Ethan, the big guy who just came by, he used to be an EMT. Our doctor has been working on training some people, but only for the last couple of weeks. I doubt they'll be much use yet."

Jonas nodded. "Well, any port in a fuckin' storm, and all that. Those two kids are in a lot of pain, and I'd bet the beer money that their wounds are getting infected."

"Bill will do everything he can." I reassured him. "We have pain medicine and antibiotics, so we should at least be able to make them comfortable and treat their infections. Do you have medical facilities at Fort Bragg?"

"We do, but I was worried that we wouldn't be able to get those two back in time to save them. Whatever happens, I'm grateful for the help."

"You can thank us after Bill gets done with them," I replied.

I found out later that Bill gave the two soldiers a strong dose of Oxycontin to ease their pain. He and Andrea spent nearly three hours pulling nails and scraps of metal out of the two soldier's legs. The wounds were as numerous as they were painful, and the soldiers had lost a lot of blood. There was nothing we could do about that, but thankfully none of the shrapnel caused permanently debilitating injury. Bill approached Lt. Jonas at his command tent after he finished stitching the last injury. He had taken off his blood-stained scrubs, and changed into a flannel shirt and a pair of jeans. Swollen, puffy circles hung beneath his weary eyes.

"How they doing, doc?" Jonas asked.

"As good as can be expected, given the circumstances. I wish we could get them to a proper medical facility, but..." The old doctor held up his hands and shrugged.

"I understand, sir. Thank you for offering your help. Do you think they'll recover?" Jonas asked.

"They should. They had a lot of puncture wounds, but none of them were deep enough to cause any serious damage. My main concern is blood loss. We will have to make sure that they get plenty of fluids and food, so that their bodies can replace what they lost. I stitched them up as best I could, but they are going to have a lot of scarring. Not much I can do about that. I've started them on a round of antibiotics to treat their infections. If they can bounce back from the blood loss, they should make a full recovery. That being said, it's likely to be two to three weeks before they're back on their feet again. When were you planning on heading back to Fort Bragg?"

Lt. Jonas grimaced. "I was planning to stay out on patrol for another three weeks before those two got hit. Do you think I should go ahead and take them back? We have better facilities in the safe zone."

Bill shook his head. "There is not much else that can be done for them at this point, regardless of where they are. If you need to keep searching for survivors, you can leave them here and we'll look after them. They should be up and walking by the time your patrol is over, and you can pick them up on the way back to Fort Bragg."

Jonas considered it for a few seconds, and slowly started to nod.

"That actually sounds like a good idea. Are you sure you don't mind? I know things are hard for you folks. I don't want you to stretch your resources on our account. We are supposed to be helping you, not the other way around."

Bill gave him a weary smile. "We've been managing okay. We have some good people here."

Jonas held a hand out to Bill. "I really appreciate the help, Doc. I can't tell you how grateful I am. You folks are the first people we've run into that didn't shoot at us and run away. I'm glad to see that you're doing well for yourselves."

Bill shook his hand, and held it. "If you really are who you say you are, then these people are going to be very happy to welcome you in. If not, and you try anything, these people know how to fight. I don't have any illusions about how it would end, but you will take casualties in the process. These folks have been through too much to bow down to would-be conquerors. Are we clear, Lieutenant?"

Jonas nodded. "Crystal."

Bill stared at him for a moment, and then released his hand.

"Well, once you boys are all set up, come on in. We put together a nice dinner for you."

Jonas smiled. "That sounds wonderful."

The meal was a hodge-podge of venison steaks, canned vegetables, dried pasta, flat bread, and wild edibles scavenged from the forest. I helped myself to a hunk of deer meat, bread, and a bowl of slow cooked pinto beans. Bill sent Emily and Justin to fetch a few cases of wine and some plastic cups. As the wine flowed, the mood became festive in the compound. The soldiers were more than happy to sit down with other survivors and eat something other than MRE's for a change. The compound's residents were anxious for news from the outside world, and peppered Lt. Jonas and his men with a barrage of questions.

Stacy brought plates to the two injured men, but no wine. The painkillers in their blood made it too dangerous for them to drink. They thanked her, and tore into their meal with gusto. Stacy sat down and kept them company while they ate. A warm meal and a pretty girl to talk to picked their spirits right up. I couldn't help but wonder if Stacy was just being kind, or if she was avoiding me. Or both.

While we were clearing out dead bodies from the housing development a few miles away, I found a beautiful Taylor six-string, and brought it with me back to the compound. I'm no Eric Clapton, but I can play pretty well and I have a decent singing voice. To take my mind off of Stacy, I fetched my guitar and offered to play a few songs during the meal. I got a round of applause before I even picked the first note.

The show started with a paced acoustic version of *All Along the Watchtower* that got people tapping their feet, and bobbing their heads. I followed that up with a couple of Dave Matthews tunes, and a rendition of *Good Times* by Charlie Robinson. That one got people out of their chairs and moving. Andrea surprised the hell out of me by disappearing into her shack and returning with a violin. Or a fiddle, as she called it. Her husband bounced little Aiden on his knee in time to an impromptu acoustic version of several Flogging Molly and The Dropkick Murphy's songs. I had no idea that Andrea liked Irish punk rock.

Before I knew it, people were breaking out private stashes of booze, and Justin brought out a few more cases of wine. Bill scowled at him, but didn't say anything. He would never admit it, but I think the old man was having a good time right along with everyone else. Andrea and I played every song we could think of, and even took a few requests. After a couple of hours, Bill called in the guards on the roof. All of the people who could replace them were either drunk, or well on their way to it. There didn't seem to be much sense in leaving them up there to miss the party.

People danced, and drank, and laughed, and drank some more. A few soldiers were lucky enough to catch the eye of what few single women lived in the compound, and joined them in their shacks for the evening. A tall soldier named Bryson, who looked like an NFL linebacker, sat down next to Cody and began chatting him up. At one point, I caught Cody's eye, and gave him a smile and a thumbs up. He turned red and laughed as he held up his cup in return.

When it looked like things were starting to wind down, I called everyone over and asked them to take a seat. Once the boozed up crowd settled down, I strummed my guitar and played a slow version of It's a Great Day to be Alive by Travis Tritt. I've never been a big fan of country-western, but I like that song. Andrea accompanied on the fiddle, and by the last chorus everyone not unconscious or en coitus was singing right along. After we finished, Andrea leaned over to me.

"Do you know that old song by Leonard Cohen, Hallelujah?"

I nodded. "Yeah, I know it."

I held up a hand to get everyone's attention. "Okay folks, one last song, and then I have to call it a night."

That elicited a chorus of boos. I laughed and began to play. The opening notes rose and fell, and the drunken partiers began to sway back in forth in time with the tune. Andrea pulled heartache from her violin in slow, bitter sweet falls and crescendos. There was not a dry eye in the place by the time we got to the last chorus.

Andrea kept time with me and played the last notes on the violin in perfect harmony with my voice as I sang the last bar. Hallelujah is a long one, and my fingers were burning as I played the final chords. The other survivors were quiet for a moment, and then burst into applause. I tell you, ol' Leonard sure as hell knew how to put a song together. I looked around and found Stacy seated near the back of the audience. Tears brimmed in her eyes, and she gave me a smile and a little wave.

On the way over to my truck, I endured numerous enthusiastic back slaps and even a few hugs from the soldiers. Stacy pulled me aside and gave me a long, heartfelt kiss.

"That was beautiful," she said.

"You're beautiful," I replied.

We laid down in her bed and fell asleep to the sounds of the last revelers settling down for the night. I felt better than I had in a long time. As I fell asleep, I wondered how long it would last.

Chapter 16

Last Straw

The next day, nearly everyone in the compound woke up with a hangover. For once, thankfully, I was not one of them. While everyone else was pounding the booze, I was sipping water to keep my voice from getting raw. I left Stacy sleeping and quietly slipped out the door to the common area. What few people that were not still snoozing and groaning moved around preparing a simple breakfast of flatbread and thin lentil soup. I spotted Lieutenant Jonas squatting down on his heels next to the two men that Bill had patched up the day before. They looked somewhat pale, but seemed to be doing much better. I made my way over to them. The Lieutenant stood up and smiled as I approached.

"That was some damn fine singing last night," he said.

I tried to say, "Oh, it was nothing.", but all that came out was a hoarse croak. I had to clear my throat several times before I could talk.

"Sorry, guess I overdid it." My voice sounded like glass shards in a tin can. Jonas laughed.

"Well, you should probably go get yourself some water. I don't think you're going to be giving another performance any time soon," he said.

I smiled ruefully and shrugged. "Hey, I can still play the guitar."

Jonas laughed again, and clapped me on the shoulder. "Now that's what I like to hear. I wish some of these useless slugs had your kind of gumption," he said, gesturing at the rows of sleeping soldiers laid out in their bedrolls.

"Come on LT," a voice behind me said. I turned and recognized the speaker. I had seen him barking orders at the soldiers setting up the barricade around their convoy yesterday.

"These guys have been through the wringer. They deserve to cut loose once in a while," he said.

Jonas sighed and relaxed his posture, planting his hands on his hips. "I suppose you're right Sergeant. That was a damn fine dinner last night, and I can't remember the last time I drank a decent glass of cabernet. Give these apes another half hour, then rouse them up and get some of that damn disgusting coffee into 'em."

"Will do, sir," The sergeant said, half smiling. He had narrow, craggy face that did not look at all accustomed to good humor. Seeing amusement in his expression was a bit like seeing the sun poke through a storm cloud. He turned to me as Lt. Jonas made his way over to Bill.

"Sergeant Will Cartwright, United States Army," he said, extending one large hand.

"Eric Riordan, financial analyst, musician, and entrepreneur." I shook his hand.

"Entrepreneur is it? What business are you in?"

"Not sure yet, but when I find out I'll let you know."

He let by another quick smile, and turned back to the recumbent forms of his comrades. "You got anything planned this morning, Mr. Riordan?"

"Not really. And please, call me Eric."

"Fair enough, Eric. Call me Will. I don't suppose you'd mind helping me brew up twenty two cups of the worst instant coffee ever to plague the face of the Earth, would you?"

I chuckled. "Tell you what, let me get a cup of tea down my gullet, and I'll even bring you a stove and a teapot."

The sergeant nodded, and set off toward the tables where Emily and a few others were serving breakfast. I stepped around the sleeping soldiers and walked over to my truck. I changed into a fresh set of clothes, strapped on my boots, and took a few minutes to look over my weapons and supplies. It had become something of a routine for me at that point, and I felt a lump in my throat at the thought of not having this as a part of my day anymore. I strapped on my load-bearing harness, holstered my pistol, and slung a rifle over my shoulder. Ethan had scheduled me for guard duty from seven until eleven in the morning. After that, I would get some lunch and say goodbye to everyone.

After lunch.

No sense leaving early. Someone would have to take my watch, and that would just be lazy. I could stand one last shift. That would give me time to tell everyone how much they meant to me, and how much I cared about them. How much it killed me to leave them. I wasn't worried, though. With the soldiers here, they would be in good hands-

"Holy sh- *AAAAUUUUGHHHH*! *Get if off me*! *Get it the fuck off me*!"

Without realizing it, I had been staring at the ground. The shrill scream snapped my head up. I sprinted toward the other side of the warehouse, clutching the grip of my rifle. Sergeant Cartwright was standing half in the doorway and half out, grappling with a man in a brown shirt, like the color of dried…fuck.

"CREEPS IN THE BUILDING! GET UP! EVERYBODY UP!" I shouted as loud as my abused throat would allow.

A couple of seconds later, the door to Ethan's shack slammed open and the big man moved toward me with a speed that belied his size. He brought his fire axe with him, and switched into a two-handed grip as he ran. Steve appeared out of nowhere brandishing his pistol in one hand. I skidded to a halt ten feet away from the struggling figures, trying to line up a shot. It was impossible. The doorway was too narrow, and the Sergeant thrashed desperately as he tried to break the powerful grip of the infected attacking him.

"Fuck, I don't have a shot. Steve?"

"No goddamn it," he swore.

"Guns down! I got it!" Ethan shouted.

He sped in front of us, and we both lowered our weapons. The front of the Sergeant's uniform was covered in blood, and he was holding the revenant's gnashing teeth at bay with one hand by pushing against its throat. Another ghoul appeared at the entrance and tried to reach over the one attacking Cartwright to get at him. Ethan shoved the handle of his axe beneath the ghoul's jaw and pushed backward. His shoulder and arm muscles bulged under the strain. The creature snarled and redoubled its efforts to bite Cartwright again. Ethan bared his teeth, and pushed with everything he had. He managed to get the infected's head far enough away to hit with my rifle. I took a few steps forward and to my right.

"Close your eyes and look away," I ordered.

Ethan complied, and I lined up the sights. The report was deafening inside the confines of the warehouse. A jagged hole appeared low on the creature's forehead, and as it slumped to the ground, Ethan fired a powerful front kick to the chest of the ghoul behind it, which bought him enough time to drag the Sergeant inside and shut the door. He slammed the bar down, and Cartwright sagged against the wall behind him. Ethan took a few shaky steps back, his chest heaving. Sergeant Cartwright gripped his right shoulder just below the collarbone and slid slowly to the ground.

"I'm fucked," he said. Cartwright stared at his shoulder for a few seconds, then grimaced and bashed his head backward into the wall.

"FUCK!" he shouted.

"Hey Eric," Steve said.

I jumped. "What?"

Steve pointed at my rifle. My finger was on the trigger with the barrel pointed in Cartwright's direction.

"Shit, sorry," I said, quickly lowering the weapon.

Bill hustled up from somewhere behind me with a first aid kit in his hand. "Ethan, you're covered in blood son, get Andrea to clean you up. Steve, you got a knife on you?"

"Yeah, right here." He handed over his pocketknife.

Bill took it and kneeled down beside Sergeant Cartwright. He sat the knife down and pulled a pair of latex gloves out of the first aid kit. As he began to put them on, Cartwright held up a hand.

"Don't bother, doc. Ain't no point."

"I don't remember asking for your permission, Sergeant," Bill said. "You're a guest in my home, and you are in need of medical treatment. Now take your hand off your shoulder and sit still."

Cartwright hesitated, then did as Bill said. Bill used Steve's knife to cut away Cartwright's bloody shirt, exposing the torn and bleeding flesh beneath. He opened up a pack of gauze and pressed it into the wound. The Sergeant grimaced, but did not cry out. I looked away, and let my rifle dangle from its sling.

The rest of the compound and all of the soldiers were standing in a loose gaggle, staring at Bill and Sergeant Cartwright. I wanted to yell at them to close their damn gaping mouths and show some respect, until I saw Stacy standing among them. She held a hand over her mouth and looked to be on the verge of tears. Lieutenant Jonas, to his credit, was the first to recover. He began firing orders at his men and galvanized them into action. Steve took control of everyone else and got them moving again. Those who were sober enough to do so went back to preparing breakfast. Everyone else dispersed into red-eyed clusters, whispering and holding each other. I slid my rifle around to my back and walked over to Stacy. She put her arms around me and buried her head in my chest. We just stood there for a while, holding one another. Noah Salinger stared at us for a moment, then turned away and walked into his shack. His expression was not a happy one.

Bill finished dressing the sergeant's wound and had Justin put his bloody clothes in a plastic trash bag. Cartwright got to his feet and staggered shirtless to the front of Bill's shack. He looked pale from blood loss, and was clearly in a great deal of pain. I let go of Stacy and kissed her on the head.

"I meant to ask you about something last night," she said.

"What's that?"

"Remember when we were getting ready to go into Alexis? You said something about the creeps following you?"

I went rigid, and my blood turned to ice. How could I have forgotten?

"Son of a bitch." I whispered.

"What?" Stacy asked.

"You're right, Stacy. I should have remembered."

I turned and walked toward Lieutenant Jonas, cursing myself for a fool the whole way. He was in front of Bill's shack speaking in low tones with Sergeant Cartwright.

"…so what do you want to do?" Jonas asked.

"I…I don't know. Give me a minute to think about it, LT."

Jonas nodded and stood up, his expression carved out of flint.

"It's your choice, Sergeant. Take your time," he said, and walked away.

I caught his arm as he walked by. "Lieutenant, could I have a word with you in private?"

He stopped and glared at me. After a tense moment, he looked down and his expression softened. "Certainly, Mr. Riordan."

I led him to the other side of the warehouse near my truck.

"How long have you been on the road?" I asked him.

"About two weeks or so. Why?"

"How long do you typically stop for?"

"No more than four hours, usually."

"Have you ever noticed any infected following you?"

Jonas frowned. "Well…they always seem to be nearby, wherever we go. I don't know if they were necessarily following us. I just figured that because there are so many of them…" He trailed off.

Jonas was a smart man. The light of realization slowly began to dawn on him.

"Oh my God. I led them here."

I put a hand on his shoulder. "Hey, it's not your fault. I've seen this kind of thing before, I should have remembered."

Jonas shook his head. "How could I have missed that?"

"Lieutenant, I have something I think you need to see."

"What?"

"Hang on a second."

I climbed into the bed of my truck and rooted around in a couple of boxes. I found the original copy of Gabriel's manual on how to fight the undead, and handed it to Lt. Jonas. We sat down on a couple of empty five-gallon buckets and I told him everything I knew about Gabriel, Aegis, the Phage, all of it. When I finished, he stared at me as if seeing me for the first time.

"That's quite a story friend," He said in a small voice.

I nodded. "Don't I know it."

"So what do you propose I do?"

"I propose you keep that manual. I propose that you read what is in it, and train your men accordingly. I further propose that you take it with you back to Fort Bragg and disseminate additional copies to your leaders, as well as everyone who has taken shelter there. I've managed to stay alive by following the lessons laid out in that document, and so have the people here at this warehouse."

"Where is this Gabriel character? I would like to speak with him," Jonas asked.

"Why? Everything he would have to say to you is right there in your hand."

"Still, he might have valuable information."

"Gabriel left the military for a reason. He wants to be left alone, and quite frankly, Lieutenant, he's earned it. If he wants to contact you, that is his choice."

For a long moment, Jonas glared daggers at me with hard, granite colored eyes. I could tell what he was thinking, and I felt my bowels turn to water in my gut. I kept my gaze steady, and prayed he would flinch before I started sweating.

"Fine," He said, heaving a sigh and looking down at the binder in his hands. "Does your friend know a way to stop the infection from taking hold?"

"I'm afraid not."

Jonas lowered his head into a weathered hand and massaged his temple on one side.

"Then I have one shit-fuck of a day ahead of me."

I didn't know what to say to that, so I gave him a pat on the shoulder and walked away. I found Bill near Stacy's shack and asked to speak with him.

"So what do you want to do?" I asked.

"About what?" he said.

"About the infected."

"The Sergeant hasn't turned yet," he snapped.

"I'm not talking about him."

"Then what are you...oh...right."

I took a half step closer and leaned in. "They probably followed the soldiers in. I spoke with Jonas, and I don't think he knew what was going on. There weren't any guards up this morning to sound the alarm, so God only knows how many more of those things are out there."

"This is all my fault. I never should have canceled the guard," he said, miserably.

"Damn it, Bill, this is not your fault. Now I need you to think, okay? What do we do?"

Bill looked ready to say something nasty for a second. The moment passed, and the gears of his mind started turning again.

"We need to get somebody up top to see how many creeps we're dealing with."

"What about the rolling door?" I asked. "It's completely covered by the shipping container except for a few feet at the top. Open it up, and let me climb out there to see how many of them there are."

Bill considered for a moment, then nodded. "Good idea. Get Steve and Earl, and meet me down by the door."

I did as he said, and within a couple of minutes, the four of us were ready to go. Steve hauled on the chain that opened the door, and Earl stood with his back to the shipping container, fingers laced in front of him. I stepped into his hands and climbed on top of the container. After I slipped under the door, I reached a hand down for my rifle. Bill handed it up to me stock first.

I got to my feet and looked around at the crumbling concrete lot beyond the warehouse. About thirty or forty undead started that damned awful croaking when I stepped to the edge of the container. Five minutes later, there were almost a hundred of them, reaching and moaning and straining. I raised my H&K to my shoulder and went to work. The anger and despair that had been growing in me over the past few months boiled over as I fired into them again and again. Without realizing it, I had started shouting and cursing at the infected as I put them down. Normally it would have been distasteful work, but anger can make anything easy. I stayed on the container for a couple of minutes waiting, hoping for more undead to show up. When they didn't, I took a few deep breaths to calm myself before I climbed down and went back inside.

"It's clear," I said to Bill. He and the others were staring at me.

Bill went back to the other side of the warehouse to let Lt. Jonas know that the infected were gone, and to ask for his men's help clearing the bodies out. I dug a folding stool out of the back of my truck and sat down on it. Ethan came over and sat down next to me on an empty bucket.

"That was a good shot earlier," he said.

I stared down at the concrete between my feet and nodded.

"You okay?"

"I'm pretty fucking far from okay, Ethan. So are you. So is the world."

Ethan shrugged. "That doesn't change anything. We still have a job to do."

I looked up and glared at my friend. "And what job would that be, exactly?"

"Living. Putting one foot in front of the other. Taking the next breath. Eating the next meal. Dealing with the next heartache. Fighting the next crisis. Not giving up."

"Tell that to Sergeant Cartwright," I said, and looked down again.

Ethan put a heavy hand on my shoulder for a moment, and then he left.

The soldiers got themselves together and swept the area around the compound for half a mile in every direction. They put down several dozen more undead. Bill set another watch, and Lt. Jonas volunteered his men to assist. Will Cartwright got progressively worse, but he refused all offers of pain medicine. Jonas kneeled down in front of him and leaned in close.

"Sergeant, I am not asking you, I'm ordering you. Let the Doctor give you something to ease the pain."

"With all due respect sir, go fuck yourself." Cartwright's grimace morphed into a pained grin.

"You've been waiting for years to say that to an officer, haven't you?" Jonas said, smiling.

"Yep, sure have. And it couldn't have happened to a nicer guy," Cartwright replied, laughing.

"It won't make you less of a man to let the doctor make you more comfortable," Jonas pressed.

"No, it wouldn't. But it would mean less pain medicine for the living."

"You, sir, are still alive," Bill interjected.

"No I'm not," Cartwright said. "I can feel it inside me. I'm getting cold, which means that the fever is about to start. It's like I have a million little jagged worms in my veins, crawling around under my skin. My head is getting fuzzy, I can't think too clear."

"You want out, say the word," Jonas said. The sadness in his expression belied the evenness of his tone.

"Nope. Not today, no sir. You folks might want to take me outside though. I'd hate for someone to get infected on my account."

"I hate to say it, but he's right," Bill said.

Jonas closed his eyes and gave a short nod. Two of Cartwright's soldiers helped him to his feet and half carried him outside. They laid out a bedroll for him near the supply truck and laid him down on it. He shivered uncontrollably, and I could hear his teeth chattering from ten feet away.

"Anything we can do for you Sarge?" One of the soldiers asked.

"A b…b..blanket w..would be n…nice."

The soldier climbed into the truck and came back with a couple of Army issue wool blankets. He laid them over Sergeant Cartwright and stepped back, unsure what to do next. I heard footsteps behind me and turned around to see Lt. Jonas walking toward us.

"I'll take it from here, men. First Sergeant Ashman will be taking over Sergeant Cartwright's duties. Go report to him for your work assignments."

The soldiers saluted and jogged back toward the warehouse. Jonas drew his pistol and sat down cross-legged next to Cartwright. He laid the pistol on the concrete beside him.

"You know what's going to happen, right?"

Cartwright nodded.

"I'll wait until you give the word, then," Jonas said.

I sat down on the concrete on the other side of Cartwright. Jonas looked up at me with a furrowed brow.

"I've got this, Mr. Riordan."

"I know. I'm just here to lend a hand, when the time comes."

Between shudders, Cartwright asked Jonas to tell his mom and his fiancé how much he loved them, and that were in his thoughts at the end. Jonas swallowed a couple of times and nodded. Cartwright shivered and shook for an hour before the convulsions started. I helped Jonas roll the stricken soldier on his side to keep him from hurting himself. Finally, after what seemed like an eternity, Cartwright went still. It was the first time I ever heard a death rattle.

We rolled Cartwright over onto his stomach and took a few steps away. Jonas lifted his pistol and fired a single round into the back of Cartwright's head. I helped Jonas carry him into the factory and load his body into the incinerator.

"I'll take care of this part, Lieutenant. You should go say something to your men," I said. Jonas nodded stiffly and walked away.

Once Cartwright's remains were taken care of, Bill called a meeting and invited Lt. Jonas and his men to attend. We set out chairs for everyone, and Bill started things off.

"I know everyone is shaken up about what happened this morning," he said. "I take full responsibility for what happened, and I want to apologize for my mistake." The old man had black circles under his eyes, and he looked twenty years older than the day before.

"That's nonsense, Mr. Cooper," Lt. Jonas said, and stood up from his chair. He walked in front of the assembly and stood next to Bill.

"If anyone is to blame for Sergeant Cartwright's death, it is me. I am his commanding officer, and any harm that befalls my men is my responsibility. I knew as well as anyone that not posting a watch last night was taking a major risk, and I did nothing about it. I should have known better, and a man is dead because of my poor judgment."

No one spoke for a few seconds. As much as I hated to admit it, the Lieutenant was right. He could have ordered a couple of his men to take the watch, but he didn't. He should have put two and two together and figured out that the undead were following his convoy, but he didn't. Not until it was too late. As a military man, those were not the kinds of mistakes that he could afford to make, even if he was only trying to do something nice for his soldiers.

"While my actions were inexcusable, for the time being I still have a job to do," Jonas continued. "Mr. Cooper here has been kind enough to offer his hospitality to Privates Dodd and Walbach. While they recuperate, my men and I will continue to patrol for survivors over the next two weeks. After that, we will retrieve our men and head back to Fort Bragg. I want to thank you for your kindness, and your hospitality. Sergeant Ashman, you have the floor."

Jonas went back to his seat, and Sergeant Ashman took his place. Ashman was every bit of six foot four, and probably weighed about two hundred and forty pounds. He had a shiny bald head, and darkly tanned skin.

"As many of you may have heard already, what is left of the Federal Government has retreated to Colorado Springs and taken refuge at the NORAD facility there. We are still in communication with them, and they have asked us to deliver a message to any groups of survivors that we encounter. A large contingent of the U.S. military is working to clear out the undead immediately in the vicinity of Colorado Springs. They have established several fortified operating bases, and expect to have the infected population under control in a matter of months. Anyone who wishes to do so, may make their way to Colorado and join the military in their efforts to expand the safe zone. Once Colorado Springs is secured, we will attempt to make a full assessment of the damages caused by the Outbreak, and we will begin stepping up our efforts to find survivors.

We have a huge job ahead of us, and to be bluntly honest, we need all the help we can get. Right now, we are accepting new recruits on a sign up basis. What that means is that you take the Oath of Enlistment, and when we come back through here a couple of weeks from now, we will take you with us back to Fort Bragg to begin your training. Anyone with significant prior military or law enforcement experience may apply for a field commission upon completion of whatever training is deemed necessary for them.

For those of you who choose to serve with us, well…I'm not going to blow sunshine up your ass. It's pretty damned bad out there. You can expect lousy food, and not enough of it on most days. You can expect to risk your life on a daily basis doing difficult, thankless work. You can expect to be sent into dangerous situations and asked to accomplish nearly impossible missions with extremely limited resources. Right now, guns and gear are in good shape, but as time goes on that will most likely change. I realize that I'm not exactly painting a rosy picture of military life, but for those of you who want to help, I want you to know exactly what you are getting yourselves into. That being said, I hope you decide to join us.

Now that my recruiting bit is over with, you folks need to know about the deteriorating condition of the nuclear power plant in Huntersville. The President ordered the plant shut down, and it was. Problem is, when they took the reactor offline, they basically sunk it in a giant water bath to keep it cool. Well, now that there is no one around to keep the water circulating in the bath, the containment unit overheated and blew its top. The explosion spread dangerous levels of radiation over a wide area. According to our Geiger meters, this region was not badly affected, but a shift in the wind could change that at any time. I can't force you to come back with us to Fort Bragg, but if you stay here, you will be in constant danger of radiation exposure."

Ashman paused for a few seconds to let his words sink in. People began whispering worriedly to one another. The meeting went on for another two hours, consisting mostly of Ashman answering the same questions over and over again.

Could the radiation reach us here?

Yes, it could.

Could we have been exposed already without knowing it?

No. If we were exposed, we would have noticed by now.

How many other survivors had they found?

Not many. Estimated at less than a hundred.

What were things like at Fort Bragg?

Tense, but stable.

What about overseas, did the infection spread there?

Yes.

How?

Multiple sources. Ships fleeing the U.S. overrun with infected wrecking on the shores of Europe and Africa. Planes with infected in the cabin crash landing in Asia. Hawaii had managed to prevent any outbreaks, but conditions on the Island were deteriorating. Civil unrest. Fear and panic. Food riots. Things did not sound good for the Aloha state.

Switzerland was doing okay, and so was Australia. There were outbreaks in both countries, but they had time to prepare, and kept them from getting out of hand. The rest of the world was not such a pretty story. Most of Europe was a dead zone. The UK was dealing with multiple outbreaks and losing the fight against them. Africa was a total loss, as was most of Asia. I thought about the billions of people in China, India, and Southeast Asia and shuddered. That was a lot of infected to have to fight.

The most disturbing news was from the Middle East. Apparently, Pakistan and India engaged in a limited nuclear exchange, as had Iran and Israel. No more than ten bombs in total detonated. I shook my head at that. The whole world was being consumed by the walking dead, and these people still found reasons to annihilate one another. Depressing.

When Sergeant Ashman finished, Bill called an end to the meeting. It was only mid-afternoon, but I was exhausted. Jonas ordered his men to rest up for the day, and get prepared to move out in the morning. I thought that sounded like a good idea, and made my own preparations.

That night at dinner, I broke the news to everyone at the compound that I was leaving. No one was surprised, least of all Stacy. She didn't talk to me very much, and avoided eye contact with me for the rest of dinner. Bill looked disappointed, but wished me well all the same. I went to sleep alone in my bedroll that night, and wondered if I was making the right decision.

The next day I slept late. Ethan came by at about eight in the morning and woke me up for breakfast. I ate flatbread and Spam with canned beans while Andrea spooned baby food into Aiden's mouth.

"I really wish you would reconsider," Ethan said for the umpteenth time. "I'm going to sign on with the Army. You should too. You would make a great soldier."

"Ethan, you have a family, dude. Are you sure joining the military is a good idea?" I said.

"What the hell else am I going to do? You heard that Sergeant yesterday about the nuclear plant. We can't stay here. What else am I going to do at Fort Bragg?"

"You're an EMT. You have medical training."

"Exactly. I could be a field medic."

I shook my head. "I'm sorry Ethan, but I don't have any interest in joining the Army. I think you have a lot of guts for volunteering, but it's not for me. Andrea, are you okay with this?"

She looked up at me with her clear blue eyes and gentle smile. Damn, but she was beautiful. "Not really, but I can't very well watch other women's husbands do all the hard work, now can I?" She turned and went back to feeding Aiden. "The Army needs help, and Ethan has a lot to offer them."

I didn't like it, but I couldn't argue with her logic. Ethan could do a great deal of good for the Army, especially considering how strapped they were for people with medical training. When I finished eating, I said goodbye to Ethan and his family. Ethan gave me a handshake and a clap on the shoulder. Andrea gave me a hug and made me break out in goose bumps with a kiss on the cheek. Aiden smiled at me and slapped me in the forehead when I picked him up to hug him. Kids. Gotta love 'em.

I made the rounds and exchanged a few words with everyone I had gotten to know over the last couple of months. I learned that Stan and Cody, along with Earl and his wife Jessica, planned to head out west to Colorado. I wished them luck. Steve, not surprisingly, rejoined the Army and intended to apply for a field commission once he reached Fort Bragg. Lt. Jonas reinstated him at his old rank immediately, and put him in charge of the squad Sgt. Cartwright had once led. Several other people, men and women alike, volunteered to join the military. Everyone else who did not enlist signed a letter of intent stating that they would go to Fort Bragg with Jonas' unit when they came back through. Justin showed Jonas all of the supplies that the compound had amassed, and the Lieutenant offered to help transport the most useful stuff back to Fort Bragg with them. He agreed to let the compound's people retain ownership of everything, and divide the supplies up evenly once everyone was safe behind the wall at the base. I found Bill up on the roof with the watch and offered him a parting handshake.

"You know, you're a hell of a good leader, Bill," I told him.

The old man smiled and shook his shaggy grey head. "Son, I wish like hell that were true. Might be a few more folks still alive, if I were."

"You did the best you could under the worst of circumstances. No one else could have done any better, and most would have done a hell of a lot worse. Every person in this building owes you a debt of gratitude."

Bill thanked me and let go of my hand. "You should say goodbye to Stacy, before you go," He said, his smile fading.

"I'll do that. You take care, Bill. Been nice knowing you."

I stopped outside the door to Stacy's shack and hesitated for a moment before knocking. When she opened the door, her eyes were red and puffy, but she managed a smile for me.

"I've been dreading that knock all morning," she said.

"Stacy, why don't you come with me?" I replied. "It's safe, where I'm going. We could…"

"We could what? Get married? Raise children? Is that what you want?"

I didn't answer.

"Eric, you are a sweet, brave, wonderful man. I love you, I really do, but I can't leave my father and I can't leave these people. Some of the children here don't have parents anymore. Who will look after them if I run off with you?"

"I don't know," I said, and looked down.

Stacy placed a hand on either side of my face and stood on her toes. I kissed her for the last time.

"Do you love me?" Those four words again.

"Yes."

"Then don't forget me. Stay alive, and don't give up hope. Find a way to do some good. Understand?"

I was not sure if I really did, but I nodded anyway. I said goodbye to her, and tried very, very hard not to let any tears fall as I walked away. I was not terribly successful. Ethan caught up with me a few minutes later and gave me a five-gallon can of gasoline and a map.

"I've plotted out the best routes to get where you're going. Between this and what fuel you already have in the tank, you should be able to get there just fine," he said.

"Thanks."

We stared at each other for a moment, and then Ethan smiled and lifted me up in a bear hug. I laughed and slapped him on the back a couple of times.

"You take care of that family of yours," I said, as he put me down.

"I will. I hope I see you again someday Eric. I'm glad I met you."

I wanted to say something heartfelt and meaningful, but I couldn't get it out past the lump in my throat, so I just smiled. Ethan walked away, and a piece of me went with him.

The drive to Gabriel's place took two days. Most of the roads Ethan plotted out for me were in bad shape. The storm that came through on my first night at the compound knocked down a lot of trees. Several times, I had to double back and consult my map to find a different way forward. I spent the first night camped out on the roof of a small country store, and marked its location on my map. There were still some good supplies in there that I could come back for. The next day, after dispatching a dozen or so undead who wandered up during the night, I spent another nine frustrating hours navigating around on back roads. I had to stop a few times to siphon gasoline, or kill infected that got too close. It was nearly six in the afternoon on the second day before I finally reached the narrow two-lane road that winds its way up the mountain to Gabriel's cabin.

My truck kicked up a plume of dust behind me as I pulled into his driveway. Gabriel was sitting in a rocking chair on the front porch, whittling knife in hand, carving a length of hickory into a short axe-handle. Next to him, leaning against one of the posts that held up the small awning in front of the cabin, was a large assault rifle. I recognized it as a SCAR 17 battle-rifle, a serious piece of hardware. I got out of my truck and walked up to the porch. Gabe still looked like Gabe. Same black, unkempt mane of hair, same two or three days' growth of beard, same scars, same scowl.

"Took you long enough," he said. "Been expecting you."

I chuckled and sat down in the chair next to him. The sun was just starting to set in the distance, painting the far mountains in hues of red, amber, and gold. The leaves in the trees were a brilliant carpet of sunset colors beneath the afternoon sky.

"I got held up," I said.

Gabriel just nodded and reached down into an egg crate beside him. He put a bottle of Maker's Mark and two tumblers on the small table between us and poured a couple of fingers in each glass.

"I was going to give you one more day, and then I was gonna drink this bottle my damn self."

I smiled. "How many times have you told yourself that?"

One side of Gabriel's face twitched into half a smile. "'Bout every day for the last two months."

I nodded. "How you been making out?"

Gabe shrugged. "Not bad. It's been quiet, for the most part."

"That's good."

"What about you?"

My smile faded. "Ran into a little trouble, here and there."

"I thought as much."

We didn't say anything else for a while. We drank our whiskey and watched the sun go down behind the hills.

"I'm glad you made it, Eric. I was starting to get worried," Gabe said, breaking the silence.

"Well, I'm here now. You can stop worrying."

I put my empty glass on the table and Gabriel filled it up again.

"So what now?" I asked.

Gabriel was silent for a long moment before answering. "Now we stay alive, and work on making this place more defensible. Unless you have a better idea."

"Nothing comes to mind, at present."

I told Gabe about the nuclear plant in Huntersville, but left out anything else. The wounds were still raw, so to speak. I could sense that Gabe had questions, but he kept them to himself.

"Well, nothing we can do about it from here. I doubt that any radiation will make it out this far. Most of the fallout should have been washed away by wind and rain, at this point."

"How do you know?" I asked.

"I read a lot."

I left it at that.

"So what all goodies to you have in the truck?" Gabriel asked.

I got up and lowered the tailgate. Gabe helped me unload all my gear and stow it in his underground shelter. The sun was down when we finished, and brilliant stars lit up the night sky next to a nearly full moon. The cold autumn air was clean and crisp, and smelled of fallen leaves. Gabe started a fire in the stove, and we settled into the two recliners he had placed in front of it.

"Well, welcome home," Gabe said, as he poured us both another whiskey.

I held up my glass, and Gabe clinked his against it.

"To surviving the end of the world," I said.

"To surviving the end of the world," Gabe repeated.

We sat in front of the fire late into the night, sipping warm whiskey, and trying not to think. The next day, we started work on the fence.

Epilogue

I'm sitting in a chair beside the wood stove, watching as Gabriel reads the most recent chapter of my memoirs. Two months have passed since I started writing about the events between the Outbreak, and my arrival here at Gabriel's property. A cold February wind is howling outside the cabin, no doubt sending a tall bank of snow against the northern wall that we'll soon have to shovel.

Gabe seems a bit troubled by what he's read. I figured that such would be the case, and have prepared defenses to the many criticisms undoubtedly headed my way. Gabe's brow is furrowed, and he is absently scratching at the thick growth of beard that covers his scarred, weathered face. He is a fierce-looking man under the best of circumstances, but when his is confused, hurt, or angry, his countenance can be downright terrifying to those not used to dealing with him. Lucky for me, I am well accustomed to Gabriel's volatile temper.

"What I don't get," he says as he closes the laptop and pinches the bridge of his nose between two thick fingers, "is why you never told me about any of this."

I look up from my notepad and give him a level stare. "Are you really saying that to me? Really? Mister 'I know about a bacteriophage that can destroy the world, but I'm not going to tell you about it until it's too late'. Are you fucking serious?"

Gabe glares angrily at me for a moment, but I meet his gaze with a little anger of my own. It is not long before Gabe looks away.

"You're right. I should have told you sooner. I'm sorry."

I can see the weight of all the untold miles, and all the crippling guilt he feels written on his broad, rough face. Gabriel has deeply carved lines around his mouth and eyes, chiseled there by painful memories and years of violence. I have known Gabriel long enough to understand that he is a man relentlessly haunted by his past, and by the legacies of his actions. For all of his massive strength, knowledge, and intelligence, I frequently find myself pitying the big man.

"Not that it makes any difference now," I reply as I return to my writing. "We are where we are, and there is no changing that."

"You say that a lot, you know."

"It's the truth."

"Doesn't make it any less depressing."

"Depression is an emotion for which I have not the time, or the inclination, to expend my mental resources," I say flatly.

Gabriel barks a bitter, mirthless laugh.

"How do you do that? One minute you talk like a backcountry redneck, and in the next breath, you sound like you could make print copy for ribbed condoms read like fucking Robert Frost. Which one of those Eric's is the real thing?"

I look up from my writing, and set the pad and pen down on a small table beside me.

"All of them. None of them. Honestly, I don't know anymore. After spending the better part of two years trapped on an isolated mountain with no one but a surly, monosyllabic curmudgeon for company, I find myself caring less and less about what specific persona I should be striving to embody. You want to know the truth Gabe?"

"Probably not, but I have a feeling you're going to tell me anyway."

I stand up and begin pacing around the room.

"I'm fucking losing it. When the Outbreak happened, I went into denial. I didn't let myself think about how bad things were going to get. I ignored the suffering all around me. I didn't let myself be angry, or sad, or frightened, or anything else about it. I just went numb, because that is what I had to do to survive. Now, in the middle of winter, ironically enough, the ice inside of me is thawing. I think about all the people who died agonizing deaths during the Outbreak and I want to scream. Every time I kill an infected, I want to cry for the person that they were, and will never be again. I think about all the creature comforts I had before the Outbreak, and I feel guilty for missing them. I remember all the women I slept with over the years, and I think about how nice it would be to fuck something other than my hand for a change. For all of that, the thing that is driving me out of my goddamn mind the fastest is the knowledge that there is no fucking end in sight. As long as we are stuck here on this God forsaken mountain, this," I gesture at the cabin walls around me. "is all that our lives will ever be."

I walk to the kitchen, place my fists on the counter and stare down into the sink.

"I have to get down off this mountain, Gabriel. I don't know how much longer I can do this. Survival isn't enough. Humans are social animals. For better or for worse, I have to try to find other survivors. I have to find some semblance of society to join, or I may as well jump down the side of the mountain and join all of our little friends down there busted against the rocks. At least down there I'll have some company."

I hear Gabriel's chair creak as he stands up from it. The door of the wood stove squeals as he opens it and tosses in a couple of fire logs.

"I know what you mean," he says.

He is calm. His movements are deliberate, efficient, and strangely graceful. Unlike me, there is no nervous energy to him. No buzzing, thrumming, maddening tension. If you did not know him as well as I do, you would never see the subtle signs of his desperation. There is a tightness in his shoulders that was not there before. An intensity and pressure behind his eyes that bores holes into everything he sees.

Gabriel is a sniper. He is an expert at self-control. He is disciplined, careful, patient, and deadly. I know that venting my frustrations does nothing to improve our situation, or my friend's mood for that matter, but I can't help it. My mouth has become a whistling steam valve that bleeds off the boiling anxiousness eating away at my sanity.

"I'm having a hard time of it myself," Gabe says, heaving a sigh. "I think this past Christmas is the last time I can remember being in a good mood. I'm tired of being cold all the damn time. I'm tired of living behind a fence, and sleeping in a hole in the ground. I was never a social butterfly before the world went to hell, but as least I always had the option, you know? I could drive into town, get a beer at the tavern, listen to conversations, laughter, arguments...I could be around some fucking life. Up here, we aren't really living. We're just waiting to die."

I turn around and lean back against the counter.

"After the spring thaw, then? No more doubts, no more arguments, no more 'Maybe we should just stay where we are, we have a good thing going, at least we're safe up here?' We are really going to load up the trailer and get the hell off this mountain?" I ask.

Gabriel nods. "I'll start getting back on the HAM radio a couple of times a day and see if I can get any news. You should keep writing. It seems to help you, when you write."

"It does. I think I've written as much as I can from my perspective alone, though. If I'm really going to tell the story, I need to start including things I learned after the fact. Things I did not see firsthand. Maybe I could get you to make a few contributions. You may not have a gift for writing, but you need to tell your side of the story too."

"I suppose you're right."

Gabe stares into the fire and settles back onto the floor with his legs crossed beneath him. He looks like a brooding gargoyle hunched over in the middle of the room.

"It's going to be hard, you know, getting to Colorado. God only knows what we're going to run into between here and there," he says.

I nod and move closer to the fire. I was away from it for less than a minute, and I can already feel the cold penetrating my clothes. The stove warms my hands as I hold them over its dark iron.

"I know. It was certainly not a fucking picnic just getting up here. I'm willing to take the risk, though. You're cool and all, but I need someone else to talk to. Preferably female. And pretty," I reply.

He glances up at me. His smile is grim and brief before he turns his eyes back to the floor. "No more doubts then. After the spring thaw, we go west."

I nod. "We need to agree on a load-out."

Gabe groans and rubs his forehead.

"Not this argument again. For Christ's sake, the trailer can haul a lot of gear. If you don't want to drag it, then just fucking cover me, and I'll pull it to Colorado."

I laugh at the mental image of Gabriel harnessed up like a Clydesdale with our aluminum cart trundling along behind him.

"Gabe, just because there is room for it doesn't mean we need to bring it."

It is an old argument between the two of us by now. Gabe wants to haul half of his damned armory out west, and I think we should bring only what we need to survive. I favor a strategy of packing light and moving quickly, scavenging what we need as we go along. Gabriel wants to pack up the trailer and bring as much weapons, food, ammo, and tools as we can possibly fit into the thing. Like most arguments between us, it will probably end in some kind of compromise that doesn't make either one of us happy, but that we can both live with.

"You need to think about what we're going to do once we reach Colorado," he replies. "Just making it out there isn't the end of it. We will need weapons and lots of ammo if we are going to survive beyond just a couple of years. There are millions, hundreds of millions, of undead out there. The human race is outnumbered at least a thousand to one, and that's just here in the U.S. alone. Not to mention all the fucked up marauders, murderers, and assorted evil bastards that managed to survive. The undead will not be the only or even the greatest

343

danger that we'll face. When it comes to fighting the living, we are going to need options. We can't run away from everything. There will be times when we will have to stand and fight, and when that happens, I don't want to be stuck with just a damn .22 pistol to defend myself with."

I glare at Gabriel for a moment, and then sit down in my chair.

"I never said we should just bring the .22's."

I generally favor ammo that is light and plentiful, and the guns used to fire it. Gabriel, being the giant of a man that he is, prefers weapons that can drop a bull rhino from four-hundred yards. I freely acknowledge the range and stopping power of powerful ordnance such as the 7.62mm and the .338 Lapua magnum, but that shit is heavy, and so are the rifles that fire it.

Gabriel says, "I understand, and agree that light ammo is a good thing when it comes to putting down the infected. If all you're worried about is a head shot from within a hundred yards, then that stuff is great. But what you need to understand, Eric, is that living people are a lot harder to hit than one of those stumbling shitheads, and that heavy ammunition does a lot better job of stopping a living person in their tracks than those little plinkers you like so much. I had to learn that particular lesson the hard way, just in case you forgot."

I hold my hands out palms up in a placating gesture. "Okay, fine, you win, we need to bring some heavy hitters. Balance that thought against weight concerns and come up with an efficient load-out that doesn't break my freaking back when it's my turn to pull the cart. You are, after all, a solid sixty pounds heavier than me."

"When I get finished rigging up that cart, you'll barely feel the weight. Trust me."

"My father always told me never to trust anyone that says 'trust me.'"

Gabriel frowns at me, then gets up from the floor and sits down in his chair. It creaks in protest under his bulk. Both of us have lost weight since the Outbreak, but Gabe is still at least two hundred and fifty pounds of solid muscle. I imagine that if it were not for all of the dried venison and beans that we stored up for winter, he would have lost a lot more weight than he has. Same for me, for that matter. The last time I stepped on the scale, I was a hundred and eighty-seven pounds. That is about twenty pounds lighter than I was when I got here, and even then I was lean. My body has burned up what little fat I carried and a significant amount of muscle mass trying to keep me warm through the harsh winter.

Speaking of, I have seen the seasons change in the high county many times, but none so bitter as this one. Winter set in very early this year, and judging by the weather over the last few weeks, it may last several weeks longer than normal. Gabriel has a theory about that unhappy fact that I find immensely disturbing.

Nuclear winter.

As if we didn't have enough problems.

The wind outside has died down, and the sun is getting low on the horizon. Darkness comes quickly in the high country, and the pile of wood beside the stove is too low to last the night. Furthermore, the snow piled up against the side of the cabin is not going to shovel itself. I stand up and start to pull on my boots.

"We should bring in some more wood and shovel that damn snow before nightfall. I don't want to be out there after dark, it is too freaking cold at night these days."

Gabriel gets up from his chair and grabs his boots.

"I hate it when the sun goes down," He says. "I got nothing else to do but huddle under a blanket in the dark, and wait until I'm tired enough to crawl down into the bunker. I know it is a safe place to sleep and all, but I look forward to the day when I can sleep above ground without having to worry about getting eaten."

I stop lacing my boots for a moment and look up at Gabriel. "You really think that's ever going to happen? What with the world being the way it is now?"

Gabriel shrugs, and the ghost of a smile crosses his face.

"A man has to have something to hope for, doesn't he?"

I stare down at my hands for a moment. They are dry to the point of being cracked and bleeding. It used to bother me, but I have grown accustomed to the pain and barely notice it anymore. I am always amazed at the things I can become inured to when I have no choice. With every day that passes, I grow more convinced that suffering, and strength for that matter, are all a matter of choice. I will wake up every morning, probably for the rest of my life, and face mortal danger. Do I let that stop me from trying to live? If I do, then I'm as good as dead already.

"I guess you do. Either that, or you just give up. Maybe that's what hope really is. Having something to look forward to," I reply.

"You looking forward to shoveling some snow?" Gabe asks as he opens the door.

Frigid wintry air blows into the cabin, bringing with it the smell of cold and the earthy, iron scent of the frozen mountains.

"No, but it needs doing," I reply.

Gabriel smiles, and the shadows around his eyes seem to lift for a moment.

"Story of my life, amigo. Story of my life."

I laugh at that as we step out into the frigid twilight.

About the Author:

James N. Cook (who prefers to be called Jim, even though his wife insists on calling him James) is a martial arts enthusiast, a veteran of the U.S. Navy, a former cubicle dweller, and the author of the Surviving the Dead series. He hikes, he goes camping, he travels a lot, and he has trouble staying in one spot for very long. Even though he is a grown man, he enjoys video games, graphic novels, and gratuitous violence. He lives in North Carolina (for now) with his wife, son, two vicious attack dogs, and a cat that is scarcely aware of his existence.

65922867R00193

Made in the USA
Lexington, KY
28 July 2017